Stephen Powers

Muskingum Legends with Other Sketches and Papers Descriptive of The Young Men of Germany and The Old Boys of America

Stephen Powers

Muskingum Legends with Other Sketches and Papers Descriptive of The Young Men of Germany and The Old Boys of America

ISBN/EAN: 9783743383487

Manufactured in Europe, USA, Canada, Australia, Japa

Cover: Foto ©Andreas Hilbeck / pixelio.de

Manufactured and distributed by brebook publishing software (www.brebook.com)

Stephen Powers

Muskingum Legends with Other Sketches and Papers Descriptive of The Young Men of Germany and The Old Boys of America

MUSKINGUM LEGENDS,

WITH

OTHER SKETCHES AND PAPERS

DESCRIPTIVE OF

THE YOUNG MEN OF GERMANY

AND

THE OLD BOYS OF AMERICA.

BY

STEPHEN POWERS.

———

PHILADELPHIA:
J. B. LIPPINCOTT & CO.
1871.

PREFACE.

ONLY four of the five legends have their action on the banks of the Muskingum, and to none other than one native there, perhaps, would they seem entitled to christen the book. The scenes of the few simple stories told in these pages range from the Elbe to the Sacramento, but among all the included streams there is none to me half so dear as the little Indian river, the little "winking river," which flows past my father's house.

In explanation of the word *young*, as applied to the Germans in the title, I have only to say that if an American, wearied and disgusted with the janglings of home politics, will visit the continent of Europe for a season, he will find himself greatly refreshed by the *youthfulness* of political discussions and platforms. And, in their enthusiasm for all noble learning, are not the Germans ever young? To Franklin, I believe, is attributed the remark that a people never grows younger in crossing the ocean.

If one will compare the Americans in California, who
may be said, in a certain sense, to have made the entire
circuit of the globe, with the Chinese, who have remained
almost stationary near the origin of the human race, he
will feel that our countrymen are, in many respects, the
oldest people in the world.

S. P.

San Francisco, March 9, 1871.

CONTENTS.

IN THE GREAT WEST.

HISTORICAL.

MUSKINGUM LEGENDS.

LEGEND OF FEDERAL BOTTOM.

What verse can sing, what prose narrate,
The butcher deeds of bloody fate,
    Amid this mighty tulzie!
Grim Horror grinned, pale Terror roared,
As Murther at his thrapple shored,
    And hell mixed in the brulzie.
BURNS.

Now let us sing, long live the king,
    And Gilpin long live he;
And when he next doth ride abroad,
    May I be there to see.
COWPER.

AMONG the tributaries of the Beautiful River which flow down through the Buckeye State, there is one celebrated for its picturesqueness. It is known by the Indian name of Muskingum. And a jolly, twinkling, little river it is on a summer's day, winking at all the old, red-jowled farmers, winking very slyly with one eye at their red-cheeked maidens, and with the other at the broad-shouldered, gawky hobbledehoys; winking at the sleepy villages, and the many fields of dark-green maize; winking at the great white-armed sycamores and the willows, whose leaves dance all day in a silly flutter of delight at such flattery; winking at the bright May-weed, and the spring beauties, and yellow dandelions along the grassy bank; winking at the huge eyes of the coal-mines, which glower blackly down upon the little river as it goes dancing, bobbing, blinking, skipping, and winking along.

On the bank of this river there abode a community which was renowned for its patriotism.   In the first place, the name of their county was Washington.   In the second place, the half-moon level, formed by one of those beautifully superfluous sinuosities which the Muskingum loves, was called by them Federal Bottom.   Lastly, the little creek which empties into the river at the lower extremity of this half-moon bottom received the patriotic christening of Congress Run.   Thus impregnably intrenched in a loyal nomenclature, they abode long years in profound and tranquil security before they were overtaken by disaster.

On the opposite side of the river is the precipitous river-range known as Tick Hill.   This name is explained by local etymologists from the fact that, so great is the sterility of the hill, the early settlers were compelled to buy and sell exclusively on tick.   On its summit there stood a tree, famous far and near as the Crooked Tree, which was so very crooked that no farmer who looked at it could ever strike a straight furrow afterward.

Just a mile from the river, up the dismal hollow of Congress Run, many years ago,—so long ago, indeed, that the memory of man ran not to the contrary,—a queer old codger cleared away a little space among the lordly sugar-trees, and built a log-cabin beside the creek.   He was known for many a mile around as Daddy Childs, and his clearing, which never grew any wider, was called Childs' Place.   Strange and wonderful were the stories told to children and superstitious persons about Daddy Childs. Among other things, it was said that his wife, when she made his clothes, spread the cloth upon the floor, laid him down on it, and cut them out by the shape of his body.

In consequence of this, his trousers were so very loose and bagging that you could have introduced into the seat of them a bushel of beans.

His feet were very red, long, and flat, and he never wore shoes in any season. Neither did he wear a coat, and always had his waistcoat and shirt opened on his breast, where the hair on a triangular space grew so abundant that when he came into a neighbor's house in a snow-storm his breast would be as white as his silvered beard. He was a stout, little man, with very red hands and face, albeit the latter was almost hidden by his snow-white hair, which contrasted strongly with his brown and shaggy breast. He always had his yellow woolen shirt-sleeves rolled up to his elbows, displaying forearms as hairy-black as a bear's, though he never did any labor. His black hat was rolled up with great precision on two sides, and he always laid it off the last garment before he got into bed, taking it with both hands, and carefully placing it bottom side up; and when he got out of bed in the morning, he put it on first, with both hands, and invariably with the same end forward.

He was always walking about with a white hickory staff, and often went to tattle with the neighbors; but nobody could tell what in the world Daddy Childs did for a living. Most people considered him a losel, worthless fellow. His cabin stood in the center of his unfenced clearing, without a bush or a stalk of maize about it, and thus it seemed to have stood forever.

But the thing about which observing farmers puzzled and cudgeled their brains most was to "contrive" how the stumps were all extracted so quickly and so completely. They could not have rotted away so soon. More than one simple soul believed there had been some witchcraft about that stump-pulling. There it was, that smooth, stumpless, grassy plat; the path down to the spring; the cabin in the midst, with its puncheon door, and the latch-string hanging out; the knees and the weights on the roof; and the enormous stone chimney outside. Not a shadow or vestige of anything else; no evidences of housekeeping, not even a long-handled gourd swinging against the logs.

When did Daddy Childs come there? Nobody knew. He had always been there.

Some of the most inquisitive spirits of the neighborhood visited the house several times, but they never could find Daddy Childs doing anything. His wife was always sitting glum in the chimney corner, rocking in her chair—

" Gathering her brows like gathering storm."

Strange and terrible stories were related of the house, and certain timorous souls would never, on any account, pass it after nightfall. One narrated to gaping auditors how he had seen a head of flame thrust out of the chimney in the evening, with drops of fiery blood dripping from its severed neck. Others had, at the dead hour of midnight, seen Daddy Childs driving a yoke of fiery-eyed oxen over the hill, drawing a bob-sled, on which his wife was riding. But nobody could find out anything positively evil concerning him, so he was permitted to remain, —a mystery to some, a terror to others. Some questioned, "What good does such a man in the world?" We shall see.

One day, in the hay-making month of July, Daddy Childs suddenly seized his hickory staff, and started down the woody hollow of Congress Run. He walked very briskly, with his head stretched forward and his white hair streaming long down his shoulders, while with his staff he kept time with his left foot. He trudged through the majestic groves of sugar-trees, and passed the pellucid pools of the creek, where the great-bellied cows stood deep in the water, cooling their udders and sleepily ruminating; nor did he glance aside even when little Bunny whipped up a lofty tree, and squatted on a limb fifty feet overhead, cocking his brush gayly up over his back, peering down at him with one eye, and saying, "Squk, wuk, wuk!" None of these things did he regard, but walked right on.

At last he approached the little creek-meadow, in which the hearty old bachelor, Halford Pinbury, was raking hay into windrows on the hillside. Now, Halford Pinbury, bachelor though he was, was renowned for the mince-pies, the rich old cheese, mustard cider, and hickory-nuts kept in his house; and seeing Daddy Childs climb over the fence, he was reminded of his mustard cider, went and lifted a wisp of hay off the oaken firkin, and took a judicious swig. Then he squatted down, struck the tail of his rake into a summer-crack, wiped the perspiration from his forehead with his arm, winked wickedly with his right eye, and laughed to himself. He watched Daddy Childs, as he shuffled along, breaking the stubble down with his naked feet. The old man did not approach him, but passed along at the foot of the hill, and when he was opposite, he waved his white staff above his head, and cried out, without stopping,—

"Beware of Jim Crow and his rebel rout!"

Upon this, Halford Pinbury rose up, standing six feet high, winked mischievously with his right eye again, and laughed. Then he leaned on his rake with his left arm, and called after him,—

"Hillo! Say, now! It's in the old of the moon. Come up. 'Tisn't going to rain to-day. Come up and try some. By hokey, what's the use in worrying so this hot day?"

The old man did not pause for a moment, but turned his head back, waved his staff again, and cried out aloud,—

"Beware of Jim Crow and his rebel rout!"

Halford Pinbury squatted down by his rake again, and watched the old man, as he hurried away, until he saw him ascend the hill, climb another fence, and disappear. Then he arose and went about his work, muttering to himself, "Humph! what is the old luney after now, I wonder?"

As the old man ascended to the top of the meadow, he came in sight of Tick Hill, and the ample fields of the river-farms lay before him, in all the splendid ripeness and richness of the yellow harvest-time. Oh, beautiful valley of the Muskingum! in thy summer wealth of farms, between the green and sunny rims of thy hills; with thy evergreen-embowered houses amid the golden fields; and thy hearty, old-time farmers, challenging each the other to a friendly combat with the ringing of the whetted scythe; or the long cohorts of contending harvesters, with the swift and whirring swoop of their cradles through the yielding grain; while the whistling quail keeps time upon the fence—did ever human eye behold a lovelier!

But Daddy Childs heeded none of these things. He only strode right on across the stubbly wheatfield, swinging his hairy-black arms. Under a mighty mulberry there sat a squad of Farmer Pinbury's jolly harvesters at their forenoon luncheon; but when their eyes fell upon Daddy Childs, they all began to hoot, and whistle, and utter cat-calls. Hagerman, who was a facetious fellow, cried out,—

"Well, old cock, you look pretty red around the gills

to-day. You'll have to walk faster than that, if ever you ketch up with your wits ag'in. Seen 'em pass here long ago, in the hind part of the morning. But they was so monstrous little, you'll never find 'em without puttin' on your leather specs."

Then he tossed up a mulberry, and it descended through his huge black whiskers straight into his cavernous mouth. He looked at the old man again, and said, muttering to himself, " The devil is in him."

Daddy Childs gave no attention to these taunts, but turned his head, swung his white staff, and cried out, mournfully,—

" Beware of Jim Crow and his rebel rout !"

Then all the jolly harvesters, with one accord, hooted in reply, and said,—

" Sho ! Daddy Childs."

Little red-headed Danny was bringing out a jug of dogwood beer to the laborers, whistling like a quail, and taking one short step and one very long one, while the jug bumped along against his legs. As soon as he saw Daddy Childs he dropped the jug, and ran and hid himself in a wheat-shock.

When the old man passed down the lane near Farmer Pinbury's house, the little farmer was mending a gate. He did not stop for a moment, but waved his staff and called to him,—

" Beware of Jim Crow and his rebel rout !"

The little farmer, with his smooth-shaven face and his soft, pleasant eye, looked after him several moments in wondering silence, and then began to whistle under his breath, as his manner was in a brown study, and went on tinkering his gate.

When he passed Colonel Dobley's house, the venerable colonel was hobbling along in his yard on his crutches.

He stopped a moment, straightened himself vigorously up on his sound leg, and looked scowlingly at Daddy Childs, for the colonel, though nobly kind-hearted, had a countenance which, when wrinkled in meditation, looked frowning and severe. The old man glanced through the fence, and called out loudly, for he knew the aged colonel was slightly deaf,—

"Beware of Jim Crow and his rebel rout!"

But the noble old testy colonel frowned still more at this, and answered him quite loudly,—

"What sense is there in talking so loud?"

But stout little Mr. Boonder, with his glossy tile, his far-looking gray eyes, and his fatherly, thoughtful ways, mildly said,—

"But, perhaps, Colonel Dobley, it would be well enough to make some arrangements, in case there *should* be any danger."

Near the river the old man passed a merry group of school-children, tumbling in the grass, under a magnificent lofty apple-tree, vast as any white-oak of the primeval forest, and eating the little yellow sheepnoses. All the smaller children ran and hid themselves in the grass, but two big brothers stood their ground. Daddy Childs called to them, as to everybody,—

"Beware of Jim Crow and his rebel rout!"

The smaller children peeped at him from behind the trunk of the tree, but the older ones, when he was far enough away, pelted him with rotten apples, and hooted,—

"Sho! Daddy Childs."

How the old man crossed the river has never been satisfactorily ascertained. Old Alpha, the fisherman, declared he swam across, passing hand over hand along his trot-line; but nobody believed Old Alpha, because he once said he caught a catfish weighing ninety pounds. Others affirmed he slid across on a film of petroleum; but that would be a greasy slander upon the waters of the beautiful Muskingum which cannot for a moment be tolerated. In any event, he did cross, and climbed up the rocky, sterile steeps of Tick Hill, toiling up laboriously with his hands on his knees, or clutching the whortleberry-bushes for a support. Once upon the summit, he paused, turned about, and gazed mournfully down upon the surpassing rich and noble valley he had crossed, but in which he had been received with so much flouting and contumely. He struck his staff into the ground and leaned on it for a moment, while his eyes wandered over its peaceful and tranquil homes. Then he cried out yet again, and his voice rang strangely and sadly wild over that whole great valley,—

"Beware! beware! I warn you faithfully, and deceive you not. Beware!"

Then all the people heard him, and they listened now to his words, and their souls were smitten with a sudden and sharp terror, as if they heard already the thundering hoofs of the dreadful and direful cavalcade. Every one stopped still in his place, and dropped the work he was doing, and they all, with one accord, lifted up their voices and answered him,—

"Thou art faithful, Daddy Childs. Thou warnest all."

And, indeed, this dreadful and fearful host was already very near, and was even then hastening with fatal swiftness down the hollow of Congress Run. They were already passing the lowly cabin of Daddy Childs, from which the raging flames leaped and hissed, and snapped their fiery tongues in the very face of the gorgeous sun in heaven.

Now this Jim Crow was a man of the Dark and Bloody Ground, famous in all that region round about for his astuteness in swapping horses. It became a monomania

with him.   When the great and terrible war came on between the two countries lying on opposite sides of the
Beautiful River, this strange infatuation became tinged witn
patriotism.   He pondered the matter so much that, like a
certain famous knight, his reason became partially unsettled, and then it was his disordered brain conceived the
daring and brilliant project of bringing the enemies of his
country to utter and ignominious defeat and irretrievable
ruin, by compelling them to swap all their horses.   He
would ride through all the length and breadth of the land
with a numerous following, force everybody to swap horses
with him, and so ride all hostile horseflesh into a state of
exhaustion and heaves, and terminate the war.   Whether
it ever occurred to him or not, this would have effected a
great saving of human lives, and was therefore a plan
which should have commended itself to all humane souls.

Jim Crow was a man of exceeding fierce and unconsti-
tutional aspect.   He was dressed throughout in gray, and
his coat had a tail treasonably long, because the fashion
of his country's enemies was short.   In his belt he had four
pistols and seven knives.   His eyes were gray, like his
clothes.   It is said that he whetted his knives every morning, and then took his eyesight out and whittled it, by
which means he made it so very sharp and fierce that, when
he looked at one of his country's enemies, with both eyes
at once, they made a hole quite through his head.   His
black moustache was so long that he could lap it around his
head and bring the ends together in front.   On the narrow, upright collar of his coat he had golden stars, which
symbolized the loftiness of his character, though others
affirmed that they denoted the phenomena which appeared
to the eyes of his enemies in battle.

And now, his dreadful and fearful host had crossed the
Beautiful River, traversed the Hoosier State, and a good

part of the Buckeye State, and was now hastening down the hollow of Congress Run. Just as Halford Pinbury had taken a draught of mustard cider, and covered the oaken firkin with hay, the tremendous and multitudinous thundering of their hoofs was heard, and a great cloud of dust ascended above the sugar-trees. In a few minutes more they emerged in sight, and then what an appalling spectacle petrified his vision!

Horned horses, horses with brazen hoofs and eyes of fire, headless horsemen, some with their heads tied on behind their saddles, two-legged horses, which advanced only by a kind of kangaroo jumps. The better to accomplish the diabolical purposes hereinbefore set forth, many of them caused their horses to go forward, not in the usual manner, but by a continuous series of somersaults, by which violent motions many of the poor beasts had jerked off their ears, and looked very hideous. Many of the riders were young, and often fell asleep, when they would be jounced violently off upon the ground; but they would run and clamber on again. Most of them had bales of calico and strings of shoes flung over their horses' backs. Jim Crow rode in fierce and terrific splendor at the head of the cavalcade, and his horse had a horn of brass on his forehead, and his eyes were of a peculiar, traitorous color, and from his nostrils there issued smoke of sulphur and other disloyal substances.

For a moment, Halford Pinbury stood and gazed in speechless amazement; then he simply ejaculated, "Well, now, by hokey!" and dived down hill at the top of his speed, to save his fat, old, sorrel horse, which stood hitched to a little locust. Snatching the halter loose, he leaped upon his back; but the infatuated animal, whinnying frantically, ran with all his might to join the dreadful cavalcade. Finding himself, despite his most desperate efforts, about to be carried, irresistibly, into the fatal and direful host, Halford Pinbury dismounted in hot haste, abandoning the beast to his miserable fate, and fled up hill to his firkin of mustard cider, where, seeing he was not pursued, he stopped.

Leave we this dreadful procession, for a moment, to note the assembling of the Home Guards at the little frame schoolhouse in the valley. Roused by the last solemn warning of Daddy Childs, they had hastened to this place of rendezvous, with their arms and accoutrements. Stout little Mr. Boonder, with the far-looking gray eyes, and his fatherly, thoughtful ways, was there to assist in "making arrangements." His voice was always heard by the neighbors in times of peril. Little Farmer Pinbury, with his smooth-shaven face, and his soft, pleasant eyes, was there in a brown study. He was walking to and fro, whistling under his breath, with his hands behind him under his coat-tails. Stout-hearted old Colonel Dobley had also hobbled there, to show the young men how to fight. There, too, was the stately, but languid, Miss Jemima Boonder, with the pleading eyes and the ripe, pouting lips; and Miss Jerusha Pinbury, with the earnest, pretty, brown eyes, and the tight little mouth, like an elongated knot-hole.

While the inspection and loading of arms were in progress, Mr. Boonder "made arrangements" with red-bearded Captain Dobley about a supply of gunpowder, then passed along the line, speaking a fatherly word to each, and showing the awkward how to load their rifles more quickly. Presently, Farmer Pinbury stopped whistling under his breath, and began quietly to build rail-pens for barricades. Colonel Dobley stationed himself at the end of the line, straightened himself vigorously up on his sound leg, sighted along the line, motioned with his crutch toward the middle, and commanded, in stentorian tones,—

"Dress up in the middle there!"

Captain Dobley then stepped forward, and, with a terrific and portentous sternness on his brow, which was peculiarly militia-like, commanded,—

"Dress up,—company!"

Upon this, the grand old veteran colonel scowled, struck his crutch hard upon the ground, and said, very loudly,—

"What sense is there in talking so loud!"

Meantime Mr. Boonder and Farmer Pinbury had consulted together as to the height the rail-pens should have; then Mr. Boonder and the captain consulted about the probability of any of the squirrel-guns bursting; then Mr. Boonder "made arrangements" to have the brave boys supplied with the necessary nutriment.

"Colonel Dobley," said Mr. Boonder, "did you hide your horse in the smoke-house or the cornfield?"

"I tumbled him over the bank of the river," replied the colonel, twitching a soldier into line.

Miss Jemima Boonder had, however, in the mean time, acting upon her own sweet and patriotic will, brought a generous supply of blackberry turnovers, which she was distributing along the line, while Miss Jerusha Pinbury, not to be behind, was cheering the defenders of their country with fresh, cool well-water. As these two dear creatures moved along they dropped several tears. When the boys had eaten the blackberry turnovers and drunk the well-water, they felt nourished, and waxed patriotic and fierce exceedingly. They gave three cheers, and loaded their shot-guns double.

And now, when the dreadful procession ascended the meadow-hill and beheld the noble valley spread out before them, what a spectacle awaited them! Horses' tails sticking out of hen-houses, horses' ears sticking out of haycocks, horses whinnying down-cellar, where they were complacently munching the last shriveled remnant of last year's apples. The children ran into the house, crowded under the bed, and plugged up their ears with their fingers. The hired girl hurried up-stairs and went to bed, covering her head with the clothes. Rosy-cheeked little Mrs. Pinbury seated herself in her rocking-chair, and pulled out her hair-pins, so that, when the dreadful noise began, she might faint without doing herself bodily injury. The cat popped into the hole. The old Shanghai cock set off at the head of his harem, but knocked his knees together, and plumped headforemost into the puddle. Then the direful procession swept along, and all the horses, summoned by the irresistible fascination of the great leader's voice, issued from concealment, and joyfully hastened to swell the calvacade.

Long before they approached the little frame school-house, the Home Guards discharged their pieces into the atmosphere, at an angle of about forty-five degrees, and effected a masterly retreat, "to draw the enemy on to destruction." None were left behind but the three old unarmed citizens and their two brave daughters. After looking for a few moments at their fleeing defenders, Mr. Boonder remarked,—

"I think, perhaps, Colonel Dobley, we had better make some arrangements to run."

Farmer Pinbury pointed toward one of his strawstacks, and said, quietly,—

"We might find a refuge there; but if they shot at us, I fear they might fire the stack, and then my cattle would have no shelter next winter."

But stout-hearted old Colonel Dobley scowled till his face looked terrible, struck his crutch fiercely on the ground, and said,—

"We'll stay and fight it out here! My crutch is worth a dozen of the chicken-hearted fellows."

And there they stayed. And Miss Jerusha Pinbury and Miss Jemima Boonder, when they saw their defenders and their lovers all running away, cried out, "Oh, were ever good blackberry turnovers so wasted!"

Hastening down to the river, the Home Guards embarked in skiffs and rowed across. Taking a safe station, so that no bullets could disturb them in their important labors, they commenced excavating rifle-pits and felling trees. It was a profound movement of strategy; they were changing their base. One smooth-faced, white-headed Simon Pinbury was the first to secure a strategic position, wherein, with his head barely visible above the ground, he called upon his countrymen, in passionate eloquence, never to yield to the vandal invader, but rather to die in the last ditch. Then he leveled his rifle, took deliberate and deadly aim, fired across the river, and totally killed and abolished a small dog.

In commemoration of this great victory, the patriotic maidens of that neighborhood caused the rifle-pit to be inclosed with an iron railing, which remains to this day, an imperishable monument to the heroism of their country's defenders.

After securing all the horses, the marauders hastened on to the river, and crossed over. Ascending Tick Hill in the track of Daddy Childs, they found that faithful but despised guardian of his people waiting to complete his mission of deliverance. He conducted them straightway to the Crooked Tree. And now, behold, what a wonderful thing was wrought! As soon as they looked at the Crooked Tree, their eyesight became distorted, so that no two of them any longer clave together, but they rode each his several way. Thus was the great sovereign and inviolable Buckeye State delivered out of the hand of the spoilers.

TWINKLE OF THE MOOSE'S EYE.

The red man came—
The roaming hunter-tribes, warlike and fierce,
And the Mound-builders vanished from the earth.
. . . . All is gone;
All—save the piles of earth that hold their bones,
The platforms where they worshiped unknown gods,
The barriers which they builded from the soil
To keep the foe at bay—till o'er the walls
The wild beleaguerers broke, and, one by one,
The strongholds of the plain were forced, and heaped
With corpses. The brown vultures of the wood
Flocked to those vast uncovered sepulchres,
And sat, unscared and silent, at their feast.
Haply some solitary fugitive,
Lurking in marsh and forest, till the sense
Of desolation and of fear became
Bitterer than death, yielded himself to die.
Man's better nature triumphed then. Kind word
Welcomed and soothed him; the rude conquerors
Seated the captive with their chiefs; he chose
A bride among their maidens.

BRYANT.

MANY centuries ago the tribe of Shawnee Indians, a member of the great nation of the Lenni-Lenape, were emigrating across the continent toward the Ocean of the Rising Sun. It was long before any paleface had ever trodden its western shores, or even ventured out on its trackless highways, and while yet the race of the Mound-builders still existed, unscared by these fierce hunter-tribes of the red Mongolians. This was the vanguard of that great ancient migration which swept them off the earth.

(24)

In that peerless valley which now immortalizes their name, the Miamis, their kindred, in a sacred and irrevocable alliance with them, had utterly extirpated the effeminate and fallen Mound-builders; and now their warriors were come to assist in the conquest of a certain noble and goodly valley, of which reports had brought them information. Luxurious, degenerate, and debased by an effete and horrible religion, the Mound-builders dwelt only in the valleys, which they had reddened with the blood of human sacrifices, while they had cowardly abandoned all the fortresses once maintained by them on the crowning summits. Beyond the river-ranges all the face of the earth was still somber with the ancient gloom of the forest, and penetrated only by the bear and the ferocious panther.

At length the Shawnee scouts announced their near approach to the valley. Leaving their squaws and papooses secreted in the recesses of the forest, they emerged cautiously upon the brow of a woody mountain, and looked down, with grim exultation, upon the valley which was theirs to conquer. Directly below them was one of those mysterious and ancient barrows which the Mound-builders elevate above their chieftains. The river here sweeps grandly around in a semicircle, and in the middle of this spacious plain they beheld a white-walled village, defended only by a feeble rampart of earth, crested with wooden palisades. In their indolent and pampered degeneracy, the Mound-builders of the east had ceased to fortify their cities with those imposing bulwarks of earth, the remains of which have lingered to this day in the valley of the Father of Waters.

All the inhabitants, for miles above and below, were gathering into this village in direful haste, for a messenger had just arrived with the heart-sickening tidings from the Miami.   As these fierce and cruel hordes stood and looked down with gleaming eyes upon their coming harvest of massacre, the smoke of burning habitations went up, and here and there a fleeing family were seen, with all their household goods in a wooden-wheeled cart, mothers and children crying as they went, over the ruin of their little homes, while the father goaded on his team of crooked-kneed, shaggy bisons.

The Shawnees gathered upon the brow of the mountain, and awaited the approach of sunset.   As soon as the huge shadows of the mountains stretched full across the valley and commenced climbing the opposite side, they descended, and crouched in a gloomy ravine, until a scout, who had crawled to the summit of the barrow, brought word that all lights were extinguished in the village. Then their great prophet and medicine-man, with his drum, his snakeskin rattle, and his medicine-bag, advanced alone to the top of the sacred burial-mound, muttered a solemn invocation to the Most High God, took a magic arrow from his quiver, placed it in his good ashen bow, and sped it on a long and lofty flight through heaven toward the village.   With an eager and a hungry motion the barbed arrow cleft the mellow air, slipping through the darkness on its curving course, until it reached its highest flight, when the heavens opened with an appalling glare, the arrow shone in a globe of white lightning, and terrifically the awful thunders roared in the valley.   To the awe-stricken warriors, as the majestic figure of their prophet stood blackly out for an instant against the quivering heavens, there seemed to flicker around his head and uplifted bow a lambent, pale-blue halo.   Then the solemn tones of the prophet were heard through the darkness,—

"By the impious and horrible sacrifices of their bloody

religion our enemies have exhausted the long patience of Heaven. The thunders of the Most High God shall bring swift and terrible succor to their destroyers.''

Then the Shawnees sent their allies, the Miamis, around in two bodies, above and below, to intercept any fugitives at the fords. This done, they themselves lay quiet till near daybreak, listening to the slow rumbling of the thunders.

When their watching eyes beheld the morning-star for one moment twinkle with a watery luster amid an oak-tree on the mountain, they arose and rushed down across the plain, and in that self-same hour the arsenals of the Most High God were opened. With horrid and heart-sickening yells they leaped the phantom stockade, and the lurid lightnings guided their swift tomahawks not amiss. The Mound-builders yielded up their wretched lives like sheep before the slayer. Not more swiftly did the murderous stones descend upon the heads of unresisting victims than the quick and forked cross-lightnings hissed and hurtled from heaven. The torrents of warm rain which gurgled in the streets glared crimson beneath the continuous bolts, and all their purple bubbles winked like bloodshot eyes in the face of the lightnings. The tempest swept over and the thunders lulled, as if the vengeance of Heaven were palled and glutted, and yet the weary savages paused not, though forgetting even their yells of triumph, so that in all the village there was no sound but the dull and thudding crash of the tomahawk. Only when the great sun looked out, with his angry and lurid eye, through a chink in the morning clouds, did the village rest in silence, and the butchers cease, because there were no victims.

So great was the multitude of the Mound-builders !

And after that the Shawnees gathered much plunder, and sent for their squaws to serve them, and they feasted, they and their allies, and made merry. Afterward, it happened that a band of Shawnee warriors, wandering over the village, found a house wherein was a maiden hidden, and yet alive. And there was with her a young moose, which had been tenderly nourished by her hand, and now lingered about her hiding-place. Upon the approach of the Shawnees it ran a little way off, then returned, and darted into the house which secreted its mistress, and moaned piteously, and turned its pleading sad gaze upon the warriors, as if beseeching them to show mercy. Thus it revealed to them the hiding-place of the maiden, and she was dragged forth, lifeless with terror. As soon as it saw her, the little animal ran toward her with a plaintive cry, pressed its silken, glossy neck fondly against her, and cowered timorously beside her, looking piteously into her face for protection, and crying and moaning; then it looked again at its strange captors, and ran a little way off, then turned and gazed again, with such infinite pitifulness, toward its mistress, and such dumb, helpless wonder at the savage warriors; then ran to her again, and so, backward and forward. The dainty little foot-taps on the floor, as it trotted about its beloved mistress; its soft bleating; the sad and piteous terror of the poor innocent, as it turned its great, lustrous eyes upon its captors; the dear and tender caresses of its glossy neck against the insensible form of the maiden; the tremor of helpless terror along its velvety flanks—ah! could even the voice of the mistress have pleaded more eloquently?

Even the grim savages were touched,—all except one, who brutally struck the poor, crying innocent, and dashed it to the ground. They bore away the maiden, and left the stricken pet where it fell. But, after a time, it recovered, and, guided by the unerring instinct of its kind, limped away toward the river.

The youthful chief, Pallenund, was fascinated with the beauty of the maiden, whose name was Opimya, and he ordered the bearers to carry her away to his wigwam. But now, continues the tradition, hardly had the stricken moose disappeared, when the very heavens seemed to scowl wrathfully, and lowered with gloom. All the thunders were fearfully reawakened, twofold more terrific than those which drowned the shrieks of the murdered city, and the lightnings blazed and quivered on the ground and over the bloody ruins. The dead Mound-builders arose and pursued their murderers with horrid yells, and with their cold and stringy fingers clutched their naked bodies. Their hideous livid faces glared with hate and fury. The very scalps writhed in the slippery clutch of the savages, and flapped, bloody and clammy, in their faces. The brutal wretch who struck down the moose was specially singled out, and pursued by corpses with sunken eyes, and bodies covered thick with carrion flies. The vultures, disturbed at their banquet, screamed above their heads. The wounded moose appeared before them with a body of flaming fire, but turned upon them the same sad and piteous gaze as before.

Then was heard again the solemn voice of the great prophet, crying through the gloom and the raging of the storm,—

"The Most High God is angry. He dwells in the air, and the clouds, and the lightnings, and the beasts of the forest, and the wound given to the moose is given to Him likewise. He has given us the animals for our necessary meat, therefore has He taken away their voices, that they should not cry unto the slayers; but the fierce lightnings are his also, and fearfully does He plead for His creatures when they are cruelly entreated. We shall not escape these thunders till we have made expiation; howbeit, if

3*

the moose be dead, He will plague this man with the torments of an implacable vengeance."

But the maiden, Opimya, had arisen, and wandered weeping for the slain innocent. In the horror of the great darkness and of the lightnings, she fled among the Shawnees, that lay stricken to the ground in terror, and sought the bank of the river, where she was wont to fondle with the fawn in the summer days. In the middle of the river was a little island, covered with pale-green trees, and opposite this she sat down under a great sycamore. Night came to deepen the tempest, and the darkness became thick blackness. Sitting and leaning her head against the friendly tree, she cried out, piteously,—

"Ah! my pretty, my pet, my innocent! How often have I watched my face and ranged my braided hair in the light of thy eyes! How often hast thou fondly leaned against me, in thy pretty, helpless terror, when I swept in my little, light canoe across the water! Ah! pretty, my pretty, my pet! would I were dead now, and laid beside thee!"

The young chief, Pallenund, was passing, with a band of his warriors, searching for the moose, that they might appease the wrath of Heaven, and they heard the wailings of the maiden, and approached. Pallenund drew near, and spoke kind words, and lifted her gently in his arms, but she only bewailed herself the more. Then suddenly one cried out, and pointed to two little gleams in the edge of the water, fiery-red and immovable, as if they were blood-red stars dropped from heaven into the river. But Pallenund no sooner looked than he uttered a joyous shout,—"It is the twinkle of the moose's eye! It is the twinkle of the moose's eye!" And one dashed into the water, and fetched it forth, amid songs, and shouting, and dancing, and great rejoicing, but the maiden fell upon its neck, and wrapped it about with her arms, and laid her cheek against its neck, and pressed it silently to her breast, while her tears trickled fast over its glossy coat.

Heaven itself rejoiced at that spectacle, for, as the tradition relates, the clouds were riven asunder and vanished, the shadows of night were rolled back, and the sun returned on his course, to lighten the earth in that glad moment.

Then said Pallenund to his warriors, "Heaven is appeased hereby, and we shall be saved if we cut off the offender from among us. Therefore let the name of this river be The Twinkle of the Moose's Eye, and so shall it be called Moos-ken-gum, and the moose shall be sacred unto us for evermore."

So they returned with great rejoicings to the encampment, bearing the maiden, with the recovered moose still tightly clasped in her glad embrace.

On the morrow they made a joyful feast for their deliverance, and sacrificed to the Great God, and the maiden was given to Pallenund. And when, afterward, Pallenund and Opimya stood together beneath a mighty beech, before the assembled tribe, and the venerable prophet gave them a double ear of maize, in token of their union, and also in token of her proper industry, subjection, and providence, while the little pet stood with its great eyes wonderingly gazing at the unwonted spectacle ; then Pallenund made a solemn vow, and attested it before Heaven, that, so long as the golden sun should light the land the Great God had given them, and so long as the uncounted eyes of the Moose-Eye River should twinkle and wink adown its course, the faithful and unforgetting Shawnees would lift up hand no more, wantonly, against a moose.

ST. TAMMANY.

Perhaps it was right to dissemble your love,
But—why did you kick me down-stairs?

BICKERSTAFF.

TAMMANY was a friend to the pale-face. He desired to abide with him in peace in the country of the Great Waters; but his tribe would none of it, and he yielded to them, removed from the land of his ancestors, and journeyed toward the setting sun.

Slowly and sadly he paddled his canoe, amid the fleet of his tribe, up the broad, blue waters of the River of the Burning Pine; then they traveled on foot over the great, roaring mountains of the Appalachites; fashioned bark canoes again, and teetered away down the swift and bubbling River of Falling Banks; passed the Place of a Head; then floated many and many a golden summer day down a mighty stream, which, gliding down in the majesty of its smooth and oily rolling, between the never-ending colonnade of pale-green trees, and around the stripped and ravaged islands which attested the greatness of its savage energy when aroused, with here and there a dead branch thrust up out of the water like a palsied arm that would drag their canoes under, seemed to them to be indeed, as it was named, the Beautiful River. Then at last, after floating down through all the long and pleasant Moon of Strawberries, they joyfully dragged their canoes upon the sand where this majestic stream receives the waters of the dimpling, little, winking Moose-Eye River, and journeyed no more.

(32)

We cannot follow Tammany's people through all the vicissitudes of their history, the fierce and horrid battles in the echoing forest, the triumphs, the defeats, the treaties, the alliances, which at last established them securely in their new dominion. The legend has business with another matter.

The tribe waxed great among the nations of the aborigines round about, and became impregnably colonized on the banks of the Muskingum. In the course of their history it had now become necessary to choose a chief sachem to rule over them. It is to this memorable event that this legend relates, for by it were laid down the rule and precedent for all coming generations of American politics. By this transaction the great American science of How to Get into Office (politics) was established forever on fundamental principles, in contradistinction to the useless art of How to Get out of Office (statesmanship).

By his well-known friendliness to the pale-face, Tammany had raised up enemies in his tribe, who composed the opposition. In accordance with their respective sentiments on this issue, Tammany's party were recognized as the White Eyes, while the opposition were designated Red Eyes.

The point of junction of the rivers, where now stands the pleasant village of Harmar, is the place where this momentous event occurred. Hither, on a designated day, repaired all the multitudes of the tribe. All the squaws and papooses came, even those which were borne upon the backs in wicker baby-baskets; and all the superan nuated warriors, who could no longer walk, but were borne on stretchers of bearskin (for Tammany gave the bearers wampum); with all the gallant and stalwart braves of a hundred fights, with nodding plumes of feathers of eagles and of redbirds, and stained quills of porcupine twisted in their hair, fiercely painted with smears and streaks of scarlet ochre, and gorgeously bedecked with flowing robes of figured wolfskins, and beaded moccasins, with chinking and jingling strings of purple wampum, and flint-headed arrows of hickory. From many a somber fastness in the wood along the shores of the river called Beautiful, and from many a patch of shining corn beside the Moose-Eye River, and from beneath the shadows of the Great Mound, the ancient and mysterious, they came in numbers, fearlessly leaving their growing maize and their wigwams without even a dog on sentry, for the matchless prowess and diplomacy of Tammany had made all tribes to fear them.

The wigwams of Tammany and of the chief of the Red Eyes were pitched about a tomahawk's throw apart, at the great encampment.

Whenever Tammany beheld a company approaching, he would advance about an arrow-shot to meet them, stop short before them, look earnestly and steadfastly into their faces, then salute them: "Welcome, my children. May the Great Spirit guide your minds, that you may vote with wisdom." To this they would reply, if they were White Eyes, "The Great Spirit is in you;" but if they were Red Eyes, "Ugh! ugh!" Then he would conduct them into his wigwam, pour a little fire-water into a gourd from a porcupine-skin, taste it himself, and hand it to all his guests in succession, each of whom remarked after tasting it, "Ugh, ugh!" After that, they would seat themselves in a circle, and he would take down a bladder of tobacco, fill the bowl of his red-stone Kanawha calumet, and pass it around the circle. All these solemn and decorous hospitalities were interspersed by Tammany, occasionally, with brief, judicious observations, such as, "Ugh, ugh!" "May the Great Spirit guide you!" "The Red Eyes are fools," "Maize well watered grows fast."

These ceremonies of hospitality being finished, the braves would visit likewise the wigwam of the Red Eyes, partake of the hostile chief's fire-water, and smoke his calumet.

Meantime Tammany would go abroad, and mingle familiarly, yet with dignity, with the assembled braves of his tribe. To the younger ones he gave strings of wampum, fine embroidered moccasins, pipe-bowls, beautiful ashen bows and arrows, and whatever other things are either pleasant to see or to possess. If an aged brave was almost deaf, he told him that people did not speak so loudly nowadays as in former years, when he was young. If any one was blind, he led him by the hand, and spoke to him many words of kindness. He struck his tomahawk into a tree, so low that the youths could all leap over the handle, and told them they could all spring as high as Tammany could in his lustiest youth.

Two days the braves were in assembling together, and on the morning of the third day there was a mighty multitude. When the hour drew near that they should elect their chief sachem, Tammany caused a long and a strong blast to be blown on the hollow thigh-bone of a. moose, which was heard far and wide throughout the encampment. All the braves thereupon gathered about his wigwam, and squatted on their haunches beneath a wide-spreading beech.

Then Tammany issued forth, arrayed in gorgeous and barbaric splendor, with seven extra smears of ochre on his face, an imposing coronal of feathers on his head, two carved and beaded clam-shells depending from his ears, and robes and moccasins of great magnificence. Standing before his wigwam, he made that oration which caused him to be canonized as the patron and great tutelary saint of all American politicians. He took a blackberry into his mouth to moisten it, and then spoke as follows:

" Men are not ruled by wisdom. My arms are not long, but I can reach above my head. My feet are not nice, but they carry my head wheresoever it goes.

"A full bladder gives no sound when it is struck. When the wolf howls he is empty.

" The deceit of man is great. The coon's tail is in the pond, but his body is on the log. The crawfish get a nibble of his tail, but the coon eats the crawfish.

" No man has eyes in the back of his head. I can see farther than I can reach. It is easier to pierce the heart through the back than through the breast.

" Go not too far. A man can sleep in a small sapling. If he climbs to the top it bends to the ground.

" Every man has a place made for him by the Great Spirit. A deer cannot climb a tree. The jay sits on the topmost bough. The arrow of the brave slays them both.

" It is easier for fools to go forward than backward. The cat can climb a tree, but she comes down tail first. A wise man does not go forward till he sees how he can come back. The duck dives after the corn, but its neck . sticks fast in the net.

" If two braves contend for a squaw, and one wins her, does he give the other her beads? They are his own. What brave is there who kills his enemy and does not take his scalp? If he did not, men would count him no better than a fool and a squaw.

" A man cannot pull up a tree by the roots, but if he climbs to the top he can bend and break it down to the ground.

" Is anybody wise who is Tammany's enemy? He is

a fool. The Red Eyes are fools. This I know. They are knaves. The Great Spirit has told me this. Truth is not to be divided. Can you split the sun with a tomahawk? Are there two moons? The sun is in all things, and when fire springs forth from wood it is the sun. There is one light.

" When the Evil Spirit seizes a man, and torments him with fatness, do not men bleed him with flints? It is wise. Also, when the Evil Spirit seizes him, and he madly thinks to become a sachem to whom the Great Spirit has not given it, wampum is taken from him. These things I know well, and the custom is so. But there is no blood in a dead man. When he is dying he is not bled, but he is cast out, and men leap and dance on his stomach, and beat him with sticks. These things are true.

"A wise brave does not strike his enemy's war-club, but his eyes. A dog has a long tail, but a squaw can cut it off. She cannot pluck out his teeth.

" The chief of the Red Eyes is an enemy of his people. This I know. If he were a friend to his people, he would be a White Eye. If you choose him to be sachem, the Great Spirit will be wroth, and our tribe will talk with owls, and become acquainted with bats. If the Red Eye chief becomes sachem, we shall take counsel with screech-owls. We shall seek the haunts of dogs, and find them. The grass will grow in our wigwams, and our sacred places will be deserted and silent. The howling of the wolf will be heard in our lodges, and in our ancient villages the fox will dig his hole unscared.

" Humbles are something, but wampum is greater. Tammany has wampum. Tammany is wise. The chief of the Red Eyes is a fool. He is also a knave. This I know well. He wishes to ruin his people. Tammany wishes to save them.

"The words of Tammany are ended."

The conclusion of this oration was received with very general exclamations of "Ugh, ugh!" as indicative of assent and applause. Then the multitude arose and gathered about the wigwam of the opposing chieftain, who came forth and stood before his door. After looking sternly and immovably toward the great warrior for some minutes, he slowly raised his right hand, pointed scornfully toward him with his forefinger, and began in a deep and solemn voice, scowling darkly:

"Tammany is not wise. He has not spoken the words of wisdom. The sound of his voice is as the west wind when it blows in the winter. Beside the noise of the blowing, there is nothing else at all."

At this point, Tammany strode majestically to the side of the speaker, confronted him with a lowering and terrible mien, and imparted to him his opinion of the entire misapprehension of facts under which he evidently labored. Thereupon the chief of the Red Eyes informed Tammany that his statement was diametrically opposed to the requirements of strict veracity, and that that virtue abode not in him. Upon that Tammany enlightened his adversary with an expression of his convictions respecting his personal character and descent, and the character of his mother, to which the chief of the Red Eyes replied with a reciprocal piece of information.

Thereupon Tammany drew near to him, and smote him with his fist between his two eyes, knocked him down, and spat in his right ear.

The assembled multitude greeted this triumph with prolonged and vigorous exclamations of "Ugh, ugh!" and at once Tammany was chosen sachem by acclamation.

ST. SHODDY.

Gars auld claes look amaist as weel's the new.

BURNS.

IN the previous legend we have been permitted to rescue from oblivion a portion of the career of the great tutelary divinity of American politicians. Now be it our delightful task to preserve, through written record, so much as has been treasured up by immemorial tradition of the life and tragical death of St. Shoddy, known and recognized in all our Christian world as the great patron saint of American speculators.

St. Shoddy was born in the valley of the Muskingum, on the left bank of the river, near the little village of Smartville, situated in the township of Getmore. The precise hour of his birth is not recorded, but that auspicious event is supposed to have occurred in the night-time, since the infant is reported to have looked hard at the whale-oil lamp, and blinked with both eyes,—which circumstance was regarded by his nurse, in subsequent years, as indicative of the child's wonderful keenness for a speculation.

Very early in youth, while yet most children are wickedly devoting themselves to kites, tops, hobby-horses, and other reprehensible amusement, St. Shoddy developed a most commendable ability to " make money." Having been orphaned at a tender age, he was assigned to the guardianship of a remarkably shrewd uncle, who fostered the boy's speculatory propensities. The earliest known instance of the development of this precocity occurred in the following manner:

The boy's uncle frequently sent him to the village of Smartville, to carry to market poultry, vegetables, dairy products, etc., in order to educate him to shrewdness in dickering and shifting for himself, for he despised schools. One day he ordered him to take a dozen fowls, and, in order that he might start early in the morning, he bade him catch them off the trees overnight. The youth obeyed, but, with remarkable shrewdness, caught only such as had bright red combs, which denoted that they were laying eggs. These he put carefully into a large crate, carpeted with straw, and early in the morning he hitched the old dobbin into the wagon and started. The wagon was very small, and had no springs, and the boy took pains to drive it over the hardest and stoniest road he could find. The consequence was, when he arrived at the market, there were in the straw twelve new-laid eggs, warm and white. This was what he had expected when he drove the wagon over the stony road.

These he justly considered his own property, and, instead of spending them for foolish and wicked toys, such as kites and tops, or, still worse, for books, he bartered them for a terrier pup. This was not for play, but for profit, as will soon appear. His uncle, in order further to teach him to "look out for number one," was very close with his crumbs, so that the animal often howled full sore with hunger, and his ribs were grievously constricted. But the boy secretly nourished the pup, by taking him into the barnyard and milking the rich strippings into his mouth. He was well rewarded for all this prudence, for when the pup waxed to a good stature, and his teeth were well grown, he brought his young master a revenue of fifty-seven ratskins and two minks, worth several dollars.

The lad also, while he was yet in his extreme youth, concocted a sort of unguent or salve, wherewith to anoint people's corns. It was very active in its operations, being composed largely of aquafortis. Indeed, it was so very active in its effects that the lad presently procured for himself a sound beating, and he was obliged to put aside his corn-salve for the present.

By all these youthful speculations, and many others not here enumerated, he at length accumulated enough to purchase a large stock of candies and sweetmeats of all kinds from the village, which he brought out for sale to a children's picnic on a May-day. He also procured quite a quantity of materials for the manufacture of lemonade. Then, by his influence with the parents and older children, he caused the picnic to be celebrated in a certain grove, where there was only one spring to supply them with water. He sold his sweetmeats to them at a low price, quite as low as they could have purchased them from the village confectioners, which caused the children to eat heartily of them and become very thirsty. Meantime, in some mysterious manner which has never been fully explained, his terrier dog, which was now quite aged and feeble, fell into a corner of the spring, so that the children could no longer drink the water. Thus they were compelled to purchase large quantities of his lemonade at a high price, by which St. Shoddy received great profit. The dog having fallen into a *corner* of the spring was remembered by St. Shoddy when he grew to manhood, and gave rise to an expression which has become exceedingly famous among speculators.

But the one great and mature enterprise of St. Shoddy, for which all this was only preparatory, and which procured for him canonization and immortality, is now to be related. His speculative brain conceived a mighty project. Looking about him, he beheld thousands and tens of thousands of his fellow-mortals engaged in making clothes, at such pitiful rates of compensation, especially in the case of young seamstresses in great cities, that the slow wasting away and destruction of human life were melancholy to contemplate. But, saddening as was this circumstance to his mind, there was another yet more painful—the waste and utter loss of a great quantity of clothes. Month after month he beheld bundles of raiment, often only slightly abraded or soiled, cast aside at the imperious mandate of fickle Fashion, thrown out to be trodden under foot of mankind, sodden by the rains, defiled with mouldiness, and reduced to ignominious mildew, pulp, and decay. He regretted so much wastefulness, but, above all things beside, he beheld herein an opportunity for acquiring immense profit. He considered in his mind the principle, that there is nothing new on earth.

"The cabbages," said he to himself, in his thrifty musings, "grow up, flourish, and decay if they are not utilized ; but they return to the earth, and, in the mysterious laboratory of Nature, they are transformed from death into life, and appear again as cabbages, to gladden the appetite, and minister to the lusty strength, of the farmer. Nature cannot supply our artificial wants ; cannot, in short, either originally fashion, or subsequently transmute, our clothes ; but we can imitate her methods, and be instructed by her wise economy.

"I will cause old clothes to be converted into new. I will bring about a condition of affairs on earth, among civilized men, wherein all useless and cumbersome sheep, cotton-plants, hemp, flax, ramie, silk-worms, and whatever other fabric-producing animals, worms, or plants now occupy so great a portion of the earth, to the exclusion of factories, mills, and other evidences of civilization, may be wholly discarded. I will thus make living-space on earth for millions of people, now excluded by these plants and animals. I will relieve untold misery and penury among the laboring poor, by giving them new garments for their old, for a slight compensation. I will exterminate the heartless monopolies of clothiers, who crush the very life from the wretched seamstresses whom they employ.

"And, in doing all these things, I shall accomplish marvels for myself. I shall put profit into my pocket. It will be one of the greatest speculations of history. There is money in it. In short, it will pay."

Thus much he devised within his thrifty mind; but how to bring his great project into execution was a puzzle. He set himself to devise some invention. How could old clothes be renovated? How could the threadbare places be thickened, and the holes in the elbows bridged over? How could the color be restored? And then, too, it would not answer, in every case, to restore the original color, because the owner would weary of wearing the same always. Besides that, the fashions were continually shifting, and, if his invention was to be of any avail, it must be capable of taking the discarded garment the moment the fashion changed, and making it entirely over.

But at last he contrived an invention of marvelous ingenuity. He constructed a curious and intricate machine, into which old clothes could be fed, with water, and ground into pulp, then spread out thin in beautiful cloth, better than it was before, from which, by means of other wonderful machinery, the garment could be entirely reconstructed. And, most wonderful of all, he discovered that the oftener a garment was ground over the better it became. At first he was alarmed at this discovery, as it promised eventually to bring the garments to such a pitch of excellence that they would never wear out, and thus his occupation would be gone forever. But the goddess Fashion quickly came to his relief, and whispered to St. Shoddy that, so long as she held supreme dominion over mankind, he should never lack employment for his invention.

Then, to establish himself and his descendants in the control of this invention for all future time, he procured from this goddess a writing called a patent, which secured to him the exclusive right throughout the world to grind up old clothes. Not only were all the remainder of mankind strictly forbidden to grind up an old coat, but they were not even permitted to mend it. So powerfully did the goddess Fashion contribute to the subsequent apotheosis of St. Shoddy.

Need the sequel be chronicled? Need it be related how St. Shoddy received immense contracts from his government, during a war which then unhappily raged? How he furnished a mighty army with fine new garments? How, when their old clothes could not be gathered up amid the whizzing bullets, he even, in his ardent patriotism, ground up hair, ropes, old paper, and skins, and made them into clothes, that he might fulfill his contract? How the gallant lads loved him, rejoiced, and were proud in their radiant new garments? How thus the army was saved, and enabled to inflict on the enemy a bloody defeat, because when *their* old clothes were worn out they had no St. Shoddy to grind them over? How he became enormously wealthy, such as man never was before in all this goodly land?

St. Shoddy waxed very great, and the fame of him was enlarged exceedingly. He caused a grand house to be constructed of pressed stone, and plastered to look like marble, and the pillars of it were of hollow iron, also marbled. The rooms thereof were paneled with pine, and grained like laurel, and all manner of precious woods of Brazil; and his furniture was veneered like mahogany and rosewood.

He also caused a library to be built, and he gave out a contract for the purchase and manufacture of many thousands of books—one thousand to be six inches long, for the upper shelf; one thousand seven inches long, etc.; and all to be beautifully gilded or marbled. He also instructed his librarian to cause a large number of letters to be written, in different handwritings, and signed with the names of philosophers, statesmen, literary men, and the like, that his visitors might wonder at the greatness of his correspondence. But the letters from the greatest men St. Shoddy wrote best himself, because, as he remarked to his librarian, he had never learned to write.

St. Shoddy also took unto himself a wife, a woman who was fleshy and red-faced, and had on her fingers many flashing diamonds very ingeniously made of clarified paste (for St. Shoddy sought to encourage ingenuity in all men), and she rode in a splendid chariot, with mulberry panels, bearing, as a heraldic device, the representation of St. Shoddy himself benevolently offering a poor mechanic a coat of his ground cloth in place of one made in the ancient manner. She also patronized learning greatly, and even permitted a poor schoolmaster to live in her elegant mansion; and encouraged him by her daily presence. She went much further in her benevolence, and employed a poor girl, paying her a considerable stipend, to serve as her amanuensis.

And now, alas! it remains only to chronicle the melancholy and tragical death which caused St. Shoddy to be canonized. The architect whom he employed to construct his mansion was imbued with his own great principles of enterprise and rotation, and, in the erection of a house, he observed the same general plan followed by his illustrious employer in the fashioning of garments. In short, he reasoned that the oftener a house was constructed the better it became. He therefore very ingeniously built this mansion of pressed stone and plaster without iron girders, in such a manner that, when the rain descended upon it in great quantities, the pressed stone dissolved, and the house fell in with a mighty crash. But he had neglected to inform his employer of the great principle which he had discovered, and he was crushed beneath the ruins. And for his epitaph there were written these words: "Thou hast no speculation in those eyes." So it came about, from the memorable and melancholy manner of St. Shoddy's death, that there arose a superstitious tradition in that country, which was, that it was dangerous for one person to possess over seven tenement-houses, for that one of them was certain to fall upon him and destroy him.

PAPERS FROM GERMANY.

THE MISSING LINK RESTORED.

A STORY FOR BOYS.

'Mid pleasures and palaces though we may roam,
Be it ever so humble, there's no place like home.
HOME, SWEET HOME.

ONCE upon a time, a number of years ago, there lived in the Oldenburg hamlet of Donnersheim a sturdy peasant, named Christian Thurngauer, with his wife Katharine, and their only and hopeful son, Hans. They dwelt in one of those little old, quaint houses one may see so many of in North Germany, with a frame of wood, and all the space between filled in with brick, then the whole plastered thickly over, inside and out, with coarse mortar, and sicklied all over with a greenish-yellow wash. The walls bowed this way and that, like jolly old burghers at their beer, albeit they were so thick that the small square windows with their four panes looked more like holes punched through for the extrusion of cannon, in case the hamlet needed defense.

All along the street these mud-walls were ranged in order, with the gables sharpened steeply up, and little pigeon-holes, and holes of windows for the drowsy cats; each house leaning to or from the street in a manner entirely peculiar to itself; and all strung along together

(47)

in such a funny kind of way that the street was as crooked as the limb of a crab-apple tree.

Christian Thurngauer owned a little plot of land outside of the village, which was large enough to produce all the cabbages he needed for sauer-kraut, and more than that, had a pond where the geese could flounce and puddle at will, and then pick grass around the edges on little scraps of shores. Every day Hans had to let the geese out of the pen in the morning, and watch them while they picked, and bring them back at night. One day, in March, when there was a cold, nasty wind, which made his face and hands look as blue as skimmed milk, he had been out all day, and having had no dinner but a piece of bread without beer, he was impatient with the geese as they came slowly waddling home, and flung a pebble at an old gander, which broke its leg.

Great was his dismay thereat, for he knew he should not escape his father's wrath. He caught the gander, and tried to carry it, but it made such a squalling and flapping that he was obliged to let it go. It dragged itself along to the pen, and then set up such a screeching that his father came to see what was the matter.

"How did this happen, Hans?"

"I—I—— He kept a peckin' the other geese, and wouldn't go along."

"Ah, Sacrament! I see how it is." And with that he fetched him a smack on the face with his hard, broad hand, which sent him spinning away over the bank, and down into the ditch, where he fell top downward, and jabbed his head into the mud so deep that it was only after a considerable flouncing about that he pulled it loose.

Hans's Teutonic blood was up now. Before, he had felt sorry, and pitied the old gander; but now he cried for very rage. His mother came to him, and tried to soothe him. She was a patient, kindly, daft little body, with a pale, thin face, and soft, Saxon blue eyes, around which many sorrows and the boisterous temper of her husband had imprinted deep lines of grief. She loved Hans, as her only remaining child, with all the intensity of which her nature was capable; and many a time shielded him with her own person from the choleric bursts of passion to which his father so often gave way.

Now, she soothed and caressed him with more than her wonted tenderness, washed his face, and kissed away his tears, in a vain attempt to check their flow. Hans was inconsolable. His soul was full of rebellion. They went into the room, and sat down around their little supper. There was a great platter of boiled potatoes, with a cellar of salt beside it, into which each dipped his potato, and a pan of bonny-clabber. That was all.

Hans tried to eat, but he could not. Now and then a tear would trickle out and run all the way down along his nose; and he kept heaving long sobs, and the potato would not go down.

So, after the meal was finished in silence, Hans crept away to bed, but not to sleep. He kept turning over and over, and muttering to himself as nearly aloud as he dared, for he did not quite venture to speak out even to himself the naughty things he was thinking about. He was planning to run away, and was determined to go to America; but he would have to slip out through the back door, and he could not for his life think how he could get through the goose-pen without stirring up the geese and making a great uproar. He thought the matter all over a great many times, and finally he remembered a hole in the wall, about as high up as his head, where he could crawl out without getting among the geese. So he got up carefully, after all the house was still, dressed himself, and crept slyly out, and crawled through the hole and got safely into the road.

The moon was shining brightly overhead—as brightly as it ever does in blue old Germany--and Hans, in order not to make tracks in the road, walked along on the grass under the great spindling poplars. He did not know where America was, but he had heard old Herr Hund-bacher, in the village, talk about it often enough, and he knew people had to go to Bremen to get there, and he knew the road to Bremen very well.

All night long he walked as fast as he could, and never thought once of his mother, nor of anybody else behind him. Before morning he got pretty hungry, and a little after daybreak he stopped at a house where they gave him some crusts of black bread. He was very tired, and sat down by the roadside to nibble them, and then he thought about his mother's bread, and he could not help thinking that if he were at home she would not give him hard crusts to eat; and while he thought about her he cried a little, but then there came back to him the broken-legged gander and the ditch, and they made him feel spunky again.

Presently he overtook an old peasant, with his long sheepskin coat and staff, trudging along in the middle of the road, shuffling his wooden shoes along, and making a prodigious dust. Hans began to talk with him.

" Mein Herr, is it very far to America?"

" Oh, little one, Sacrament! America! That's more than a hundred miles from here!"

" But when I get to Bremen I'll be pretty near there, won't I?"

" Tut, little one! Bremen isn't more than half way there. They have to cross the big water first, where there's great wall-fishes, with holes in their heads on top."

" Is them wall-fishes very big?" asked Hans, somewhat alarmed, "and will they catch anybody?"

" Yes, they're long as that house yonder. But what are you doing; going to America? I'm afraid you're running away, little one?"

This question confused Hans not a little ; but he was too honest to lie, so he muttered and mumbled something, but the old peasant's understanding was so obtuse that he paid little attention. More than that, even if he had, he would have been only too glad to be young himself, and on the way to America. Presently Hans mustered courage to commence again.

"They telled me in our village that in America the clouds is barrels, and it rains beer sometimes, so people only has to set kegs under the spouts."

"Potztausend! little one, don't you believe none of them foolish stories. But I'll tell you true stories about America. There's men there that gives men money just as soon as they comes ashore, and shakes their hands, and gives 'em plenty of beer, and takes 'em to nice houses, and takes their old German money, and gives 'em American money, lots of it, more than five times as much as they had before, and all new money, too. They are so glad to see 'em come."

" Well, I hope they'll give me some money," said Hans, with childish honesty, "'cause I ain't got much."

"And then, when Germans has been there two or three months, they takes 'em again, and gives 'em more money for nothing at all ; but all they has to do is to take some papers, and some little pieces of papers, and go and put it all in boxes. They treats 'em like brothers, and shakes their hands every time they meets 'em."

"But what's all them papers and boxes for?" asked Hans.

"Oh, they're just to get beer with. If they gets enough papers into the boxes, the men that gets the most buys beer again."

And so they talked and walked together, Hans and the peasant, till noon, when they sat down on a grassy bank, and the peasant gave Hans some bread and sausages out of his handkerchief, and they ate together and drank some beer from a flask.

Hans had to sit down and rest many times that afternoon, and it was not till about sunset that he reached Bremen. He knew nothing whatever of the big city, so he went wandering about the thronged streets, among the crowds of people so strangely and brilliantly dressed, his great eyes rolling about in his round, pudding-sack face, like those you may see in a little Dutch clock in a jeweler's window. By a most fortunate chance he fell in with a Bavarian, with a great red face and yellow beard, who was going to America on the next vessel, and agreed to take him along if he would live with him in New York and learn to brew beer. Hans readily agreed to this, and in a few days they went down to Geestemünde, and went on board.

It was a sailing vessel that they embarked upon, and they had a great deal of tempestuous weather on the voyage. Ah! how sick was poor Hans! He would sit by the taffrail hour after hour and gaze down upon the sea, which looked just as the soapsuds used to in his mother's washtub; and then he would keck, and retch, and strain until he thought he would turn wrong side out.

When the ship would go up, his head would feel as heavy as if there were a big gander on top of it; and then it would go down, down, down, so far and so fast that it seemed as if his stomach had slipped right up into his mouth, and as if his hair were coming loose and flying up into the air, while all around him it would look yellow and ghastly, and he would feel so desperately sick that he could scarcely keep hold of the ship's rail. Ten thousand times when he sat crying, and felt that he would almost as lief fall into the water as not, he wished he was back again minding the geese at home.

The fare on board the ship was very wretched. In the morning and at evening it was nothing but miserable watery soup and mouldy bread, and at noon they would get some greasy, rancid meat and beans, or perhaps some spoiled and stinking fish, that made Hans sicker than the ship did in rolling.

Many grew sick and died; his friend, the Bavarian, was sick and thought he should die; the storms were terrible. Nearly every day Hans saw them tie up some emigrant in a sort of sack, with a heavy piece of coal at his feet, and slide him over the rail into the dark cold ocean. He was afraid to look over to see what became of them, and he soon became afraid to sit by the edge of the ship at all and look down upon the water. He was so weak he could no longer walk about the deck, but he would crawl out for an hour or two to look at the beautiful sun once more, when it shone out dimly through the clouds, and wonder whether his mother were thinking of him, and whether the same sun he saw stood over his dear old home. Then he would weep bitter tears, and wish he, too, might die, though he did not want to be thrown down into that cold black sea.

Then he would crawl back into his black and filthy room, and one of the emigrants would lift him up into his berth. There he lay without any covering, and all night he would have to keep hold of the edge of the berth with both hands lest he should fall out. The ship plunged about so that he would sometimes almost stand on his feet ; and then he would go back the other way and butt his head against the wall so hard he thought he should break a hole through after awhile, and fall out into the brine.

Poor Hans ! Did he not wish ten thousand times he had stayed at home, and minded his father? By the time he got to New York his plump round face was all pinched together, and he had to be carried ashore. They carried him through the streets of the great swarming city, and laid him in a bed in a quiet room, where, after many weeks, he got well.

We will here skip over a long interval in the life of Hans. Suffice it to say, that after he recovered he became an apprentice to his friend, the Bavarian, with the great red face and yellow beard ; stayed with him till he was of age ; then went out to San Francisco, dug gold, became wealthy, and finally took unto himself a frau.

But all the while he kept thinking of his father and mother, and wondering what his mother would do, and after he had quietly settled down to business in San Francisco he determined to write home. He wrote, and in due time received a letter from his father, in which he told him that his mother had died many years ago, soon after he ran away, for grief at his loss. He had supposed Hans was dead, but had long ago forgiven him, and he begged him to come home and visit him without delay, "For," said he, "I might be sleeping under the grass before you come, and so die without beholding your face."

Hans wept when he read this letter, and he determined to go at once to his father before he died. He went to

New York, sent a telegram home, telling his father by what steamer he should sail, and went aboard.

He was now a fine and manly figure; his yellow hair had darkened into a beautiful auburn; his face had lost something of its expressionless and boyish fatness, but was clear and fresh with the ruddy flush of health. His huge brown beard had changed him so that nobody who saw the yellow-haired, white-faced boy carried through the streets of New York would once have thought that this was the same.

"I wonder," said he to his wife, as they sat on deck one morning, "I wonder if my father will know me?"

"Oh, I suppose so. Why not?"

"Because I am not Hans any longer; nor am I a German even, but an American."

"But your father has grown old, too; and don't you suppose his recollection of you has grown old as fast as he has?"

"No; when he last saw me I was a mere sprig of a boy, with a round whey-face and yellow hair. Every time that he has thought of me since, even if it was twenty years afterward, he thought of that same boy with the yellow hair."

"But then he will remember how he himself looked at your age."

"He might, perhaps, if he had before him an exact picture of himself at thirty."

"Has he one?"

"He has none at all. Nobody can have the least recollection how he looked when he was a boy or a young man, unless he has a picture which was taken then. If one should look in the mirror twenty times a day all his life, he would only remember how he looked the last time."

"Well, we shall soon see."

"At any rate, I believe my mother would know me; but, alas! she is dead, and it was I that killed her by my ingratitude."

Here Hans turned away to conceal his emotion.

It was a wonderful thing for old Christian Thurngauer to receive a telegram from his son in far-off New York, which seemed to him on the other side of the world. He believed it was all a trick and a jest they were making upon him. "He will sail to-morrow in the steamer *Quadratic,* and here it is to-day yet! Tut, tut, all nonsense! People in these days has run clean mad with their jimcracks, and lost their senses. 'Twan't so in my young days. They didn't have no such fool doins in them days. Sail to-morrow, and here 'tain't night yet! Tut! such foolishness!"

So the old man talked on, and it was not till the burgomaster of the village came down and explained the whole matter to him for an hour or two, and gave him some money to go down to Bremen, that he would believe anything. Even then he would not believe their stories; but he said "he would go down to Bremen anyhow, for he'd never been there once in his life, just to see what foolishness men could do in these days."

After a long but pleasant passage in the month of June, the good ship *Quadratic* hove anchor in the harbor of Portsmouth, England, and sent ashore some mails and passengers. Next morning she continued on her way through the German Ocean.

It was now, the captain said, the last day of the voyage, and everybody was out on deck to watch the coming land and take the pleasant sunshine. Pale, limp ladies, who had suffered unceasingly during the voyage, were gently helped on deck, and sat in shady corners, fanned and refreshed by the cool salt breeze. The fidgety old gentleman brought up his little packages, and canes and coats, and set them down a minute, then straightway moved them somewhere else, and so kept fussing about, and moving them fifty times an hour. Little knots of passengers gathered over the forecastle, and all along the ship's rail, and pointed out to each other each fresh object with all the feverish delight of children.

The very wheels seemed to partake the general animation, and, eager to rest once more, lashed the yielding waves into two long streaks of snowy foam; while the graceful old *Quadratic*, with great politeness in her manners, went—

"Bending and bowing o'er the billowy swells,"

waving her "silent welcome" to the shore; and the great white sails above now bellied slowly out with a sounding flap in the breeze, as she careened, then slackened down all flaccid and lazy, as she righted.

Hans and his wife, with their little Carl, sat alone on the quarter-deck while he pointed out to her, one after another, the objects which he still remembered. They sailed among myriads of small white fishing-smacks, which rocked and teetered on the waves so much like toys that Carl was delighted, and clapped his hands in childish glee.

At last the long white line of the surf lifted itself slowly out of the blue, far, far off; and in an hour more they began to plow the muddy waters which flowed out of the river Weser. Then the long flat coast spread out infinitely before them, and on it the quaint old boxes of houses, huddled together in villages, and the ponderous windmills swinging around their four long arms in a sort of boozy way, as if they had taken too much schnapps.

As all these familiar objects drew nearer, Hans became sad and silent, and left his wife and Carl, that he might pace the deck alone. He could not forget that he should see his mother no more on earth, and that it was his base ingratitude which had brought down that dear, sad face so early to the grave. As the hour drew near when he should stand in the presence of his once stern father, his heart was filled with the most melancholy recollections, and with an indefinable dread, lest he had not been fully forgiven; and, strong man though he was, as he drew nearer to that beloved yet dreaded face, he felt as if he had gone back through all the years of his wanderings, and stood again before him with the awe of a little child.

At last the deep-voiced cannon boomed from the forecastle its salutation far and wide over the level land, but there came back no echoing response. As the smoke lifted above the bowsprit there came up the long, rumbling clank of the great chain as the anchor shot swiftly down to its miry rest; and to Hans the sound was like the rattling of the clods upon his mother's coffin, burying that pale, sad face he should see no more forever. The vessel stood still at last, and rested from her long tossing, and to him the strange and unwonted cessation of noise was like the silence of his mother's grave. The little tender came out swiftly from the shore, dancing and bobbing over the waves, rounded to, and quickly came alongside the mighty hulk, like a little, affectionate child eager to greet its mother.

Even before the tender was made fast, the yearning eyes of Hans discerned his father amid her passengers, leaning upon his staff—the same old staff as of yore—and gazing, with a bewildered look, upon the huge monster.

Feebly the old man climbed up the stairs, supported by a friendly hand, for Hans could not trust himself to go down.   He stepped upon the deck and gazed about him, seeking the face of his long-lost wanderer.   But in all that throng his dim eyes rested on no familiar form.   All the passengers knew the history, and they stood in respectful silence.   The son stood near, in an agony of suspense, but not daring to approach.

But at length he stepped forward, and reached him his trembling hand.   Mechanically, the old man took it, and looked in his face with his dimmed and milky eyes, but gave no sign of recognition.   The stricken prodigal quivered in every limb, and seemed about to sink to the deck, but his tongue could not utter a word.   His voice all stuck in his throat.

"Ah! my father, my father, speak and say I am forgiven!" he would have cried, in the anguish of his soul, but his tongue refused him utterance.

At that moment little Carl came running to him, crying, "Papa! papa!" clasped him about the knees, and looked up in innocent wonder into the grandfather's face.

The old man glanced down upon the child, and in an instant his doubts were dispelled.   *The missing link was restored.*   He saw at his feet the little white-haired boy he had coddled thirty years before upon his knees.   He fell upon his son's neck in a passionate embrace, and together they mingled their glad tears and their sobs.

Many a face amid that throng was turned aside to conceal a moistening eye.

AWAKING IN THE OLD WORLD.

Fair scenes shall greet thee where thou goest—fair,
But different—everywhere the trace of men,
Paths, homes, groves, ruins, from the lowest glen
To where life shrinks from the fierce Alpine air.
Gaze on them, till the tears shall dim thy sight,
But keep that earlier, wilder image bright.

BRYANT.

HOW we got to Bremen I know not, for it was midnight. Neither do I know any other thing whatsoever save that I awoke in the morning, lying, or rather half sitting up, on a prodigious bolster, under the featherbed instead of on top thereof. The bed was tucked away in a most dainty little niche, curtained off, with luxurious accommodations for sleeping, but the most contracted space for breathing. And the counterpane was so exquisitely smooth and silken that it had a distressing propensity to slide off to the floor during my slumbers. And the bed-tick was so delightfully pulpy and plump with feathers that I had the utmost difficulty in inducing it to remain perpendicularly over my person, as much as if it had been one sack of flour superimposed upon another.

I arose very early, and went down to take my first observations of the Old World. After a long sea-voyage, with what a dazed, wandering, and uncertain gaze one treads again the "strong base and building" of mother earth! One's head feels like a spent pegtop, swimming in the air. In the first movements one unconsciously braces one's legs, as if to resist the ship's lurching, and

(60)

one is fain to clutch at the ratlines, as if the deck were about to come up again into one's face.

My first visit was to the market-place. How queer it is for the first time to have the porches of one's ears filled with the unintelligible, buzzing hum of foreign words, with which one has only a book acquaintance! Why, these people stand there, with their graphic and changeful countenances, and gesturing so naturally that I ought to understand them. What is the matter? There is a word I understand. There is another. The first thing one knows one smiles at himself for his eagerness, as if he had caught himself smiling and nodding to a person whom he thought he knew, but did not. He runs on in a jack-o'-lantern chase after these words, now and then bobbing up, that he understands, and thinks he is about to catch the whole meaning, but "every something, being blent together, turns to a wild of nothing."

How immaculately clean, and square, and regular, and prinked-up everything is about the streets! Every square stone in the flagging is just as large as every other, and looks as if it had been dusted with a brush of peacock's feathers. And the barouches glide over them so tenderly, so smoothly, so noiselessly! Every house is precisely as high as its neighbor, to which it is joined, and all of them alike are sicklied over with that creamy-yellow stucco. It is wearisome to behold.

And then you never see anybody in the streets, as in great, roaring New York, even on Broadway, swinging his arms along, with his sleeves pulled up to cool his wrists. Indeed, nobody wears a linen coat at all. And so much profound bowing and doffing of shining hats! These two soldiers, in their bright light-blue uniforms, salute each other with as much punctilious courtesy as if they were major-generals. Stop to speak to this laborer, in his blue linen blouse, and—presto! his cap is in his hands and he stands uncovered till you, in your American disgust, bid him put it on again.

How lightly this tenor-drum is tapped as the soldiers move along to guard-mounting! And the very locomotive pipes in a thin, delicate, little whistle, as if it feared to scare somebody.

Except these gouty, old merchant burghers, with their glistening tiles, everybody seems to be only half a man. The people seem to be scared, as if they were afraid of doing something. One thinks of poor little Mr. Chillip, who would slip through a door sideways to take up as little room as possible. A wild and bloody American feels greatly tempted to get in the middle of the street and give a lusty yell, and swing his hat, so that he can hear a good hearty noise once more.

Ah! Bryant, well might you conjure the departing Cole to keep that "earlier, wilder image bright." Heaven be thanked that we have that image!

But to me one of the most amusing and yet touching of all spectacles was that of the thousands of collected emigrants, waiting for a passage to America. Here they all were: the hard-featured Brandenburger, in his sheep-skin cloak; the Saxon, with the mild, blue eye and pudding-sack face; the Bavarian woman, with her enormous bearskin shako, like a grenadier; the jolly, laughing Suabian, in his knee-breeches and shad-bellied waistcoat; the pretty Bernese maiden; the Tyrolese chamois-hunter, with his conical hat and cock's feather, a simple-hearted *terræ filius*, gaping in a loamy-faced vacuousness at everything. But the thing which was above all amusing was to see how the leaven of the far-off liberty was working already, and to watch their uncouth friskiness.

All at once you shall see a lumpish fellow, with his

clouted shoon, jump straight up a foot high, like a hare when the hound runs underneath. There is no visible incitement whatever to this sudden and gratuitous proceeding. Then he will shoot out his hand, and poke his fellow in the ribs, whereupon they will both throw up their heels and laugh immoderately. What has so suddenly made all these old, spavined plow-horses into merry-andrews? Why, they are going to America.

And then they were so amusingly and so unusually profuse with their snuff and tobacco—peasants who, for many a year, perhaps, after a hard week's toil were barely able to scrape enough together for Sunday to purchase a very small *schoppen* of small beer. Whenever I went among them they insisted I should partake. At first I took a pinch and sniffed at it, but it was so very strong that I sneezed my hat off, whereupon the simple fellows were like to fall upon the ground with the violence of their laughter. Why have they thus suddenly become so shockingly extravagant with their snuff and their schnapps? Oh, they are going to America, where there is a plenty and to spare. And have they not collected in divers fragments of cloth marvelous store of little, greasy, dingy coins, "hoarded long and counted oft;" besides pillow-cases, and long strings of sausages, and tin cups, and tobacco and snuff of mighty potency?

For once, and, perhaps, the first time in their hard lives of poverty, they have an unbroken holiday, and many of the more sober ones wander vacantly about the streets, in a sad perplexity what to do with themselves. Others, collected under the spreading lindens, sought to cheat dull care,—

> " While many a pastime circled in the shade,
> The young contending as the old surveyed."

Untutored freedmen of the Old World! They scarce knew yet how to employ their new-found faculties. How touching to an American to watch these uncouth gambols of these newly unyoked oxen—so uncouth because so un-accustomed! With what strange and unheard-of antics may we not imagine the children of Israel, as they went out, bent, and stiffened, and galled with their hard bond-age in the brickyards, gave vent to their first rejoicings! Infinitely more precious to an American does his native land become when he beholds how it is yearned for by the peoples abroad. Alas, that their anticipations are destined to encounter so many rude brunts, and the hopes of some of them so many bitter disappointments!

Then I strolled back to the hotel, and when I arrived the proprietor sallied forth to meet me, with an abundance of ostentatious civilities and kind inquiries, as if the love of me were greatly shed abroad in his heart. His multi-plied blandishments and bowings quite overwhelmed me, and made me feel ridiculous, as if I were an individual of mighty consequence. But to a meek-spirited man, who may have felt somewhat aggrieved and wounded by the "insolence of office" of the regal snobs who do clerical duty in our American hotels, this is worth more than his passage-money to Europe, for he feels that he is now ap-preciated for once in his life. Why, this landlord is a genius, and you feel that he understands you.

Entering the hotel, I found I was going in the same passage used by the horses. They are driven on into the hotel court, however, while the guest turns aside, just be-yond the porter's lodge, from which that high functionary is always peering out through his glass walls, ready to issue forth on the instant, and extend to the arriving guest all the courtesies and assiduities learned from his master.

I passed through a long hall, which conducted to the *café* or breakfast-room. In an instant, before I was even well seated, two attendants were at my elbow, arrayed in fastidiously elegant suits of black, with immaculate white neckcloths. They received my orders with a profound obeisance, and the remark that they were "beautiful" (*schönn*), and set out to execute them with the most commendable alacrity. In one corner of the room there was a white earthenware stove, towering nearly to the ceiling, and polished to a most icy and forbidding glitter. The little tables were profusely littered with newspapers, but how lonesome and homesick I felt for a moment when I found on all of them, instead of the familiar faces of my inseparable friends, the fat, dowdy hieroglyphics of the German alphabet!

Under the conduct of my German friend, I went, a little later, to visit the old cathedral, being then under the delusion which most novices in European travel experience, that I must conscientiously visit, scrutinize, and identify each and several of the stones, bricks, crucifixes, and ancient and desiccated mummies in every city. This also is a delusion to which the guides are nowise loth to minister. Although afterward I should have rated this cathedral a very slender spectacle, and even, as Byron says, irreverently and contemptuously held my nose in gazing upon the mummies, I am bound to record the powerful impression which they produced upon me then.

Designed originally as a simple nave and intersecting transept, it has expanded through seven hundred years, straggling wide around; adding here a chapel, a sacristy, or a porch; there a vestry, or a mausoleum for a warrior, bishop, or some glorious old soldier of the Lord; and shooting up into airy pinnacles, and blossoming with gables rich in colored glass or stony foliations. Beneath, in the vast and gloomy crypt, our lightest footfall echoed and re-echoed along the mouldy alleys, and among the shrunken mummies, which grin repulsively out upon us from their linen cerements. Welcome, indeed, was the voice of the living here, even though it was only the indescribably drowsy droning of the wrinkled beldam.

Whether we move along the majestic aisles, in the religious and mellow dimness of their tinted light, or among the gigantic columns, towering far up and reaching each other their strong arms overhead like a forest monarch, or pause under the great groined arches of the transept, or penetrate the inmost sacristies, where a sacred and secret solitude holds undisturbed dominion, everywhere we are surrounded by a concourse of silent monitors,—patriarchs, prophets, apostles, martyrs,—who all, from out the canvas seamed and dimmed with years, look down upon us with the same unchangeably sad, earnest, and tranquil mien.

Ranged below them, the marble effigies of those who partook their triumphs or their tribulations, even unto death, kneel meekly with upturned eyes, or lie recumbent along their stony couches, with folded hands, in that quaint, and straight, and stiffened, and yet most touching simplicity which only the childhood of sculpture could have fashioned. No studied graces of posture; no punctilious disposition of folded drapery; no dainty curves, or smiles, or dimples, but stark, and rigid, and meek they sleep. No futile effort to cheat the grim destroyer of his terrors, but stiff, and still, and mute they bow before him.

Whether in the sculptured monument, or enshrined in storied urn, or on the dimmed and somber canvas, or within the imposing pomp of the mausoleum, or beneath the dull, cold pavement, they are preachers more eloquent than the living. These you may mock and put to silence, but, standing before those, you dare not mock. The living die, and their words are heard no more, but when you toss on the couch of death, the eyes of those dumb witnesses shall still turn upon you their sad, earnest, admonitory gaze.

From their places on the wall, looking out through their dull, rayless sockets, they have watched the cycling generations of the living; they have seen the infant carried to the baptismal font; they have beheld him, in the full pride and strength of youth, kneel before the hymeneal altar; they have followed him as he doddered, feeble and sightless, before them, to listen a last time to the voice of sweet music; they have seen him borne, in slow and solemn march, to his rest. Revolutions, and religions, and kingdoms, and empires have arisen, and flourished, and fallen into oblivion; but there they have unremittingly maintained their silent vigils. The watchman on the mediæval citadel may have slumbered on his sentry, and neglected to warn the sleeping garrison of the incursion of the enemy; but these sleepless sentinels on the outlooks of time have failed not to warn the careless dwellers within of the approach of the King of Terrors, and, through "an innumerable series of years and the flight of times," have ceased not to utter to each passing pilgrim their voiceless admonition,—"So shalt thou rest."

RIDING BY RAIL.

Rumpas bellorum lorum,
Vim confer amorum
Morum verorum rorum,
Tu plena polorum!

LONGFELLOW.

AS we passed out from the hotel in Bremen all the waiters in the establishment, cut and long-tail, were drawn up in military array. In their immaculate swallow-tailed coats, and white neckcloths, ranging from biggest down to littlest, who looked so funny in his clerical attire, they stood with their hands clapped on their trousers seams, bodies as rigidly erect, and countenances as solemn and austere, as an "awkward squad" in the terrific presence of the drill-sergeant.

As each traveler dropped a trifling gratuity in the extended hand of each, he acknowledged his gratitude with a profound and silent obeisance, at the same time looking at his benefactor with one eye and three-quarters of the other, while one small corner squinted down at the money in a way that was very amusing. Poor machines and sticks that they are! it offends the soul of a wild and savage American to be fussed over with so much servility. And then there was the last and supreme fuss of the proprietor, the supple and smooth blandishments, the smiles, and the unctuousness of farewell flunkyism.

We got through it all at last, stepped into a drosky, and —just then the *commissionnaire*—may his tribe decrease!— came rushing breathless down-stairs to dun us for his fees,

(68)

when we had paid him in the cathedral, at the same time we did the ancient beldam. He thus put us to open shame before the multitude, though one would have believed from his manner that it nearly broke his heart so to distress us, and, as the engine had already whistled, we were compelled to pay him again.

What a wonder to our' fresh American eyes was that palatial station, with its indented battlements, interlacing arches, turrets, groined arches, and colonnades! If only it were not everywhere sicklied over with that maudlin, drab-colored stucco of Germany! It was some relief to this to look upon the long, latticed piazzas, covered with screens of luxuriant ivy, so copious in its growth that it often clambered to the very battlements and crept through the indentations. If one of those brave old cavaliers who jousted in Aspromont or Montalban could stand before this splendid palace, he could almost believe that he might still, "ycladd in mightie armes and silver shielde," ride forth beneath the portcullis, intent on "knightly giusts and fierce encounters."

A large number of uniformed officials were sauntering up and down the spacious saloons, mingling among the passengers, as if they even sought occasions for extending to them every possible civility and information. How cheerfully and smilingly they bow the willing ear to any inquirer! How elaborately they lengthen out the pleasant answer, "*Ja wohl, mein Herr,*" instead of the grumpy "Yes" or the surly and contemptuous nod of our American sovereigns! Verily these be servants of the people in no metaphorical interpretation. Many of them seem to feel positively grateful to you that you have given them an opportunity of doing something to entitle them to their wages and a full discharge and acquittal of conscience.

Let us inspect the passengers arriving, and we can grade them pretty accurately according to caste.

Here comes a clownish peasant, in his coarse gabardine and thumping wooden shoes, half running or trotting, staggering under a mighty chest, which bends his head far forward, and bumps cruelly about his brawny shoulders. Surely he will ride third-class.

Next there sweeps up, with great ostentation, a carriage glittering with silver and with gilding, the curveting steeds flinging the gravel disdainfully aside with their dainty hoofs. The lackey flings himself off, nearly throwing himself to the ground, in his absurd flummery of assiduity, by treading on the tail of his ridiculously long coat, lifts his high, glazed hat, and assists the inmates to alight. It is Mr. Americus Shoddy, and he will ride in the first-class, of course, with the other kings, fools, and Americans. He has the "genuine money-making countenance;" his collar has not been changed since we sighted land, and his slouched hat is pulled down on one side. The footman, still standing uncovered before him, addresses him some inquiry, "with 'bated breath and whispering humbleness," to which he replies, taking out one of his hands for a moment from his pantaloons pocket, and motioning with it, "Take them fixins in the depot."

Immediately following this is a modest drosky, from which springs out a rosy-faced little merchant. He makes the coachman hand him the *Fahr-tariff*, which he had cunningly secreted under the cushion, ascertains for himself his compensation, quietly counts out the precise amount in the infinitesimal coins, hands them to the fellow without allowing him a word, puts his cigar in his mouth again, and walks away. He is sensible, and will ride second-class.

Next comes a well-favored, rubicund, merry-eyed priest,

with his shovel-hat, and his long cassock flapping and fluttering inconveniently about his legs, as he runs forward at the sound of the whistle. He does not omit to carry the purse and the scrip for his journey, and in a piece of penitential-looking old cloth he has a suspicious bottle rolled away. He rides with the peasant, with whom he cracks a joke as well as a hard-boiled egg, and seems nowise concerned to inquire as to the condition of his soul.

In one of the largest saloons the passengers are busily unrolling on a low counter, and displaying to view, their wardrobes, "ruff and cuff, and farthingales and things," while on the other side the officers are leisurely inspecting them. Good nature ripples over most countenances, for even the veteran officials cannot wholly divest these proceedings of a certain aspect of ludicrousness.

They utter scarcely a word, quietly nodding and smiling assent, yet allowing nothing to pass unopened, though they sometimes merely give it a pinch with the thumb and forefinger, as on the corner of a bandbox; and sometimes, again, without any conceivable reason, plunge in an arm elbow-deep, and rummage far and wide underneath, till they ferret out a box of pills, perchance, and unwrap it persistently, cover after cover, despite all explanations, to the innermost core and center of mystery. Heart knows under what a solemn responsibility these officials labor, for if, through their remissness, any incendiary potions or evil mixtures and concoctions, or other "perilous stuff" whatsoever, should be imported into the kingdom, who knows but it might burst, or otherwise crack off, or produce a destructive combustion, and alarm his Majesty! Oh, who would be an officer of the customs? "Neither the front nor the back entrance of the custom-house opens on the road to Paradise," says the Salem Surveyor.

One notices that the most inexperienced travelers, especially of the tender sex, stand most pertinaciously on the defensive against the exposure of certain highly innocent and exquisite articles of the wardrobe. They explain, protest, expostulate, and thus induce a number of embarrassing contentions, half comical, half vexatious, and only make the inspection more rigid. Women are natural smugglers.

About a minute before the departure of the train, the doors were opened, and the passengers surged frantically through upon the platform. Then came a spectacle, on a small scale, of a "paternal government." Accustomed as we are to see our railroad officials standing about in the most grouty and contemptuous unconcern, it was not a little amusing to see these German officials, many of whom were of dumpy stature and of considerable obesity, and flushed with excitement, racing anxiously up and down the platform, with a paternal solicitude lest some misguided traveler should go astray. Here one plucked a passenger by the sleeve, and pointed out to him the proper car; there another shouted at the peasant, "*Steigen Sie heraus!*" and twitched him out of a second-class car; yonder, another ran along before a very red-faced, elderly gentleman, who trotted and waddled after him, like Mr. Pickwick at the ice-pond, till they came to the proper car, into which he whisked him with such unseemly haste that the old gentleman sprawled flat on the floor of the car, flinging his bandbox against the opposite door, while his legs projected out into the depot.

Said I to myself, after I sat down in the car, What figure can such a people ever cut in self-government, when they interfere, with so much fuss and meddlesomeness, even in the most trivial affairs?

We found ourselves in an apartment splendidly upholstered, extending quite across the car, and separated from all others by partitions reaching to the ceiling. There were only two seats, so that the occupants sat facing each other, one-half riding backwards.

Now, herein is a phase of the German character admirably illustrated,—to wit, their sociability. In an American car there is a universal sweep from end to end, containing whatever multitude it may on a common understanding; but here each compartment contains its little coterie, half facing half, for conversation. It is an intensely disagreeable arrangement to most Americans to have their faces set square over against strangers, only four feet distant; but I have seen German peasants, after they had temporarily exhausted their stock of small talk, or had it drowned in the "*morum verorum rorum*" of the train, sit fifteen full minutes gazing into the depths of each other's eyes with a most profound and serene vacuousness that was refreshing to contemplate.

It was our fortune to be assigned to a compartment filled with ladies, and it was with immense consternation that I heard the conductor of our car bolt the door and announce that it would not be opened till we reached Hanover. I had thought to enjoy without interruption these my first broader glimpses of Germany, and had provided myself with no books or newspapers. Great was my disgust, therefore, when I found that, through my own remissness and my friend's mischievous plotting, I was packed like a sardine in the middle of the sofa, with ladies on both sides of me, and likewise opposite.

The Prince of Morocco declares to Portia that he would "outstare the sternest eyes that look" to win her regards; but what would he do confronted by the most bewitching? The young lady opposite me had such eyes, wonderfully soft, and blue, and melting; hair of that golden hue of which Ouida seems to have a monopoly; and delicate, almond-shaped nails.

I scrutinized the architecture of the ceiling overhead, the loops, knops, and scollops, and other paraphernalia. I narrowly inspected the ventilator over the door, with a gaze as intent as that which a photographer's client fixes on a polyanthus pinned to a curtain. I rummaged my valise for articles I was certain it did not contain. After looking a long time at a fly on the ceiling overhead, scraping and polishing his thighs, and screwing his head on, I would accidentally look at my *vis-à-vis*, and—pop! our eyes would cross. Then I would look steadfastly out at the cabbages, streaking past us in a gray line, as if they were about to run their heads off, and so fall to musing on the beauties of German agriculture, and of a rural life in general, and at length attempt to sweep diagonally across from the lower corner to the opposite upper one, when— pop! our eyes would cross again.

I made repeated endeavors to create a diversion in my favor by engaging my friend in conversation, "*nutans, distorquens oculos ut me eriperet,*" but he cruelly preferred to appear wholly absorbed in contemplating the scenery without.

It's a far cry to Lochow, but Hanover was reached at last; several of the ladies alighted, and I took good care, in the redistribution of sittings, to secure one next the window. The vacant places were taken by a couple of extremely elegant and finical young Berlinese, who, to the astonishment of us Americans, deliberately took out their cigar-cases, extracted therefrom each his cigar, lighted them, and began to whiff out voluminous rolls of smoke, without even saying to the remaining lady, "By your leave."

That feature of the landscapes which most vividly impressed me was the inexpressibly wearisome air of constraint, of silence, of rigid precision. In all that dreary land, where "nor fosse nor fence are found," absolutely and interminably level, over which we clattered all that April day, we saw not a single

> " Wild and wanton herd,
> Or race of youthful and unhandled colts,
> Fetching mad bounds."

Here, perhaps, was a great crooked-horned cow, led to pasture with a rope along the roadside, or a few sheep, nibbling the close-cropped grass on a flat as big as my hat, or some geese, guarded by a blue-cheeked, carroty-haired child,—everything rigidly watched and tended. How I wished that those poor, cribbed, cabined, and confined animals could break away somehow, leap, and jump, and stand on their heads, if they so desired, and throw up their heels without getting a permit therefor from the Prussian government!

There was not a singing bird to be heard anywhere. What heart had they to sing, or to do anything else whatsoever, in a land without trees, or containing only poplars, so absurdly straight and erect that they could not build in them?

The whole face of the land, as far as our eyes could extend, was just like a checker-board, being divided into an infinite number of tiny plats, parti-colored with various grains and vegetables. But on that April day there was a "frown upon the atmosphere." It was not the frown of a leaden heaven, but of an old age, cheerless and saddened by penury. A single rich, creamy cloud would have been a mighty relief to the landscape, but they were all skimmed off, leaving the atmosphere indescribably bleak-looking, poor, and blue, like thin skimmed milk.

But along the railroad the labor expended in ornamentation was wonderful. Now the train rushed, without slackening speed in the least, over a bridge embellished with elegant carvings in stone, and which trembled no more than the solid earth. Then it bowled along an embankment whose slopes were shaven like a lawn, and planted with diamond-work of boxwood rows. Then it whirled through a shallow cut, whose unsightly edges had been sodded, and ornamented with slender pavements of stone, in the shape of geometrical figures or of branching trees.

Every half-mile, or oftener, the train rumbles past a tiny brick cottage, sometimes half hidden in ivy, and always surrounded by pretty parterres of vegetables and homely flowers. Here resides the patrolman, who takes his station with punctilious precision before his house, and presents arms with his baton.

By an ingenious contrivance of telegraphy, a clear-toned bell, perched in a little isolated belfry, announces in measured strokes our arrival at a station. The same contrivance causes a tiny clock-hammer, fastened to the station, to give forth a rapid musical tinkle while we halt, and when we start again the bell tolls as before.

Thus our humble journey becomes like the triumphal progress of a crowned and sceptered sovereign through his dominions. The patrolmen accord us military honors as our train sweeps majestically before them; watchful attendants make haste to bar all crossings against the approach of vulgar vehicles, and even against irreverent curs, which might disturb the decorous and stately advance of our royal equipage. Even the lightning yields loyal obedience to our high behests, heralding our approach, recording the interval while we graciously deign to pause, and, when we take our departure, intoning us a sonorous and pompous farewell.

But it is now almost time to relinquish the enjoyment of this fancied homage and these imaginary triumphs, for we are rapidly approaching the Prussian capital. The shadows of the night have long since settled calmly down around us, and the silvery flocks of heaven, in their noiseless march above us, look down in tranquil silence upon our noisy and tumultuous flight.

Far before us, across an extended plateau, an uncertain and tremulous luster, as of the aurora in September, stretches in a long arch across the eastern horizon. But it is not until we sweep around the jutting skirt of a pinery that the great metropolis looms in midnight resplendence before us, across its enveloping waste of sand and swamp.

Now our royal courser, as if he had husbanded his powers for his imposing entry into the capital—for does not everything belong to the king?—neighs exultingly in the pride of his unsubdued strength. How his single great eye drinks up the darkness before him! Fiercely does he drag his burden after him, swaying to and fro in the gloom.

Thus we entered at midnight into great Berlin, and poured out into a surging multitude, in which the gilded helmets of the *gendarmes*, glittering in the gaslight, are all that I remember. Out of this tumultuous and jostling throng some skillful hand caught us up into a drosky,—I know not how, I know not where,—and we were whirled away through a long, silent, cavernous street.

Since these arms of mine hath seven years' pith,
Till now some nine moons wasted, they have used
Their dearest action in the tented field;
And little of this great world can I speak,
More than pertains to feats of broil and battle.

OTHELLO.

RETURNING one afternoon from a visit to the Thier-garten, I sauntered under the great Brandenburg Gate, and then along the magnificent boulevard, Unter den Linden. It was one of those indescribably sweet and sunny days of early spring, a kind of beatific accident, which sometimes, for a few hours, "breathes through the sky of March the airs of May," so grateful to the inhabitants of a great city.

Along the middle track, the Rotten Row of Berlin, military officers reined their glossy, curveting Poles, leaning forward in the saddle with that distressing lack of ease and confidence which marks the German horseman. Hundreds of brilliant equipages glided along the flagged highways, with tops opened to scoop in the mellow sunshine. It was Corso day, and all the haughty nobility of Berlin was abroad, with many princes; and from out the landaus flashed those apple-red faces of the beer-drinkers, with that mottled white-and-red which seems to be daintily painted on, and not suffused from the blood beneath.

Even the lordly merchant, slipping along the pavement with that easy, level gait of the German, relaxed a little his buttoned-up complacency and his upright neck, let out the business wrinkles from his brow, and glanced about him with a kind of retail satisfaction, as if he were almost apologizing to himself for smiling. How the sweet sunshine warms up even his soul, and makes him linger !

All along the street, in front of the *Conditoreien*, the potted shrubbery fenced in from the pavement long, narrow retreats, whence the sippers of the bitter goat-beer glanced out through the green leaves upon the happy idlers. The winter haunts within were all deserted and silent, but there came out now and then a chilly puff of yesterday, mingling in the sunshine, and reminding them of January. How joyously they laugh and quaff—these witty Berlinese,—half hid in their leafy screens, and swig off mug after mug of that inexpressibly bitter beer ! The Englishman, when he feels merry and wants to inform mankind of that fact, like the Fat Boy of Dickens, "likes eating best," but the German says with Wollheim, when he has a gala-day,—

> " Bring' mir bairisch Bier,
> Ewig bairisch Bier !"

A little beyond the university I stopped to admire, for the hundredth time, Rauch's magnificent equestrian statue of Old Fritz.

There is not in all Europe such another noble, comprehensive, and imposing constellation of architecture—though not so brilliantly grouped as that one beholds in standing by the Egyptian obelisk in the Place de la Concorde—as that which surrounds the great Frederic. That university which is the greatest in the world, and that arsenal which is the mightiest ; that academy of art and science which is the most learned ; the palatial Old and New Museums ; the Protestant and Catholic cathedrals, side by side ; the vast, gray pile of the Schloss ; the

Royal Library and the Royal Opera, the most richly musical and scenic in Europe; and the palaces of the kings, —these, all within his sight,—these, to use one of the ambitious phrases of Berlin, are the exclamation-points upon the illustrious past, and the interrogation-points upon the great future, of the Prussia which he created.

The martial atmosphere which floats over this noble boulevard is terribly significant. From the Goddess of Victory on the Brandenburg Gate, who conducts her fierce steeds homeward, through all its course, to the statues of the Lion-tamer and the Amazon guarding the portals of the Old Museum, the Unter den Linden resounds like the Iliad with the clang of arms. Grouped around Old Fritz, or standing near him on humbler pedestals, are the Great Elector, worthy of his Roman son; old Marshal Forward, Von Blücher, who spoke at Waterloo "in Prussia's trumpet tone," side by side with Gneisenau, his Patroclus, and former of those campaigns whose execution made them both immortal; Scharnhorst, whose genius gave to Prussia that unequaled system which made her a "people in arms," and thereby the savior of the Fatherland; and the great captains, Schwerin, and Winterfeld, and York.

Eight marble statues on the bridge over the Spree portray the tutelary deities who lead forth young Fritz to a long and glorious career; defend, support, and inspire him through its arduous warfare; reward him for its triumphs; and crown at last with laurel the brow of the dying hero when his course is finished.

The citizen of Berlin, when walking in this great boulevard, may almost fancy he hears the silver clarion of Virgil:

> "Multa quoque et bello passus, dum conderet urbem,
> Inferretque deos Latio, genus unde Latinum,
> Albanique patres atque altæ mœnia Romæ."

It may even excite a smile in the beholder, in a thoughtless mood, to note how often the martial gods are called in to the exclusion of the softer deities. Pallas appears twice, and three times does exultant Nike bestow upon him her acclamations and her laurel chaplets. Even peaceful Iris is impressed into Prussian service as a gentle *vivandière*, and presses to Frederic's feverish lips the nectareous cordials of Olympus.

The very Caryatides and the brawny-shouldered Atlantes on the façades of some of the government palaces are relieved on guard by hussars, cannoneers, and their similars.

But the thoughtful gazer can hardly smile, for it is one of the saddest spectacles of Europe, thus to observe how a peace-loving people have been, all their national life, driven to "feats of broil and battle" by the bitter necessities of self-defense, and to rescue Germany from the evil and miserable quarrels imposed on that unhappy country by its hordes of little princes. Above all things else, let not the "red fool-fury of the Seine" shake her gory locks at this peaceful people, upon whom her hellish lust of dominion has forced this loathed habit and custom of battle.

While Frederic was yet alive, and occupied his favorite palace in Potsdam, his subjects were accustomed to assemble under a certain linden which flourished near the window of his work-cabinet, with their petitions in hand, waiting to gain his attention. As soon as he chanced to look that way, up would fly the petitions, fluttering into the air, and off would come the caps of the petitioners. He would nod a friendly recognition from the window, and forthwith dispatch one of his stalwart hussars to fetch in the documents.

When I visited Potsdam, a century after the great monarch had been carried to his grave, the famous old "petition-linden'' was still living, but seemed likely to topple over in the first hurricane.

But it was no longer needed. The palace where it stood was no longer the favorite abode of the Prussian monarchs, and with their removal migrated also the tradition of the brave old linden. The very bronze which preserved the lineaments of the grim Frederic became the successor of the venerable petition-linden, and, as it were, the patron of the suppliants. Who had a better commission to plead for mercy to the poor and humble than the terrible old Fritz?

By accident or design, the statue was planted very near the window of the little work-room of the reigning monarch. It was so close that he could, as he sat before his writing-table, discern the countenances of the petitioners standing at its base.

It was the custom of King William to spend many hours every day in this his favorite work-room, writing, giving audiences, or perusing and dictating telegraphic messages by hundreds. When he was reading dispatches, or talking with auditors, he generally sat beside the little window, leaning his arm along the sill. He would cast frequent glances down into the street, and invariably return with a friendly nod or beckoning of the hand the salutations of his humblest subject. Everybody in Berlin knew where to look for the "King's window,'' and seldom did anybody ever pass it, at whatever unseasonable hour, without glancing up to see if it was occupied by the august scrivener, for he was a most indefatigable worker.

If he sat writing at his desk, they could just discern his head and shoulders. But nobody could ever mistake that broad face, those half-closed eyes, that Burnside beard, that clean-shaven chin, shining almost like the razor with which it was daily polished. It was a heavy face, and a fluffy, but sensual-kind, with beetling eyebrows, and inclined to a scowl, serious, but not severe, when in repose. It was eminently a negative face, the scowl seeming to denote a painful labor *for* thought rather than *with* thought.

But if beside him were visible the figures of ambassadors or others, the citizen would pause for a moment and begin to cudgel his brains. Your humdrum, home-keeping Cousin Michael is a thorough Paul Pry, ever "plucking the grass to know where sits the wind." Who knows but something may happen! Only think of it,—if something *should* happen! Wonder if there'll be war with Napoleon? Look, neighbor, that messenger has a red stripe round his *kepi*. I believe there *will* be war with Napoleon. O fie! see, it's yellow. He's from Austria. Don't you remember, three weeks ago the king refused a mug of Vienna beer? If *that* doesn't mean war, I should like to know what does.

But these wiseacres seldom arrive very near the truth with their guesses; for the Germans are anything but brilliant in setting "romance on the throne of the Cæsars."

Among the multitudes who press along in endless procession past the statue of Old Fritz as I stand there, comes a notable man, tall and spare, with the inclined head and stooped shoulders of a professor. What eyes! They are set under eyebrows where order and locality are large, and so far back in his head that he looks right out from his brain. Beard or moustache has he none, and his face is furrowed with delicate hair-lines, like the spider-webs of his wonderful strategy, wherein he catcheth the crafty.

That is the "old schoolmaster," silent in seven languages. He flogs the naughty nations without even letting them behold his rod. All Europe is mapped on that subtle brain. Shut in his little closet, his eyes look inward upon that map, and order battles. He fingers the electric wires, and a quarter of a million soldiers move in obedience to his commands.

That man gripped Benedek at Sadowa, and ground him as between the upper and nether millstones. He coiled his legions like a boa round Metz, and crushed it in his folds. He took an Emperor in a trap, and Paris, the world-city, in a mouse-trap. That is Moltke. Yet how modestly and pensively he walks along, with his hands behind his back !

Now here comes another of Prussia's great ones, as we may know by the profound deference with which he is greeted. He strides along like a grenadier, with an erect and daring mien, towering above most men a head and shoulders. He is a major of dragoons, with a white cap and yellow band, black-blue, double-breasted coat, and a great mass of black silk wrapped close around his muscular neck almost to the chin.

He is not in a smiling mood to-day, but his face is darkened, Mephistophelian, with "a laughing devil in his sneer" at all humanity. The high and massive forehead, the peculiarly square-cast features, the half-closed eyes, the enormous ears, standing far out from the huge, close-cropped head, give the beholder an idea of an almost Satanic energy, and of an immense, audacious courage. No words can convey a true impression of the unscrupulous daring, the amazing strength of determination, which dwell in that grim countenance. It is the pure Scandinavian brawn, not Teutonic, but the heaven-daring and earth-defying audacity of the old vikings, which exulted in danger for its own sake. It is "steel and blood," with very little blood.

Not in all my life have I ever looked upon another human being who, when not relaxing in the moment of social intercourse, seemed to be so absolutely devoid of a conscience. Hating none, fearing none on earth or in heaven, neglectful and even scornful of personal appearance and of most of the conventions of society, he seems the nearest human approach to Mephistopheles, except that in the sublime grandeur of his daring he more resembles the Miltonic Satan.

In fact, Bismarck resembles Goethe's great creation most in his "malignant mirth" upon occasion, which yet is hardly malignant, because, like Milton's Satan, he has an egotism so vast and an ambition so immense that he hardly appears conscious of wickedness. To repeat, Bismarck's character, though sublime in its audacity and in its colossal intellect, appears to contain no ingredient of conscience. Yet it has no element of cruelty, which lurked in the Italian nature of Bonaparte, making him a vile and dastardly assassin in Syria. Bismarck is like Cromwell, but greater.

Thus he strides on, in his large indifference, shouldering his way through the obsequious multitude, not deigning a single glance toward the king's window, passes on over the Spree bridge, and enters the Schloss.

Meantime, a considerable number of persons of humble degree have collected about the iron railing which incloses their great advocate. For the hour is near at hand when the battalions of the garrison will march past to the afternoon parade, and they are certain then to catch a glimpse of King William. The battalion drums, colors, and standards must all be brought from the little room beside the king's, where he scrupulously keeps them under his own lock and key, and where an unexpected visitor has sometimes found him with board and pins, busy at the game of war, like a seven-years' child ! Here it was, also, that he humbly bowed himself upon his knees, and wrestled earnestly in prayer with his Maker for three hours, before he departed for the campaign in Bohemia.

When the troops defile before his window, therefore, he never neglects to appear to their vision, in uniform as scrupulously correct as a martinet's, with his regulation-coat closely buttoned up to his ample chin, and the ribbon of the *Ordre pour le mérite* hanging down over the lappet. This is, for petitioners, the auspicious hour, between the outward march of the troops and their return.

Here is the Rheinlander, in his bright-blue linen blouse; the Westphalian, with his white great-coat, and a piece of ham in his pocket; the Pole and the Silesian, in their untanned sheepskins; the widow in her weeds; the pensioner on his wooden leg, with a petition, perhaps, asking permission to beg in the streets.

To be sure, they are congregated right in the middle of the main thoroughfare of the city, and are exposed to the danger of being dashed under the wheels, or beneath the feet of the prancing steeds. But there, too, rides Old Fritz high aloft, looking grimly to the west, and flourishing his sceptre with authority, bidding the multitude part to right and left. This is highly inconvenient, no doubt, and productive of delays to the gay and feathered occupants of the coaches which glide along; but the people will have it so, and the people are king sometimes, even in Prussia.

It were a high-handed outrage, forsooth, if these honest provincials could not be permitted to prosecute their æsthetical culture by gazing on the statue of Rauch's workmanship!

The citizens of Berlin are spirited, and noted for their persistence in defending certain minor prerogatives, while they allow the greater to slip through their fingers. They will resist with tooth and nail a rise of a penny in the price of beer, but quietly submit while the king takes away their liberties. In 1848 they made a desperate charge on the city officers, under the ringing slogan, "Liberty, Equality, and the Right to Smoke in the Thiergarten!" and carried their point. So here, they insisted on the right to study High Art in the Unter den Linden.

The government not only yielded gracefully, but provided a number of select policemen, designated as " controllers of petitions," whose duty it was sedulously to foster these æsthetic cravings. They were to be always in attendance, and look to it that nobody was run over while he was gazing at the Father of his Country.

And now the king is seen to rise from his writing-table, disappear in the next apartment, then present himself, smiling and uniformed, before the casement. Off in a twinkling go a score of hats,—tiles polished, tiles fuzzy, plush caps, sheepskin caps, cloth caps, sweaty and frowzy, —while several large blue-and-white mottled handkerchiefs descend, with many a pensive and melancholy flutter, gently down to the ground. Out of these caps emerge petitions, soiled and greasy, which twinkle on high.

All manner of familiar, cabalistic, and blandishing gestures, winks, nods, and beckonings woo his Majesty. The eager petitioners elbow and jostle one another, and barely escape being thrust out and trodden down by the horses.

The king nods pleasantly, and smiles, and sends down one of his gigantic orderlies to bring up the petitions. This official kindly offers to take the documents in charge, and pledges himself to convey them in his own person into the king's hands.

But—unaccountable perversity—five out of ten of the

suppliants wholly reject the offer!   It is absolutely indispensable that each individual should be presented to his Majesty in his own proper person and essence, in order that his "little matter" may be accurately propounded and thoroughly elucidated to the king.

"Would the porter have the goodness to inform his Majesty that Hans Wurst, from Blitzendonnerhausen, had arrived?   If his memory was a little treacherous, he might remind him that he once drank a porringer of his brindled cow's milk, and smacked his lips afterward, when he was riding on a hunt.   Would he also please inform him further that Conrad Rumpelschirmer's mooly ox had unlawfully and feloniously broken into his (Hans Wurst's) cabbage-garden, and abstracted, purloined, devoured, and injuriously munched forty-three heads of the cabbages aforesaid; that the court had refused to requite him of the offender; and that he had come to Berlin to ascertain if his Majesty could not issue a proclamation in behalf of his faithful and liege subject, Hans Wurst aforesaid, compelling said Conrad Rumpelschirmer to make full and complete restitution to him for the felonious purloinings and endamagements aforesaid?

"Then, too (plucking him mysteriously aside and whispering in his ear), he could assure him he should be no loser if he would procure him such audience, as he had brought up four crocks of nice sauer-kraut to present to his Majesty; but that he would give him one, provided he would not reveal the transaction to his Majesty."

The porter smiles blandly an official German smile (the blandest on earth), but informs his countryman that his Majesty has a good many "little matters" claiming his attention.   And so at last poor Hans Wurst dolefully consents, and reluctantly gives into his hands the greasy and rumpled document, elaborated in hard and staggering characters, and worn nearly through in his hat in coming from the far province.

As soon as the king receives the documents, he holds them up before the window, and nods and smiles pleasantly to the suppliants below, as an assurance that their petitions shall receive attention.

And now the soldiers are returning from parade. They defile with stately tread and mighty clangor of brass before their sovereign, move on down the great avenue, beneath the acacias and the lindens, encompassed by a great cloud of citizens, who have come out to follow them, and listen, with the ever-new delight of their nation, to the inexpressibly rich, mellow, glorious music of Germany.

The king vanishes from the casement, the petitioners are swept away in the music-loving multitude, the twilight slowly darkens in the streets, its pale, wannish glimmers flicker off the windows, and Old Fritz rides high aloft and alone on guard.

PROFESSOR DOCTOR KINCK VON KINCK.

In Berlin, says he,
Be you fine, says he,
And make use, says he,
Of your eyne, says he;
Knowledge great, says he,
You may win, says he,
For I've been, says he,
In Berlin.

HÖLTY.

THERE are few things which afford me more pleasure than to wander about those great old libraries of Europe and rummage among their quaint and curious volumes of forgotten lore. I highly value the privilege of being allowed to sit at leisure in their alcoves, and pull down one ponderous dusty tome after another, "bound in brass and wild-boar's hide," or in beechen boards and blue, and turn them over, catching now and then from their crabbed black-letter pages some whimsical conceit, or reading some story of those ancient worthies, the best that ever lived "thorough the unyversal world."

Nowhere has this pleasure been oftener tinged with a certain pensiveness or melancholy than in the libraries of the Germans,—a feeling almost as sacred as that which should attend the visitor in their village churchyards. Above all other people, the German finds his best companionship in books; and the circles of a society he has found so pleasant he wishes to enlarge, until they shall embrace the whole mundane brotherhood.

(90)

He willingly relinquishes the enjoyment of social intercourse, his beloved mug, and all the innocent and connubial endearments of his frau, to give himself up wholly to his unselfish labors.   With an unwearying and more than paternal affection, he gathers and digs from innumerable sources the choicest roots, buds, and blossoms of the True, the Beautiful, and the Good, to furnish forth and embellish therewith the pages he is writing with such fond and confiding assiduity.   Each volume we behold on these shelves informs us of some such earnest life; informs us, perchance, of long years of penury and pain, of nights of sleeplessness and days of hunger, all endured with cheerfulness in the sweet hope of fame, "that last infirmity of noble mind."

And now he is dead, long dead; and the book which he wrote, and of which himself was the principal reader, has lived its appointed life, and is found no more among the living, except in these dusty alcoves, or amid the heterogeneous and musty collections of the antiquarian. But when the thoughtful soul passes the antiquated book, or stops awhile to explore its pages and ramble among its obsolete constructions and its queer old cranky involutions, he will not mock him who lived all these laborious days to write what nobody now possesses.   It is the counterpart of the author's better self; the faithful Horatio whom the dying Hamlet piteously adjures to linger yet awhile, and in this harsh world draw his breath in pain to tell his story.

> "He gave the people of his best;
> His worst he kept, his best he gave."

Here, then, in this great library, is a city of the dead. Through its populous recesses we should tread with a greater reverence than along the more pleasant and sunny alleys of the churchyard, for here repose, as it were, the remains of the soul, while yonder is only the mouldering and loathsome body. And while the separate particles of the latter return, by the chemistry of decay, each to its native dust, and appear again, after an innumerable succession of years, to gladden our eyes in the "forms and hues of vegetable beauty," who can tell what seeds of thought may have been planted in fruitful intellects by the mere passing glimpse of a title, or by a casual perusal of these dead and forgotten pages?

One day, after a number of hours thus spent in the Royal Library of Berlin, I sauntered into the reading-room. Among the numerous busy inmates, I had my attention particularly attracted by a robust and rosy- or, rather, pink-faced gentleman, who the librarian kindly informed me was none other than the celebrated Professor Doctor Kinck von Kinck.

He kept buzzing and bobbing over a great number of large books bound in blue pasteboard, plucking out from a hundred places snippets of sentences and paragraphs, which he industriously transcribed into a memorandum-book. He was quite short-sighted, and as he turned over the pages rapidly, thrusting his nose and green spectacles deep down between them, his motion reminded me of that of an athlete jumping through empty barrels, set on end in a series.

My mind recurred at once to the scene so delightfully described by Irving in his "Art of Book-making," and I supposed these persons, as in that sketch, were all professional authors. What was my surprise when the librarian informed me they were all popular lecturers, wholly distinct from the hundred ninety and seven regularly employed in the Royal University!

This bit of information piqued my curiosity to know

something further concerning them, their audiences, and subjects of discourse. I asked the librarian if it was not a matter of great difficulty to procure audiences for such a multitude of lecturers. He replied that it had become very difficult, and that the lecturers thought of petitioning the Prussian government to institute military levies in their behalf.

Even while we were speaking, there presented himself in the library a collector of subscriptions for a series of lectures soon to be delivered "for the especial benefit of the laboring-classes." He was a stout little man, with a rather dirty neck, and two small and very rosy-bright patches of color on his white cheeks, in the manner peculiar to many beer-drinkers. The librarian was a very pale, thin-featured gentleman, with preternaturally large black eyes, and one leg so crooked that he seemed almost to step on the knee.

The stout little man deliberately hung his overcoat and hat on the rack, set his cane beneath them, approached, and bowed very low before the librarian, smiling all over his face. The librarian bowed quite low, smiled an official smile, and extended his hand.

"Good day, Herr Doctor," said the little man.

"Good day, mein Herr," replied the librarian, in a very bland but non-committal voice.

The stout little man wore a kind of gray jerkin, gathered tight by a band behind, and edged around the neck and pockets with green binding. From an inside pocket of this he now produced a very thin green memorandum-book, as broad as it was long, with leaves of intensely blue smooth paper. This he handed to the librarian, open at the subscription page.

"Herr Doctor," said he, "it gives me the greatest pleasure to inform you that Herr Professor Doctor Kinck von Kinck will lecture to-morrow, at seven o'clock P.M., in Hypothenuse Hall, on the Satires of Horace. I have the honor to say, Herr Doctor,"—here he bowed quite low,—"that he has commissioned me to solicit the honor of your subscription."

Upon that the librarian bowed, and smiled that painfully polite official smile, so exquisitely and so inexpressibly less than nothing, so far as meaning is concerned, that such an attack as this must slip off it as rain-drops off a duck's feathers.

"Mein Herr," he replied, "it gives me great pleasure to learn that the Herr Professor Doctor Kinck von Kinck will lecture. I need not assure you, certainly, that none knows better than myself how to value the opportunity thus afforded of profiting by the Herr Professor's acknowledged great learning, if my official engagements would permit."

Here both bow quite low again, and smile, and the stout little man resumes :

"The price of admission, Herr Doctor, has been set very low; only four silver *Groschen* per ticket."

Again that exquisitely and excruciatingly polite official smile—the only answer the honored Herr Doctor deigns to give to a suggestion so immeasurably and so insufferably contemptible as that relating to money. The little man now trains on him his last battery, and very complacently, for he knows it will succeed.

"Herr Doctor, I believe your next lecture is to be ——?"

"A week from to-day, mein Herr," says the learned Herr Doctor librarian, promptly.

"And the subject, I believe——?"

"On a singular mass of fused flint recently found in the ashes of a burnt haystack." The Herr Doctor announced this with more animation and positiveness than he had yet shown, having been hitherto exceedingly negative.

"Ach, yes!" The little man utters this in a tone of the most profound remorse and self-abasement, to think he should have forgotten, and strikes impatiently before his face, as if he were killing a mosquito.

"*Pardon*, Herr Doctor. I may do myself the honor to remark that the Herr Professor Doctor Kinck von Kinck observed, a few days ago, in my presence, that he certainly intended to be present at your lecture."

At this point the learned Herr Doctor librarian bows, and both of them smile very pleasantly. Need I add anything further? The little man knew the librarian's weakness, and that the certainty of having one auditor was a bait at which he would inevitably catch. He knew that he could have secured his subscription with the lure of half an auditor (like the forty professors of Erfurt, who had, in 1805, twenty-one students), having him sit in a partition, with one ear opening into one room and the other into another; but he chose to be generous. Of course he got his subscription, and went away with many bows and smiles.

Next day I was leisurely sauntering along Subjectivity Street, and stopped before one of the wooden pillars erected at the street-corners for that purpose, to read the latest bulletins of lectures. Among them was one announcing "a gratuitous course of lectures for the special instruction of the laboring classes;" and a few of the topics were as follows: "The Diseases of Chinese Silkworms," "Salubrity of the Climate of Beloochistan," "The Figures of Equilibrium in Liquids."

Now, thought I to myself, is this all a philanthropic humbug? or are the "laboring classes" of Berlin possessed of such immense learning as to be able to comprehend these things? Goethe makes one of the characters in "Faust," on hearing a revolutionary song, declare his gratitude to Heaven that he is not responsible for the preservation of the Holy Roman Empire. But what government on earth can stand, when such ponderous boulders of knowledge are pitched promiscuously about its bases? Surely Prussia is in danger!

While I was thus musing, whom should I behold but the famous and learned Herr Professor Doctor Kinck von Kinck! He whisked past me on a keen run, and, turning round, I observed, a few rods in advance of him, a person whose blue linen blouse showed him to be a member of the "laboring classes," and of whom the learned Herr Professor was evidently in earnest pursuit. Being an elderly gentleman, of a very considerable obesity, he waddled along with much difficulty, and was constantly losing ground. I was certain it was he, from the immense roll of smooth greasy-blue manuscript which protruded from his pocket.

Well, now, thought I to myself, upon my word, he's running after that workman to get him for an audience! He wants him to listen to his lecture. This is no longer the pursuit of knowledge, but the pursuit of ignorance, under difficulties.

I determined now that nothing should deter me from hearing the Professor's exposition of Horace. On the appointed evening, therefore, I found myself in the spacious Hypothenuse Hall on Subjectivity Street. There was not a soul present except the usher; but presently the pale librarian with the crooked leg arrived, and halted painfully up the aisle. He was followed by the little agent himself, with the dirty neck and rosy-mottled cheeks. Then came two other persons, one of whom had wads of jeweler's cotton in his ears, and the other had black hair and blue spectacles. We five composed the audience.

The learned Herr Professor Doctor arrived very promptly. He was, as before remarked, of a short stature, and quite obese, very fair-skinned and ruddy-cheeked, though the color, as with many of these beer-drinkers, looked almost as if painted on, and not suffused from beneath. His hair was yellow, parted high on his head, combed behind the ears, and cut straight off all around. In the lobe of each ear was a very small ring. Around his neck there was wrapped a very portentous black neckcloth, in many a fold, covering his neck thickly from his ears quite down to his shoulders. He moved up the aisle with that peculiar German pace or gliding motion, consisting of short level steps, which, as the novelist Richardson describes it in his own case, seems rather to steal away the ground than to get rid of it by perceptible degrees.

He was evidently gratified by the warmth of our applause and the size of the audience. He bowed low, then untied the blue pasteboard covers, and read as follows :

" Meine Herren : The lecture, as announced, will consist of a running commentary on Satire 9, Book I., of Q. Horatius Flaccus, popularly elucidating that amusing composition in the hodigetico-exegetical method of Westner. The subject of the satire, as you well know, is the encounter of the poet with a persistent Roman bore.

" If you will carefully observe the first verse of this admirable satire, you will discover in it a most beautiful instance of the adaptation of the rhythmical structure to the sense of the passage. The poet was ascending the Sacred Way, which is a brisk slope upward from the Coliseum, and the halting movement of the words *Ibam forte Via Sacra* fitly represents the laboriousness of the ascent. On the summit of the ascent, before you descend toward the Forum, stands now the Arch of Titus, where Horace probably sat down to rest himself, a movement which is beautifully represented by the cæsura in the verse, where we pause, or, as it were, sit down, in scanning. Then the line concludes with the soft, liquescent words, *sicut meus est mos*, which indicate the ease of the descent.

"You will observe, meine Herren, that the third line, which records the approach of the garrulous fool, contains four words of two syllables each. Now, here is a remarkable beauty of composition. In the first line, where Horace was still alone, the words are mostly of one syllable; in the second line, where he descends into the noisy Forum, the words swell out into a turbulent length; but in the third, where the poet and the fool are together, a majority of the words are of two syllables. [Applause by the man with the defective ears.]

"Next, I will call your attention to the remarkable words, *O te, Bolane, cerebri felicem !* O Bolanus, happy of your head ! I need not tell you, meine Herren, that this celebrated passage has given rise to innumerable virulent controversies among the learned, beginning as early as the time of Permixtus, in the second century. Everything hinges on the case of the substantive *cerebrum*.

"First, as to the reading *cerebri*. By this we must understand the poet as saying that Bolanus is happy *of* his head, in possession of his head, that is, in having any head at all. But we can form no conception of a man happy *without* his head ; hence this reading seems to attribute to the poet an impertinence, and I condemn it as spurious.

"With regard to the reading *cerebro*, we know that poets are licensed to give the ablative the sense of *in*, without employing that preposition. From this we should have the reading, happy *in* his head. But the usual sense of the ablative is privative, denoting absence, ablation, or abstention. Understanding it so, we should read, happy *out of* his head. But it can hardly be supposed the poet would write in this manner, though, as a purely psychological fact, people are often happier out of their heads than they are in them. [Profound silence.]

"I do not attempt to deny that there are also many difficulties connected with the reading *cerebrum*. The phrase, happy *in respect to* his head, would indicate that he was peculiarly felicitous in regard of some peculiar quality of that organ. If this were a serious composition, we should be bound to suppose that Horace meant to congratulate him on his acumen or brilliancy; but, since it is satirical, we are unsettled from the usual base of criticism, and compelled to seek for outside historical information. There is, indeed, an inherent probability that the poet meant to felicitate Bolanus on his obtuseness, since that quality would have shielded him (Horace) from this fool's infliction.

" But this theory, unfortunately, is controverted by the positive historical statement of Mallonius (ii. 27), that Bolanus was a remarkably astute advocate. On the other hand, however, Trebonius affirms with equal positiveness, in a fragment discovered in Brindisi in the fourteenth century, that when he dined with Bolanus on one occasion he had peacock in the third course and boar's-head in the fourth, and ate his celery with sweet oil. This would seem to indicate that he was a person of a rather imbecile understanding. So this important question still remains *sub judice*.

"*Misere cupis abire*, You are monstrous anxious to get away, says the inexorable bore to the poet, as he writhes

and wriggles.   I desire, meine Herren, to call your attention to the profound metaphysical or psychological knowledge here displayed by Horace.   He might have written
vis, You wish to get away; or *petis*, You seek; or *desi-
deras*, You desire; or *niteris*, You struggle; but not one of
them would have conveyed the nice shade of meaning
expressed by *cupis*.   *Wish* denotes pure and simple volition; *seek*, muscular volition, as that of a stag-hound;
desire, intellectual, or, oftener, moral, volition, without
cause or reason expressed; *struggle*, strong and violent
volition, accompanied by kicks, blows, flinging of stones,
and the like.   But *want* denotes intense, interior, subjective volition, a movement of the intellect seldom found
among the superficial and objective Italians, or even among
the ancient Romans, but more frequent among Northern
nations.   *Cupis abire!*   It is very expressive.''

During the delivery of the above paragraph, the Professor seemed temporarily to lose himself in a profound
metaphysical abstraction.   He gradually lost sight of his
manuscript, and began to pace slowly up and down on the
platform.   Presently he fell into the national attitude of
meditation, to wit, the left hand laid gently across the ab-
domen, the head thrown slightly to the right and upward,
and the right forefinger placed alongside the nose.   In
this attitude he remained in a deep meditation for some
moments.   Then he began, in a dreamy and pensive
strain, to repeat what he had uttered, but with his right
side toward the audience, and his eyes directed upon the
side wall of the room, as if he were abstractedly apostro-
phizing an imaginary audience.

Here I ventured to commit a breach of decorum to
which the student of human nature is sometimes tempted.
I turned back and looked into the faces of the audience
of four persons.   Any one who will perpetrate this piece

of ill manners in a theater, or when listening to a comical speaker, will be rewarded with an interesting phenomenon which will repay the loss of some of the finest passages. The facial muscles of the most impressible people in the audience, especially in Germany, seem to play in sympathy with the speaker's, assuming the same smiles and distortions. These movements sometimes extend, among Germans, even to the neck and arms, causing them to gyrate in unconscious and gentle accord, as if in an effort to assist or supplement the thought of the speaker.

In like manner, one may often observe little children at play, earnestly intent on some circular or twisting motion, industriously following it up with their lips or tongues. As Horace himself says,—

> "Si vis me flere, dolendum est
> Primum ipsi tibi."

So now, graven on the bewildered face of the poor fellow with the black hair and blue spectacles, I saw the word *cupis* in all its pregnant significance. Let the reader only consider what a dreadful thing it was for a member of the "laboring classes" to have this intensely psychological word written upon his lineaments ! I was mightily alarmed for him, lest it should strike into his system.

The Professor presently faced his audience again, and resumed upon *cupis :*

" I seem to myself, meine Herren, to see them now before me,—the irrepressible bore in his luxurious toga and perfumed, flowing locks, leering with a grin of exultation on the unfortunate Horace, who 'sweats even down to the ends of his toes,' and looks piteously about for Apollo or some compassionate mortal to hasten to his rescue. The taunting tone of the impudent snob in that word is quite untranslatable. *Cupis abire. Cupis*—ha, ha! *Misere cupis*—ha, ha, ha!   [Great laughter.]

"When Horace tells this impertinent chatterbox——"

Here the Herr Professor Doctor was suddenly interrupted by a deep and prolonged groan, followed by a heavy thud, as of a man falling to the floor. Hastening to the spot, we found that the unfortunate laborer with the blue spectacles had fallen under a paralytic stroke, and was insensible.   The kind-hearted Professor hastened down from the platform in deep concern, and ran with great precipitation to fetch the sufferer a draught of beer. In the mean time we carried him gently out into the open air, and then across the street, into an apothecary shop, to await the arrival of a physician.

Seeing the lecture was hopelessly broken off, I started homeward, then lingered awhile on the pavement, while the relatives and sympathetic friends were administering cordials, rolling the unfortunate man on a barrel, hammering him on the back, and performing other well-meant operations.   A physician arrived presently, and, after glancing at the sufferer, took his companion aside to question him as to his habits of life and the probable cause of the stroke. I overheard only the concluding sentences.

"Did you say it was the honored Herr Professor Doctor Kinck von Kinck's lecture you were listening to?"

"It was, Herr Doctor."

"Ach, Donnerwetter! Then I can do nothing for him. It is a hopeless case."

Next morning I read in the newspaper the coroner's verdict: "Came to his death from an excessive and untimely administration of *cupis*."

STUDENT RAMBLES IN PRUSSIA.

I.

Hamlet. I am very glad to see you.   Good even.
  But what, in faith, makes you from Wittenberg?
Horatio. A truant disposition, good my lord.
HAMLET.

BUT Wittenberg breeds "truant dispositions" no more.   No more does the German student, round-faced, broad-shouldered, in his immense cannon-boots, and with his little skull-cap gayly cocked on one side of his head and brilliant with as many colors as a poppy-bed, saunter with his level gait through the narrow, crooked, cobble-paved alleys of lonely Wittenberg.   No more do the *Bierburschen* prowl through the streets on midnight missions of sign-lifting, hoisting one the other upon his shoulders before some grocery door, or scattering like frightened rats at the alarm of the police "rattlers," diving higgledy-piggledy down the darkened alleys. No more in lonely Wittenberg does the incarcerated sign-lifter turn his leaden eyes from the depths of the university dungeon, as he hears in the court the footfall of some comrade who was fleeter than he, and sees his shadow flit across the narrow grating, and dolefully sigh, *O beatus ille !* No more in Wittenberg does the hapless fag, the freshman "fox," sigh for the day of his legal emancipation,—the great, the pregnant day which shall usher him into the miseries and the mysteries of the condition of "singed fox," when his emancipators shall

(103)

dance and yell around him, paint on his face a pair of
whiskers, and sing the song of his deliverance:

> " Ich mal' dir einen Bart, dass du hinfort geartet
>   Sollst sein, nicht wie ein Kind, das noch ganz ungebartet."

Then, in due process of time, the "singed fox" became a "young boy," then an "old boy," and, last of
all, arrived at the tremendous dignity and responsibility
of a "moss-skin," a free person, *inter pares primus.*
Then he could wear his. sword of authority, and play the
absolute tyrant over the luckless "schoolworms," "boo-
bies," or "yellow-bills" in the classes below; compel
his freshman to run on errands, to feast him without return, to lend him money without hope of repayment, to
fight with the street-boys for his amusement, or to pommel for him the "obscurants" or "stinkers" who obstinately refused to yield to his tyranny by entering the
secret societies.   And if the wretched fag refused to obey,
the lordly "moss-skin" could beat him with the flat of
his sword.

Evil days were those, albeit the golden age of "academic freedom," and sad dogs were many of the gradu-
ates who went home to their elders.   The old song says:

> " Wer von Leipzig kommt ohne Weib,
>   Und von Halle mit gesundem Leib,
>   Und von Jena ungeschlagen,
>   Der hat von grossem Glück zu sagen."

Gone forever and forever by, not alone in Wittenberg,
but everywhere, is that German student whom Kobbe
limns with a touch of fond and tender pathos: "Ah!
where are ye, happy times, when the German student was
a being who considered himself lifted above common
mortals, and who looked down upon the life of a citizen
with unspeakable superciliousness and contempt?   Like

the ancient Titans, he gazed down upon the puny generation that crept, and crawled, and wept upon the earth,
regarding them as so many ants which existed only for
his service.

"Bestowed in his immense cannon-boots; his pipe,
with its long, swinging, gay-colored tassels, resting its
bowl on the floor before him; and his jaunty little cap
tipped to one side, what was the world to him, or he to
the world? Or, as he sat in the cellar before the beer-
table, while his voice swelled high in *Gaudeamus* or in
Landesvater, and the backsword hurtled through his hat,
and the glasses clinked around him; or, mayhap, as he
swung his lusty arms to a *Hoch lebe* or a *fiducit*, how all
things else in the outer world sank into prosy vulgarity
and nothingness! Or, again, when he sat in his little
chamber—his throne his bed, his footstool the Pandects
piled high around him, all in confusion, wherever he could
find room; the beermug beside the inkstand, and on the
broken plate, as the song says, 'with the potato a herring;'
his table an altar to Bacchus; and from the midst of all
a dense savory smoke ascending from his pipe—how its
delicious fumes wrapped him in sweet forgetfulness of the
dull world!

"Behold him again in the intoxicating hour when he
stands before the chalk-line on the floor, and the gleaming rapiers cross and clink before him—O world! ye do
not know his exultation. Or the yet greater felicity of the
day when he gave audience to his freshmen! There he
sat in his fleecy robe, stretched far back in his soft easy-
chair, the pipe in his mouth, his weather-soiled cap
cocked upon his head; and before him, clad in black
from tip to toe, all ruffled and frizzled, and with *galanterie-*
swords by their sides, his *chapeaux d'honneur*, like cham-
berlains, awaiting the beck of their Serenissimus; while

before his mental vision there floats a coach drawn by four or six prancing steeds, postilions with their clanging horns, marshals of honor, seniors and Præses on horseback—a long train in brilliant array !   Now he is king for the last time ; for the last time a free man, one of the elect ; and they are escorting him forth with honors into the busy world.   But it existed not for him.   .   .   .

"Nowhere else than in Germany, in the land of dreamers, could have existed, could have arisen, such a being as the old German student.   Nowhere else than in old Germany could there have lived such an exclusive freedom. In that land alone where no freedom was, could men feel themselves attracted to this fiction of freedom."

Ah, yes ! these enormous ramparts, which encircle the little humdrum town, grass-grown, and clean-shaven as a lawn, and so lofty that the sentries on them almost overlook the town, as they pace their appointed beats, with their polished bayonets and their *Pickelhauben* flashing in the sunlight,—these are Chancellor Bismarck's latest revised edition and commentary of that old "academic freedom."   These gleaming cannon, which, with their single grim eyes, Cyclops-like, glower down from the grassy parapets,—these are the big exclamation-points of sarcasm which King William writes at the end of that brilliant phantasmagoria of liberty, that "fiction of freedom," conceived in dreaming professors' brains.   Germany needed a little "blood and iron" to startle these academic troglodytes out of their political hibernation, and make them lift their noses for a moment from between the pages of commentaries, that they might comprehend true liberty, which comes only from strength, which comes only from union.

But there is no change since Hamlet's time in these little greenish-yellow, mud-and-cobble houses, the everlasting stucco of Germany, sicklied over with a maudlin wash, but so enormously thick-walled that the small square windows look like portholes for cannon. Here, on a market-day, one wanders whithersoever the current bears him—now jostling among wagons and pedestrians sheer in the middle of the alley; now nearly overturned by a low cabbage-wagon, guided by a stalwart, red-faced woman, and tugged along by a dog, barking and screwing his tail in his impatience. You had better take care, or he will knock you down among the cabbages.

Still carried along in the devious windings, unable to see ten rods ahead in the crooked crevices called streets, seeming to be only earthquake-cracks among the houses; sufficiently grateful if one escapes being borne down by an Amazonian market-woman bending under an immense hamper of vegetables; looking before and behind, and dodging fearfully under horses' noses.

The quaint sharp gables are ranged along like so many huge saw-teeth, or the red-tiled roofs slope toward the street, reaching down through several stories, with rows of dormers to each, and all black-spotted by time or smirched with splashes of lichens. In one of the dormers is a mousing grimalkin, which stretches its neck eagerly up, and moves it round and round, following the flight of the pigeons close above. What a queer, funny way these houses of old Germany have of standing along in a row like militia!—some with backs to faces, others with backs to backs, others sides to sides, and every one leaning in its own peculiar direction.

But to-day there is only an occasional peasant-woman, in a very short dress, stumping along with her wooden shoes, and rattling over the cobbles, as she shoves her toes in at every step; or one of Bismarck's boys, in his dark-blue uniform with red facings, and his fascine-knife dangling in its broad sheath against his legs, while he munches a sausage which he holds in both hands.

Once out of Wittenberg, I journeyed on along the ancient royal highway, between the ever-welcome colonnades of stately poplars, planted that the kingly head might never be scorched by the sun of summer. The sun shone as brightly as it ever does in blue old Germany ; but what a weary, weary land to my eyes, on that pitiless May-day, was that sandy champaign, almost utterly naked in its hopeless sterility ! So indescribably blue, and cold, and pinched was it, without any vegetation but a forest of planted pines, which, after a quarter of a century, had struggled up with their wretched, scraggy trunks only fifteen feet. The very soil looked blue and thin and skinny, and the rye looked blue, and was so meager and chilled that it could not conceal the ground or the knees of men who plucked up the weeds.

All the dismal immensity of this fenceless, hedgeless, houseless waste, except an acre of rye in a hundred, was given up to the sorrel, the lichens, and the quitches. The very air seemed poor and attenuated, like old skimmed milk. All the houses were clustered together in little villages, far apart, where they huddled close, as if for warmth. Their dead, dull peat-fires gave forth no cheerful wreaths of smoke. In all the desolate and bleak waste there was scarcely a soul abroad.

The faces of the carroty-haired children, who were occasionally watching some geese, were mottled with blue, and purple, and goose-pimples. If a man ventured abroad to pluck up weeds in the stunted rye, which seemed to shiver with a kind of rustling, starved chilliness, his hands were bluer than the air.

So utterly worn out, so bluish-wan, and weary, and lean with the lapse of untold centuries seemed all the earth and the air of that Germany which I looked out upon on that dismal May forenoon.

Lamartine says the blood of the Germans is blue, but that of these Brandenburgers must certainly be sour.

It will readily be believed that I did not undertake a pilgrimage through this inexpressibly bleak region in search of fine landscapes. I wished only to visit, by their own firesides, and in their own fields, that hard, grim, Puritanic race to whom Prussia is primarily indebted for all her greatness.

It was hours after mid-day before the spires of Wittenberg vanished below one of those broad sand-knolls, which swell broadly up with a thousand acres. The afternoon was far spent, and I began to cast longing glances ahead in quest of an eligible tavern. I had come up with a thumping lout of a young peasant, who strode along with his "clouted shoon," about a yard and a quarter at a stride, whose voice blubbered and gurgled up out of his stomach in such a manner that the fierce wind whisked it away, leaving me only an occasional horse-laugh (whereupon I would also laugh, though I had not the remotest notion of the matters whereof he was discoursing). By his advice I passed several tolerable inns, though I found afterward, to my sorrow, he was looking only for the cheapest.

At last we came to one which was the meanest of all, but I was too weary to go a step farther. It bore the pretentious name of the Inn of the Green Linden. It was an absolute hovel, built of cobbles and mud, tawny-yellow within, greenish-yellow without, with an earthen floor and benches around the walls. Above the door were twined some twigs of Whitsuntide birch, which I had noticed during the day on the peasants' hats, wagons, and everywhere.

Around a pine table were eight or ten men and hobble-dehoys, each with a *Schoppen* of terribly stiff beer before him, and most of them smoking the long, swan-necked porcelain pipe, while four were intent on cards. The men were hard, gristly-faced, sour-blooded fellows, who only muttered now and then a monosyllable, which I could seldom understand. The youths looked on with the most vacuous loamy countenances imaginable. So intent were they on the miserable game that they gave no heed to our arrival, and when I endeavored to ascertain who was the landlord, I received only a blank stare, or a gesture of impatience.

I sat down and waited, and I confess, for a few minutes, my enthusiasm for the Prussian character fell absolutely to the freezing-point.

After about half an hour the landlord seemed to be disturbed in his mind by a suspicion that I was a foreigner, drew near, and ascertained that fact. Whereupon he brought me some vile black coffee, and a couple of excellent wheaten *Semmel*, such as you seldom fail to find in Germany, and which do much to atone for the execrable coffee.

The players continued at their game far into the evening, and though the stakes were of the most trifling amount, often only half a penny, they displayed a fierce and obstinate eagerness which was surprising. They would rise up on their feet, lean far across the table, and smite the same with astounding violence. When they at last desisted, and were preparing to disperse, they collected about me, and, finding I was an American, listened to me awhile with a kind of drowsy, immovable passiveness, while the smoke lazily twirled above their heads. Unlike the lively Suabians, and the joyous drinkers of the sunny wine of Freiburg, they scarcely asked any questions, or expressed any interest beyond grunting their assent or wonder.

At last the host and myself were left alone. Then he proceeded to prepare the only couch he could offer, by shaking down on the floor a bundle of clean rye straw. He tucked me all up as carefully as if I were one of his young *Buben*, shook the hand which I reached out from the straw, and left me with a cheerful "*Schlafen Sie wohl.*"

There, in the inexpressibly dense and bitter smudge of the tobacco smoke, and the fumes of that terrific beer, cold and shivering, I grabbed frantically the livelong night at my persecutors.

In the adjoining room a lusty fellow stretched himself on a bench, pillowed his head on a portentous loaf of rye bread, without having even inserted that useful article of diet into a pillow-case, and there he snored—*stertitque supinus*—the long night through, in a tone so exasperating that I was greatly tempted to arise and· introduce a wisp of rye-straw judiciously into his windpipe.

When I sat up on my couch next morning, pulling the straw out of my hair, I said to myself, "Oh, I have passed a miserable night!" I had not had any "fearful dreams," nor, for that matter, any sleep, that I was aware of; neither had I had any "ugly sights," because it was too dark to see them; but I felt them. They appeared to be greatly rejoiced to be able, once in their lives, to extract blood from a man's veins instead of beer.

The next day I passed through spectacles of the most wonderfully minute and unceasing toil. In a planted pinery, where the trees were become too large to be plowed, there were men on their knees weeding them. Others, in long sheepskin cloaks, inherited from the time of Tacitus, were weeding great fields of flax. In a royal forest a woman was culling the merest twigs for fuel. Others along the roadside snipped off the close short fleece of grass, bunched it up in mighty bundles on their backs, and carried it to the village for the stalled cattle. Here a stalwart yeoman lazily leans his chin on the top of his crook, guarding three sheep as they nimbly nibble! Peasant women going to the village to hawk their little stuff, shuffled along with their wooden sabots, making a prodigious dust, and chatting cheerfully with their stolid lords, though they were half bowed down to the earth beneath the intolerable weight of vegetables. And the infamous tyrants trudged on beside the poor women, never offering to touch their burdens with so much as one of their fingers.

The women and the cows of Germany perform all the labor in-doors, and a third of that done out-doors.

At this point I will introduce a few statistics, taken from the Prussian *Jahrbuch*, showing the industrial condition of the monarchy in certain aspects. By the latest census (1863) there were in the entire kingdom 1,216,919 independent landholders or farmers, while the number of dependent laborers, of all sorts, on these farms was 1,911,861. How different is that from England, where there are only some 30,000 landholders !

The relation between the number of independents and dependents of the rural districts is quite variable. Thus, in the Stralsund district, there are 5·40 laborers to one farmer; in the Berlin district, 3·32; Potsdam, 2·58; Königsberg, 2·73; Magdeburg, 2·06; Erfurt, 1·24; Cologne, 1·05; Aix-la-Chapelle, 0·82.

The reader will detect a singular and apparently paradoxical fact in the above figures. In the Westphalian and other fertile provinces along the Rhine, the proportion of laborers is much less than in the sterile eastern provinces. In other words, in those fat and merry provinces where Catholics are most numerous and wine abounds, the number of dependent laborers is smaller, proportionately, than in these sandy barrens I am traversing, peopled by a grim, Puritanic, beer-drinking race. This appears to be contrary to what one would naturally expect.

The explanation seems to be, that these eastern provinces have been longest under the iron rule of Prussia, and that the onerous taxes which have been necessitated by her military system have forced many farmers to sell their little patrimonies, and become hirelings to the nobility. If so, it is the hard and bitter price which Germany has to pay for union, because nothing else in the world but the grim military system of Prussia can ever stamp out the infernal janglings of the little princes of Central and Southern Germany, and make one great nation, respectable and strong. The world will never know, until it is fully set forth in history, the infinite indebtedness of Germany to those few, early, Puritanical provinces of Prussia, and the mighty burdens they have borne in their poverty in building up, in spite of itself, the greatness of the German nation.

When Germany is fully united and strong externally, she will become liberal to her own citizens. Louis Blanc said, in 1840, "Germany becomes Prussian to-day, to become democratic to-morrow." With this agrees Bismarck: "None but a completed commonwealth can afford the luxury of a liberal government."

I think the Germans will never "witch the world with noble horsemanship." The horses of Prussia are splendid animals for the farm, strong, and glossy, and round, equal to the heaviest Clydesdales; but the people seem to care very little to mount them. After all my travels in Prussia, I have yet to see a man riding on horseback in the country, and in the city it is chiefly the military officers who prance along the boulevards. The great superiority of the Hungarian cavalry over the Prussian was abundantly demonstrated in the Bohemian campaign of 1866. The dreaded "Three Uhlans" of Edmond About were often Poles.

It is said that the sovereigns of Germany, when paying visits of ceremony at foreign courts, seldom omit to take along with them a favorite charger or two, to whose paces they are accustomed, that there may be no blunders or embarrassments in the reviews. It would be a dreadful thing if his majesty should be planted on his august head by an uncourtly Gaul.

These poor peasants here evince little more confidence than do their majesties. The outrageously unprofessional and awkward manner in which they treat the noble brutes would enrage a horse-fancier beyond endurance. To save toll at the gates, they often hitch only one horse in a two-horse wagon, so that the tongue bruises and thwacks his shins in a disgraceful manner. And then to hitch the head of one gallant horse to the tail of another—bah !

In the village of Beelitz I had an amusing adventure, resulting from my ignorance of the customs of the country. Upon entering the village, I began to cast about me for some eligible tavern, wherein I might take my customary mid-day repast. The first one I approached was the Inn of the Black Horse; but there were rather too many frowzy, unwashed children and dingy geese tumbling about; besides, the sign hung down from one corner. The only other one was the Inn of the White Eagle, which was scarcely any better, but it was Hobson's choice. It was so extremely small that I was in doubt whether it was a public tavern or not; so I rapped.

Only the clink of the dinner-knives responded.

The operation was repeated with a certain amount ot vigor. There was a kind of objurgatory remark made inside, and in a moment the door was opened about two feet, and an immense brawny arm, bared to the elbow, was protruded out around the edge of the door. The arm alone was visible, no body seeming to be attached thereto. In the fingers there was clutched a hunk of some substance which appeared to solicit my closer inspection. A single glance at this substance revealed to me the pleasing and interesting fact that it was bread. It was undoubtedly bread.

This was an unexpectedly prompt response to my desires, and presented an opportunity for the acquisition of a limited amount of provisions cheap, but one of which my conscience would not permit me to avail myself. Howsoever, I scrutinized the bread with quite a lively interest. It was manifestly good bread, that is to say, it had been good bread at some former period of time, but was now somewhat dry. Indeed, I think I may safely affirm that it was totally devoid of moisture.

Presently the hand holding this article of diet executed a sudden movement of impatience, or, as it were, of beckoning or blandishment, as if I were expected to take this bread and masticate the same. But as I still hesitated, the arm was suddenly withdrawn into the tavern, there was a very audible remark made inside, and then the brawny hostess owning the hand presented herself at the door, and appeared to have made an astounding discovery.

Tableau !

A substantial dinner of pork and cabbage. Many apologies.

Moral: In a country where beggars are numerous, never knock at the tavern door.

*   *   *   *   *   *   *

I will end this chapter with a translation of part of a curious document I came upon in my rambles. It is entitled "Leipsic Beer Code," and is the body of rules accumulated from tradition upon the subject of beer-drinking in the Leipsic University. It will show better than a treatise could to what a system the devotees of Gambrinus have reduced their orgies:

I. Subjects of the Code.

1. All persons, under the operations of this Code, are divided into beer-boys and foxes.

2. A fox becomes a beer-boy, either by the lapse of two semesters, or by beer-trial. The beer-trial is conducted in the following manner: the song beginning,

> "In Leipzig angekommen,
> Als Fuchs bin aufgenommen,"

is sung; and if, after the first and the last stanzas, the candidate drinks a whole, and after each of the others a half-pint, he is solemnly proclaimed a beer-boy.

3. All kinds of beer are constitutional under this Code, but other drinks are not recognized.

II. Drinking Challenges.

4. To increase the jollity of drinking-bouts, it is an immemorial custom for the beer-boys to drink to each other about a round-table, even if it is only the plain beer-table of the jovial student, for thereby the reproach of the "solitary swig" is removed. When Müller says to Schulze, "I come to thee, I challenge thee, I drink to thee a half, a whole," or so, Schulze will be so carried

away with enthusiasm that he will involuntarily accept in the usual words.

5. As to the acceptance of the quantity named, Schulze is bound under all circumstances, both morally and by the beneficent rules of the beer-shame, to do so at once, and in the following words: *"Profit,* drink it, swig it, it's right." Mere winking or nodding does not suffice. Even the expression "Swig it double" is not forbidden, only Schulze is not to guarantee that it is actually done. If Shulze delays to respond *"Profit,"* etc., then Müller can demand it of him with the words, "Schulze, say '*Profit,'* " etc. three times. If Schulze, after this demand, does not at once accept the quantity named, he goes into a beer-shame. If Müller drinks before Schulze accepts, the latter is not bound to follow up. But if Schulze has his throat so well in order that he feels the need of a drink, he cries out with a loud voice, "Müller, I follow you up," whereupon the latter gives vent to his unspeakable joy.

6. One is not bound to accept a challenge from a beer-debtor. The constitutional quantity ranges from a quarter-pint to two wholes.

7. Should several beer-honorable souls, as Müller, Schulze, Lehmann, etc., wish to express their liking for some one, they blow him in the air with so or so many wholes or halves,—that is, each of them drinks the same quantity to Richter, for instance. Richter must now drink this quantity to each of them in return, at intervals of five beer-minutes (three minutes). Foxes cannot blow in the air this way without the participation of at least one beer-boy.

8. To promote universal jollity at the beer-table is the object of the very useful custom called " Drinking to the World." Richter, after drinking his quantities, retaliates

with the same (at least a half-pint) upon every one at the table except Müller, Schulze, and Lehmann.

III. Beer-Duels.

9. A beer-duel is a duel in which the weapons are beer, and the conqueror is he who first drinks a certain quantity in a constitutional manner.

10. As in every duel, so here, there must first be an offense given. After every offense a challenge must be given within at least five beer-minutes. The offense is of two sorts, "sage" and "beer-baby."

11. In case a beer-boy is called "sage," he can either challenge the offender, or, when he thinks the offense was involuntary, or proceeded from some other cause, he can reply with "Doctor." The other must then challenge him, or reply with "Pope." After "Pope" a challenge *must* be given. In case of a duel on "sage," each party drinks a half; "Doctor," a whole; "Pope," two wholes.

12. When a beer-boy is called "beer-baby," a challenge must be given, and each party drinks a half.

13. Each principal must choose a second, and the second of the challengee an umpire. The challenger's second commands, "Let the Popes (or Doctors) seize!" the challengee's second says, "Attack!" the other replies, "Out!" In a duel on "beer-baby," the challengee chooses an umpire, who equalizes the weapons. The challenger says, "One;" the challengee, "Two;" the challenger, "Three;" whereupon they begin to drink.

14. The umpire declares him in beer-shame who drinks unconstitutionally, or who was the last to say "beer-baby." To drink unconstitutionally is, to begin to drink before the word "Out," or "Three;" to slop out beer (bleed) during the drinking; to leave a little (called

Philistine), enough to cover the bottom of the mug ; or, to break the mug in setting it down.

15. Seconds and umpires must be beer-honorable beer-boys, and the umpire is bound on *Grand Cerevis* to decide according to his best knowledge and belief.

IV. Orders Ex Pleno.

16. Every beer-boy has the right, in certain cases, to order a fox to drink as a punishment. This is called an order *ex pleno*. It is usually resorted to when the foxes carry their tails too high, and long experience has demonstrated it to be the best means for keeping them in a proper state of humility.

17. The order *ex pleno* is given in the following manner : The beer-boy calls out to the culprit fox, " Müller, drink *ex pleno*" once. If the fox delays, this order is given a second and third time, and if he still refuses, he is at once declared in a beer-shame. Idle excuses are not to be accepted. If the beer-boy calls out, " It is remitted," the fox is released from further drinking ; but if he compels him to drink it all, he is bound to drink at least one swallow with him, under pain of the beer-shame.

18. Should a fox think he was ordered to drink *ex pleno* without sufficient ground (which is hardly conceivable), he can, after he drinks his quantity, ask the other why he ordered him to do it. If he still thinks himself wronged, he can then take oath before any impartial beer-honorable beer-boy, and through him have a beer-court assembled.

19. In beer-villages, that is, in every place outside of Leipsic, except in corps-bouts and regular beer-cellars, a man of a higher semester can order one of a lower to drink

ex pleno.   If the latter refuses, the other can punish him by shaking his mug of beer out over his head.

V. Grand Cerevis.

20. The *Grand Cerevis* is the highest form of affirmation in all beer-cases.   It is, therefore, to be given as the last and indefeasible testimony, when no other kind can be adduced for lack of witnesses.

21. Since the *Grand Cerevis* is principally employed when jollity has reached its acme, by reason of the unlimited swigging, and when, by consequence, it is no longer to be expected that general attention will be paid to what is passing, it is necessary, in order to prevent a frivolous use of it, that it should never be given negatively. In other words, one must never affirm on *Grand Cerevis* that another did *not* do so and so; but, at the utmost, that he did not hear or see him do so and so.   One *Grand Cerevis* must also never be given against another.

22. The only case where the last clause above given is violated is as follows : When one accuses another of having given his *Grand Cerevis* falsely, he must establish that fact through two beer-honorable witnesses, who are bound on *Grand Cerevis* to declare truthfully what they have seen or heard.   If the defendant is proven guilty, he goes into the highest beer-shame.

*   *   *   *   *   *   *

I cannot follow up this quaint document further.   It contains eighty-three sections, describing beer-courts, beer-conventions, beer-punishments, the beer-shame, etc. There are twenty-two beer-crimes which lead to the beer-shame, seven which conduct to the sharpened beer-shame, and four which terminate in the perpetual beer-shame, or gallows, at which point the offender may be forcibly ejected from the drinking-bout, if he refuses to enter a beer-trial for the sake of drinking himself back to a beer-honorable estate. Although hanging on the gallows, he can still return, if he will drink enough within a certain number of minutes.

STUDENT RAMBLES IN PRUSSIA.

II.

All that's moisture
  Drink with cheer;
Only water
  Touch with fear.

GOUNOD'S OPERA FAUST.

STANDING just outside the mighty ramparts of Magdeburg, looking south, I saw only a green infinity of grass. Not a tree for the birds to perch in and sing. "*Daz tuot den vogelînen wê*," as the ancient Walther sings. How grumpy they were, although it was June, as if they felt sour toward the Lombardy poplars for shooting up their branches so straight that they could not build in them! Even when they wanted to alight, they had to clutch a perpendicular twig desperately, and stand out horizontal, to their great disgust.

Imprimis, let us observe this circumstance. The superb old Lombardy poplars, regally useless, and planted in the times of "divine right" notions, are here fast yielding place to sweet-scented apples and cherries. It is the triumph of modern utilitarian democracy over royalty. Every poplar destroyed is one more infinitesimal kingling gone. "Off with his head!" Well done for him.

Walking down between these blooming and sweet-smelling rows—here a king, there a score of democrats—you shall see, far out on the magnificent long sea-rolls of brown loam, gangs of laborers, seventy or eighty in a

(122)

row, men and women together, dressed in blue Saxon linen, hoeing in the beet-rows, which reach away till they disappear below the blue horizon. It is the same sad, hopeless, trip-hammer stroke which one might see, some twenty years ago, in our own sunny Carolinas. There is the overseer, too (how much he looks like Legree!), moving to and fro along the line.

It is not that there is such an excessive amount of physical suffering, except in winter and in unusual cases; but the circumstance most deplorable is, the intellectual vacuousness, the lubricity, and the utter crushing out of noble ambitions wrought by this never-ceasing drudgery for another. It degrades human nature to be always a hireling.

As the sun nears the horizon, and "*procul villarum culmina fumant*" with supper-getting, many a wistful glance wanders thither. When the village bell rings, forthwith they throw up their heels, leap, and jump, and stand on their heads, and butt one another like bellicose rams, showing that they lack much of exhaustion. But their toil is not ennobled by the sacred ambitions of ownership, and such toil is inevitably brutalizing.

For this reason it was that, in the village inns, although the peasants who flocked in to fuddle themselves with beer in the evening were more glib and oily in speech than the sour-blooded boors about Wittenberg, they were far more lascivious. The unchastity of the South Germans is partly accounted for by their softer climate, but here the same temperature prevails as about Wittenberg.

The Germans seem to suffer in their moral nature, under a purely hireling system, more than any other people of Christendom. Manifestly, they are not to be compared with the Italians as to the absolute descent, because they fall from a higher level ; but they are a nobler race, and are correspondingly more brutalized by peonage.

The laborers on these beet-plantations live in immense barracks owned by the planters, and in the towns those employed in the sugar-factories live in the same manner, but in still more deplorable squalor. They live largely off beets and other vegetables, and greens snipped out of the fields, in consequence of which their faces are very fluffy and pulpy. They seem to have in their veins the colorless lymph of fishes. The little carroty-haired children, tumbling on their heads in the streets of Stassfurt, have the ophthalmia to a distressing extent. Nearly all of them look repulsively blear-eyed and watery, as if they were just about to dissolve away.

I talked with one of the laborers on the plantation, who was a trifle more intelligent than most I tried, but his utter ignorance of political liberty was astonishing. Said I to him :

"Couldn't you get along without a king, think?"

The question almost shocked him, and he looked quite vacant.

"The king gives alms to the poor." It was the strongest argument that occurred to him.

"But, suppose you should elect your king, and allow him regular wages, such as you get yourself, only higher, in proportion to his place?"

The poor fellow's countenance was really troubled, and he answered softly, as if afraid he might be overheard :

"Oh, I think that would be bad, for then the poor would get no alms."

"Is that all you fear? Suppose your Diet in Berlin paid him wages—not half so much as he now gets—and saved the rest for the poor?"

He gave a glance, to be sure we were not overheard,

and then he considered the notion of electing a king, which seemed to be peculiarly strange and terrible to him. Then came the argument which was convincing.

"But, if we did not vote for this king, but another, his police would come and catch us, and put us in prison."

The poor, scared, starved soul! So utterly impossible was it for him to place himself back of the notion of the king as the source of all things earthly. He seemed to be as incapable of conceiving of anything whatever existing without the consent of the king as we all are of understanding how the Almighty has existed from eternity, self-created. I questioned many, and found this notion of royal almsgiving was always uppermost.

Here it becomes necessary to write a thing which may seem terribly un-American and undemocratic. A vast majority of the masses of the Continent are not "sighing for liberty" at all. They do not even know what liberty is. The root of the matter is not found in them. They are dimly conscious, like a linnet hatched in its wicker-cage, that there is something lacking in their little lives; but, if they long to come to America, an honest analysis of their minds would evolve the unheroic fact that most of them are distinctly conscious of no higher purpose than to be able to acquire a more ample quantum of meat and mustard for a smaller outlay of labor.

The war between Prussia and Austria was just in its incipiency, and Stassfurt was full of belligerent talk. As the villagers sat around their little tables, I thought many times they would certainly fall to breaking one another's noses. First, one would leap up, lean far across the table, and beat it very earnestly with his fist, or strike wildly into the atmosphere, as if in the prosecution of severely personal hostilities against a June-bug; then the other would do the same; then they would both jump up, put their countenances close together, and discourse very violently and simultaneously for many moments together.

Close by the roadside, on an eminence commanding a prospect far and wide over the plains, stood a sandstone monolith, which, to the seeker after the dark ways of character, was a better guide than ever Number Nip served to the wayfarer.   It appears that the Duke of Anhalt, on whose territory it stood, some twenty years ago, when his excessive taxes had reduced the people to beggary, was graciously moved in his paternal heart to order the construction of a ducal turnpike, to enable his subjects to keep the wolf from their doors.   This was all very good and pleasant to a philanthropic mind, but the weak point of the German character appears on this monument, in the following inscription, among others :

"Wanderer, as you pause here, let us joyfully declare to you that Love fashioned this column, as a memorial of our lealty to him."

The principal circumstance to be noted in this inscription is that certain something of servility, of adulation and incense-burning to sleek rank rather than to starved and penniless genius, that "too-much-ness" of loyalty of which Coleridge accuses the Germans.   Compare the German *Domkirchen* with the cathedrals of Italy.   In the latter are tens of thousands of statues, statuettes, busts, pictures, cartoons, in which the children of genius do each other noble honor above all ribboned potentates; but in German churches there are few grand tombs, except to coffin the purple, few sublime frescoes, except to celebrate the heroism of the blue blood.   How true, how pitifully true, even of the genius of Germany, is that bitter sarcasm of Bismarck : "If the people had money enough, every one of them would have his king." Or that acrid word of Moltke, as he stood before the splendid portraits of Bazaine and McMahon in Versailles: "I think we Prussian generals have about as much merit as these gentlemen, but they will not place any of our portraits in a Pantheon at Berlin." Of all nations of Europe the most peaceful, and the most unhandsome on a horse, they have the most absurd disproportion of equestrian bronze in their streets.

When will the Germans cease to worship kings, and build for the Fatherland a true Walhalla, wherein shall be gathered their real Einheriar?

What more contemptuous term of reproach in the rest of Europe than "German count?" In their journals they quote the sayings of their great statesmen far oftener than we in America do, but it is merely the tribute of bookworms,—the conceit of learning. It is egotism. Egotism and skepticism are one. And it is a curious commentary on the value of most modern skepticism, that the most skeptical people of Christendom are the most devoted king-worshipers.

A skeptical people can never maintain republican government. They are too absolute; they must push every principle to its ultimate results; none of the imperfect systems, which alone, in this fallen world, can be carried on among men, will be tolerated by them. They would pick it to pieces, and establish in its stead such a Utopian complication as was sought to be made, in 1848, in Frankfort. There is no elasticity in the German character, no spirit of compromise, none of our easy American *laisser aller*, which is indispensable to self-government. The German loses his temper in politics, and strikes blindly about him. German minorities always protest. They have no patience with political offenders. "Shoot them down like mad dogs," said Luther of the rebellious peasants.

But we have wandered a long way from our sandstone pillar. Yes, here is Hettstadt.

The landlord of the White Swan was a tall, slender, meager-faced man, and he received me with much solemnity. We sat down on opposite sides of the polished earthenware stove, he with a hand on each knee, and I looked at him, and he looked at me, and we both looked at each other. To keep up the conversation, I was obliged to set forth unto him my whole history in order, interspersing the same with divers instructive accounts of American wheat and rye. But when the young people came in, as usual, in the evening, to refresh themselves with a little beer, his tongue was loosened. His preternatural gravity had been superinduced only by the profound cogitation in his mind, whereby he was lifting himself to the realization that he had a genuine live American under his roof.

He rehearsed to them, with an almost childish eagerness, all my noble qualities, together with those of American vegetables; every man the while looking at me with his two round eyes, with many ejaculations of admiration, until I began to feel, as Hawthorne said he did once when lionized, very much like a hippopotamus. I had to drink an alarming quantity of beer that evening, and answer several hundred questions about America.

Eisleben stands on one side of a picturesque, valley, not very deep, and about a half-mile wide, looking across to vast accumulations of copper slag, heaped among the knolls.

Directly I deposited my traveling-bag in the Golden Ship, I set out to seek the birthplace of the great monk. And what a disappointment! Elizabeth Goethe says:

" The individual is buried in consecrated ground. So should one also bury great and rare events in a beautiful coffin of recollections, to which each can return to commemorate the remembrance." But how all my youthful and rose-colored imaginings of Luther's birthplace were mildewed !

Conceive a mud-and-cobble house, of the natural earth-color, jammed in between two others so tight that it shoots up into two full stories, though scarcely more than fifteen feet on the ground, looking like a little boy in a spelling-class, standing on tiptoe, with his arms squeezed close to his body. Not more than five corpulent old burghers could walk abreast in the alley before it, and right in front of the stone step, worn down many inches by centuries of use, trickled along a film of sewerage. The tiny window on the right of the door contained nearly a hundred pieces of stained glass, about three-fourths of them square, and the others puttied together in kaleidoscopic fashion. Over the door was a black medallion bust of the Reformer, a modern work, with leaves and grapes twined around it, and this dubious legend written above :

> " Jedes Wort ist Luther's Lehr,
> Darum vergeht sie nimmer mehr."

The door consisted of two rough unplaned boards tacked together, and the walls were of almost Cyclopean thickness, the same within as without. In one corner there was a huge uncouth structure of hewn logs, whereby we ascended to the upper story.

This is low, and the walls are partly covered with ragged paper, partly with frescos, and partly with paintings, chiefly by Cranach and Albrecht Dürer, referring to scenes in Luther's history. They are in the quaint, pre-Raphaelite style ; the trees looking like toy-trees drawn by school-children, with occasional dabs of leaves without any visible means of support, and the trunks sometimes failing to make connection with the ground; and the people reaching their arms out of their breasts, as in an Egyptian wall-picture. One of them depictures the Diet of Worms under Biblical forms, being divided into three compartments: that on the right showing Nebuchadnezzar (Charles V.), and the three young Jews (Luther, Spalatin, etc.), with the corpulent form of Tetzel among his councilors; that in the center, the golden image (Popery); and that on the left, the Jews in the burning fiery furnace.

These paintings are full of bigotry. They are as Luther describes himself, "Rough, boisterous, stormy, and altogether warlike, born to fight innumerable devils and monsters, to remove stumps and stones, to cut down thistles and thorns, and to clear the wild woods." The guide shows a mediæval coin, which, as you hold one side up, presents Leo X., but when the other is turned up, there appears a moderately correct likeness of the devil.

It will be remembered that the "profoundly learned lady, Catherine Luther, his gracious housewife," bore to Luther six children. Of his numerous descendants, living in Halle, nobody knew anything whatsoever except the simple fact that they existed. "Alas for thee that thou art a grandson," says Goethe.

The memory of the mighty monk is not cherished as it deserves to be, either by the Prussian government or by the German nation. Not in all the city of Eisleben, with its two daily newspapers, could I find a photograph of the Reformer, and it was with difficulty that I found two of his house in an obscure *Buchhandlung.* The stone step of his humble dwelling is little worn now by the tread of reverent pilgrims, and the cobwebs stretch athwart the stairs. That the house exists even is due to its Cyclopean walls. It is built better than was Shakspeare's.

Germany has erected a few statues to the honor of genius,—to Guttenberg, and Faust, and Schoeffer; to Goethe and Schiller; but most are in apotheosis of sashed and ribboned idiocy, bestriding the horse which the Germans of all men sit most ill, and only great "by the grace of God," or the titular additions of flunkyism. France writes on her July Column the names of *all* her immortals; Italy fashions from enduring marble, with the long patience of centuries, and places in her Pantheon of Milan the forms of *all* her illustrious sons; but Germany, which is full of bronze kings, who, in their generation were tyrannic idiots, plants no worthy statue to Luther, or Humboldt, or Beethoven, princes of eloquence, of science, and of music in all our Christian world.

Peaceful as she is, and plodding in all practical matters, Germany is the *youngest* of all civilized peoples, and, like a young girl, her imagination runs on military brass and spangles.

The next day was Sunday, and we attended service in the little chapel wherein Luther preached his last sermon. Its rough walls were cracked and crumbled away in many places, giving chinks for the chattering rooks, and checkered around the bottom outside with memorial tablets of stone bearing the names of deceased members. The high-backed perpendicular seats were thoroughly of the American pioneer sort, in their discomfortableness. They remind one forcibly of that ancient meeting-house wherein one was wont to sit, listening to

> "The humming of the drowsy pulpit drone
> Half God's good Sabbath,"

with one's little legs projected straight out, like a couple of marline-spikes, now sleepily blinking at the flies dancing a mad cotillon in the air, and now munching a caraway-speckled cooky, surreptitiously slipped into one's hand as a preventive against childish ungodliness.

The congregation rose to their feet during the reading of the text, and bent their heads reverently while the Lord's Prayer was recited, as did also the pastor, removing his skull-cap. I was surprised to see, on the pulpit beside him, an old-fashioned hour-glass. It was matter of surprise, because the Germans are noted for the brevity of their discourses, and are never so long-winded as the seventeenth-century English divines, with their "sixteenthly" and "seventeenthly" elaborated with "Episcopal pertinacity," as Sydney Smith says.

I had an interesting conversation with a young editor of the town on the scarcity of fuel in Prussia. It is certain that this has a very benumbing effect on the intellects of the peasants, who consume such quantities of cold beer besides. The picture of a sour-blooded peasant shivering over his still, dead, smokeless peat-fire, is not one suggestive of brilliant brain-work.

Dr. H. P. Tappan, a distinguished metaphysician, said that when he wished to compose on an abstruse topic he shut himself in a cold room ; but there is no logic in an unintermitting congelation. The terrible rigors of Dun Edin are doubtless well suited to the production of steely treatises on "Fixed fate, free will, foreknowledge absolute," if there be judicious alternations of roaring fires ; but the poor blue-nosed peasant, with never a jolly blaze before him, raps on his frosty mind, and finds no foreknowledge in it at all.

In the village of Querfurt I was burdened and overwhelmed by the hospitalities of the people when they discovered I was a child of *die mächtige Republik.* In the evening I effected the acquaintance of a musician who had returned from our happy land, with daughters and dollars, and he rallied a circle around me who kept me up till the stroke of midnight, and were rapping at my door directly after cockcrow. All that forenoon, I remember, and until three in the afternoon, we ranged about the village, visiting the ancient round-tower, and— well, I believe that was the only antiquity, but we made up for that by visiting it at various angles, to complete the perspective; and each time we emerged from it we discovered an entirely new and convenient beer-garden, whereinto we entered, being weary, and rested, and refreshed ourselves with a little beer. My musical friend had indoctrinated his fellows in the American custom for this particular occasion.

In *The Traveling Student*, Schneider has the following discourse:

"Quiet, Freshman! You are to keep still when old moss-heads speak."

"O Lord! I can't stand so much drinking of healths. It's killing me."

"Hold your tongue, Freshman. You have taken only nineteen *schoppen* of vile *cerevisium* yet. That is nothing. Study three years, and you'll bring it up to twenty-nine."

Like the luckless freshman, I thought it was a good time to stop, between nineteen and twenty-nine. But such genial and overflowing hospitality!—one cannot be boorish.

What a tempting way the Germans have of arranging provisions in the show-window with rural scenery: boiled hams, daisies, links of sausage, sweet-williams, sprouting pinks, sweet fountains, and moss-banks! Try this glass of *maitrank*, an innocent beverage, new to Americans.

My friends, we all shakes our hands. Sausages hanging in the woods.   Fine portrait of General Scott on the wall. General Scott fought for his country, and whipped the Mexicans.   You cheers for General Scott.

It was long after noon before I could by any means get away from the importunate hospitality of these pleasant people.

Like the young editor of Eisleben, my musical friend accompanied me many miles, and insisted on carrying my traveling-bag the entire distance. It was an extremely warm day in June, and he was quite a stout little gentleman, yet he clothed himself with a heavy overcoat before he started, and, to my astonishment, wore it the whole afternoon, but laid it off directly we entered the cool hotel in the evening. Of course, after our arduous labors in exploring the round-tower, we frequently became fatigued, whereupon we would enter into a little inn, and refresh ourselves with a little beer. There was an inn every half mile, and my friend was quite impartial. At first I kept him company, but presently I was obliged to skip every other inn, and at last to refuse, sternly and absolutely.

The German capacity to drink beer is positively amazing. Yet I can truly say that I never saw an habitual drunkard, or even a drunken man, in Prussia.

Next day, when I parted from my stout little musical friend in Freiburg, he seemed considerably affected. His eyes moistened, his voice trembled, and, before I was in the least aware of his intentions upon me, he imprinted a very warm, soft, and broad kiss on my forehead. There was no doubt whatever of the sincerity of his affection, yet I confess I almost staggered with amazement. But this same man, the day before, when we came upon a poor woman who had fallen in the road beneath a mighty bunch of grass, which she had reaped and stacked upon her neck, passed her by with contemptuous unconcern. It did not seem to occur to him for a moment that she was the victim of an infamous domestic tyranny.

So strangely susceptible are the German people of the deepest attachments known on earth, and yet so destitute of gallantry, and often so tyrannous over their women and children !

At Naumburg I had two hours to wait in the station, and I imprudently took out my map and newspapers, and commenced reading the war news from Bohemia. Presently a broad-faced *gendarme*, with a short stout sword in his scabbard, and trousers which fitted his legs as if the latter had been molten and poured into them, came and gently tapped me on the shoulder. He asked to see my " papers," meaning my passport, but as he could read no word in it—though I could hardly keep from bursting outright with laughter at the intense and inscrutable solemnity with which the fellow perused it awhile—he requested me to accompany him to police headquarters.

As nobody there could read English, we went next to the burgomaster. This personage was a blue-eyed, rather long-featured, and exquisitely bland gentleman, seated behind a desk, on which was a mountain of documents bound in the inevitable blue, official pasteboard covers of Prussia. He questioned me pretty sharply. He could by no means comprehend what any rational individual should be doing, walking about over Prussia and writing down matters in his book, without some ulterior *Zweck.* He was greatly concerned to know what my *Zweck* was. *"Was haben Sie denn zum Zweck ?"* he asked me several times.

I explained to him, as well as I could, that my *Zweck* was to acquire useful and interesting information for my-

self, and also to impart the same to inquiring minds.
But he was not satisfied, and presently he bethought himself to call in his wife, who could speak English.

"*Liebe Frau,*" said he, "*herein.*"

This lady spoke English very sweetly, and it was all the
more delicious from her exquisitely musical and liquid
German accent.   It was worth more than an hour's arrest
to be questioned by such a charming inquisitor.   At his
command she perused my note-book pretty thoroughly,
but when she found, instead of descriptions of fortresses
intended for the use of the wicked Austrians, such peaceful and innocent observations as that the King of Prussia,
for instance, squinted when he laughed, and that two
gallons of goat's milk in Eisleben made a pound of strong
cheese, she smiled feebly, and handed the note-book back.
To convince her I was an American, I handed her some
letters.   She turned them over and over, and then looked
at me with a puzzled and dubious expression.

"But they are not opened," she said, with the faintest
tone of expectant triumph in her voice.

The burgomaster also looked at me more sternly than
he had ever hitherto done, as if demanding that this dark
mystery should be solved at once.

I squeezed one a little in my hand, causing it to gape
open at the end, where it had been merely slit.

They were both so chagrined that such a simple device
should have escaped them that they at once dismissed the
case.   The lady explained to her lord that the contents
of my note-book were not dangerous, and that she was
convinced I was by no means an incendiary person, a
roaring democrat going about seeking helpless monarchs
to devour; and so at last they sent me away, with very
sweet and bland apologies and expressions of regret.

STUDENT RAMBLES IN PRUSSIA.

III.

Thus I wag through the world, half the time on foot and the other half walking; and always as merry as a thunder-storm in the night. And so we plow along, as the fly said to the ox. Who knows what may happen? Patience and shuffle the cards.

LONGFELLOW.

AS I left the cathedral of Frankfort, its great chime of bells were pealing out wild and wide and swift over the old imperial city their clangorous summons to matins. What a stirring and imperious voice is that of the morning bells wherewith, all round the world, the Church of the ancient Eternal City speaks yet to her worshipers!

The Prussians had occupied the city only a few days before, and Frankfort was ebullient with wrath. As I walked down the street I saw a ragged urchin run after a Prussian officer with a lady on his arm, screaming and yelling with laughter, "*Kuckuk mit'nem Schmetterling!*" (Cuckoo with a butterfly), until the officer became so enraged that he dropped the lady, drew his sword, and pursued the screeching youngster most furiously. He ran into a crowd, who protected him.

I walked on, past the house of the good *Rath*, wherein was lived that "rich and manifold life, without any positive moral tendency;" past that lordly statue from whose troublous brow looks out the grandest mere intellect since Shakspeare; past the statues of those three men of whom

12*   (137)

Louis XI. said, in wonder, that they spent all their time in making "*plusieurs beaux livres.*"

In a twinkling, almost, I popped out from the narrow, reeking alleys of the old city into the superb beauty of this immensely rich metropolis.

On one of its broad avenues, so surpassingly rich in shade-trees, among the lordly piles built with "Christian ducats," but inhabited by men scarcely known beyond the bulletins of the Frankfort Bourse, there nestles in a bosky labyrinth one little white-walled cottage, to whose owner Czar and Cæsar and Kaiser do homage. It is the house of Rothschild. It is rather Oriental in shape, looking in front as if one low, flat-roofed house were placed upon another, the lower being much the wider. Across its whitewashed front, between the upper and lower ranges of casements, trails its one ornament,—full of significance to its pretentious neighbors,—a slender moulding of flowers and cornucopiæ intertwined. It was a pleasing spectacle, to find this descendant of a race once "God-beloved in old Jerusalem," now persecuted and homeless on earth, dwelling in unaffected simplicity, and content to observe that outward modesty which, like mercy, is "mightiest in the mightiest," and so beautiful in contrast with the tawdry pomp of his people's hereditary oppressors.

Once out of this wonderful wealth of suburban greenery, I entered upon the great champaign of the valley of the Main. It is early June, and a mellow, drowsy glamour spreads like an enchantment over the plain, softening the outlines of the low Wiesbaden mountains. Far down, athwart this sunny, dreamy plain, roll the light-green waters of the Main, the ancient, while the spotless cope of the heavens spreads high and wide above, resting down upon the hills, "with peaky tops engrailed," with which it is blended by the haze into an almost unbroken oneness. The stately poplars of the Prussian highways shade the roadsides no longer, but are wholly replaced by stout-limbed apples, wherein the birds, exultant in the grateful warmth after a chill and rainy week, twitter and chirp and shake out their feathers and twiddle their tails, and jump up and down over their callow young a hundred thousand times a day.

Whether on a noble and lordly estate of the dimensions of a house-yard, or on a bloated and grasping monopoly of a full-rounded acre, each peasant is tilling the ancestral ground, separated from his neighbor by no unsightly fence or unsociable hedgerow, and molested in his operations by no plows or cultivators, or other inconvenient and troublesome gimcracks of modern ambition. Every hamlet and every hovel is to-day deserted and silent. All the occupants are laboring in the field this sunny weather, the woman side by side with her lord, brother and sister together, chattering maiden and lover a little apart. If the clumsy hobbledehoy discovers an injurious potato-worm close by the little pink toes of his beloved, and slashes at it with his mattock to see her jump and give a pretty scream, whose business in all the world is it but his own, I should like to know? Here one group, with measured and laborious stroke, swing the heavy, two-pronged mattock among the vines; others collect the wandering tendrils and teach them to clasp the espaliers; ι woman moves along the highway with erect and steady tread, bearing on her head a mighty bunch of grass; there one drives a lumbering water-tank backward and forward, while a helper slings the liquid manure far and wide over the young meadow.

At frequent intervals along the wayside still stand, in neglect and decay, the memorials of a religious devotion from which the living generation appear to have grievously lapsed. The wooden crucifixes, some of which were erected over a century ago, and bearing effigies of the Redeemer in his dying agony, beneath which are still dimly discernible such legends as, "At the name of Jesus every knee shall bow," now stand forsaken and dismantled, and, to the eye of taste, repulsive. Kneeling penitents no longer wear away the grass around them, or piteously beat their foreheads on the ground, or adorn their weather-stained arms with garlands; and when a summer breeze plays over the field, it sways the bending stalks of rye full against them, these *ædes labentes deorum.* The peasants dare not lay sacrilegious hands upon them to remove them, but they allow them no more to crowd out their barley.

From the dark and fertile alluvium in which Frankfort is situated the soil gradually changed, as I mounted higher upon the plain, into an ashen whiteness, and the full mid-day glare of the summer sun was reflected from it with that flickering brilliancy which almost blinds the eyes, as in parts of Lombardy and Venetia—the perfection of a vineyard soil. About one o'clock I reached the celebrated champagne factory of Hockheim, and found within its long cool walls a most grateful refuge from this fervid, shimmering incandescence.

I found the only proprietor who was present a thoroughly courteous and affable gentleman, rather short of stature, and with a sharp, American, "genuine money-making" countenance. That German wine manufacturers are not incapable of accomplishing remarkably shrewd things will appear hereinafter.

We visited first the "hot room," which is not hot at all, being unheated, but is so called to distinguish it from the "cold room," or cellar. At first I was under the

guidance of an intelligent clerk, too intelligent and frank
by far, for the proprietor soon came and relieved him,
evidently fearing he would expound too many processes.
Here, as we passed along, our taper dimly revealed on
some of the butts and tuns the outlines of quaint and fantastic devices,—vintage festivals, wild junketings of fauns
and satyrs, bacchanalian carousals,—many of them de-
pictured at life-size on the immense heads of the vessels:

> " Old Silenus, bloated, drunken,
>   Led by his inebriate satyrs:
> On his head his breast is sunken—
>   Vacantly he leers and chatters."

There, in the weird solitude and darkness of that old
wine-hall, these creatures hold their fantastic orgies undisturbed, ready to salute each new explorer with the
same leering grins and grimaces if he will only rewake
them to life by the gleam of his little wax taper.

At this point let us begin at the beginning, and trace
the lordly juice through its various transmigrations, until
it astonishes itself and other people by its wonderful acquired qualities. The hilarious labors of crushing and
pressing the grapes must be performed in the field, lest,
if the bunches were conveyed anywhither in a cart, some
of the tender skins might be ruptured, thus mingling the
juices of the stem with those of the berry, or the internal
structure of the juices might be disorganized, and their
tartrates jolted into nitrates or phosphates. With what
incredible carefulness and painstaking the bunches are
handled ! Not a crate of King Dagobert's eggs would be
lifted more softly, borne more tenderly. After culling
out all the stems and straws, and whatsoever other conceivable matters might mar the quality of the juice, the
vintners press the grapes without an hour's delay, for if

this should ensue, those berries which are red would impart that color to the juice. Grapes which are slightly crimson communicate to the wine a richness which the paler berries do not, but they must be crushed directly they are picked, if white wine is desired.

The juice thus procured is brought to the factory and poured into some enormous wooden tanks. Here it remains throughout the winter, fermenting, mingling, and distributing the ripest and sunniest juices through those which are paler, so that the whole mass is concocted into a uniform consistency, and purges itself of a large quantity of impure matters, which are precipitated to the bottom.

With the earliest warm days of spring the fermentation has sufficiently advanced, so that the must may be taken from the tanks and bottled. Pure and wholesome as it now appears, it is still loaded with impurities, and is execrably sour. The smallest mouthful will produce a lamentably unhandsome countenance on the impatient drinker.

Up to this point all varieties of wine, the still and the sparkling, the noble and the base, have pursued a common course, simply fermenting as natural juices. Henceforth they part company. First we will follow the baser sorts, which are to be converted into sparkling wines or champagnes. These are not bottled yet, but are conveyed from the tanks into the great tuns and butts above mentioned, where they can be compounded, nurtured, and "craftily qualified" to evoke within them the treacherous and delusive sparkle more readily than if they were in bottles. We went, for form's sake, into the room where these operations are performed, and found a great quantity of suspicious-looking funnels, sections of hose, chambered stoves for nursing the juice, and gallipots filled with mysterious decoctions and distillments for imparting the

"delicate aroma" which the too fleeting German summer
failed to communicate. Here, by the aid of these subtile
elixirs, *viellesseur*, *pomard*, distillation of potatoes, and
heart knows what, they concoct a vintage as mean as
Scuppernong into a liquor fit for gentlemen's tables in
America. After allowing me a few moments of silence
to gather such information as I might from an inspection
of harmless vessels and of labels that told no tales, my
sharp-faced proprietor, usually so voluble, but here so
ominously silent, led me hastily away.

All the varieties now go below, in bottles, into the
"cold room,"—the sparkling with all those mysterious
concoctions admixed; the still wines containing only a
little white beet-sugar, the purest essence of sweetness
produced by human art. Only a very small portion of
the vintage is rich enough to be used for these noble
wines. We go down with them into the vast subterranean
vaults,—down a first flight of steps, down a second flight,
into the profoundest deep of deeps, a dungeon more terrible than that where Bonnivard wore his life away.   In
the first vault into which we descend the champagne
variety is still frisky with fermentations, and frets and
chafes within its narrow prison-house like the Æolian
winds in their cave,—"*indignantes magno cum murmure
fremunt*,"—while the workmen vainly seek by daily turn-
ings to mollify its rage,—"*mollitque animos et temperat
iras*."   Instead of being appeased by a reversal of position, it is often impelled into a more towering passion,
and resents the high offense against its dignity by flinging
the ragged shards of its broken dungeon hurtling about
the eyes and ears of the workmen, who would certainly
suffer for this their *crimen læsæ majestatis*, but for their
strong visors of wire gauze. All these noisy outbreaks,
however, the workmen contemplate with the same quiet

complacency and satisfaction with which the farmer watches his prankish young herds; and, indeed, if they were mute and motionless, they would be greatly concerned.

Farther below there is much less clatter and whizz of shivered bottles, for the haughty spirit that inhabits them, no longer able to resent the vile decoctions that are eating his heart away, has abated his fiery ardor. Still lower down, he rests quiet, broken-hearted, and submissive, thoroughly crushed and subdued by the cold damps of his prison-walls, and the heartless rigor of his incarceration.

When the wine is ripe and old, it is hoisted from the vaults with the carefulest of motions, cork downward, to prevent the sediment on it from mingling again with the liquor. A workman then takes a bottle in his left hand, cuts the cord, which lets the cork shoot out, together with the sediment and a teaspoonful of wine, then claps his thumb deftly over the mouth, and hands the bottle to another. This one fills the little remaining space with sugar, cognac, and very old wine, mingled in secret proportions, and the bottle is then ready to be corked for a last time, wired, labeled, and dispatched to America or Calcutta.

What, now, is the result of the two processes,—the honest and the dishonest? On the one hand, fresh, crisp, sparkling Moselle, which sends up a thousand little beady silver-specks from the bottom of the bumper, quivering up in dainty, tender effervescence, fascinating to the eye, and deliciously cool in the mouth like a breath of soda; but it is a cheat and a delusion. All the glorious heart of ripeness and mellowness is eaten out of it by the manifold concoctions through which it has passed. On the other hand, the honest process, aided alone with a little quintessence of sweetness,—the beet-sugar,—gives us the noble, old, inexpressibly rich Hockheimer, still, and deep, and calm, and satisfying to the soul of man. The first is the ever-restless, nomadic, brave, ardent American; the other, the ripe, old, mellow, dreaming soul of the German philosopher, infinitely rich, soft, and full of mazy fantasies. And it is precisely that flippant and lively wine that is sent to America, while the wise and cunning old Germans retain the other. Knowing I was an American, this shrewd proprietor caused many varieties of the sparkling juice to be set for my approval, and but few of the better sort; and he tried various devices to induce me to pronounce in favor of the first. "All your countrymen prefer it," said he, impatient and almost offended that I persisted in liking the still wine better.

To reduce this matter to dollars and cents, which may make it more comprehensible to certain minds, I may say that the confiding young clerk told me that the average price per bottle of the best sparkling wines sent from this factory to America is only forty cents, while the still varieties, such as the genuine Hockheimer, a great part of which goes to the royal cellars in Berlin, cost, at the factory, $1.50 to $1.75 a bottle. Steinberger, another still wine, which was the favorite of the Dukes of Nassau, costs $9.72 a gallon at the factory! We know nothing of good still wine in America.

I may add, in conclusion, that I fully felt the important responsibility devolving upon me, as a committee of one, for the investigation of the qualities of Rhine wines, and that I prosecuted my researches with that thoroughness and assiduity befitting one charged with the rendition of a verdict so weighty. But I distinctly recollect that, as frequently happens also when profound minds are engaged in the adjudication of legal questions, the more I investigated the less I came to any clear conclusion.

Then at last I left the great champagne factory, and hastened forward, eager to behold the Rhine for the first time at the approaching sunset. At the summit of a little hillock, which the road passed over, I came suddenly in sight of the valley, just after the setting of the sun, and seated myself on the coping of a roadside wall to enjoy the noble vision. Imagine two vast and beautifully undulating plateaus, each a league in width and a dozen long, inclined toward each other with a uniform and gentle slope, and their surfaces covered with an infinitely subdivided mosaic of white-walled villages, dark-green pasture, yellowing grain, light-green barley, and somber pineries. And down between these vast slopes glide the silken, sea-green waves of the historic, the legendary, the romantic Rhine.

As far away to the left as the eye can extend the majestic river begins its course, and travels league on league directly toward me; then sweeps in a slow and stately curve before me, where his green waves laugh among the willows, as they go down to the sea; rolls his great flood past a hundred villages, which strew his shores like baubles; then, curving northward, hews his giant highway through the mountains, and sinks from view. The noble Rhine disdains, in the pride of his Teutonic strength, the effeminate purple drapery of the streams of luxurious Italy, and enrobes himself in an atmosphere tinted with emerald, as if the very radiance of his own shining waves were diffused upward through the lower heavens.

And now, over all these green-and-yellow-mottled, far-slanting plateaus, and vine-grown slopes, and murmuring villages, and along all the meandering margents of the willows, there creeps the hallowing enchantment of the daylight dying. The gorgeous segment of light that arches across the west is the sole lingering fragment of the broken empire of the king of day, and it crimsons with the blood of his impetuous hosts, who fiercely struggle for its occupation with the dusky legions of the queen of night. But they contend in vain, and slowly and reluctantly retreat before the darkling masses of their adversary, and sink silently down, down, down. The drowsy and soothing murmur of human avocation mellows down to a peaceful stillness, across which the silvery trill of some clarionet is wafted like a melodious echo in a dream; the far, white walls of silent cities glimmer vaguely in the thickening darkness, and sink at length beneath its encroaching floods; a myriad household fires, like shining points, spring one by one along the glooming slopes, countless as the stars which hold their noiseless march above; and I sit in the brooding darkness, alone. After the painful incandescence of noon at Hockheim, how sweet to my aching eyes were the changing glories of that unequaled sunset!—waning successively from the softest emerald to orange, from orange to crimson, from crimson to leaden night.

In Mayence, as always, I went first to visit the cathedral, guided thither by the tumultuous and mighty clangor of its great bells. In front of the gorgeous high altar two or three priests, robed in soiled white cassocks, were performing their drowsy rites; now swinging a smoking censer before the altar, now before the people; kneeling mechanically in various places, and touching their foreheads to the altar; exposing with ostentatious solemnity a gilded image to the worshipers; then intoning a chant in a rapid and monotonous sing-song, while a loud blare of instruments peals down from some hidden gallery. Most of the peasant women, who composed a large proportion of the worshipers, had come in from the market-place hard by, in their short, work-day dresses, and they were constantly coming and going. Most of them brought their huge baskets and panniers with them into the slips, where they kneeled a few minutes, counting their rosaries. Some hurried right away, others proceeded to extract from their pockets divers rags, from which they took out dingy little coins, the gains of the morning, and counted them over and over again with laborious accuracy, while others wandered through the gorgeous aisles and the transept, lugging their uncouth baskets, and staring, perhaps for the thousandth time, at the lustrous fringes of velvet and gold, the ivory effigies, the golden candelabra, and all the splendid paraphernalia of their religion. Nothing is more singular and more notable among the South German peasants than their almost infantine devotion to tawdry ornamentation.

This was well illustrated in a little village near Mayence, whose single street, when I entered it, was furbelowed in an astonishing manner. Scores of streamers and banners, of endless variety, were stretched across the street, while the front of every dwelling was lavishly decorated with festoons and garlands of flowers, miniature flags, and an innumerable and indescribable multitude of devices in colored papers. They were momently expecting the arrival of their bishop (Catholic), who was on his periodical tour through his diocese, to confirm the children of three years and upward. Presently his coming was heralded by the booming of cannon, and then a great procession of children, young men and maidens, went out to receive him, and brought him in beneath a gorgeous canopy of silk, the while chanting a solemn anthem. In the evening the successful termination of this ceremony of holy anointing of children was celebrated by booming cannon, the incessant rattle of musketry, an open-air speech from the bishop, uproariously applauded, and finally, by an alarming outpouring of beer. On the evening of this religious festival I saw at least a score of peasants who required to be lifted into their wagons, or steadied through the streets, mumbling and maundering like a calf—more than I saw in all Prussia besides !

In the village of Ober-Ingelheim there was also a festive occasion which was well illustrative of South German character (for these peasants here are no longer like those in Protestant Prussia). It was the birthday of a certain great man of the village, who died and was buried, and they assembled to do honor to his memory in the graveyard ! A speech was made by an orator standing on his monument ! So great was the crush of the multitude to hear the eulogium that there arose a contention at the gate, wherein walking-sticks were freely used and broken over the people's heads, and when they were all at last well in, there was a most unseemly surging and swaying to and fro, right over the graves, which were shamelessly trodden and beaten down.

Then a band of music came in, and, standing before certain graves, discoursed some of the mellow, glorious music, the inexpressibly sweet and solemn threnodies, of Germany, as it were a mournful serenade to the spirits of the dead. Again the abominable desecrations and trampling of graves ! It was not done by vulgar clowns, but by cultivated villagers, men and women who had in them the soul of music, even to intense devotion..

If there is one thing notable above another in a South German city, it is the studiously artistic, or rather artilized, nature of the ornamentation of the cemeteries. Great prices are paid for large pieces of coral, or stalactites and stalagmites, or fantastic shapes of Oriental alabaster, to place upon the graves, whereon ivy is taught to

13*

climb in imitation of nature. And yet people of such finely artistic perceptions, so passionately fond of music, and so exquisitely capable of judging it, will tread thus ruthlessly over the grave, which the English or American child is taught so reverently to pass around. And yet English and American graveyards are gloomy as death compared with the South German! It is a mystery, a contradiction, one of those innumerable paradoxes of the German character.

The South German mind is utterly hollow and vain, sacrificing utility or noble reverence for gauds at any time. Why do not the multitudes tread over the grave beautiful with ivy and coral or natural alabaster? Simply because of their devotion to the form of beauty. The graves are not ornamented even because of affection, but because of a devotion to the gay, the brilliant, the beautiful in superficial things. Says Louis Ehlert: "The hasty demands of life do not stop to inquire whether it be Sabbath or not; they surprise man amid the worship of the Beautiful, and scarcely give him time to refrain from profanation of the altar." But the South Germans sacrifice everything upon the altar of the Beautiful, even piety to the dead, and worship there alway.

Between Bingen, "dear Bingen on the Rhine," and Ehrenbreitstein, the Rhine traverses a defile which, though far less sublime and elevated than Harper's Ferry, reminds the American of that historic pass. Wherever there is the smallest sunny bank or handful of earth amid the towering ledges, the industrious peasants have terraced it with walls and planted it with vines, so that the innumerable little zigzag walls and cross-walls have the appearance of an immense honeycomb.

Everywhere else are the somber pines, while

" Above, the frequent feudal towers
  Through green leaves lift their walls of gray,
And many a rock which steeply lowers,
  And noble arch in proud decay."

He who has never voyaged from Bingen down the Rhine, between these time-old walls, where it moves in majesty, may well believe that when a German cradled on its banks relates its natural glories, he does but speak with a fond and filial exaggeration ; and that the artist who has labored to portray them has sought rather to repay a debt of gratitude than to sketch a truthful panorama. But when he comes and beholds the object of these seeming adulations, his incredulity straightway vanishes. Whether gazing on the "walls of gray" which crown many a towering crest, or on the giant palisades in liveries of softest, richest brown, or on the sloping ledges and vast, overthrown boulders whose emerald tints seem only a deepened reflex of the silken, sea-green waves which glide beneath them, he declares in his rapture that these un-hewn walls yield hues more noble than the artist ever spread upon his canvas. However bleak, and cold, and gray the hand of nature may have penciled ledges in drier and higher regions, here they seem warm, and soft, and glowing. However hard and grim may be the sur-roundings of the Rhine where it is cradled among the thundering avalanches and the savage granite of Alpine solitudes, it flows down at length in the tranquil majesty of its greatness, along exuberant and picturesque valleys which its own green waters have fructified, and through mountain gorges which its own humid influence has soft-ened and green-limned with beauty.

THE KAISER'S RESOLVE.

I.

Sweet are the uses of adversity,
Which, like the toad, ugly and venomous,
Wears yet a precious jewel in his head.

SHAKSPEARE.

IN 1848 three crazy words from France created such an earthquake in Austria that the imperial succession made a long skip. Uncle, father, were both set aside, in that year of rejuvenescence, and the boy Francis Joseph reigned Kaiser of Austria. The House of Hapsburg, however, did not skip as many traditions as years, and Hungary revolted. But the struggle of revolution went sore against her, through treachery and division, and the end was now daily awaited.

One evening the young Kaiser, unutterably disgusted and bewildered with the state business to which he was so little used, was reclining languidly in an easy-chair before the fire in a small private parlor of the old Burg. With his feet resting across a footstool cushioned like an ottoman, he slipped far down in the capacious chair, crossed his hands over the arms, turned his head wearily to one side, snuggled it deep into the rich downy velvet, and was soon lost in sleep. From this he was awakened by a messenger, bringing a telegram from Pesth, they having orders to bring him such at whatever hour. Muttering a petulant curse upon the lackey, he sleepily reached out his hand, took the message, dropped it, cursed the

(152)

lackey for his awkwardness, took it again, and laid it on the cushion, without once lifting his head.

Some time after the messenger went out, a brand of fire fell down, startling him a little, when he remembered the telegram, stretched it out with both hands, and read :

ARMY HEADQUARTERS, PESTH,
October 7, 1849.

To His Imperial Majesty the Kaiser.

Since Görgey's surrender at Világos, the whole province has been tranquilized. The rebel soldiers have been dispersed to their homes, and quiet prevails. Yesterday the nine generals were shot at Arad.

HAYNAU, FZM.

"So! then it is over. Pity nine had to be shot," soliloquized the young Kaiser half aloud; and then, after heavily and drowsily blinking at the paper three or four times, he rolled his head over again, snuggled it into the velvet, and slowly the uplifted hands drifted down, down, down, till they softly rested on the chair again, and the paper slipped from their nerveless grasp, and fluttered to the floor. Weariness prevailed, and he was slumbering again.

Whither wandered the dreams of the imperial sleeper? Did his roving imagination return to the hated work-cabinet in the vast and lonely Burg, whence he had just escaped, to drag him again through the thousand arguments and cross-arguments with which his ministers and dispatches from his jangling provinces daily distracted his pampered young life?

No; the remembrance of the message still lingers, and he wanders in dreams far away to the battle-fields of unhappy Hungary. He gropes his way among the hideous and blackened ruins. The vultures, scared from the unburied corpses, flap and scream around him. Human heads, bloody and horrible with their protruding eyes, stare at him from the tops of poles. He stops at last before the patriot generals doomed by his command to death. The files of executioners stand stolidly before them. There are the faint words of preparation, each slightest sound being terribly distinct in the awful stillness. He hears the muskets click. Then a second word of command, low but plain. The fatal crash of muskets is heard. They fall, writhing and ghastly, and the bright blood spirts on their gorgeous Magyar uniforms. The young Kaiser leaps to his feet, with a shudder of unspeakable horror, catching his breath convulsively !

The low buzz of commands was only the purring of the fire ; the crash of musketry, the brands falling again ; and the bright streams of blood, the flickering, expiring flames.

Thus was announced, and thus was received, the news of the downfall of poor Hungary, and the beginning of one of the most hellish retributions recorded in history.

II.

Eighteen long years rolled away, and some of them left their imprint in wrinkles upon the face of Francis Joseph. Its boyish roundness was gone, it had grown longer, apparently, and was pulled down and pulled together into something very like an habitual scowl. It was a small and delicate face, but there was little meaning in the eyes, except a kind of querulous appeal to be let alone. The cares of his bedlam of provinces, forever wrangling and bickering, and the unvarying succession of disappointments, defeats, bankruptcies, and disagreements with his ministers, had soured his temper. He was always suspicious that somebody was about to overreach him. His eyes, looking out from their slender setting beneath faint eyebrows, seemed to be always glancing toward one side or the other, never straight forward.

Kossuth, the noble, the generous, the confiding, was pining in proud and hopeless poverty as a teacher in Turin. Görgey, the infamous, after having dragged his Fatherland down to an earthly hell rather than abate one jot of his satanic pride, had retired, detested and abhorred, as an obscure professor in Styria, haggard with a remorse which came too late. Haynau, the Austrian Hyena, whether in a spirit of demoniacal mockery, or attracted by the splendid chivalry and magnanimity of that people whose best sons he had butchered, declared his purpose to become an Hungarian; and put to the practical test their great-hearted forgiveness by riding on horseback, with a single attendant, through the length of the land. With the wonderful elasticity of that people, they had recovered everything, except their liberty and their unforgotten dead.

And now the black war-clouds commenced drifting heavily down from Berlin, and there was sore apprehension in the old Imperial Burg. The tempest was also gathering in Italy. The Hungarian Parliament beheld its opportunity, and prepared and forwarded to the Kaiser a proposition for restoring them their ancient constitution, and a separate army and treasury. This was too much, or rather, it was too soon. The Kaiser had been well scourged at Solferino and Magenta, but those events were so distant that the lesson of them had slipped from his memory.

An Imperial missive was quietly sent down to Pesth, informing the members of the Parliament that the exigencies of public affairs, fortunately, were not so pressing as to demand their further attention ; and that therefore his Imperial Majesty graciously accorded them permission to go about their private business.

III.

Francis Joseph went to war with King William. Or rather, as a matter of history, his man Benedek stayed supinely in Bohemia, and let the war come over the Giant Mountains to him. About the first day of July, 1866, Marshal Benedek telegraphed earnestly to his Imperial master substantially this: "I beseech your Majesty to make peace on the best attainable terms." Benedek was an Hungarian, and he saw well, what was hidden from the Kaiser's eyes, that his compatriot Magyars in the army had no heart in the bloody business which was approaching.

But no peace was made, and the two great armies stood up to the battle. Two days after the above dispatch, about nine o'clock in the morning, there came to the Burg the following message:

ARMY HEADQUARTERS, KÖNIGGRÄTZ,
July 3, 1866.

TO HIS IMPERIAL MAJESTY THE KAISER.

The decisive battle of the campaign was joined this morning. Everything is going well.

BENEDEK, FZM.

At ten o'clock there came another brief message:

"The battle is raging all along the line. Our troops are steadily advancing, and the enemy is falling back. Everything is going well."

This was true up to that hour, for the two Prussian

armies had not yet effected a junction. But the telegraph talked no more. All day long it was obstinately silent. The Kaiser, no longer the listless boy disgusted with affairs, in his impatience repaired to the office in the Burg. At his command they shot messages off to the battle-field, but they dived off the end of the wire, and clicked in deserted offices, or were drowned in the mighty roar of battle. Where was Benedek? was the agonizing question. And still the messages which they lanced at him danced off the end of the wire into nothingness, lost in the great void of the world, and brought no response.

But at last, about ten o'clock at night, oh, joy! the instrument began to rattle, as if it wanted to say something. All ears were erected. The operator called off, "Hohenmauth." Then he slowly repeated aloud to the Kaiser what the wire was saying,——"Click, click, click!—— . . . . at—first—the—retreat—was—conducted—in —good —order,—but—finally—the—soldiers—were—panic - stricken—and—the—retreat—became—a—rout.—Hundreds—perished—in—the—Elbe."

The Kaiser's heart sank within him. Feverishly his finger sought for Hohenmauth on the wall-map. Hohenmauth? Hohenmauth? Perdition catch these German maps! They are so covered with little fine names that nobody can find any place. Ah! here it is! Sick was the heart of the Kaiser when he marked it. A long way more than a score of miles south of Königgrätz! All that long flight since ten o'clock in the morning!

Never in history or in story will the narrative of Königgrätz be told more graphically than Marshal Benedek pictured it to his Imperial master, in that single date, and that fatal sentence, "Hundreds perished in the Elbe."

Then all the remainder of that dreary night the Kaiser

lingered in the telegraph office in the Burg, alternately dictating dispatches to his "good brother" on the Seine, and listening to his replies. All night long, without intermission, the wire hummed and buzzed between Paris and Vienna, and it was long after sunrise of that summer morning before the Kaiser entered his carriage and drove out to the palace of Schönbrunn. And not many hours afterward, the tricolor of France waved over beautiful Venice. The Kaiser flung the burdensome province out of his left hand, that he might withdraw it to the succor of his right.

IV.

Before he drove out to Schönbrunn, however, he was able, by this cession of Venetia, to telegraph to the Archduke Albert, in Verona, to set the South Army in motion in all haste for Vienna. And right well did the heroes of Custozza obey the command, for they longed to meet a foeman worthier of their steel. One long train after another, crowded with the gallant lads, thundered over the great Semmering Pass, and bowled away down the valley to Vienna. Never in history has another immense army been hurled as that army was hurled from Italy into Bohemia. With a proud heart might the Kaiser have looked down from the south windows of the Burg, to behold the trains rumble in, for never was grander achievement of human energy; but, alas! he was filled with dismay when he looked from the north windows. Swiftly as his gallant lads were hastening to save the tottering monarchy, the fierce and dreaded Prussians were rushing more swiftly to overthrow it.

The watchers perched far aloft in St. Stephen's tower, straining their eager eyes across the valley of the Danube toward the low mountains and hills of Moravia, already caught with their glasses the long and glittering lines of the *Pickelhauben* amid the blue mountain passes. Gay, thoughtless Vienna for once forgot to laugh, and looked on in silence, while one immense train after another rolled away toward Pesth, loaded with archives, and jewels, and bullion, and with the fleeing nobility.

V.

Then came another night when there was sore trouble and unrest in the old Imperial Burg. In his little cabinet sat the Kaiser, surrounded by a few faithful counselors, who pleaded with him as they plead whose life hangs in the balance. The irresolute and yet obstinate monarch, goaded almost to distraction by this unparalleled succession of sudden and overwhelming calamities, and protesting he was betrayed by every one, declared his determination to put himself at the head of his gallant army, lead it to victory, and save his dynasty, or perish in the universal ruin. They entreated him, on the contrary, to follow the example of his illustrious ancestor, go down to Pesth, and there throw himself on the generosity of the great-hearted Magyars.

Now he would start impatiently across the floor, exclaim aloud against his enemies and betrayers, uttering impotent and puerile threats; then he would sit a long time moodily silent, listening doggedly to their arguments and entreaties. It was long after midnight, and the wan and flickering camp-fires of his four hundred thousand soldiers had hours since ceased to be reflected in the twinkling waters of the Danube, or among the forests of the Moravian hills. The sentinel paced his beat to and fro alone in the shadow of the grim arsenal. Still the humiliated monarch hesitated.

The great bell in the tower of St. Stephen, with a deep and measured clang, slowly tolled the stroke of three. In the solemn silence of the night, the sonorous reverberations floated in to those sleepless watchers in the cabinet with awful distinctness. Suddenly the Kaiser started up, as if alarmed by its ominous voice, advanced to a window, and looked out upon his slumbering capital. What said the great bell to him, with its after-vibrations? "Go—go—go—o—o—o—o!"—faintly ringing, ringing, dying, in the midnight void. It was as the voice of the city, of those eight hundred thousand human beings who were asleep, reposing their destiny in his hands. In that solemn hour their voice was heard; his better self prevailed. Turning suddenly to his counselors, he said, "I will go."

When we remember the fatuous persistency with which Louis Napoleon saddled his own incompetency upon his army, thereby crushing it into hideous disaster and ruin, let it be remembered, to the praise of Francis Joseph, that, weak and obstinate as he was, he listened to wholesome but bitter counsel. When we consider the galling humiliation it was for a Hapsburg to go and plead like a mendicant before the haughty Magyars, whom he had so cruelly spurned and destroyed when *they* petitioned, let it also be remembered that he accepted even this penance.

VI.

The Kaiser went down to Ofen. In the ancient and sacred capital of the kingdom of St. Stephen, he met the Magyar chiefs. They received him with cold and haughty obeisance. Happy for him, in that moment of keen humiliation, he did not yet know that no standards were lost at Königgrätz, except by Magyar regiments. In all the Oriental splendor of their native uniforms,—what of them had been spared by the mean and beggarly proscription of 1849,—which are not equaled in Europe for their picturesqueness, they stood before him, to listen to his appeal. In their own rich and melodious tongue, and with a frankness which astonished them, he pictured to them his tottering monarchy, and entreated them to hasten to his succor.

They listened to his words in stern silence. He pleaded for that Austria with which, for eight hundred years, their traditions and their glories had been united. He pictured to them, in the best eloquence he could summon, the consequences of defeat, the disruption of the empire, and their own probable absorption into Russia. They listened to him with astonished eagerness, and yet with the most lofty outward unconcern and the immobile gravity of the Orient. Not once was he rewarded with such a ringing outburst as followed the appeal of Maria Theresa. His heart was dismayed.

Then he spoke, lastly, of his family, and, in soft, tremulous tones, he pleaded before the Magyars as a father speaking unto fathers. In the earnestness of his plea for his innocent little ones, he forgot, for the moment, the monarch, his feelings overmastered him, his eyes moistened with tears, and he turned away his face, and was silent.

Then at last the haughty Magyars made reply. They, too, were not unmoved, but it was not a time for scenic display. It was a time for justice. They could not forget the fearful crime of 1849. They, too, spoke plainly. Never before had the hearts of monarch and people been so uncovered to each other's gaze. It was an hour of mutual reasonings, not of reproaches, but of noble and solemn admonitory eloquence, addressed by them to their

humbled monarch. They, too, had had children, and seen
them cut down in hideous butchery before their eyes.
After eighteen years, they remembered those things no
longer vindictively, but with a mournful and unforgetting
bitterness; and they spoke to him with that lofty and
patriarchal dignity native to the children of the Orient.
Each of them could say:

> " Time has laid his hand
> Upon my heart, gently, not smiting it,
> But as a harper lays his open palm
> Upon his harp, to deaden its vibrations."

They offered him a crown for a constitution. He accepted.
Before he left them, Hungary was restored.   How great
happiness it was given to that man to bestow, within a
few days, upon two peoples,—the Venetians and the
Magyars!

In that hour, how greatly and how signally were the
Magyars avenged! They had not only recovered, by a
peaceful triumph, what had been wrested from them with
cruel and bloody violence, but they had seen a Hapsburg weep.

Thus it is that the kings' extremities are the people's
opportunities.

NOTE.—All the main events set forth in the preceding narrative are
matters of historical record; but it is necessary to state, for the sake of
accuracy, that a few of the minor incidents and details rest on no higher
foundation than the gossip of court circles in Vienna.

KAISER HANS.

There was a king of Yvetot once
But little known in story;
To bed betimes, and rising late,
Sound sleeper without glory;
With cotton nightcap, too, instead
Of crown, would Jenny deck his head,
'Tis said.
Rat tat, rat tat, rat tat, rat tat,
O what a good little king was that!
Rat tat.

BÉRANGER.

ONCE upon a time there was a good little Kaiser called Kaiser Hans, who ruled over the land of Albeeria. The name of his capital city was Circumstadt, and his favorite summer palace, near by, was called Maulhaus.

Now, one morning this good little Kaiser awoke at eight o'clock, and opened his eyes. He rung his bell for the attendant, and ordered him to bring in a small cup of black coffee, which he drank reclining in bed, and then covered up his head with the sheets, and took another pleasant nap.

Afterward he awoke again, and winked three times, and rubbed his eyes. Then he arose and dressed himself all over, and wound up his watch. After that, he caused the attendant to put his slippers on his feet, and then he sat down before the fire and ordered them to bring 'im a mug of *Klein-schwechater* beer, which they brought, and he quaffed the same. Then his Majesty held out his feet

(163)

to the fire, and toasted his toes, and rubbed his stomach, and felt very snug and comfortable.

At ten o'clock and fifteen minutes, this good little Kaiser Hans pared his nails.

Some time afterward he sat down to his piano, and played the little love-song, " *Come questo care,*" from *Don Bucefalo.* This seemed to recall old and pleasant memories of the youthful life of the Kaiser, and he sat some time absorbed in deep reflection.

At eleven o'clock the Kaiser partook of breakfast, which, on this occasion, he was pleased to eat alone. He partook of a deviled Manx chicken, with the quality of which he expressed himself well satisfied.

Soon after this he proceeded to the White Chamber, where he presided over a council of ministers, assembled to consult upon the main business of the day. Directly he took his seat upon the throne, the Kaiser arose, and stated to his ministers that the question for their consideration that day was the very important one of military reform. Complaints had reached his ears, he said, through petitions from his faithful and well-beloved subjects, that they were grievously burdened and distressed by the present military system. The welfare of his people lay ever very near his heart. He was deeply moved by these appeals. He had assembled together his trusted ministers, on whose wisdom he had depended so often, and not in vain, that they might assist him in devising some thorough measure of relief. A sovereign's greatest crown of glory, he believed, was in his tender nurture and protection of his people. He invited all his ministers to express themselves freely.

When his Majesty the Kaiser ceased speaking, his Eminence, Prince Moritz von Mettler, Minister of Other People's Affairs, a tall, dark gentleman, with black whiskers, arose and craved his sovereign's indulgence. He said, if he might be permitted by his august master, he would suggest that a pressing necessity for reform existed in the present color of the infantry uniform trousers. It was well known that scarlet was a dangerous color in battle, as it virtually invited and guided the enemy's fire, thus causing wounds in the shins, which incapacitated the soldier not only from all further service, but from future usefulness in civil stations. He would suggest that green trousers be substituted, as being more like the color of the fields.

His Eminence Count Johannes von Pumpenhausen, Inspector of Bungs, a well-favored German, with spectacles and blonde hair, begged to suggest that the white coats of the uniform also be abolished. Battles were seldom fought in winter, as the learned Dr. Conrady had demonstrated in his great history (vol. ii. p. 136), hence the white coats were conspicuous in the landscape, and scarcely less dangerous than scarlet trousers.

At this point of the proceedings, his Majesty's favorite spaniel, King Charles, bounded into the council-chamber. He was exceedingly delighted to see his kind little master, and whisked and jumped about, and wagged his tail to such an extent that his whole body, from his ears back, seemed to be one elongated tail. Kaiser Hans was also much pleased to see his favorite, and stooped down and patted his head, and called him by name. Thereupon the dog waggled his tail again. The attendants finally had to remove him from the chamber.

His Majesty then said he was pleased to listen to these suggestions, and considered them valuable ; but they were not in the direction he had anticipated, since they did not steadfastly keep in view the welfare of his people, whose prosperity he always had earnestly at heart.

His Excellency the Minister of Other People's Affairs begged to remind his Majesty that green cloth was cheaper than scarlet, and would therefore lessen the expenses of the military bureau, and enable the taxes upon the people to be very materially lightened. He had no doubt that each pair of green trousers substituted for the scarlet would save a peasant the value of two chickens.

His Excellency Baron Rothkopf von Rothkopf, Minister of Belligerency, a gentleman with fiery red hair, begged to be allowed to suggest that neither of the noble gentlemen had struck at the root of the matter. The measure of reform must go deeper, and deal with profounder questions than any which had been mooted, or the empire of Albeeria was bankrupt. The present was a time which demanded the most searching investigation into the errors and corruptions of the past. The empire, as all the noble gentlemen well knew, was even then struggling in the very throes of—he had almost said dissolution; but no, it was a healthy effort, the effort of a great body to free itself from the *materia peccans*, the evil influences of bad legislation and bad administration. Albeeria was not a corpse, Heaven be thanked, but only a convalescent struggling with its great natural strength to shake off disease.

The measure of reform which seemed to him most urgent, was one in relation to the soldier's personal welfare. How often, his Excellency asked, during the recent disastrous campaign which shook Albeeria to its base, how often had the soldier been seized by his beard, and thus held while he was beaten ! How often had his beard become the harbor of dust, fog, and consequent disease ! How often had he bled to death, because his cumbrous and useless beard prevented the surgeons from reaching his wound in time to stanch the flow of blood ! The noble gentlemen must certainly be aware that the learned

Dr. Krackmeyer, in his great work on the Human Whiskers (p. 1407), had demonstrated that one-half the throat diseases of soldiers are caused by their beards, which they are too indolent to keep purified.

He would, therefore, humbly suggest to his Majesty that the projected reform should begin with the whiskers of the army. He would propose, in fine, that the soldier should be required to shave off his beard.

His Majesty said he must ask the eloquent minister the same question as before. In what manner would this reform benefit his faithful and beloved subjects? He was unable to perceive.

His Excellency begged to reply to his sovereign, ever anxious for his people, that whatever benefited the soldier must indirectly benefit the subject. It would give occupation to thousands of barbers, now languishing in utter penury for lack of employment. But, far more than this, it would restore the efficiency of the army, insure Albeeria victory in the impending great conflict of arms, and, therefore, give the whole nation prosperity, where now all was ruin.

His Majesty was pleased to say that he was deeply impressed by the views which the minister had urged so eloquently.

His Excellency the Minister of Other People's Affairs, nervously stroking his beard, and speaking in a husky tone, asked whether the noble gentleman had intended to cast any slur upon his colleagues by his vehement and very pointed tirade against beards.

His Excellency the Minister of Belligerency sharply replied that he could, with as good reason, ask whether his Excellency the Minister of Other People's Affairs had intended to cast any slur upon him (the speaker) by his attack upon trousers of a certain color.

His Majesty said it grieved him to see two of his ministers descend to sharp and undignified personal allusions. He could not permit two of his most distinguished subjects to become involved in an affair of honor upon such trivial matters.

Under this paternal rebuke from their sovereign, the two noble gentlemen made ample apologies and retractions, and finally shook hands very amicably.

After some further unimportant discussion, his Majesty caused a decree to be drawn up, and then dismissed the council.

The decree was as follows:

Hans, by the grace of God Kaiser of Albeeria; King of Essen and Trinken; Prince of Sauer-Kraut, Schnapps, and Pumpernickel; Archduke of Brod and Kartoffel; Duke of Bratwurst; Margrave of Rindfleisch; Count of Klein-Schwechater; Grand Commander of the Order of -Hans; Chevalier of the Order of Zechen, Kneipen, and Scherzen; etc. etc. etc.

It is Our pleasure, and We hereby decree:

1. Every subaltern officer and soldier in Our army shall abate, remove, abolish, and shave off his whiskers.

2. Every commissioned officer in Our army shall, at his option, shave off his entire beard, or only that part of it situated, lying, and being between two lines let fall perpendicularly from the corners of the mouth.

Given in this Our capital and city of residence, Circumstadt.

HANS, m.p.

ALLGEMEINE ZEITUNG.*

Gazettes, if they are to be interesting, must not be restrained.
FREDERIC THE GREAT.

In a free commonwealth both language and reason, word and thought,
must be free.
TIBERIUS CÆSAR.

HAVING solicited and obtained permission to visit,
at their office, the editors of the *Allgemeine
Zeitung*, of Augsburg, I took good care to keep my appointment punctually. At an early hour in the forenoon
the train set me down at the depot, and I started out
to wander, without as much as the mythical thread of
Ariadne to guide me, along alleys more tangled than the
streets of Troy, and among the historic memorials that
still bear their majestic witness to a once fabulous opulence. After an illustrious career of eighteen hundred
years, this Imperial City has seen its scepter depart forever; and over its once populous and resounding marts
there hovers now a tranquil stillness. Where once the
lieutenants of Augustus led out beyond the walls their
long legions, with glittering helmet and cuirass; and
where the gorgeous retinue of a monarch, greater than
ever ruled in the Eternal City, moved in imposing and
solemn grandeur along its winding streets, to hold their
august tribunal for a continent, there the web-footed

---

* Reprinted, by permission, from Harper's Magazine.

tribes hold now their noisy musters undisturbed. I wandered on, past the "Three Moors," where once the Fuggers gave audience to spendthrift sovereigns, but where the traveler now resorts to taste its famous, sunny wines; under the great clock-tower above the gate in its ponderous walls; past arsenals, and ancient, gloomy palaces, and long, monotonous fronts of modern barracks; past the mediæval cathedral, whose jagged, crumbling walls are the home of chattering ravens, but whose interior is still resplendent with the offerings of a wealth gathered from the ports of a world.

At last I came suddenly upon it, hidden away in a labyrinthine recess, little less difficult to penetrate than that in the vicinity of the London Printing-House Square. On a quiet, grass-grown alley a long, low building lifts its gray front toward the south—it is the home of Germany's "Great Thunderer."

Passing through a spacious entry-way into the large, quadrangular court, I found an obliging individual who conducted me at once to the apartments of the editor-in-chief. An atmosphere so cheerful, so domestic, so tranquil pervaded everything around me that I seemed to myself to be in a private residence; and, half yielding to the impression, knocked on his door. He opened it himself, for he was wholly without attendants.

In a twinkling the voices of both of us were drowned in a fierce chorus from his little favorites—black terriers and tan, white spaniels and black—whisking about our feet and making an extraordinary uproar. Presently he succeeded in calming them so that we could hear each other speak. I presented him my card, and was received with the most cordial kindness.

"*Ich bin gekommen, Herr Redacteur, um*"—here a fresh scurry of yelps deafened us for a moment—"*um—*

um—to visit your newspaper establishment, in accordance with your very kind invitation."

"*Ja, ja; ich sehe. Ein Amerikaner.* Come in, come in, sir."

Oh, who shall ever fully know and honor the benevolence of his brother-man? What more noble proof of it than the commiseration with which two persons not of the same language regard each other when they meet? How kindly and how patiently each assists the other by speaking to him in his language!

Thus there ensued for a moment a running skirmish at cross-purposes: "Take place, sir; take place," said the editor, pointing to a great arm-chair covered with rich velvet.

"*Ich wünsche, mein Herr, nur—nur——*"

"You are a journaleest, I think—a correspondent; not true, sir?"

Seeing the venerable editor was intent on speaking "Engleesh," I quietly abandoned the benevolent contest, for, like Wellington in French, he spoke "with the greatest intrepidity," while my German was rather labored.

The editor-in-chief, Dr. Altenhöfer, was a gentleman of stout, short stature; the muscular neck, small gray eyes, and strong lower development of the head denoting that he was fond of the good things of life. He reminded me not a little of the portrait of Sir Walter Scott, only there was not that wonderful Scotch top-head. The somewhat misanthropic and heavy expression of his thoroughly Suabian features would not have pointed him out as the author of the quietly humorous paragraphs I knew him to have written. A head equally and compactly rounded, rather than large or prominent in any point, thinly covered with gray hair, with a forehead not high but full, seemed to be the home of a certain dogged but immense power rather than of any brilliancy of imagination.

He wore a bright parti-colored dressing-gown, rich as that of "Lusignan;" a Turkish *fez* of crimson velvet, from the top of which swung a long black tassel; and an incredible mass of black satin, wound about the neck until it became more formidable than a Prussian regulation stock.

I was surprised to find even an editor-in-chief occupying, as a work-room, such sumptuous apartments. There were three rooms—parlors, I had almost written—all laid with the choicest Brussels carpets, furnished with luxurious sofas, velvet-cushioned easy-chairs, mahogany center-tables, book-cases with richly carved walnut mouldings, busts, engravings, and several gems by old masters, Cranach, Holbein, and others. The books on the shelves were numbered by thousands,—modern volumes in dainty bindings ranged above; worm-eaten and dusty tomes of ancient lore drawn out below in solemn phalanx. The deep recesses of the casements were the hiding-place of pleasant flowers; and the clambering vines, covering nearly all the window, bathed the rooms in a soft, green radiance. As well expect sturdy political disquisitions to issue from these dreamy, Platonic abodes as to look for madrigals from the grimy, garish, sweltering attics of our American editors.

The chief editor had four lieutenants, only one of whom occupied the spacious suite of rooms with him. After a few minutes of conversation, I suggested that I could not allow myself to interrupt their pressing labors (though the elegant walls contained no curt admonitions to the visitor), and that nothing would be more agreeable to me than to be permitted to be a silent spectator of the various stages of growth of a German newspaper.

They accordingly seated themselves at their tables, and began to rummage among the heaps of newspapers and letters before them. The veteran chief seized first upon a quantity of letters from his correspondents, lifted his large green spectacles a little higher on his nose, and commenced chasing the scraggy hieroglyphics to and fro across the page, addressing me now and then a question. But a German editor cannot so completely make himself two men at once as an American. In a letter from Berlin his quick eye detects a paragraph that might cause his correspondent to be expelled from his Majesty's dominions, and he quietly buries it under a long, black, oblivious furrow,—"*allinet atrum traverso calamo signum.*" To another he affixes a brief note of explanation, or of total disavowal. A little further on he pauses doubtingly upon a quotation from Lucretius, glances a moment into a thick quarto within easy supporting distance, then passes on content. In a market quotation that has traveled over the wires all the way from Bombay he seizes upon a geographical name that seems to violate the analogies of Sanscrit terminology. A brief reference to a ponderous lexicon at his right elbow confirms his suspicions, and he washes his hands clear of it with an ?-mark.

Now, after deigning it scarcely a glance, he contemptuously tosses a letter into a capacious wicker-basket. "Death loves a shining mark." The German editor is utterly intolerant of "eloquence." My indignation waxed warm against him. Presumptuous and vain man that thou art, has thy little lease of power thus emboldened thy thoughts and steeled thy heart, to wage such cruel and Herodian warfare upon these innocents of the brain?

While he is thus burrowing through a hill of "diplomatic correspondence" and English newspapers, his lieutenant in the adjoining room is laboriously quarrying through a mountain of "occasional correspondence" and German journals. The other three, in their apartments, are industriously mining in all the other leads of Europe,—France, Italy, Spain,—all except Turkey and the Slavonic languages. The crude metals thus obtained they hammer, and purge of all dross, and beat into the smallest possible compass.

All these busy workers are what Confucius modestly called himself, "transmitters, not makers," for they very seldom delve in the dangerous and unprofitable mines of original composition. The atmosphere of Germany is of a nature so peculiar that literary mining may be prosecuted with the greatest safety; but in political shafts there always collects a body of highly inflammable and destructive gases, which are liable to explode without a moment's warning, and hoist the workmen in irretrievable ruin.

Returning presently from a cursory inspection of the rooms, I was pained and dismayed at the disastrous havoc that had been wrought among the helpless contributors. There were letters from far Oamaru, in the South Sea Islands, written by the uncertain flicker of a rush-light; from Hong-Kong, penned by the glare of a burning joss; from Helsingfors, where the atmosphere was still luminous at midnight; from wherever in the world there is a German,—and where is there not one?—all written with laborious accuracy, most of them furnished forth with apposite ornaments and choice morsels of wisdom from Horace and Cicero, and all of them framed with a highly-commendable terseness; yet all, all consigned without favor and without compunction to the insatiable basket.

I asked the editor if his conscience did not sometimes reproach him for the wantonness with which he thus deprived mankind of so much valuable advice and information. He replied that it had ; that he had often regretted the hard necessity that was imposed upon him ; that he was every day made aware that it is the inalienable privilege of every German to write and publish a letter ; and that his countrymen carried with them a high sense of their prerogatives to the remotest confines of the earth. He believed they received as many as eighty communications daily, aside from those relating entirely to business concerns.

Besides these countless stationary contributors they employed two special correspondents in the Austrian camps in Bohemia, and one in the Confederate army campaigning on the Main ; but the latter the Bavarian Prince Charles, Commander-in-Chief, expelled, together with all his comrades, detailing one of his aids to transmit by telegraph the "necessary news!" This was a return to the system of the Roman government, for Suetonius relates that Julius Cæsar appointed a military editor for the *acta politica diurna* (some interesting fragments of which Petronius has preserved in his "Supper of Trimalchio"), and that he ordered copies of it to be dispatched by couriers to the provinces. This was certainly a more generous undertaking than that of the Bavarian prince. In his earlier campaigns Cæsar wrote and published his own journals, which have survived eighteen centuries—a destiny certainly not reserved for the ephemeral records of the war of 1866. In the modern instance, as in the ancient, there appears to have been no detriment suffered, but a benefit gained, by the substitution of a military for a civilian journalist, for the dispatches of both were equally laconic, while those of the former narrated events with military accuracy.

A German correspondent, who witnessed the great

battle of Custozza, spurred back to Verona in furious haste, took down his annotated edition of Schiller, seated himself among his lexicons, furbished his dusty spectacles and then covered a large page of foolscap with a history of the battle, which he prefaced with an admirable quotation from "The Robbers," and illustrated by two instructive references to Grotius's work on the Rights of War and Peace. The modern German, like the ancient Roman, studying the idiom of camps, abhors prolixity; but what should we say if Cæsar had introduced his concise description of his battle with the Nervii, and embellished a number of passages in it with elegant extracts from "Antigone" or "Prometheus Unbound"? Conceive him making a destructive onslaught on the left flank of the Sequani with a quotation from Alcæus!

After lingering a short time among the editors, I proceeded, under the guidance of the foreman, through the light, airy rooms in which the compositors were at work. There were between seventy and eighty persons, many of them small boys, ranged before a series of elevated desks, sloping toward them, and partitioned into a great number of minute compartments. The number of these compartments is necessarily great, since the erudite editors and correspondents, whose compositions the printer must follow as scrupulously as an ancient Jewish copyist his manuscript, pillage all languages and enrich their own with its spoils. In one series of them are the German letters; in another, the Latin; in another, the Greek; in another, the Cyril; while others contain single letters or symbols from the French, Italian, Swedish, Dutch, and numerous others. Over all this grimy mosaic of tongues hover his busy fingers, choosing with incredible rapidity here one piece, another there, and shaping them into words, some of which speak to him in familiar accents, while others utter only a vacuous myth. Poor, patient, plodding printer—groping, guessing, comparing, earnestly anxious to know the mind of the master whom he serves, but who often addresses him not only in a foreign idiom, but so crudely and so uncouthly in his own that his servile understanding cannot follow—who oftener maligned, who more conscientious than the German compositor ?

Although they were employed almost exclusively by daylight, a large proportion of them had seriously impaired their vision. Whether induced by neglect of sanitary requirements and excessive use of acid vegetable diet (which is most probable), or by close application to a vicious alphabet, the prevalence of ophthalmia among South German printers (which is much more universal than in Prussia) is a subject of serious concern to their physicians and philanthropists. The appearance of so large a number of young boys and youths, with the full, round, and almost colorless faces so peculiar to German apprentices, disfigured by their uncouthly-large green goggles or spectacles, would have been highly grotesque if it had been less melancholy. Five full years these mere children must plod through this irksome and ceaseless drudgery—for the German compositor, not less than the American, knows little of Sunday—before they are released from the restraints of apprenticeship; and when this long probation has at last passed away, it often leaves them with an eyesight incurably impaired. But they cannot escape even then from bondage, for they are dependent on their daily toil for the merest sustenance, and it is too late to turn back and devote another sixth part of a lifetime to the acquisition of another craft. There is no avenue of escape but that which leads out to the New World; and that, unhappily, is too often closed by the poverty which it alone could alleviate. And yet they labor with cheerfulness; and I saw pale-faced boys, bending over their grimy "cases," cast occasional glances of deep enjoyment upon the little pot-plants in their windows. So strange did these sweet flowers seem amid the indescribable dinginess and smut of a printing-room!

Having now visited the principal rooms, I returned to the parlor of one of the junior editors, who gave me a "complete day's history of a German newspaper."

The editor sips his black coffee or chocolate, and arrives in his parlor nearly as early as the clerks, instead of at eleven o'clock, like the American. First he reads over the proofs of the afternoon edition, although they have been read already very thoroughly by the proof-reader. Then he busies himself in his letters, as above described, until about noon, when the afternoon paper is out, a copy of which, still dank and reeking, he takes in his pocket to read while seated at his dinner. Thus early has he acquired a vigorousness of appetite which does not come to his American congener until the middle of the afternoon; and he accordingly partakes of a very leisurely and substantial repast, followed by a number of *Schoppen* of Munich's best, or by a half-flask of Johannisberger.

The afternoon is occupied in the preparation of the morning edition. Sunset finds his labors for the day substantially ended, and the main body of the paper in type at an hour when its great contemporary of London lingers yet half in the inkstand. While the "Great Thunderer" composes himself for a night of placid and bucolic repose, his English brother keeps up all night his growls and his grumbles.

Nightfall, then, brings relief to most of the tired laborers, whether with head or with hand, and the profound rural stillness that settles down over the great establishment is broken only by the slow and measured tread of the solitary watchman, moving to and fro in the light of the dim taper, or by the squeaking and gibbering of some literary mice. One editor remains alone in his parlor, but, instead of writing for dear life beneath the flaming gaslight, or making great garish head-lines over the telegrams swarming in upon him, he is probably absorbed in the latest romance by Auerbach. By ten o'clock, or earlier if he choose, he turns his light down low, and snugly bestows himself in his luxurious couch. If, perchance, a trusty compositor still lingers, employed upon a brief dispatch from Berlin, as soon as it is finished he follows the comfortable example of his superior. Instead of that row of flaming-bright windows in the fourth or fifth story, which, in America, shine out until nearly morning over the darkened city, all here is deep and blissful repose.

Perhaps at midnight a dispatch comes from Paris (for those naughty Frenchmen will never go to bed, and let honest people sleep), and the messenger comes pounding at the editor's door. He rouses himself in his night-robe, reclines in bed in that attitude beloved of inveterate novel-readers, gazes dreamily on the jumbled and sometimes hopelessly meaningless words before him (for European operators make bad work with news), reads them forward and then backward, as they did the Delphian oracles, conjectures, expurgates, and punctuates, until they assume at least a constructive meaning, then sends them to a compositor, who has also to be awakened. After three o'clock nothing further can be introduced into the morning edition, and the editor's slumbers are thenceforth undisturbed.

At early cock-crow the forms are set, without stereotyping, in the cylinders, which are then put in motion. The great sepulchral press-room, hitherto so quiet, now speedily becomes "distraught with noise." What a weird, Plutonic, diabolical thing it seems,—that black-looking, many-cylindered, many-jointed monster,—clanking there in its power; swallowing down bale after bale into its insatiable maw, and flapping off its iron-feathered pinions the printed sheets! What demoniacal business or sorcery manufacture is prosecuted here? Is it an abode of wizards and hobgoblins, or is it a laboratory of Doctor Faustus? Near by the glowing furnace flings a ruddy glare over the faces of the workmen; the engines hiss and quiver under their own superfluous strength; the sooty feeders move hither and thither, carrying bales, as if, like fell ministers, they sought to propitiate with votive offerings this paper-devouring Moloch.

Such is a brief narrative of my visit to the home of this village *Weltblatt*, this village oracle, which is so great in Germany. More than any of its contemporaries, more than any other paper in Europe, it is the workmanship and noble monument of a single man, John Frederic Cotta; the outgrowth of a single great thought, followed with an unwavering fidelity, to which, in the political sphere at least, the history of Germany affords few parallels.

A man of incorruptible integrity, great learning, accurate, reticent, and an utter contemner of the tuft-hunting and sycophancy of his time, Cotta saw with pain the press of his Fatherland sunk in abject vassalage, sloth, and scurrility; whispering with bated breath the permitted chronicles and scandal of fifty courts, and absolutely devoid of political intelligence not copied from the *Moniteur*, and he determined to rescue it from a servility so ignominious.

In 1798 he, together with a kindred spirit, established this journal, and in the first issue announced that it would be the mouth-piece of none but himself and his correspondents. For a creed he proclaimed the great word, facts—facts—facts. Germany was astonished and incredulous, and the courts set all their snares to entrap him. His name was mentioned with scoffing not unmixed with concern, but an unbroken silence was his only retort. This almost divine patience and silence under reproach and injury were something so unusual among his too-passionate countrymen that they attracted curiosity, and, eventually, that admiration that is never denied to conscious strength. No word was suffered to appear in his columns that had not previously received his personal scrutiny. Everything scandalous, trivial, or dogmatical he expurgated so rigidly, and every one who furnished him accurate and sententious descriptions—if it were only five lines—of what he himself had seen or learned from the most unimpeachable witnesses he remunerated so generously, that he not only eluded all the stratagems of the courts and the espionage of the police, but surrounded himself gradually with many friends in every station. The princes and princelings, seeing he did not come to them, and that his proclamations were rapidly becoming more weighty than their own, followed the prudent example of Mohammed and went to him. Five years after the foundation of the paper the remote Pasha of Egypt forwarded him semi-official communications, together with a respectful solicitation for insertion. Early in the century the French court was the only one that maintained an official organ; but from 1818 to 1820 this paper supplanted even the *Moniteur.* No cabinet in Europe could claim its columns exclusively as it own; nor was there one but was fain to seek at times their now powerful assistance. But a triumph far more gratifying to their owner than this conquest of kings was that of the great names of Goethe, Humboldt, Fichte, Schelling, and others, all of whom, in speaking through them to their countrymen, thought themselves not less honored than honoring.

Many years before his death Cotta had the satisfaction of seeing the journal he had built up with such incredible labor the acknowledged leader of Continental journalism; and what was greatly better, he could affirm that it was the voice of his beloved Germany, while its only great rival was only the voice of the king who "ruled the hour"—to-day Louis XVI., to-morrow Robespierre. As he lay on his death-bed he could say, truthfully and with noble pride, that his example had contributed more than the wars of Bonaparte to vindicate the freedom of the press in his Fatherland. The poet Goethe, though a citizen of an inconsiderable t wn, compassed the sublime thought of a universal literature; but Cotta, with a truer perception of human possibilities, created a bond of German liberty and German concord more effective than the poet's own august memory.

When Goethe approached his final hour he could nominate no follower to continue his sublime labor, and his works were his only successor; but when Cotta passed away from his labors, that must be renewed day by day, would they not go down with him into the grave? No; for a work so beneficent is self-perpetuating, and imperiously summons a pupil to follow in the footsteps of the master. The glazing eyes of the dying Cotta still traced the familiar lines, and his stiffening fingers still guided the correcting pen, even though it were grasped in the hand of another.

No, the labor of his hands has not perished; neither have those hands, though turned to silent dust, ceased to guide it onward. In a land always torn with intestine feuds, always groping in search of an unknown good, it has moved tranquilly on amidst the wrecks of broken monarchies, unshaken, by the brunts of revolution, unmoved by the menaces of monarchs, unawed by the approach of contending armies; never threatening, never desponding; yet more eloquent than all the clamorous partisans around it, more eloquent than all the imperious oracles of courts.

"It is the voice of a god" is no longer the idolatrous acclamation of the multitudes; but, on the contrary, when a monarch's voice is heard speaking through that which the people have consecrated to liberty, it renders it fatally and forever odious. He who speaks the king's words is soon fain to eat the king's bread. In those sleepless outposts of German liberty, the book-stalls, the voice of the dead Cotta still speaks; but the voice of the living king is not heard there. No news-vender offers you the king's paper; you must go to the publication-office for that.

The greater popularization of knowledge in America, which is both the cause and the result of the newspaper, is shown by the greater comparative rewards of its writers. Thus, for instance, Prussia pays her English ambassador $29,400 a year, while the best-paid editors of Berlin receive only $1000 or $1200. On the other hand, the highest salary received by an American ambassador is $17,000, while New York editors receive from $2400 to $6000. The editor-in-chief of the *Allgemeine Zeitung* has a yearly stipend of only $998.

The characteristics of German editorials are the same, in general, that mark the literature of the country. The Horatian·maxim which teaches that "knowledge is both the foundation and the source of correct writing" is the guide of the ambitious feuilletonist no less than of Kant and Schelling; while the American practically obeys the advice of Cicero, first to acquire words, and afterward thoughts. "Fine writing," therefore, which is only a paraphrase of Hamlet's "words, words, words," that is, words for the sake of words, finds no place in the German's ambition. There is a species of wretched diplomacy practiced in our American law-courts, called "speaking against time," known also to thriftless collegians on examination-day, under a slightly modified form, as "mouthing," which is also not unknown to journalists of slender intellectual resources, when they sit before a vacuous, hungry page that must be filled.

This is a device having its origin in a peculiarly American combination of insincerity and fertility of invention, and to the less ingenious but more conscientious German is wholly unknown, for he is always profoundly in earnest, even though the topic to be treated is not more elevated than the proper care of shoe-leather.

If a German editor has no original thoughts to offer his readers—and it is exceedingly seldom that he has none—he by no means refuses to allow Aristotle, or Scaliger, or Grotius, or Jean Paul to speak in his stead; nay, so great is the benevolence of his nature, and so honorable his sense of comparative merit, that he often permits them to speak so frequently that neither himself nor his topic can be perceived to have said anything at all. "Wonderful erudition, but no logic," as Victor Cousin once said of Ralph Waldo Emerson. If you will only give a Vienna feuilletonist leisure and lexicons, he will array a subject so humble as that of city drainage in apparel of the most faultless texture and classical elegance; yet it will not be discoverable that he has said anything in particular in regard to city drainage. Into his short newspaper-woof he will weave more golden threads and shreds of "sky-tinctured grain" than enter into the fabric of the sacred coronation-robe of St. Stephen; but his gorgeous garment will not afford its wearer any appreciable amount of protection against a few rugged arrows of Anglo-Saxon logic.

One of the most salient features in the methods of the German editor is the feebleness and indecision with which he generalizes from passing events, in order to turn the current of the time upon the mill-wheels of thought. With two occurrences before him, the searching and vigorous intuition of the Anglo-Saxon seizes out of them a prophecy, or a formula for his future guidance; but the dreamy and skeptical Teuton, distrusting his ability to cast the horoscope of coming events, applies himself instead to ascertain whether the occurrences ever took place.

The most exalted attribute of the philosophical historian (which the journalist should be) is the imagination—not the fancy—which gives him power to summon from the dust buried generations, and revivify them with the hopes, the hates, the fears they carried with them into the grave. This endowment, this historical imagination, which is thus useful to the historian of dead men, is alone capable of seizing out the heart of meaning from the present. When exercised upon current events, this historical imagination becomes intuition into their relations, and perception of their widest import.

This clairvoyant insight into the genius of his time, into that which daily goes on around him, is denied to the German editor. It was their sympathies rather than their prophetic ken which made the German press predict success to our anti-slavery North, while the English prophesied only evil continually.

The imaginative Frenchman and the Englishman

schooled in the craft of state always seek first the con-
nections of the present with the future, but the German
first with the past; hence the press of the former hold
that of the latter in a perpetual bondage. The German
.editor feigns to hold the "conjectural politics" of his
western neighbors in philosophical contempt; yet when
their seers take their station to watch for omens in the
perturbed sky of Europe he never fails to be present, and
scans them with an intensity of curiosity that is a tacit
confession of the shortness of his own forecast. If, when
the earth is giving premonitions of disruption, and the
low, sullen mutterings of the approaching earthquake are
heard at intervals, the journalists on the Seine and on the
Thames (as the German sarcasm is) are sometimes capable of hearing the grass grow, their contemporaries on
the Spree and on the Danube often hear nothing whatever until the earth yawns along the Rhine and swallows
down a German province. On the other hand, they
sometimes harass themselves with an undefinable terror,
and predict a throng of improbable calamities, with
whose imaginary ordeals they are so distraught that when
the genuine catastrophe comes it finds them unprepared,
and overwhelms them with unresisted violence.

After the great battle of Sadowa had unsettled Europe,
and destroyed that "balance of power," to preserve
which, as French catechisms teach, is the chief end of
man, the German journals had an infinite deal of pother,
and were occupied nearly half their time, all the next
winter, in destroying the mare's-nests of Continental
alliances discovered by the imaginative Parisians.

This routinism and this very incredulity it is that makes
the German press, in the crises of history, paradoxical as
it may sound, the most untrustworthy of the Continent.
During the tranquil leisure of peace the soil of Germany

produces the most fragrant and the most copious abundance of the roses of Truth; but in the disturbed epochs of revolution it yields also the most noxious harvests of the nettles of Uncertainty. With the German, truth is the growth only of toilsome comparison and analysis, for he lacks the Anglo-Saxon's searching penetration, which adjusts conflicting probabilities at the moment, and from internal evidence alone. During the short war of 1866 the South German and Austrian press was inundated with false history; the comparative amount of truth in the published telegraphic reports sunk even below that of the marvelous bulletins that were written along the Potomac and the Chickahominy in the early, credulous days of the rebellion. There were no amazing and magnificent inventions, as among us; but lean, bald, official falsehoods day after day persisted in. The unhappy editors published everything, the chaff with the wheat, in sheer desperation, for there was no leisure to winnow it; but they published also an incredible daily edition of interrogation-points—such editions as were never read before or since in any well-informed community. None is more conscientious and truthful than the German editor; neither is any more incapable of instantly branding falsehood on its brazen front.

During those few fearful weeks when the "Black Eagle" flapped his exulting wings over Bohemia, and Germany was convulsed as it had not been since Waterloo, nothing could have been more pitiable than the German press, groping amidst the surging and raging of the battle like the blind Ajax, and crying out for light! Around a little window in Munich there gathered nightly a multitude with pale, careworn faces, waiting for the official dole of "necessary news;" far off beside the Main their sons and brothers lay already in their "cold

and bloody shrouds," or fled with a traitor prince in ignominious retreat, while each day brought the fierce
Prussians a day's long march nearer Munich; yet each
day the official journal gave them the poor, stale lie,
"No more battles at the front," and they turned away
with sickened hearts!

In Prussia, Austria, and Bavaria alike the police-officers
search suspected dwellings without a warrant, confiscate
and carry away obnoxious papers, and on their testimony
alone imprison, mulct, or banish as a public malefactor a
subject whose greatest offense perhaps was an unguarded
utterance touching the sacred person of the monarch; or,
if he will accept debasement as the price of liberty, they
suffer him to roam his Majesty's dominions at pleasure,
but voiceless.   In Prussia alone have I known such an in-
terdict enforced with such minuteness of interpretation
that a subject who had given his parole was seized and
imprisoned for a violation of it, because he had visited a
public assembly, and, "by his presence" merely, exhorted
the populace to sedition!   The mere hint of a potentate,
so inconsiderable that one may stride over his dominions
in an hour, is sufficient to procure the banishment of an
Austrian subject from Austria by Austrian courts.   But in
Prussia alone have I witnessed the amazing spectacle of a
court, composed largely of gray-haired men, publicly con-
demning an edition of the *Allgemeine Zeitung* to be burned
with fire for traducing their august sovereign!

It is notorious in Germany that the journals of Vienna
as far surpass those of Berlin in the license of their pas-
quinades on the court and nobility, as the latter surpass
the former in sturdy political discussions and in the casu-
alty lists they publish after battles.   It is the Kaiser's
good pleasure to allow the journalists to amuse the mer-
curial and merry citizens of his capital with "quips and

cranks'' which, in the columns of the austere and solemn journals of Berlin, would be *Staatsamtsehrebeleidigung !*

Another characteristic of the Vienna press, as contra-distinguished from that of Berlin, is its coquetry with French phrases and awkwardly Germanized words, such as *comfortabel, octroyirung,* etc. The dialect of Berlin may often deal in words so rugged, hirsute, and ponderous as to make the reader feel uncomfortable, but it is at least patriotic and unimpeachable German. So terrible is the Berlinese sometimes that, in a telegraph treaty made between France and Prussia, on one occasion, the French insisted on the stipulation that '' no unusual combinations of words should be permitted,'' as the operators of Berlin, to save expense, sometimes glued together such terrible big words that their contemporaries in Paris had to coil them around a cylinder to get them off the wires !

Most of the telegraph lines in Germany are controlled by government, and they do not encourage journalistic enterprise by making deductions for dispatches of extraordinary length, but rather the contrary. And it is doubtful if newspaper proprietors could be induced to accept a much greater quantity than they already receive. When such a possibility is suggested, they simply shrug their shoulders in dismay, for that which they now receive requires to be so often translated in its tortuous journeyings, and is sometimes so wretchedly rendered by routine officials, that, upon its arrival, it is frequently impossible to render it more than approximately intelligible and accurate. To the conscientious and painstaking German these uncertain oracles are peculiarly unsatisfactory and obnoxious; they perturb his philosophic equanimity, they becloud his understanding, they harass and perplex his waking hours, and thus invade and retrench the period allotted by nature to healthful repose. It is greatly corrosive of intellectual tranquillity, and wholly subversive of the principles that should control every well-regulated human life, to be compelled to lose half an hour from one's meditations on the *Corpus inscriptionum Romanarum* in an attempt to ascertain from a miserable telegram whether a colliery explosion in Wales occurred at Llwydcoed or at Llwidcoed.

But in no department of journalistic enterprise is Germany more deficient than in her Art journals. When St. Paul's Cathedral requires new windows of stained glass they must be brought from Munich; when Englishmen of culture weary of looking at the wretched, tawdry collections of the National Gallery, they flee to Dresden and Munich; yet when Germans would read of what themselves have accomplished they are obliged to subscribe for a London journal. Germany affords the most striking demonstration of the truthfulness of the old complaint, that artists do not read. Of agricultural papers Leipsic publishes over half a dozen,—in fine, there is no known country in which agriculture is at the same time better taught and illustrated and more wretchedly practiced than in Germany, especially in South Germany.

Single newspapers in Germany never attain the colossal circulations sometimes found in France and England. This fact is entirely in accordance with the centrifugal tendencies of the character of the nation. There prevail in Germany as many theories of governmental and ecclesiastical polity—all of them of the most indubitable practicability and impregnable orthodoxy—as there are separate and particular persons, viz., some fifty or sixty millions. Now every thoughtful reader must see at once that it would be very difficult—I think I might say extremely difficult—for one paper to espouse one-half of these theories, or even a tenth portion of them. It

should also be here premised that every German citizen
desires the welfare of the land of his nativity more than
he desires his customary nutriment; and, further, that he
is profoundly persuaded and convinced that that welfare
can be permanently established and maintained only by
bringing to bear upon the science of legislation a body
of preordained, immutable, and primordial principles,
axioms, and corollaries which no previous legislator or
collection of legislators of any century or country has
hitherto either discovered or applied. For want of an
understanding of those principles the fatherland is traveling hourly to canine habitations. To avert a catastrophe
so deplorable and so fraught with direful consequences,
he patriotically establishes a journal in which to propound,
elucidate, and demonstrate those principles. He also
reads it. Whether any other of his countrymen engage
with him in that patriotic and interesting avocation is a
matter of secondary consequence, for he now peruses
healthful sentiments, and feels secure.

Thus, while the United Kingdom of Great Britain
supports only ninety daily newspapers, Prussia publishes
one hundred and forty-three, and Austria seventy-two,
most of them in the German provinces. While I do not
for a moment overlook the importance of the circumstance that the journals of Great Britain have only one
government to assault or champion, while those of Germany have a matter of thirty or thereabout upon which
to employ their attention, I likewise cannot forget that
in Prussia it is perilous to subscribe for *more* than one
political journal, while in England (as also in America)
it is perilous to subscribe for *only* one. As soon as a
thriving burgher in the little village of Eichhornstadt becomes so ambitious as to presume to peruse a journal in
addition to the government organ, it will go hard but the

police will presently find it necessary to confiscate his wild-cherry book-case, together with its contents; but if the American farmer peruses only one partisan newspaper it may be a great many months after the occurrence before he learns that his party has violated the Constitution. I am fully persuaded, therefore, that it is the great multiplicity of governments alone that has been able to impart vitality to so large a number of daily journals, when they were laboring under the depressing restrictions above narrated; and in view of this fact the cruelty of Count Bismarck in merging together a number of those governments will appear in its most aggravated and heinous character.

Another notable phenomenon is found in the fact that Protestant and intelligent North Germany does not publish proportionately as many papers as South Germany and Austria. Berlin, with a population of 620,000, requires only 142,200 copies of daily newspapers; while Vienna, with a population of only 530,000, requires 142,700 copies. In other words, Berlin has a daily to every 4·39 inhabitants; Vienna, one to every 3·73. Dresden, with a population of 200,000, requires 25,800 copies; Munich, population 167,000, daily papers 77,600.

Certainly this marked disparity cannot establish a superior intelligence for the South, for every other known fact demonstrates the contrary. The true explanation is that the South publishes a greater proportionate number of small penny papers (*Kreutzerblätter*)—very minute and trivial affairs, largely filled with advertisements, and of so low a price that thrifty merchants subscribe for several of them. They contain very little political or valuable information of any description, but chiefly "wise saws and modern instances," "old wives' fables," neighborhood genealogies, chronicles of two-headed calves, and such like matters as are level with the intellectual abilities of the credulous, tattling populations of the Catholic South. The South German or the Austrian laborer awaits nearly as anxiously as the French or the American, and more anxiously than the English or the Prussian, his daily portion of small news, though he employs great economy in its purchase. You will find in his house a trifling newspaper and a well-thumbed prayer-book oftener than in that of the Prussian, but less frequently a copy of Schiller.

17

SOME GERMAN CHARACTERISTICS.

ONE of Kaulbach's colossal frescos, ornamenting the new picture-gallery of Munich, allegorizes the triumph of true art over false. Under the conduct of Minerva, the artists and scholars, some on the friendly back of Pegasus, some on the ground, are making a terrific row with a many-headed monstrosity called the Zopf. Thwacked and thumped on all sides with all manner of weapons, brushes, mahl-sticks, dictionaries, chisels, this modern Cerberus struggles to escape in every direction, but cannot, on account of the number of his heads. With frantic rage depicted in one of his hideous faces, the blustering and gasconading audacity of an Homeric hero in another, and the whimpering, sneaking grimaces of a whipped Thersites in another, this grotesque man-beast—worthy the creative genius of Spenser—writhes and writhes, but cannot escape.

Such a many-headed nondescript has Germany always been among the nations. Every one of the sixty-odd millions who speak the great language of Luther—he is

(194)

Germany. The *heart* of every one of them beats honestly and passionately for one and the same fatherland; but, alas! the *head* of every one of these sixty-odd millions is the origin and perpetual dwelling-place of an absolutely perfect system of government, without the adoption of which the fatherland aforesaid will necessarily and inevitably go, and daily and hourly is going, hopelessly to the dogs!

In the German provinces of Austria, for instance, there are six well-defined political parties—Centralists, Autonomists, Dualists, Federalists, Democrats, and Clericals. To catch the shades of difference between the platforms of some of them would require a dialectician able to "distinguish and divide a hair 'twixt south and southwest side." The Germans reduce politics to a learned science, and treat it in the methods of the scholastics. The famous Frankfort Parliament of 1848 contained a hundred and eighteen professors! But the Germans learned something in that Parliament, for they elected to the first North German Parliament only twelve professors.

The professors of Germany are the bane of its liberties. They seek a perfect liberty, a platonic liberty, such as no nation ever has had or can have. The Frankfort constitution has been fondly called the wisest ever made. It was quite too wise. The German professor says, x of taxation $+$ y of representation $=$ z of liberty; but Francis Joseph says it should be $\frac{y}{2}$ of representation. The professor says that is not a good equation. Thereupon the Kaiser loses his temper, and cancels that quantity altogether.

These professors do not understand how to vote a demanded appropriation which they know they cannot withhold, simply to save the form of right, as the House of

Commons did many a year when it was struggling with the Tudors or the Plantagenets.

In the legislatures of Berlin and Vienna one finds vast and almost encyclopædic learning; in Paris, elegant scholarship, wit, sometimes fresh and crisp eloquence; and in Florence, a legal acumen often carried to a ridiculous excess. The Germans deliver lectures in their parliaments, the French construct climaxes, the Italians quibble on points of law, while the Magyars appoint sub-committees and proceed to business.

The intense individualism mentioned above has a result which may seem paradoxical, or not legitimately deducible therefrom, and which yet is probably natural. The egotism of independence in thought and action becomes, in politics, the egotism of servility, if the critics will tolerate the phrase. In speaking to Lord Loftus, the English ambassador, Bismarck once characterized this foible of his countrymen with trenchant sarcasm. "My lord," said he, "you do not know the Germans yet. I can assure you that, if the people had money enough, every one of them would have his king."

To a member of any particular little principality, there are more "foreigners" in Germany than in England. That is to say, if a man is so unfortunate as to live outside of an imaginary circle inclosing some few thousand acres, by courtesy called a kingdom, he is, politically, an alien. One of the most notable features of Vienna journalism is the absurd violence with which any man not born in Austria is attacked as a "foreigner," especially if he is a German. The great Count von Beust, the most astute premier, and the one who gave Austria the most splendid diplomatic triumphs, since Metternich, was stigmatized as a "foreigner" because he came from Saxony.

The inhabitants of the little principality of Reuss will

resist to the last drop of their blood rather than allow the Prussians to eat a steak of venison from the princely pre-serves, though they themselves, only a little before, in a frenzy of passion, tear down the chateaus in the park made odious to them by the tyranny of the prince.

In Prussia, however, the sentiment is far broader and more catholic. The only questions asked respecting a candidate are: Is he capable? Is he a German? Indeed, when the great University of Berlin was established, learned men were specially invited to professorships from nearly the whole civilized world.

Another result, perfectly logical and natural, of this intense individualism, is found in the cosmopolitanism of the German mind. The Germans are an epitome and digest of all nations. Begin at Dantzic, and study your way through to Basle, if your lifetime sufficed, and you would never need to travel more. You would possess all that this present time has to offer, not only of exact and speculative science, but of human character.

As Dr. Döllinger says, the Germans have written better on Shakspeare than the English, and better on Dante than the Italians. Even the Italians themselves, egotistical and self-saturated as they are, confess, through Count Cesare Balbo: "These wonderful and conscien-tious Germans are, step by step, usurping to themselves all our learning." The ancient saying of Jordan, in his *Chronica de Imperio,* "For the student one place, namely Paris, suffices," should be changed now to, "For the student one country, namely Germany, suffices." Ger-many alone has the real and true university, because Ger-many alone has real and true universality of thought.

The traveled German becomes like an onion with its many layers. You can peel off one after another, each representing some foreign nation, until you arrive at last

to the original heart and core of the fatherland. The
German alone of all men can truly say, with Ulysses,—

" I am a part of all that I have met."

This intensely developed egotism and personal independence of thought makes the German continually over-
flow into one great ocean of universal brotherhood. That
is to say, he continually flies off in a tangent from the
fatherland and from all his friends and kindred, and joins
himself in sympathy to the remotest and the strangest of
the tribes of men. He loves his own country more ardently than any other human being,—and the more
ardently in proportion to its smallness,—and yet he loves
the whole world. He has the true "world-soul."

It is in illustration of this fact that Germany clung to
Latin most tenaciously of all mediæval nations, and to
French most tenaciously of all the modern. "He who
seeks to restore to use his mother tongue is considered a
lunatic," wrote Gabriel Wagner in despair. Even as late
as 1690, Professor Thomasius, in Halle University, found
the German language, as written, so little understood,
that he was compelled to exercise his classes in making
German letters on the blackboard before they could listen
to him in that language intelligently. "The most of
them," said he, "could not even construct the simplest
sentence, or write a German letter." But they were pro-
ficient enough in Latin. Even the great Leibnitz
abandoned all attempts to introduce German into the
universities.

And the German continued longest of all in the de-
grading vassalage to the French. Not only did Frederic
the Great correspond with Voltaire in French, but with
his sister Amalie. Count Ernst von Hesse and Leibnitz
exchanged none but French letters. Maria Theresa con-

sidered it unworthy of her to correspond in German. To this day German is systematically discouraged in the noble circles of Vienna, but far less so in Berlin.

Having inflicted upon the French at Sedan the most crushing defeat ever suffered in civilized warfare, still the conquerors, with the most exquisite politeness, negotiated with the fallen emperor in his own tongue! European etiquette may have demanded that, but American independence would have been rejoiced to see that language of which Leibnitz says, "It never says any but honest things," at last and for once assert itself against the lying idiom of dandies and harlots. But if King William did not, at least the harmonious cannon of Prussians, Bavarians, Saxons, Wurtembergers, bellowing together on the heights, thundered into the ears of the stupefied and collapsed braggarts the information that for once the *Unzusammengehörigkeit* of the grand old jargon was laid aside.

A German who did not begin to learn our language until he had arrived at an adult age, once told me that, at the end of five years, he habitually "thought in English." I doubt if anybody but a German would have accomplished that.

But this very comprehensiveness or fluidity of character, which enables them, as it were, to pour themselves into the thoughts of all men, is fatal to them politically. Bismarck, with his usual acuteness of perception, but with more sadness of utterance than is his wont, declares that, "The disposition of mind which causes men to grow enthusiastic in support of foreign nationalities, even when their own fatherland suffers thereby, is a form of political disease which, alas! is found in Germany alone."

The Germans of Austria outnumber every other nationality, and they have again and again, by their valor on the battlefield, subjugated every other in that motley empire, and again and again abdicated to every other in politics. "Nowhere do things happen more wonderfully than in the world," says the Princess Elizabeth Charlotte of Orleans, in one of her letters; and nowhere in the world more wonderfully than in Germany.

Of this species of moral abdication it will be worth while to give examples at some length. A pamphlet published in Leipsic, in 1867, gave a list of six hundred and seventy-four families in Hungary, who, in the two years, 1848 and 1849, caused their names to be translated from German into Magyar. This, be it remembered, at the time when to be a Magyar was to be the subject of the greatest suspicion and persecution from the Imperial Government!

It is chiefly the nobles and the middle classes who affect this thing, for the peasants remain in the ways of the fathers. For instance, Tolpy, Matray, Ballagi, Hunsalvi, and Ipolyi, members of the Hungarian Academy, thought themselves unfit to enter its august portals until they had divested themselves of the unseemly rags, Schedel, Lutzenbacher, Bloch, Unsdorfer, and Stummer, respectively. They sometimes carry the egg-shells of their Teutonic origin still on their heads, as Szonntag, Weisz, Oszwald, and Sulcz, for Sonntag, Weiss, Oswald, and Schulze. So common is this thing that they have a stanza about it, which may be rendered thus:

> "Ludasy call me here,
> In Prussia call me Kehl.
> Thus Magyar feathers grow
> From German sparrow's tail."

In Tyrol these silent conquests go on more stealthily,

and the sweet accents of sunny Italy are steadily creeping up the valley and among its mountains. The fierce old battle-cry, *Morte ai Tedeschi!* is heard there no more; but the soft air of Italy, the beaming wine of Terlan and Lagarina, and the silvery-sounding patronymics, are more potent than the red-shirted legions. There is on the border a little village with the mighty name Mezzo Tedescho Mezzo Lombardo (half German, half Lombard), which once corresponded to the fact; but it stands now far out in the ocean of Italian waters.

Honest Hans Wurst colonizes in the valley of the Adige, and straightway he and all his carroty-haired progeny are installed in the illustrious family of Calderini, tracing their genealogy back to the flood.

And this translation of German names and sympathies into Italian, strange to relate, suffered no check, but rather an acceleration, from the great German victory of Custozza. The Tyrolese seemed to say, with Cato, *Victrix causa diis placuit, sed victa Catoni.*

In Triest these conquests of the Italianissimi are more enigmatical, for they are opposed to the interests of commerce, which is supposed always to follow common sense. The Germans who are forever agitating for the annexation of that city to Italy are too well read in history not to know that, when Bonaparte joined it to that country, thus cutting it off from its natural base of supplies in Austria, the population fell to 19,000.

In the Slavonic provinces, which are the most degraded in Austria, and which are indebted to the German language for whatever culture they have, these renegades are found, as clannish as elsewhere. Herr Kaiser, for instance, in some little swinish village of huts in Carniola, dubs himself "from immemorial antiquity," by the Slavonic name of Zeravez. To set everything right on its head, he puts his given name behind the surname, and, as Zeravez Ambrosch, he feels himself a made man, *ad unguem factus homo.*

The great Bishop Strossmayer, who made such a gallant struggle in the Eternal City against the Dogma of Infallibility, and who makes no attempt to disguise his origin, is one of the most redoubtable champions of Panslavism in the Parliament of Croatia.

A German member of the Parliament of Carniola not only learned their uncouth idiom, but spoke it in preference to his mother tongue, although more than two-thirds of his audience were German, and did not understand him.   Why should a man be more Catholic than the Pope himself?

In Carinthia these renegade Germans received a merited rebuke.   They constructed for the schools an artificial alphabet, that they might study their native dialect of Slavonic.   But the children could not understand it any better than the German ; and, moreover, the parents petitioned their Parliament that the scholars might be permitted to learn German, because, even after they acquired the patois alphabet, there was no literature for them to read.

In Bohemia the German nobles become leaders of the ultra Tchech party, as against their own unspeakably oppressed and pillaged countrymen.

Enough instances have been adduced above to show forth this weakness of the Teutonic mind, which began to be exhibited as early as the time of the celebrated Philip Schwarzerd, better known by his Greek name of Melanchthon.   And it was through their respective dealings with this national foible, that Austria finally lost the hegemony in the German Empire, and Prussia gained the same.

Through the whole course of her history Prussia has industriously and persistently Germanized, but Austria has always lusted after the flesh-pots of Slavonia. Above all things else, and all other considerations, Prussia has sought to add to herself German territory, but Austria has married and conquered fourteen languages, and always anything rather than German. In the mixed provinces of that empire it has come to be regarded as axiomatic that to belong to the Government party is to be Slavonic —to the Opposition, German. It is an historical fact that the single Slavonic province of Bohemia has been allowed to furnish three-fourths of the officers of the empire, and that too when all Tchechs are devout disciples of St. Vladimir, whose most notable saying was, "It is better to live under the knout of Russia than in Austrian freedom." There are hundreds of little towns in the mixed provinces of Austria, where a little assistance from the government would enable the Germans to maintain a German school, and so save their children from becoming denationalized; but Austria never helps them. On the contrary, Prussia gladly gives such assistance in her Polish province, and in Schleswig-Holstein, to save her young German subjects, and gain others from the Poles and Danes.

In a word, then, all indications point to Prussia as the only rightful regenerator and conserver of those Teutonic forces which Austria and the petty princes have so prodigally wasted. To Prussian statesmen everything that is German is exceedingly precious, while all the other German governments, including Austria, have practically co-operated with France in scattering, dividing, dissolving, and frittering away the noblest national inheritance on the continent.

IN THE GREAT WEST.

THE COLLEGE POLITICIANS.

I'll sing the zeal Drumlanrig bears,
Who left the all-important cares
  Of princes and their darlings;
And, bent on winning borough towns,
Came shaking hands wi' wabster lowns,
  And kissing barefit carlins.

BURNS.

IN a little Western town, which, as a seat of learning, was greatly exalted above its natural importance, and whose quiet inhabitants, being chiefly descended from the Puritans, were often grievously scandalized by the wild pranks of the madcaps collected there from the great roaring cities of the West, this story has its action.

In a dingy chamber, on a certain evening, two students were seated on opposite sides of a table, conning Latin. The kerosene lamp between them, having a shade with brick-red pictures of elegant rural gentlemen gracefully bending with sickle in hand to reap impossible golden wheat, was just lighted for the evening. One of the students had his lexicon, carefully covered with sheepskin, leaned up at a convenient angle on a small wooden frame, and his *De Officiis* spread open upon his lap. He was a youth of huge stature, but very loose-knit in the joints, with a head so capacious that his almost white hair seemed to be spread over it in a single layer. His great bloodless face and forehead, and his big eyes, reminded the beholder of nothing more forcibly than a couple of eggs broken into a tolerably large basin of flour. When he stood up to make a lyceum speech, his feet were planted wide apart, and, in his gestures, his powerful arms radiated from him in rigidly straight lines, with all his fingers spread out fan-shaped.

He was a man of a massive intellect, but his uncouthness procured for him, among the pert collegiates, the nickname of Pulp.

His companion was as odd a genius as himself, but in the opposite extreme. He was short and stout, with a head like a bullet, and a singularly funny pug-nose. It seemed to have been struck, at some period of his earlier history, with injurious violence, and slightly driven up into his forehead, and at the same time flattened on the end, and bunched out sharp. He had a piping voice, which was often fervently lifted up in the class prayer-meetings; and he had a habit, when addressing his fellows, of turning his head somewhat to one side, and elevating his little eyes to the upper corner of the wall with a kind of soft, Madonna-like simplicity, while his mouth, being pursed together, caused his pug-nose to turn up in a comical manner.

He was profoundly earnest, in his narrow way; but he had the misfortune of being obliged to wear the same very short, pudgy, pale-drab overcoat all through college; —hence he had to abide a nickname also. He shall be known in this history as little Tim Pliny.

He had just shoved into the table a drawer from which he had eaten his frugal repast, and was again immersed in his lexicon. Pulp continued to fumble his awhile, then he turned his *De Officiis* over, straddling widely on the table, rose up, joined his hands behind him under his coat-skirts, and commenced pacing to and fro across the floor, in his soft shambling gait, putting down his heels first and as carefully as if he were treading on Geneva crystals. Presently he stopped, rolled his great gray eyes up toward the ceiling, and slowly repeated to himself the famous passage :

"Nunquam se minus otiosum esse, quam quum otiosus, nec minus solum, quam quum solus esset."

Then he raised his voice out of the depths of its abstraction :

"I think, Mr. Pliny, that is one of the profoundest sentiments ever uttered. *Quam quum solus esset.* Wonderful power of introspection and treasury of intellectual resources must that philosopher possess, to whom the microcosm, the little world of himself, is greater than the great world, the macrocosm of the universe! Remarkable power of introspection, Mr. Pliny."

"If he had only been a Christian instead of a heathen ! But a heathen's thoughts, not being directed toward his Maker, must be wicked and deceitful," replied little Tim Pliny, without looking up from his book.

"An inconsequential suggestion, Mr. Pliny; quite. Christianity, if absorbingly pursued, consumes the individuality. No Christian philosopher has ever possessed a more profoundly subjective idealism than the heathen speculists of Greece," rejoined Pulp, with a disdainful flourish of his arm above his head, as he seated himself.

"Do you think Cicero as great as St. Paul?" asked Tim Pliny, looking up, distressed at his chum's skepticism.

Rap, rap, rap !

"Come in," said Pulp, out of his infinite and serene benevolence.

The knocker availed himself of this invitation.

"Good-evening, Mr. Square," said Pulp, rising, and reaching him his huge hand across the corner of the table.

"Take a chair, Mr. Square," piped little Tim Pliny, and then he cackled and shook himself, and felt quite funny indeed over his jingling rhyme.

Square, with an easy familiarity, shook hands with both at once, then seated himself at the end of the table. This newcomer, although his very prominent cheek-bones and sunken cheeks gave him a triangular-shaped face, had a mathematically square and marble-white forehead. His hair was coarse and black, and in their deep, flaring sockets glowed a pair of relentless, coal-black eyes. His voice was hard and sometimes almost terrible. He was accustomed to stand up in class, and translate *De Corona* with wonderful accuracy and fluency, in a strong voice, and with more audacious assurance and pomposity of utterance than if he had been Demosthenes speaking on the *bema.* His splendid scholarship made him a favorite of the professors, but he was detested by his class.

"We were just entering upon a very interesting discussion relative to that famous passage in the lesson beginning *Nunquam——*"

"Forever *totus in illis*, Pulp. Cut that!" said Square, impatiently, lighting his cigar over the lamp-chimney. "I came here to talk politics. You never smoke, I believe. You know, Pulp, you have influence among the Neutrals in all the classes, and you ought to bear a hand for yours truly, because it will all redound to the glory of the Neutrals. You know these dapper little sweet-williams of the secret societies have had the President of the Lyceum three years hand-running, and they now labor under the delusion that they have a moral mortgage upon the same. Are you afraid of these wealthy curled darlings?

Curse the whole crew of the sick-faced, musky dandies, and lily-livered pulks! I will fight them to the last tunk, before they shall ride over our necks every year on their high cock-horse. They have whistled and snapped their fingers at us, as if we were spaniels in training, long enough; and if *I* have any influence, the Neutrals shall not crawl and whine after them, like whipped puppies and fags, any longer, by——"

"Oh, don't swear, Mr. Square!" squeaked little Tim Pliny; and then he cackled very much again, and rubbed his hands, at his unintentional rhyme, for he had meant to be very solemn.

Square looked at him, with an ill-concealed expression of contempt, then lighted his cigar again, which had gone out during the above outburst.

Pulp had listened intently, his thin-haired, lumpy head rolling heavily back; and when the orator finished, he puckered out his mouth sagely. After considerable deliberation, he said:

"*Caret tibi pectus inani ambitione*, Mr. Square? For I fear it is indeed a vain ambition. The secret societies are always reinforced by deserters from our ranks; besides which, they outvote us from the beginning. *In comittiis prevalebunt.*"

"*Prevalebunt* be——!" said Square, fiercely, smiting the table with his clinched fist. "I know there are always white-faced muck-worms enough among the Neutrals, who are groveling in the dust the whole four years of college after these insolent damned jewelers' sons and French cooks, in hope of getting an invitation to join them. They are ready to do anything they bid them,—the pitiful fags!—even to blacking their boots. But if we come out once in a body, like men, and dare to own our own souls, and fling defiance in the teeth of these cowardly snobs and bullies, they will come to us quick enough, and we can demand our own terms."

Poor little Tim Pliny had laid down his book, and simply gazed at Square with open mouth, appalled at such audacious wickedness. But Pulp was slowly kindling, for, as soon as Square finished, his great gray eyes rolled about in a fine frenzy. He was manifestly jarred out of his ponderous propriety by such daring and fierce talk, and it took him some time to recover his metaphysical condition of mind.

"You state your propositions vigorously, Mr. Square, I concede. And now I think I remember to have heard, vaguely, that the hereditary feud between the Alphas and the Omegas is more embittered than common this year. *Adversi turbine venti confligunt*, as Virgil says."

"Yes," interposed Square, eagerly; "and they have the little societies, their allies, so equally divided between them that we Neutrals hold the balance of power. Let them tear one another, the false harpies! If we will only make politics a study, as they do, and begin in time, and not be eleventh-hour vaporers and fools, we can bring them cringing to us for an alliance, and force them to give us the President this year. We can *force* them to do it, and then, of course, I shall be elected."

In this strain the discussion was continued for some time, during which Square established, from private information he had, the following facts:—That there was an extraordinarily bitter rivalry that year between the Alphas and the Omegas, the leading societies; that each of them had a good man for the Presidency, and each was determined to elect at all hazards. Both of them had, by the proffer of certain minor offices, not only strengthened their old alliances, but gained new ones, having plied all the small societies so industriously that they had ranged them all on one side or the other. Also, these two great hostile camps were so nearly equal in numbers that they dared not enter the election without some positive arrangement with the Neutrals.

Neither of them, however, expected to make any compact which should bind all the members of that body, because it was a kind of wild Ishmael of college, containing all the odd and eccentric elements which could not be carved into their likeness. Any one of the secret societies, in making a political alliance, was always able to bind all its members to the support of a certain ticket; but the Neutrals were refractory, independent, scattering, a drove of wild ass colts which never could be so penned in but that some of them would make a clean breach through the fence. There were always stragglers and guerrillas among them, prowling on the outskirts of the secret societies, seeking admittance.

After having read Square's fierce denunciation of this class, as above, it may be interesting to the reader to be informed that he had formerly been expelled from a branch chapter of the Omegas in another college! At the moment when he was heaping maledictions on all secret societies, he was wearing the Omega badge, not, of course, on the left lapel of his vest, but attached to that portion of his trousers by which he might be supposed to signify toward it his most concentrated and profound contempt.

The result of Square's energetic movements was, that a few of the most prominent Neutrals issued a call, a few days after the circumstances above narrated, requesting all collegiates not belonging to any secret society to assemble at a designated hour in the Greek recitation-room. So thoroughly had the election excitement among the secret societies penetrated the Neutrals, that there was scarcely one lacking. Square took good care not to get himself nominated chairman, and then, by being promptly on the floor, as soon as business was in order, with a motion for appointing a Committee on Elections, of course he secured for himself the chairmanship of that committee. The other members were Pulp, and a third man of remarkable insignificance. Then, through a friend whom he had charged for the purpose, the wily Square procured the passage of a resolution instructing this committee to fight shy, simply awaiting bids for alliance ; and, on no account, either to make or receive any proposition looking to anything less than the Presidency for the Neutrals.

A further result of these proceedings was, that, early the next afternoon, a delegation from the Alphas, more prompt and watchful than their enemies, called upon the Neutral Election Committee to beat the bush. The two principal delegates were Augustus and Polly.

Augustus was a handsome *brunet*, tall, slender, with a very commendable incipient moustache, and a pair of coal-black eyes. He had that easy nobility of dignity, that eloquence of mere motion, that unhesitating volubility, which proclaimed him the born orator. More than this, he had that wild and wizard quaver of the voice, that lightening of the eye, in his impassioned moments, and that electric quivering of the hand above the head, followed by a swing of the arm with that abandon which announced the genius, and which held the listeners in thrilled and breathless silence, so that they forgot to applaud until after the bewitchment of the clarion voice had ceased. And then, when they tried to recollect what he had uttered, "Every something, being blent together, turned to a wild of nothing." He was of that kind of men whom women love with a devotion that passeth knowledge.

Polly was the college nickname of a youth who should have been born a girl. He wore his hair long, had a liquid longing languor in his large eyes, and soft, long cheeks. But, above all else, he was thoroughly girlish in his impetuosity and his charming unreason, and in his passionate Italian fondness for burrowing in some harmless plot, some secret society intrigue. He was always hunting up personal facts, anecdotes, and reminiscences. He. was a walking encyclopædia of biography of all the men—at least, all the Alphas—who had ever been in college. He knew what Alpha took a valedictory in 1854, who took the salutatory in 1837, and all about it. He had postage-stamps, autographs, and an Alpha catalogue with innumerable annotations and interlineations.

These two, and a third who need not be described, met the Neutrals in Pulp's room. This apartment was, therefore, occupied by seven persons, little Tim Pliny being supernumerary, for he had obstinately refused to go out. Polly was no speaker, so Augustus was to be spokesman. But Polly was full of fidgets lest his eloquent *frater* should offer too much ; so he seated himself close beside him, slyly reached his arm around, and seized his coat-tail, ready to twitch it in case of emergency.

The Neutrals sat on one side of the room, the Alphas on the other, and little Tim Pliny at the table. Intense solemnity prevailed. Augustus rose and began, somewhat embarrassed as his manner was at the outset :

"Gentlemen of the Neutral Committee : Having been unofficially informed of the action recently taken by your honorable body, in regard to the impending election, the Alphas, to which we have the honor to belong, have delegated us to meet you, and endeavor to effect some arrangement for an alliance. Our meeting was entirely informal [twitch by Polly]—— We have no credentials to offer you, gentlemen, showing our authority to negotiate; but we demand none from you, believing that, in an affair of this description, we can repose confidence in our mutual good faith. It is unnecessary, perhaps, for me to enter here upon an extended explanation of our relations toward our ancient and hereditary enemies, the Omegas; but I think it may not be improper to request an answer to the question whether they have yet approached your committee with any [twitch]——whether the Omegas have—well, I think it is entirely safe, gentlemen of the committee, to premise that we are prepared to offer you more fraternal and generous terms than the Omegas can possibly be willing to concede. You must have perceived, gentlemen, in the course of your college experience, that the Alphas have never yielded themselves up to that blind spirit of persecution and of contumelious effrontery toward the always honorable and noble body of students you represent, which has disgraced the history of the Omegas from the foundation of the chapter [twitch] —— Gentlemen, we are instructed by our society, then, to offer you an alliance upon the following exceedingly liberal conditions: The Alphas to elect the President of the Lyceum (seeing they have not been represented in that office for a year), they pledging themselves, on their part, to vote solid for a Neutral as Vice-President, and promising also, on the good word of gentlemen, to secure to this arrangement all the votes of the societies in alliance with them. Of the six minor offices, we pledge ourselves to give you four, reserving only two for our allies. Such, gentlemen, are the very liberal terms we have been instructed to offer [twitch]——"

Augustus sat down in great disgust at this unseemly

curtailment and reduction to plain sense of his intended flowers of speech.   Square rose abruptly to reply:

"Gentlemen of the Alphas: You speak of *giving* us the Vice-Presidency and four of the minor offices. Until this moment I had not been made acquainted with the fact that the authority was vested in your secret societies, either singly or collectively, to give or withhold any of the offices whatsoever within the gift of the whole body of students.   In reply to your offer to *give* us the offices named, I have simply to state that my instructions are to entertain no proposition which does not offer the Neutrals the Presidency."

Polly glanced at Augustus, and Augustus glanced at Polly.   Pulp rolled his great gray eyes at Square in amazement.   As for little Tim Pliny, who did not at all believe in these wicked buyings and sellings, he was so indecorous as to put his head under the table and snicker.

It is not necessary to pursue the course of the negotiations, and indeed they had not much further course. After a little more parleying, with great stateliness and stiffness the Alphas withdrew.

It is well to record, perhaps, that Polly took his departure from the scene of these unsuccessful negotiations with a large-sized flea in his ear.   There entered into his mind a profound conviction, or rather, one of those prescient intuitions for which he was noted.   He had the keenness to perceive that Square, with all his ferocity, was not a mighty man among the Neutrals, and not at all to be feared ; and that Pulp was the mountain, which, not being able to bring it to him, like the prophet, he must approach.

As they went out through the wicket-gate (or the place where the gate should be, for certain evil-disposed persons had, before Pulp was put on the committee, abstracted, purloined, and secreted the same), whom of all men should they meet but a delegation of Omegas, going up to labor with Pulp? Singular what a popular place of resort that sorry chamber had suddenly become for those young aristocrats! Little Tim Pliny had hard work now-adays to get a chance to eat his dinner at all. He would hardly get well to nibbling and munching at a piece of Graham bread, when somebody would knock, and he would have to whip the bread into the drawer, shove in the same, wipe his mouth, and become intently engaged over his Greek lexicon. Indeed, it is related that a band of young politicians once came upon him so suddenly that he bolted a whole cut of sausage endways, which lodged in his throat, to the serious detriment of his faculty of speech for several consecutive minutes.

Several days passed on, and each society delegation met the Neutrals frequently, as it leaked out that one or the other had offered better terms. But a time at last arrived when each had offered its ultimatum, and had no-thing further to propose. The chairman of the Neutrals now summoned another general meeting, for the purpose of listening to the report of the committee, and taking action thereon. This evening, therefore, would be the momentous crisis of the whole campaign. If the Neutrals should determine to adhere to the resolution of instruc-tions given to their committee, it would make a " trian-gular fight," for neither society intended to offer them the Presidency for this year; but if they voted to accept the terms of either, the contest was already virtually de-cided.

For these reasons, therefore, while the Neutrals were holding secret session (for they did this, despite their de-nunciation of the societies) in the Greek recitation-room, the electioneering committees of the Alphas and the Omegas were assembled at their respective headquarters, eager to catch the earliest intelligence. Both of them had spies or sycophants among the Neutrals, who were certain to hasten to them with the result, in hope of earning the coveted membership.

In Augustus's splendid suite of chambers (for a society man could occasionally persuade himself to accept rooms on the second floor) there were, besides Polly and the third man, nearly all the Alphas congregated together, for there was no studying that night. While waiting and wondering at the unusually protracted discussions of the Neutrals, they had agitated the question in all its bearings for the thousandth time, until they had grown listless and disgusted. They were almost invisible to each other in the cigar-smoke, as they indolently lounged on the sofas, or covered all the huge French bedstead, like an army encamped, or lazily shuffled the chess-men, or lolled in the rocking-chairs, reading something out of "Verdant Green."

The ever-wakeful Polly sat at the window, looking down into the street, and occasionally casting wistful glances up it toward the college. His colleague sat near him, inspecting his meerschaum.

"I say, Polly," exclaimed the latter, "blast my eyes but those Neuts are windy to-night!"

Polly winked significantly with one eye.

"Pulp has his hands full of 'hoc job.'"

"Do you think he can make it?"

"Of course he can."

There was a slight click of the gate-latch down in the yard, only caught by Polly's catlike ears. Looking down, he saw, where the gaslight flooded the snow, three men standing behind a snowball bush, apparently consulting.

Presently they moved out of the shadow, and advanced toward the door.

"Cock's soul!" cried Polly, leaping up. "Boys, the Omega committee are coming up here! What *does* it mean?"

In an instant every sleeper was aroused; the chess-men executed some frantic gymnastics in the air, and the window went nigh to be broken by the boys surging against it. Their immemorial enemies coming to solicit an alliance! What can it mean else? It must be that they have some secret information that the Neuts are going against them. What *does* it mean? Such a thing was never heard of in college.

But no head was equal to the tremendous necessities of the occasion but Polly's. Make an alliance with the Omegas? Of course, if the Neuts were lost, but not otherwise. Victory at any cost; but victory would be twofold sweeter if it meant also defeat to the Omegas. But *quid facere?* The Omegas were already admitted, and were tramping in the hall below. If they only knew how the Neuts were going! Tramp, tramp, tramp! coming up the stairs. Polly frantically clutched his hat, and sung out:

"Delay, boys, at all hazards! Mum's the word! Tell 'em an important member of the committee is absent. Leave all to me."

With that he dashed over two sofas and a wide bedstead, knocking flat down a *frater* Alpha. He made a frantic rush for a window, opened it, and leaped out like a frog on a shed-roof, his coat-tail whipping through the sash just as the Omegas knocked. Crawling along the roof on the inside slope, he reached the outside corner, slipped down a post bruin-fashion, and found himself in the back-yard. He must make a wide circuit before coming into the street, lest the Omegas should catch a glimpse of him from the window.   While he is floundering through the snow in back-gardens, tearing through choice English gooseberry bushes and raspberries, nearly cutting his neck in two on clothes-lines, and receiving attacks in the rear from several ferocious bull-dogs, indignant at being disturbed at such an unseemly hour of the night, we precede him to the Greek recitation-room, to make some note of things which happened there before his arrival.

The Neutrals being called to order, Square, as Chairman of the Committee on Election, proceeded to make his report.   He simply stated the offers they had received as the ultimatum of each society.   He was not unaware of his growing unpopularity, and he had so often fulmined against the society men, that for once he restrained himself.

Upon this there arose a mighty wind of debate.   Some called upon the Neutrals to accept the offer of the Alphas, others that of the Omegas, and others insisted that they should go into the fight independent of either.

Pulp waited calmly until all the small orators had lashed themselves into a fury, and subsided.   Then he arose, and went all the way to the upper end of the room, in his rolling, plantigrade gait, picking his feet up and setting them down so softly, and with his head thrown back in his lunatic manner.   He stepped on the dais, planted his feet far asunder, placed his hands upon his hips, and began abruptly, the audience listening breathless:

"Buddha Sakia said, 'All men are equal,' and he received the lowly.   But the haughty Brahmins despised him, and remained aloof, saying, 'He accepts even beggars and criminals.'   They received only the great.   As a consequence of this Pharisaical exclusiveness, the Brahmins number less than one-fifth the converts of the Buddhists. Let us be instructed by this example, and shun a vainglorious but empty independence. There are three great contestants in the field. If we enter into a triangular battle, the election may last all night ; and, depend upon it, the society men will linger until the morning stars grow dim, while the Neutrals will either go over to them through sheer weariness, or go home. As a last resort, they will make an alliance, and thus, in either case, we shall lose everything,—*cantamus vacui.* But by a timely alliance we shall secure much. I give my voice for an alliance with the Alphas.''

He sat down amid universal astonishment. What, Pulp ! Of all men in college, Pulp, proposing an alliance, and that with the aristocratic Alphas ! Pulp, who had so often, in his elevated and philosophical vein, discoursed on the evils of clannishness, emulous intrigue, and the deplorable bitterness of bickering flowing from that fountain of gall, the secret societies. Pulp, the greatest intellect in four hundred, whom even the professors never contradicted, but listened to as to a superior ; Pulp, the lofty, the Baconian, the wise, haranguing in favor of a coalition with boys !

Square was furious. ''It is false !'' he cried fiercely, quivering with passion. '' It is false ! The soft-handed snobs dare not go into a fight without us. Let not these brainless dandies ' who caper nimbly in a lady's chamber to the lascivious pleasing of a lute,' pipe their *Ranz des Vaches* to us ! Has my colleague been opiated with musk and geranium ? Has he been brained with a lady's fan ? Has he been introduced into the ' first circles,' and been overpowered by the lewd witcheries of the round-dance ? Has his philosophy been turned into a jeweler's kit, and the music of the spheres, which echoed sweet and low

from his soul, been crimped into the little measure of
their creed, until his great heart beats to the ticking of a
twenty-carat gold watch, and his traitor hands mark the
time of boughten infamy? It is a lie! a gratuitous lie!
They will fight each other to the bitter end, and we have
only to stand by and await their coming, which will be
the coming of cowards, begging, ay, whining, for an alliance. This I happen to know from private——"

At this point he was interrupted by Pulp, who had
been seen to step out a moment with the doorkeeper, and
then return to his place. He stopped there a moment,
as if hoping Square would pause; but the fierce, dis-
jointed invective of the man was too much even for the
philosophic Pulp, and he held up his right hand, with all
his fingers intensely rigid with passion, each one striving
to get as far away as possible from all the others. He
spoke, huskily:

"Will Mr. Square permit me to interrupt him for a
moment? In reply to his assertion that the societies will
never coalesce, I have to say, that I have just received,
from a trustworthy source, the information that the
Omegas have gone to the Alpha headquarters, and are at
this moment in consultation with them in regard to an
alliance."

Square turned deadly pale, and uttered never a word
more. Well he might, for in an instant the room was
filled with hisses, yells, and hoots of execration. The
voices of Pulp and the chairman, calling for order, were
utterly drowned and lost, being inaudible even to themselves. Infuriated cries of "Put him out! Put him out!"
"The liar!" "The slanderer!" "The big mouth!"
mingled with stamping, hisses, groans, and cat-calls.
Every one rose from his seat. Fists were brandished
fiercely at the fallen plotter. Fiery maledictions were

hissed in his face through clinched teeth. He would doubtless have suffered personal violence, if he had not seized his hat and hastened away. Ruined forever! Never did vaulting ambition so overleap itself, and fall. He never appeared in chapel again, and he left college in less than a week.

As soon as quiet could be restored, a member moved a reconsideration of the former vote of instructions, which was carried. Then Pulp moved that the offer of the Alphas be accepted; the motion was seconded, and instantly carried by a unanimous vote. A committee-man was elected in place of Square, and then the committee was instructed to proceed at once to the Alpha headquarters with the acceptance.

Polly had hurried back to his fellows, and, as soon as he cooled his face a little with snow, and removed the impressions he had received from the clothes-lines and the gooseberry bushes, he entered, and greeted the waiting Omegas with considerable cordiality. But the Neutral committee soon arrived, and the disgusted Omegas, knowing what it signified, took their melancholy departure. They knew, without asking, that the offer of the Neutrals would be accepted before theirs.

Not long afterward came the election, and the Alphas, of course, gained the Presidency. Next morning Pulp, for the first time in his college history, was late at chapel. He walked up the aisle with downcast eyes. So unusual a circumstance turns every eye upon him. What is the matter with the man? Has he suddenly, in some unaccountable manner, become ashamed of his huge feet, that he looks at them so steadily? What is that so bright and pretty on the left lapel of his vest? It must be a butterfly. No; it is winter yet. Four hundred pairs of eyes are riveted on it. What can it be? It burns his breast as the flaming emblem of her crime, the "scarlet letter," did the bosom of Hester Prynne.

It is the Alpha badge !

Deserter ?

Yes ; and something more. Most of the Neutrals used a harsher word than that.

A week or two later, just before Commencement, Polly is talking in his chamber with a *frater* who has just returned from a long vacation.

"But I say, Polly, how in the deuce could you fellows stand it to rope in such a camel ?"

"But we had to do it to get the Neuts, don't you understand ? Then, too, he had only two weeks more in college."

"Tell me how it all happened, Polly. *Dic age, O virgo !*"

"Well, you see the Neuts put him on their committee one evening, and the next afternoon we met them, and *hæc-fatus*-ed the matter. I saw in a minute Pulp carried them all on his shoulders. So that very night we voted him in, and I rushed him hard, and pledged him about midnight, and we initiated him about one o'clock. But, of course, we didn't swing him out till election was over ; and then it was only two weeks to Commencement. We could stand it two weeks."

"Who would have thought Pulp would do it ?"

"Do you remember what Pope says of Lord Bacon ?"

TWO ONLY SONS.

HAMLET.

THERE lived once on the bank of the Beautiful River, in Ohio, two neighbors, of whose children we have somewhat to chronicle. Farmer Polney was a hard-working, God-fearing man ; but Mr. Baywood lived in an old-time, generous ease, on the interest of his money. His house stood close beside the lordly river, surrounded by a smirk white fence, with flowers in parterres, shrubbery, etc.; but Farmer Polney's house was far back amid his fields, and had a hard and naked appearance, being inclosed by a lichened fence, and by a few rosebushes, which were frequently nibbled by some extremely utilitarian calves.

These two families, being the most prominent in the little neighborhood fenced in by the river hills, led off in all the momentous school-meetings and in the various solemn conclaves and weighty businesses of the district. They contrived, by strict economy, and by having the teacher "board round," to maintain a school three months in summer and three in winter. So, twice a year there was considerable commotion in the little humdrum district, and much riding up and down of prospective schoolmistresses on wheezy, old, stiff-necked plow-horses, on side-saddles that were certain to turn over.

. (223)

Sometimes they came to see Farmer Polney, but oftener Mr. Baywood, because he was never away in the fields; but it was always Farmer Polney's horses which had to go after the schoolmistresses, and take them home on Saturdays; and it was always little white-headed Sargent Polney who had to go with them and ride behind. And invariably, when they ascended a steep hill, the girth would burst, and he would slip off behind over the horse's tail, and the saddle and schoolmistress would fall on top of him.

Harry Baywood and Sargent were always together, as absolutely indispensable to each other as the sine to the cosine. In the weekly spelling-schools, held on long winter evenings, they two and Jolie Baywood were always the last to be "spelled down." Harry was never content unless he had Sargent at his house, and the latter was so fond of Jolie that he had no trouble in going, and invariably overstayed the hour appointed by his father.

Farmer Polney's library was small, and contained principally such intensely solemn and inscrutable volumes as Drelincourt "On Death," Baxter's "Saint's Rest," and similar; while old Mr. Baywood's book-case was ample, reaching, in its grandeur of rich old walnut mouldings and gilded tomes, all the way from the floor to the ceiling, and containing "Robinson Crusoe," "Scottish Chiefs," etc. But Harry would always drag Sargent away from the books, and whisk him off out-doors to watch his mills for sawing rotten wood, his wind-mills, and all manner of automatons and moving gimcracks.

He was a merry and a lively boy, caring nothing for girls, dogs, and cats, except to torment them, hang them by the neck, or explode firecrackers in their ears. He was captain of all the school battles, but he could do nothing without Sargent for his swift-footed lieutenant. He organized all games of "shinny" on the ice, and all snow-balling combats; but Sargent always contrived to make his duty to his captain so elastic as to allow him to push Jolie's sled, or stand by her side when the snowball bombardment waxed most furious. He could not have told why it was if he had puzzled for a week, but it was nevertheless an indisputable fact that he never could play at "blindman" without catching Jolie first; and it was equally certain that she would be offended if he did not catch her first. But the strangest thing of all was, she would give him the most trouble she possibly could.

The schoolmistresses were generally selected from among the poorer "hill-folks;" hence these two boys presently got beyond their depth, and "knew more than the mistress." They graduated across the river, into the pretentious, three-story brick "college," but they were still inseparable. They crossed in the same skiff, Harry always rowing the forward oar, in which respective positions they had many a tug to try which could turn the other. They were in the same Latin classes with Bullion's Grammar, played the same games of ball and marble.

But now at last they were obliged to separate. Harry conceived, after awhile, a rooted disgust for Latin, and aspired to a steamboat. Sargent rather liked the art and science of surveying, and had vague yearnings for civil engineering, though he had once, after having his susceptible imagination strongly wrought upon by the blare of trumpets from a menagerie chariot, registered a solemn promise in chalk, upon the paternal work-bench, to devote his life to the menagerie.

Harry was too modest for a Western steamboat-captain, that pearl of all gentlemen; too modest to grapple with the rude insolence of the boiler-deck; though he had that native and graceful nobility, that dignity of mere motion, of manner, of voice, which made him the companion of his seniors and the envy of the younger. He went into partnership with an old man in a small local craft. But he rapidly mounted to the hurricane deck, and waxed prosperous exceedingly.

As for Sargent, he suddenly fell away from the binomial theorem to the cornfield. Farmer Polney had conquered his way up from poverty by hard knocks, and he still kept a strong grip upon the farm; but he was resolved that his boy must begin to prepare himself to stand presently in his stead. It was well enough for him to go to school until he "ciphered to the rule of three," but when he began to gabble algebra, and quotations from Cæsar, the farmer shook his head. He gave him "sums" to find the number of acres in a certain field; he tried to interest him in adding, subtracting, and multiplying crops of wheat. He gave him sole and exclusive proprietorship in sheep and a yoke of oxen; he induced him to clear away the forest on a hillside, and plant an orchard. But the orchard grew to brambles, and the chipmunks nibbled away all the apples thereof.

The boy would carry out his "Paradise Lost,"-the only readable book he could find, and leave it at the end of a cornrow, and when he plowed a round, he would snatch it up and commit to memory two or three verses. While he was repeating them on another round, he would let the plow gouge out a cornhill, whereupon he would most unjustly fustigate the faithful and innocent old horse, and an alarming capering about and destruction of maize would result. He named his young oxen "Noun" and "Verb;" but they recognized no such outlandish and opprobrious names, and accordingly ran away, got unyoked, and one violently extracted the other's tail, to which it had been very injudiciously attached. In trying to add some verses of Milton to the stock he possessed, while cutting corn in the field, he would grievously hack his shins. In the long winter evenings he would sit by the kitchen stove, to escape the contagious and agreeable tattle of the sitting-room, crooning over his Milton or his Latin grammar; but, after the day's fatigues, he would nod in spite of himself, and then thump his head in disgust.

His father, with the old habit of authority strong upon him, and impatient of any blundering in his sight, sought to direct the boy's doings, even in his own little crops, and in the most minute particulars, where he should have let him stumble along and learn for himself. The youth's slowly growing sense of independence would sometimes assert itself in most tempestuous phrasing, which he would afterward bitterly regret.

Thus he was gradually acquiring an unconquerable repugnance toward the farm, and groped blindly along, in obedience to some higher impulse, he knew not what. His thirst for knowledge increased, and he often pleaded with his father for permission to go to college, and wept in secret over his hopeless ignorance, and cursed his sleepy stupidity.

He received frequent letters from Harry, written in elegant commercial chirography; but his replies he was compelled to send in the accursed scrawl of the district-school, made with oak-ball ink, which dried into an unhealthy yellow color. Harry was greatly prosperous; he was adding to his bank-account many hundreds every year, more than the whole Polney farm produced. He had dined and ridden out with the Mayor, and had even been introduced to the Governor. He was sole proprietor and captain of the " Viola," and thirteen men gave obedience to his youthful behests. In short, his life was gliding tranquilly along in that smooth and uninterrupted current of commercial prosperity which afforded little of episode, or of matter for romantic or instructive narration.

But Sargent envied him none of these things, for he knew him to be nobly worthy of the best success; but it caused him to chafe more and more at the plow-tail. Jolie, the romping and mischievous, was grown into a very dignified young lady, and had gone away to a fashionable boarding-school, and he saw her very seldom. He thought she was acquiring high notions, and cared nothing more for him, a clumsy clown of the farm; and, whether she did or not, he determined, with a kind of proud and obstinate bitterness, to think she did not, and avoided seeing her. In all this he judged her very foolishly and unjustly.

His sister, Jane, had grown into a pretty farmer's daughter, with soft, brown eyes and brown hair, and a very affectionate disposition; and she often wept and wondered at her brother's stormy discontent, and sought in vain to encourage him with her innocent prattle. She pleaded for him with their father. She magnified his gifts, which to her seemed marvelous. She told the taciturn farmer, with wonder and with pride, how he would stride up and down the room, now repeating Webster or Milton, and now fuming over his enforced ignorance.

And so at last the farmer reluctantly gave his consent that the lad should go to college. But he still believed he could make a farmer of him, so he agreed to send him, on condition that, during vacation, he should come home and buckle to the farm-work. His outfit was purchased and made up, even to the checkered trousers, through which he jumped every morning about four inches too far, and the little caraway-seed silk handkerchief. At last the great and eventful morning arrived. In his characteristic way, the farmer worked and puddered about something or other, in order to lose no time, till the very smoke of the steamboat was in sight. Sargent and his sister were distracted, for he had not yet received even the money for his expenses. Nevertheless, they reached the river in season. The lad shook hands around the little circle of the farm inhabitants, his father's tenants, and then walked aboard, with his heart in his throat, and stepping very high and awkwardly on the teetering plank. The boat backed off, and then steamed grandly up past the landing, while the handkerchiefs fluttered and the farmer shook his hat. But, as soon as the steamboat was behind a tree, he turned away, and with the back of his hard broad hand dashed away a falling tear. Ah ! if the boy could have witnessed that act, he would have known and loved his hard and taciturn father better.

This succinct narration cannot follow him throughout his college career. The black and gusty clouds of civil war came up; Fort Sumter was assaulted and captured; and a great nation was delirious with frenzied patriotism and with mad passion. Hard upon the heels of this news came the thrilling intelligence to the college : "Washington is captured ; the rebel banner flaunts in insolent and haughty triumph above the Capitol ; the streets are reddened with blood, and Lincoln and Scott are captives!"

It was a bright Sunday morning in May when this evil and astounding intelligence burst upon the quiet village. The great college chapel was crowded as it seldom was on that day of the week, but not to listen to prayer.

The grand old chancellor enters. There falls upon the stormy multitude a great silence. He opens the Bible on the desk. He closes it again. He strides up and down the long estrade, with his head drooped, as if unconscious of the very existence of Bible or of students. Then he suddenly stops, turns to his audience, and, gazing abstractedly far away over their heads, as if he beheld the bloody streets of Washington itself, says very slowly, as if dreaming :

"So, young gentlemen, some twenty millions of us are without a government to-day!"

Then he pauses many moments, slowly lifts his clinched right hand, and with a swift and strong gesture, and in a voice tremulous with emotion, but thrilling in the immense and audacious greatness of its energy, he exclaims:

"But I think we know how to find it, young gentlemen !"

Never since the swift and burning rhetoric of Peter the Hermit summoned fanatic Christians to the rescue of the Holy Sepulchre has human eloquence wrought more magically than did these words upon those impassioned young souls.   The effect was indescribable.   The smoky old chapel thundered to the echo.   The ardent young patriots rushed away to a mass-meeting, and the Sabbath quiet of the strict old Puritan town was profaned by the clangor of mustering regiments.

Hark ! I hear the tramp of thousands,
And of arméd men the hum ;
Lo ! a nation's hosts have gathered
Round the quick alarming drum—
Saying, ' Come,
Freemen, come !
Ere your heritage be wasted,' said the quick alarming drum.

All day the town echoed to the soul-stirring music of the clarion and of the "ear-piercing fife," the tumultuous surging of the thousands, and the rattle of rusty bayonets.   Five student companies were organized at once.   If the rumor had not been contradicted, Monday morning had seen the university depopulated.

The farmer's son wrote home for permission to enlist for actual service. He received the following reply :

"You are my only son, and I cannot consent. I shall contribute to the volunteer fund according to my means, and send a special substitute. If you enlist without my consent, I shall follow you up and join the same regiment."

Could any answer have stopped him more effectually? He had intended to enlist without permission, if he could not get it; but to think of his gray-haired father carrying a musket beside him !

Meantime, in a far-distant camp, Harry Baywood is in the full progress of the militia drill. A soldier in the ranks as yet, his experiences are amusing, if not peculiar. "Get into two rows, you fellers, and come out here end-ways, the way you did yesterday !" cries the good-natured drill-sergeant. They jumble, they jiggle, they hobble along higgledy-piggledy, in a kind of absurd Shaker dance, galling their kibes and decorticating their shins at a frightful rate. One gets his legs tangled together, and tumbles down in the middle. Harry fortified his ankles with a pair of heavy boots, and bided his time.

When at last the poor fellows, by their scanty preparation, had been rendered meet "food for powder," and were about to start for that terrible unknown region, the front, he was elected Lieutenant. Every day brought out his merits, and made him more beloved by his comrades. He was modest and frequently blundered in giving commands, but he was never too busy in his tent to listen patiently to the humblest of his comrades. When there was no tent, he slept on the ground among his men, and not aloof, as if he were an intelligence from another world. When the wagons were delayed, and there was no baggage, he might have been seen marching the livelong day cheerfully beside his column, with his sword across his shoulder, and at night dependent on one of his men for half of his blanket. He never threw out a soldier's tin cup to make room for his box of collars.

And now the farmer's son came home for his first annual vacation. Obedient to his promise, he laid aside his scholastic gown, and arrayed himself for the cornfield. To his infinite dismay, he met Jolie, for the first time in many months, while ignominiously attired in indigo-blue trousers, much too short, a farmer's hunting-shirt, and an immense chip-hat. He sidled awkwardly around, and prayed the earth to open under him; but Jolie was very gracious, and, in the kindness of her heart, noticed nothing. She even detained him, and conversed very cheerfully for a good while about the old school-days.

It is useless to deny that Sargent was greatly encouraged. He even "went to see Mr. Baywood." In fact, he presently became quite a frequent inmate of his fine old-fashioned parlor. About dusk on summer evenings he might be seen walking rapidly up the clean gravel walk, stepping very lightly, and looking sheepishly about, greatly distressed at the unusual and gratuitous loudness of the crunching in the gravel. In some mysterious manner unknown to him—for he had never dared mention such a thing—Jolie had become aware that the sight of a very little white apron was especially agreeable to his eyes, and she never failed to appear in that particular apron. Mr. and Mrs. Baywood, anxious to assure him, would remain a few moments in the parlor, monopolizing the conversation, then presently retire, to his immense consternation. He would be obliged to propose a resort to chess, that favorite refuge of bashful lovers.

O ye kindly cavalcade of kings, and queens, and knights, and bishops, in your snowy or sable robes,

He gasped out a quick breath, and felt he was almost going.

"I was just thinking—Jolie, I was about—there! did you hear that plunge? Somebody must have fallen over the guards."

He ran to the edge of the deck, and peered down into the dark, rushing waters. It was only a log, bumping along on the hull.

It began now to rain hard, and they therefore went below, and separated for the night, both of them well-nigh in despair. After all, he didn't say it. He didn't pop.

How the Lieutenant gets on in the army, meantime, may be learned from this letter to his old schoolmate:

"PEACHTREE CREEK, GEORGIA.

"MY DEAR OLD BOY,—I have lately got promoted to Captain, and I will narrate the whole matter to you in order. Our 'ridgi-ment' (as the Johnnies say) had been five days on the skirmish line; and, by one of those blunders which happen so often that the boys are about ready to knock off, when our supports were drawn back, we were not notified, and we were left hanging right down into the Confederacy. We were two whole days without a pinch of grub, and at last Colonel —— swore he would take the responsibility of ordering us to *tack*, in short, to fall back, to save our *bacon*, or—get some. Here again was a shameful blunder (I wouldn't blab thus of my superior officers to any one but you, for it is a great relief to be able to speak my mind freely once in awhile, where none of the boys can hear me—I think I fight better for it afterward),—it was a blunder, I say, for we ought to have fallen back under cover of the dark-ness. We were lying each in a pit about as large as a bath-tub, from the which we scrambled out, and ran pell-mell back to the first line of works where we could find any grub.

"My Captain was the only man hit, falling in a little hollow. He lay only a biscuit-toss from the works, but the interval was raked by a fire in which no man could live. He was not mortally hurt, and he could have come in, only he couldn't get on his pins. He was safe where he was, and he waved his arms piteously, begging for water. We flung him can-teen after canteen, but none of them reached him, and the rebel sharp-shooters spitefully bored them through and through, like hornets stinging some luckless enemy again and again.

blessed ministrations are yours! How often do ye pur-posely entangle yourselves together, so that the fingers which move you touch the fingers of the beloved, and are thrilled with a divine electricity! How conveniently stupid ye are, and how ingeniously absurd are the moves ye make, not to spoil her dear little silly game!

But as terms and vacations came and went, and Sargent never got any further along than chess-playing, he was in a profound despair. The neighborhood match-makers lost their patience. It threatened to be a courtship as in-terminable as that of poor Lilly Dale, who is dragged through two whole volumes, and remains an old maid after all.

One evening they were voyaging down the Ohio on a magnificent steamboat, and by some unexplained chance they found themselves sitting alone on the hurricane deck. Jolie was now ripened into a stately but languishing beauty, with pallid cheeks, rather long and grave in expression, hazel eyes, with a soft and pleading lustre, and pouting lips. She still cherished a hope that the farmer's son would, in some inspired and happy hour, so far soar above the clods of this dull world as to say something which she wished to hear, and to which she encouraged him by many a gracious and languishing smile.

Smooth and still the Beautiful River lay on either side, and far back behind they could see the graceful hair-line waves widen out from the steamboat's wake, chase each other across the patches of starlight, and fade silently away on the dark bosom of the river. How gracefully and how stately the stars lifted and then sunk, as the first wave rolled beneath them, then fell to rocking faster and faster, until at last they got to dancing at such an unseemly rate that they shock their little cheeks all to pieces! Right beneath them the mighty wheel, in its slow and laboring revolutions, clawed, and thumped, and mauled the waters in the darkness, until they glistened and whitened the black night.   It was a scene by no means poetical, except to a poetical soul, but the very swish and thudding of the waters conveniently tempered his voice, so that it did not 'frighten him as it usually did when he was alone with Jolie.

Suddenly there came to him a great and indomitable resolution to say it.

"Jolie,"—then he was seized with an unimaginable terror, and looked up into the sky,—"the stars are very bright to-night."

"Yes; do you see those double stars, one red and the other green?"   She pointed to them.

"Do you think they are really—I mean, why do you suppose one is red and the other green?" he said, with a gasp.

"Our old astronomy, I believe, says they are—what is it?—supplementary to each other.   Now, isn't that the word? You haven't any right to laugh at me if you won't correct me."

"I didn't laugh at you."   This was a highly gratuitous assertion on his part, though the lamentable grimace of distress which at that moment pervaded his countenance, if it could have been seen, would have moved the laughter of devils.

"That word means they are necessary to each other, doesn't it?"

"Jolie, I was going to say—yes, it means that,—necessary."   Then, by a prodigious effort of will, he ventured to take her hand, "Take care, my dear! upon my word, you will fall over on the wheel."

"Oh, I haven't the slightest fear of that so long as you hold my hand.   You were about to say something?"

She looked toward him with a sweet, inviting smile; he was looking the other way; so it was lost in the darkness, as so many others had been before.

A pause.

Just then a great shower of sparks came out of the flues, and floated in a long and splendid sheet above their heads.   It was as if ten thousand solar systems had been ground to powder and blown in red-hot dust athwart the heavens.

"Ah, that spark! let me brush it off."

After brushing it off, he was alarmed to find his arm almost encircling her neck, and he drew it away very quickly.

"Oh! I shall be burnt up here! I do believe there's another spark on my shoulder.   Pray do look!"

Shrugging her shoulders in a dear little panic to get away from a spark which didn't exist, she leaned quite against him.   He looked, but saw nothing.

Oh, you poor stupid Philistine!   Why, anybody could have put his arm round there then and found another spark.   But you couldn't!   Oh, fie!

A long pause.

It clouded over at last, and began slowly to rain. Sargent went below, and returned with an umbrella, which he spread, for he was not yet ready to abandon hope.

"I have often wondered," began Jolie, slowly and thoughtfully, but with volumes of hidden meaning in her tones, "I have often wondered how any one person could own an umbrella with a good conscience."

"Why so?"

"Why, hold it as one will, there is a great yawning void on one side, so suggestive.   One alone under an umbrella looks so selfish!"

"Then at last I called for volunteers, and we cut an enormous log, which we rolled ahead of us until we reached the Captain. But *revocare gradum*—that was the *opus*. However, after an hour's hard work, and after having been pelted by the rebels most unmercifully, we succeeded in getting back, and brought the Captain safely in. But, at the very last moment of success, just as we were lifting the poor fellow over the works, and when one of the boys was saying to him, 'Well, Cap, you're behind good wood now,' a rebel bullet pierced his heart.

"H. B."

Another vacation beheld Sargent at work on the farm again. He was revolving plans for the prosecution of his arduous enterprise beyond the limits of chess-playing. There came to him a happy inspiration. He would summon the assistance of the Muses; not his own, but those of the "bards sublime." He made a pretext of pressing agricultural business to visit the nearest bookstore, where he became the possessor of a dainty edition of Tennyson, in which he remembered a passage suitable to his needs. He hauled it triumphantly home in his four-horse wagon. He conveyed it joyfully into his chamber; and that evening he searched out the passage, marked it with a pencil, and inserted a book-mark in the place.

Now, it happened that the affairs of his father's household were administered by a good motherly aunt, who possessed, perhaps, more than the usual modicum of feminine curiosity. Next day she espied the book, was attracted by its gorgeous binding, and scarcely less by the book-mark, which she took out to admire. Then she naturally fell to reading cursorily, here and there a little, until she turned over several pages, and marked another passage which impressed her fancy. Suddenly recollecting that the dinner-hour was approaching, she whipped in the book-mark, as it happened, at the passage she marked, laid the book down, and went bustling away.

That evening Sargent carried the book with him, to

present it to the mistress of his bashful affections.   They played chess once more, and with a zest not at all impaired by the generous goblets of sound and mellow cider brought by the servant-girl.   Jolie played so well, indeed, that the book was entirely forgotten until he was going away.   Then he reached awkwardly round and extracted the volume from his coat-tail, and thrust it at her, mumbling some inarticulate words, and was at the bottom of the great stone steps before she could return thanks.

She tripped away up-stairs, half sadly, wondering if anything more would come of this present than of the numerous others; set the lamp down, looked admiringly at the book, the frontispiece, etc., and read a snatch or two.   Ah! a mark.   She hoped there might be a note. No—nothing whatever.   Ah, yes! a passage very dimly marked.   Her heart throbbed wildly while she read:

> " I have played with her when a child;
>   She remembers it now we meet.
>   Ah ! well, well, well, I may be beguiled
>   By some coquettish deceit.
>   Yet if she were not a cheat,
>   If Maud were all that she seemed,
>   And her smile had all that I dreamed,
>   Then the world were not so bitter
>   But a smile could make it sweet."

Jolie flung the book angrily on the sofa, and commenced pacing the floor.

" Well, I'm sure he needn't have given himself so much trouble to tell me that.   'A cheat,' indeed !   Oh, yes; Captain Hayes rode out with me once in his own carriage, to be sure ! To call me a 'cheat' for that ! So dim, too ! He didn't dare mark it plain."

Then she threw herself on the sofa again, buried her face in her hands, and wept bitter tears—not of anger now, but of sorrow. A long time she remained in this position, then arose, gathered together all his presents, and commenced, very slowly, very wearily, very sadly, making them into a package. Very long did she linger over this task, never hesitating in her steady purpose, but stopping often,—ah, how often!—because she could no longer see through her fast-falling tears. At last the sad work was done, but before it was finished the first faint gray streak of daylight straggled into her chamber window.

In the morning the servant-girl carried it to the farm-house, and Sargent being near by, plowing in the field, she carried it out, and gave it into his hands. Alas, alas! that it had not fallen under the eye of the motherly meddlesome aunt! He opened it with eager hands, wondering and glad, gazed at it transfixed, then sat down on the plow-beam, and rested his forehead on his hands in his voiceless grief. Long after the girl had crossed the last field and entered her mistress's door, he quietly dropped the package beside the plow, spoke to his horses, and one long smooth furrow hid it from his sight forever.

Upon receipt of the news that the Captain was wounded in battle, so dangerously that he could not be removed from the field-hospital, Jolie nobly rallied from her sick-bed and hastened to his side, while Sargent went away, as one who is dead to the world, to his classes.

We behold Jolie sitting now, sad and silent, by the pallet of leaves and branches where her brother catches his quick and painful breath. He is sleeping for the first time in many days. The long hospital-tent is crowded with the wounded and the dying, whose faces the wan glimmer of the candle lights up with the ghastly waxy pallor of death. The attendants move noiselessly to and fro, speaking in ghostly hollow whispers, most rasping to the lacerated nerves; they lave the burning foreheads; they smooth the dank and bloody locks of the dead. The hot and breathless stillness is broken only by feeble moans, where some gallant fellow, in his last agony, fights his battles again. He struggles in the frantic surging of the charge; he feels the cold bayonet plunging again toward his heart; he sees his brave comrades fall around him, and their hot blood spurt again across his face. They reel backward, broken and beaten down and trampled upon by ten thousand yelling demons, and a frown of despair settles upon his face. But now he sees the reinforcements; he feebly swings his arms; he cries out, "Steady, boys, steady! they are coming! they are coming!" But for him they come no more forever. The Angel of Death soars on his dark wing above him, and his pallid face is still.

Awakened by this noise, the Captain beheld his sister bending sleeplessly above him. He smiled, and feebly reached out his poor bloodless hand, already growing cold.

"Jolie dear," he whispered, "tell me now, before I die, what has passed between you and Sargent, that you are estranged?"

"Ah! my brother——" She covered her face with her hand, and buried it in his pillow.

"I did not think to give you pain, Jolie."

For a moment she made no reply; then, with a true woman's devotion and unselfishness, fearing lest, in his dying hour, her brother should think aught less of his beloved friend, she made a great effort, and said, very calmly, and in a voice scarcely above a whisper:

"It was I, Harry; believe me, he was not to blame."

The Captain made no answer, but turned his eyes upon

her in one long inquiring look, as if awaiting something more. She would have answered more, but he interposed,—

"Forgive me, dear Jolie. I only thought——"

She heard no more, for suddenly there burst upon the midnight stillness the crash of musketry, and the awful thunder of the cannonade. The moon had risen, and there was a night attack. The Union troops, taken by surprise, reel back, broken and panic-stricken; the forest is filled with the fleeing and disorderly multitude; the hoarse roaring of the battle and the exultant yells of the pursuers mingle with the cries of the wounded and dying. That most heart-sickening noise of battle, the hellish blurt and howling of ragged shells, swashes with a fierce rattle through the forest. The pursuers are coming on amain. All the hospital attendants have fled or hidden. Jolie sits alone, speechless with terror, holding the still hand. The glazing eyes of the dying soldier gleam for a moment with the old light of battle. He beholds his regimental flag once more brightly flaunt above the bayonets; she feels the stiffening hand feebly clutch her own for his sword.

A single bullet, wandering far and spent through the rushing multitude, plunges through the tent. Another and another. Shall they be all in vain? Shall they not have a fair prize? This one bursts one canvas wall, but not the other. What! Jolie? Ah! Jolie! She droops— she falls! Her head lies on his pillow. She has even gone before him.

In reply to the letter which bore these double tidings of death, Sargent wrote to his sister:

"He has given his life gloriously to his country, while I live here in ignominious ease. I cannot blame our father for opposing the enlistment of his only son; but mother, dear mother, if you look down to-night from your blissful abode upon your useless and unhonored boy, you would rather see him lying on the battle-field than living here. Ah, Jolie! by some evil and inexplicable fate thou hast robbed me already once, and now this time yet again. Would that to-night I could dispute thy privilege, and sleep beside him, low in the quiet grave! His tomb should be chiseled with a wreath of laurel, but mine should be wholly blank, and it might thus, perchance, add to the honor of his.

> "'O Death, Death, Death, thou ever-floating cloud!
>   There are enough unhappy on this earth;
>   Pass by the happy souls that love to live!
>   I pray thee, pass before my light of life,
>   And shadow all my soul, that I may die!'

"O that I had gone out with my beloved comrade, and been in the front of battle, that I might sleep now beside him in the quiet grave! Then, perhaps, some one on earth, sitting alone at evening, would miss me now, and drop a tear to my memory, and whisper softly, ' But he died for his country.' "

SAN ANTONE.

THAT was the name by which he was generally known in camp. He was richly endowed with the agnomens of a rude inchoate heraldry, but this was the most convenient. Besides these was his real name; but that was German, and few had ever heard it, and fewer still could pronounce it within a half-dozen consonants of correctness. Another appellation he had was "Marine Sheeps," which accrued to him from his comical mispronunciation of the name of a certain valuable breed of wool-producing animals.

When the train was assembling and organizing on the prairies of Texas, preparing to cross the continent, and everybody was eliciting, a fragment at a time, the history of everybody else with whom he was destined to spend several months, this man was distinguished among the keen, gray-eyed, quizzing Texans by his glum seclusiveness, and he contemptuously told the loquacious little Doctor that his name was San Antonio (which became abbreviated as above), as if he took a kind of savage satisfaction in being despised as a "Greaser" by a man whom he so thoroughly despised himself. He seemed to say:

> "Scorned, to be scorned by one that I scorn—
> Is that a matter to make me fret?"

He had lived so long near San Antonio, Texas, that the flaming sun of Mexico had burned his Teutonic skin into the color of a bilious *mestiño*, so that the deception was easy; and as for the little old-young Doctor, San Antone despised him from the outset to the utmost of his immeasurable capacity for contempt.

The first time I saw this strange and terrible man, the impression he produced upon me was sufficiently vivid. The train was to leave Waxahatchie the next day, and I accordingly carried out my roll of blankets, etc., and deposited them in the mess-wagon. Beside a feeble fire near the tent crouched a man, clad in whitish-gray, slouching clothes, and a dingy-white hat, which lopped down all around, giving his eyes a kind of sinister glare. He was of a medium height, rather spare-faced, but with a body powerfully built and knit together with mighty muscles, though he had lived so much in camps that he had become extremely round-shouldered. He had the Teutonic roundness of head, but his large occiput and strong emphatic nose showed—if physiognomy be any guide—that he was not an inherently malicious man, terrible though he looked. Yet there was something in his great bloodshot eyes at times which was absolutely awful. When he was enraged—as Germans, unfortunately, become sometimes—they glared out from their cavernous sockets with a blood-curdling ferocity which made a peaceable man quite satisfied with a single glance. Add to this his haggled and matted hair, projecting from the top of his hat; his complexion, which was about an equal compound of an olive-green and a coffee-color; and his Herculean muscles, which rounded broadly out on his back, as he sat doubled almost into a half-circle, and you have a man whom most people would be disposed to let assiduously alone.

Yet he returned my salutation in a tone of voice so pleasant that I was surprised. He set off his frying-pan, brought out some biscuits and coffee from the tent, and we ate together, squatting on the ground.

"You are to cross the continent with us, I suppose?" I remarked in my most winning manner.

"Yes," said he, making a beef sandwich for himself. "Are you de man what walks afoot?"

"Yes."

"It is very much deestance to walk," he said, quite indifferently.

I looked sharply at him, for I thought his accent was anything but Mexican.

"*Sie sprechen Deutsch vielleicht?*" I ventured to remark.

"I was German born, only in Texas. I speak also German, but better English."

He was the first and only German I ever saw in America who did not gladly respond to the invitation to speak in his mother tongue. It appeared upon subsequent inquiry that he was the son of a wealthy stock-farmer in Western Texas, who had been well educated in the Fatherland, both in English and French, but had wandered to the New World, and found something congenial in Texan frontier savagery; and that this was a kind of black sheep in the flock, the only discontented one, and yet the best-beloved of his sons. He was ignorant, as he acknowledged with regret, because he had always played truant from his father's own school; and he had, by consequence, passed through some fearful experiences in the Yellow Jack hospitals, and in the Rebel army, wherein he had served as a battery soldier. He was, therefore, no mean and beggarly ruffian, but the prospective heir of broad acres and a patriarchal wealth of cattle, and he had a most savage contempt for small moneys and small economies. Yet he was fierce and uncouth enough, to be sure, to have been a Rio Grande bandit.

Probably I did not learn even these few particulars at first, for I speedily lost caste with San Antone, because he thought I was "citified." Yet I never fell quite so low in his estimation as did the little Doctor.

The fellow could swear some of the most appalling oaths, in which an Americanized German probably excels any of our native citizens; but, with all his amazing affluence of cursing, he never could invent any expression which would, in the slightest degree whatsoever, do justice to his disdain for that effeminate individual. He would sit cross-legged by the fire, cooking breakfast, and watch him dip the palms of his long apelike hands into water and pass them daintily over his face, and then he would simply ejaculate, "Humph!" He could no more. Shade of Diogenes! the unspeakable riches of scorn concentrated into that single grunt. To the last morning of our four-months' journey he would feast his fascinated eyes on that spectacle, and let his soul fatten on these pastures of contempt. He loved to live to despise the little Doctor's face-washing.

He exercised a most terrific stepmotherly tyranny over the unhappy Doctor, in divers fashions. The Doctor was a sluggard in the morning, and San Antone, after waiting the shortest possible allowance of time after *reveille*, would strip the blankets off him with violence. We lived with Spartan simplicity in our mess, having only one tin cup apiece; and if sometimes the Doctor took two, unnecessarily, our ferocious stepmother would snatch one out of his hand and put it away. This would have been simply outrageous with any other person, but the Doctor was lazy, effeminate, cowardly, and insincere; and San Antone did all this with such thoroughly straightforward and incorruptible honesty of contempt, and with such absence of any symptom of a smile on his face, that the rest of us were only amused.

Being obliged to be much with this terrific Agonistes, walking along with the train, I studied to be as barbarous as possible. I praised his cookery, which was, in fact, very good for a camp-cook, except that he would fry his steaks Southern fashion, in grease. Consequently he never vented upon me any of those outrageous indignities which he heaped upon the head of the hapless Doctor.

He displayed the most amazing energy and strength in his wrestles with the diabolical oxen of Texas. He would ride on horseback after a full-grown wild ox, lasso its forefeet, jerk it headlong to the ground, then dismount and tie it head and foot. Then he would ride down another, capture it in the same manner, hitch the rope to the pommel of his saddle and fetch it to the other, when he would, single-handed and alone on the open prairie, yoke the furious brutes together and bring them triumphantly to the corral. It was an achievement worthy of Hercules himself, and would appear quite incredible to anybody not acquainted with Texas.

Nearly every morning, especially when we had rested awhile, they had to inclose the accursed never-tamed brutes in the circle of wagons, where they would surge up and down, putting all the women and children and half the drivers to flight. But San Antone would seize the hugest ox by the horn and nostril, double his neck together, and fling him upon the ground. Sometimes we would see him in the middle of a dreadful tangle of oxen, wrestling with the hellish beasts, justling among their long shining horns, or slung around with his heels high up in the atmosphere.

I took pains to applaud him for these feats, but he appeared to care nothing about it, one way or the other. He was something more sensitive as to his cookery, and I lay the flattering unction to my soul that I produced some impression in that direction.

I began really to admire the man for his hearty and brawny savagery, and for the ferocious contempt which he manifested toward all shams and make-believes and half-hearted doings.

One thing which was especially admirable in him was his kindness toward his oxen, which stood out in noble contrast with the infamous brutalities of many Texans. He never would make the least provision for his own comfort until they had been driven to the best water and the best grazing anywhere to be found. Once only, during a long and exasperating march by day and night across the terrible Llanos Estacados, he lost his temper, snatched up a great chain, and swung it with his powerful arm like a whip-lash. Fortunately for the offending oxen, they saw it in time to leap aside, and the chain descended upon a box, smashing it into a hundred splinters. He did not spare the lash in critical places, but one strong swift blow, with the magnetism there was in his terrible voice, was worth hours of the infamous dead mauling of the miserable brigands with the other teams, who had in them no soul of power.

But as soon as they were up the hill, he would go and lean against them, put his arms around their necks—I have seen him do this a hundred times—and caress them like children. His leaders, a pair of little spotted monkeys, he almost idolized. He would go out from camp on the darkest night, and grope all about with his hands, to find whether they had any grass. On moonlight nights or in the daytime he would stand and wag his head at them, and laugh, and call them by name, and they would look up with their large mild eyes, and wink quiet winks at him, as if to say, "You're a pretty good fellow—you are !" The consequence of all this was, that he never killed an ox, while other drivers sacrificed whole teams. These things covered a multitude of his outrageous rudenesses.

San Antone began to be an exceedingly interesting study to me, as showing how completely German servility of politeness could, in a single generation, be converted into the savagest and the sturdiest of Texan frontier barbarism. Is it Landor who attributes to Benjamin Franklin the remark that a people never grow younger in crossing the ocean? But it is not true of the Germans coming to America. They do grow younger.

The other members of our mess were always occupied with the herds; and through weary days, weeks, and months, while we crawled on our slow march across the mighty plains, this rude ox-driver was my most frequent companion. What was most singular in him was, that he avoided his own countrymen. Who ever saw a German, I wonder, that did not prefer the congregation of them that are faithful to the mug, to all the tents of the beer-scoffers? But San Antone not only would not speak German, but he studiously secreted from any Cousin Michael we might meet his knowledge of the grand old jargon, and was angry if any American imparted that information to him.

And now at last his demeanor toward me began very perceptibly to soften. When, weary of vagabondizing or botanizing on the short incursions I dared make into

Comanche or Apache land, I would fall back to saunter along with the train, he would jump down from his wagon and seek to make himself sociable. He began to be my friend, in his uncouth and boisterous way, and to make me his confidant. Thereat I wondered. I had done no valorous or great thing, I had tamed no ox, I had ridden no "bucking" mustang, that I should be illustrious in his eyes. Why this change?

He seemed to be poising over the edge of some terrible revelation he wished to make; and yet he was still uncertain of me, and he would sometimes gaze at me with one long and hungry look, as if he wished to penetrate my heart of hearts. While we strolled along beside his oxen, swinging on in their slow, ponderous gait, he would talk in a monologue for half an hour, in a kind of smiling, childish, German way, telling me the story of his life, which was, like that of most Germans,—so far as disastrous chances and moving accidents by flood and field are concerned,—as insipid and colorless as can well be imagined. Thus would he talk on, and talk on, and on, until he seemed suddenly to draw near some frightful precipice, some hideous chasm in his memory wherein lay a ghastly secret, when he would shrink back appalled and horrified, glare at me to see if I had divined his soul, and then retreat into himself and become gloomy and morose.

On all sides, around and around, he had passed this hideous secret of his life, leading me to the very verge, as if to point it out, then shrinking back with a shudder, and with a strange fierceness which scared me. It seemed as if, having conducted me almost to this dreaded and mysterious revelation, he were about to slay me for having it in my possession.

Ever and again he returned, as if lured by some frightful fascination, and circled round and round this awful mystery, until at last the dreaded secret would out; with a sudden and almost frenzied movement he stretched out his arm, snatched away the curtain, and, with a livid, deathly face and a quivering finger, pointed out to me a ghastly corpse!

A murderer!

I stared at him with a feeling of unfeigned loathing and repugnance I could not conceal. But he, as if he would destroy me, now that the fatal secret was in my possession, turned upon me in an instant such an awful glare of those blood-shot eyes as made my blood freeze. In a moment I penetrated his thought:

"Your unaccustomed kindness has bewitched me, until I have made an abject fool of myself, licked the dust to you for sympathy, and absolutely put my life in your possession. Will you now turn, and put your heel on me, like everybody else?"

Then it was that there seemed to me, for the first time in all my experience, to be some meaning in that phrase of Thomson's, "fierce repentance." By every possible means I endeavored to conceal my natural dislike, and make him understand I was not his enemy. But he remained for a long time gloomy and sullen, and I heard him sometimes imprecate the most awful doom upon himself, so terrible and so bitter was his remorse. Simple-minded as he was, he seemed to be astute enough to suspect that I might be smoothing matters over merely out of complaisance. It took me many days to regain his confidence. He was not a cold-blooded assassin, and had only committed the deed in a moment of frenzied anger; but he had that strange capacity for self-torture and remorse which appears to be characteristic of the German nature, and which, as illustrated in the character of Rigolette in the "Mysteries of Paris," is more Teutonic than Gallic.

But gradually his confidence was restored, and, as it returned, his gratitude became unbounded. To me it was a most interesting and piteous spectacle to witness the struggles of that grim and savage nature to find means for expressing his grateful feeling, without making himself obnoxious to me or the butt of ridicule to the brutal souls about him. Knowing my eagerness to learn the botany of the country, he would make wide explorations through the perilous *chaparral* about camp, and bring me rare specimens, carefully secreted in his coat lest he should make himself ridiculous to the herdsmen. He would urge me to walk out, and then he would, of his own motion, scale the most precipitous and dreadful cliffs to bring me mineral contributions. He exhausted all his little stock of knowledge to tell me the popular names of flowers. Once he came to camp and conducted me, almost with the triumph and elation of a little child, to see a curious clump of cactus; and when I did nqt utter as many exclamations of wonder as he had expected, he was sadly disappointed.

When we were recruiting in camp, he would hasten to finish his kitchen business, and then come and crawl into the tent with the utmost quietness, when I was writing, and stretch himself close beside my desk, where he would lie for hours together, with a doglike patience and fidelity, waiting for me to finish, that he might talk again.

One day, after our larder had become exceedingly skinny, and even boiled dried apples were an extravagance of Sybaritic luxury which we scarcely hoped ever to indulge in again, the cook of a neighboring mess boiled some of that luxurious fruit, and brought over a cupful to his brother potwolloper. As soon as he was gone, San Antone brought the boiled dried apples into the tent where I was writing, and not a mouthful would the poor fellow touch until he had compelled me to masticate a considerable portion. I confess this simple little act touched me deeply.

When we were sitting around our bivouac-fire with the other members of the mess, he was, if possible, more savagely boisterous in his conduct than ever; but the moment he was alone with me, his voice became as soft, and his manner as gentle, as a woman's. What fascination had I acquired over this strange and terrible nature? It was a wonder to myself.

It was in Apache Pass, that gloomy and horrible pit, most darkly infamous in the bloody history of Arizona, where San Antone's great powers were fully brought to the test, and where he displayed the most fierce and amazing energy that is possible to any human being. Nearly all the wagons had to be drawn up with doubled teams, but there was one unwieldy monster which eighteen great oxen of Texas failed to take up the mountain. About a score of imbeciles had collected around them, mauling, and cursing, and yelling, and swinging their arms, and jumping up and down like a number of crippled grasshoppers. The poor brutes were lacerated and terrified; but there was no soul in all those drivers which had in it any magnetism of power.

Then everybody called for San Antone. He was reluctant to undertake the Herculean task, but night was coming on rapidly in that great horror of blackness and massacre; nobody knew but the bloodshot eyes of the Apaches already glared down upon us from the racked and battered crags, waiting for nightfall and vengeance; the women and children were crying with terror, as night came on ; and there was no other man in the train, no score of them together, who could take that wagon up the mountain.

So he finally consented, and came down into the ravine with his great whip, nearly twenty feet long. With the savage brusqueness of his nature, he ordered every man to stand aside. He fetches his long lash round and round, ending with a crack which leaps among the lofty mountains like the roar of a rifle; and all the yelling and fluttering fools fall back in silence, like an awe-stricken mob. Every voice of crying woman or of whooping teamster is hushed, that they may witness the mighty struggle.

He speaks one strong word. The oxen know their master. They bow their great crooked knees to the ground. The very mountain seems to tremble. The wagon moves. Then comes peal after peal of cracks, like a rattling volley of musketry; but above all rises that deep, terrible voice. The oxen fall—they rise again —they sway and surge—they crawl on bended knees— their eyes start from their sockets—they falter—they stagger slowly backward. A moment more, and they will be dashed over the precipice! His calm is gone; he becomes like a fiend; he seems in all places at every moment; the mere terror of his voice and the rage of his presence appall them. His one fierce will leaps into all those huge bodies, and quivers along all those mighty muscles. They recover—they move upward—they are saved!

A great and multitudinous clamor of applause bursts from the whole train. Ah! how we worship power, in whatever shape it is manifested!

I stood alone on a hill to witness this triumph of human will over brute force, and I confess I never felt more exultant enthusiasm in witnessing the most fearful and splendid bursts of heaven's artillery on the prairies of

Texas. Such was the amazing energy of that man's presence ! The few stinging lashes he gave his oxen were not for a moment to be compared with the infamous, brutal, dead mauling of the imbeciles. As soon as he reached the top of the ascent, he walked modestly away to his own oxen—an unconscious hero, worthy to be ranked with Wordsworth's Benjamin. With that worthy, he could well say to his oxen :

> " Yes, without me, up hills so high
> 'Tis vain to strive for mastery.''

But I think Wordsworth never saw, for a prototype of his Benjamin, a man so grand in his rude and unconscious simplicity. Xenophon, in the " Cyropædia," draws a pretty comparison between the horseman and the statesman ; and I think there was in San Antone the making of a better *conduttore* of states than in many a politician.

From Apache Pass to Tucson the journey was soon accomplished. Several times I had declared my intention of leaving the intolerably sluggish train at that city, to venture on alone and more rapidly, across the desert swept by the cruel and treacherous Tonto Apaches, to the Gila, where I should be safe in the Pima villages. The other members of the mess made demonstrative and wordy remonstrances, and tried to dissuade me from an undertaking which they could only consider downright foolhardiness ; but whenever the subject was mentioned, San Antone would say nothing whatever. If I spoke of it when we were alone, his voice would lower in an instant, and his single pleading glance and the few subdued words he would utter were more eloquent than ten thousand wordy protestations of the others.

It was a touching thing to witness, the mute, uncouth

pleadings of this savage nature—so all unused to pleading and so unwonted to any atmosphere of sympathetic kindliness—to detain me yet a little longer. So precious to him seemed to be the few kind words I had spoken, and yet so awkward was it for this untamed boisterousness to use the gentle arts of persuasion. He appeared to study how to make his manner more courteous and softened.

When he came to awaken me in the morning, he would turn down a little corner of the blanket with a touch as gentle as a babe's, then speak hardly above a whisper, and greet my opening eyes with a smile. Sometimes I feigned to be in a deep and refreshing slumber, and would watch him with one half-opened eye. He would come up softly on tip-toe, and stand looking at me, then stoop down and sit motionless beside me for a long time, as if he could hardly persuade himself to disturb me at all;— so wonderfully tender and gentle had a little kindness rendered this broken-hearted murderer, who toward others, in the bitterness of his despair, was so ferocious!

And now, after we had recruited and refreshed ourselves awhile near Tucson, the appointed time was near at hand when we were to separate. Many and many a pleasant summer day, through perils manifold and deadly, we had journeyed together across the great globe, and now the approaching hour of parting was one of unfeigned sadness. San Antone was oppressed and gloomy even more than ordinarily, and, but for his obligation to his employer in this hour when so many worthless hirelings, disgusted and appalled with the journey, were deserting and leaving the train-owners in desperate need, he protested he would keep me company. He saw I was in first-rate earnest in my purpose, but he tried to convince me I knew nothing of the infernal Apaches as he did; and he would have gone along for what I believe he would have counted the privilege of fighting for me, if matters came to a pinch. But his noble sentiment of duty to his employer, our well-beloved Tom, in this time of dastardly desertions, restrained him.

There was a Mexican *fandango* in Tucson one evening, which several of our mess visited out of curiosity, San Antone among the number. But he was gloomy and sad, amid the obstreperous gayety, keeping near me all the while with a doglike faithfulness. He was so unusually melancholy with the remorse he could not shake off, that he seemed to dread lest he should be provoked into some deed of violence.

The wild and riotous dancing went on almost without interruption, to the soft, voluptuous tinkle of the light guitar, until late in the night. It was a long, low, stone-floored room, with benches around the sides, dimly lighted with tallow dips, which cast a sickly yellow glare around, gleaming now and then on the polished pistol-butts, and turning the creamy complexions of the gaudily-dressed Mexican girls to the ghastly waxiness of a corpse. Occasionally the couples retired for refreshments into a contiguous room, half grocery, half groggery, where men and maidens partook together of candy, villainous wine, or more villainous *mescal.*

Among the dancers there was one particularly low-browed villain of a *peon,* short in stature, and almost as dark-skinned as a negro. He wore a United States army coat, dungaree trousers, and carried two revolvers and a murderous-looking snickersnee in his girdle. He was flushed and wild from frequent potations of the fiery *mescal,* and whenever one of the hated Americans joined in the dance, he scowled fiercely. He was said to have had a bloody affray with one recently, and he was only waiting for an opportunity to wreak a cowardly, vicarious revenge on the first one of the meddlesome race who might cross his pathway.

According to the usual custom of these rude orgies, whenever a man wished to invite a partner for the dance, he had only to advance into the middle of the floor and beckon to her, no matter how limited might be his acquaintance. She would accept or decline without further ceremony.

Few Americans, and none of our mess, joined in the barbarous revels, for all the Mexicans were jealous. At length, just as we were about to go home to camp, this *peon* came out with a partner from the dance-room, half staggered up to the counter, violently slapped the same with his hand, and demanded more candy and *mescal.* They both drank, and then started to return. I happened to be standing near them, and stepped away to avoid coming in collision with the fellow. The space was narrow among the barley-sacks and the barrels, and it so fell out that I stepped on the trailing dress of his partner. She turned about and gave me an angry glance. I said, *"Perdon, señorita!"* and bowed an apology. But the cramped position I was standing in caused it to appear, probably, that I was soliciting her company for the next waltz.

The *peon* heard my words, turned and saw me bowing, saw that the woman was giving her attention to me, and, not knowing the real cause, evidently supposed I was about to interfere and entice away his partner. This was his opportunity. In an instant, and without a word, he drew his revolver and made a lunge.

San Antone was standing on the other side of the heap of barley-sacks which prevented me from escaping, and had seen and heard everything, for the faithful fellow had scarcely let his eyes wander from me for a moment. With the agility of a tiger he vaulted over the barley-heap, knocking over a Mexican, who in turn stumbled against and threw down the unfortunate girl. He could not possibly reach the *peon* before he fired. He saw it; he saw all in an instant; with one sweep of his powerful arm he thrust me behind him as if I had been a child.

The deadly report of the pistol crashed in the close, stifling room. There was no echo in the reeking air, but a dull, deep thud, followed by a moment of awful silence. Then came a low moan from poor San Antone, and he slowly staggered backward against me, and fell to the floor. The proud soul of the man, though he was stricken unto death, yet disdained to fall prone before the base Mexican, and he convulsively clutched a barley-sack, but dragged it over on him, as he fell.

The Mexican was instantly seized.

We carried San Antone out into the cool, sweet air, and laid him gently down where the bright moon and the stars looked down upon him in pitying tenderness from heaven—that calm, grand face of Nature, so soothing, and so full of the sadness of an infinite compassion. The life of his life was swiftly throbbing away in a great crimson current. But after that first low moan of mortal agony, he disdained to utter a complaint. Some brandy was hastily brought, and I knelt down beside him.

"San Antone, my brave fellow, do you remember the dried apples? Can you taste a little of this?"

He looked at me, and tried to smile. He remembered. Then he thought of his little spotted monkeys, his leaders, around whose necks he had so often put his arms and caressed them, after they had tugged hard up the hill. He feebly whispered:

"Don't let them kill my little Spot and Ball. My poor little monkeys!"

I bowed down my head over this dying murderer, who had given his life for mine, and my tears fell thick and fast. He thought not of himself. He thought of his "little monkeys." They had been kinder to him than his fellows. No more, in the bitter, bitter despair of his remorse, should he go out, and, looking in their large, mild eyes, find that kindliness he had sought in vain among men.

He lingered but a little while. His mind wandered away in a delirium. Seeing his lips move, I bent down and caught these words, muttered in his mother tongue:

"*Dort ist Ruhe.*"

"Yonder is rest."

Was he thinking of his far-off home in Texas? or were his thoughts at that moment following his fast-glazing eyes, and roving among the stars?

There came a sharp, quick shudder, and San Antone was dead.

PIMO LEGEND OF MONTEZUMA.

LONGFELLOW.

IT was when the Casa Grande still lifted up its mud-built walls beside the waters of the sacred Gila. It was when the seven cities of Cibola were still full of warriors, strong to twank the arrow, and of the glories and the riches of many wars, turquoises, and emeralds, and many precious stones, with jewels of copper, and knives of obsidian. All their streets and market-places were still full of spinning-women ; and these had gourds, and earthen vessels, and plenty of maize and of melons, beans of *mesquite*, and painted cloths of *manta*.

Far toward the rising Sun, a great king ruled without dispute over mighty plains and sandy heaths, smooth and wearisome, and bare of wood, covered all over with herds of crook-backed oxen, swift and fierce. Toward the setting Sun, beyond the great Colorado, King Tartarrax ruled over the pleasant and sunny land of Quivera, with yellow valleys, and purple hills full of gold. The Colorado still rolled down his wide waters to the sea, unvexed by any keel of the Palefaces ; and the banks of our own river were still untrodden by any of their destroying bands of braves, or of their ancient and black-robed Fathers,

(261)

who came to take away peace forever from our sacred country, Aztlan.

It was when our strong young braves still wooed their dark-eyed maidens, and walked in purity beneath the shadow of the cottonwoods, naked, and were not ashamed; before the unclean and guilty Paleface had taught them to covet those blood-colored garments which are abominable unto mine eyes. All yet was peace, sweet peace, within the borders of our sacred country, Aztlan; but our young braves triumphed over all her enemies round about, and the Moquis brought us tribute of wolf-skins, and the terrible Apaches humbly bought our maize for the gold of their mountains. We drank the blood of the savage Yumas, and braided their long hair into bow-strings; and there was no deceitful Paleface to interfere. There was then no murrain in our flocks, no blight or mildew in our fields, and no fire-water in our wigwams. Our women were pure yet from the hated touch of the Paleface, and our papooses toddled in and out our doors, with faces clear of those horrible cankers which they bear now for the sins of their fallen mothers.

When you stand with your face toward the rising Sun, and point with your right hand, far off in that direction ruled our Great Father, Montezuma, in his city Tenochtitlan, over all the land from the sunrise- to the sunsetwaters. We had silver like rice, and gold like heaps of yellow corn, brought from the land beyond the Colorado, the land of Quivera; but we gladly gave it all to our Great Father.

In those days there came to our fathers a story, floating on the wind, that a band of the braves of the Palefaces, with certain of their ancient and black-robed Fathers, were coming from the city of our Great Father, to visit sacred Aztlan. And the hearts of our fathers were filled

with joy; and they were moved to propose a feast of welcome to those who were coming so great a distance to
visit them.   Our chief and all the young chiefs assembled
together, that they might devise how best to give them
welcome.

And, before many days, there came one of the Pimos,
running and catching his breath, and said the Palefaces
were coming.   There was a little company of braves,
bearing muskets and lances; and they came with great
pomp, and many horses, and strange and wonderful music
of silver reeds, and having upon their heads coverings, as
it were, of rubbed and shining gold.   Before them rode
their chief, with a great knife, long and dazzling, and his
horse wheeled this way and that way; and behind, sitting
upon asses, were the ancient and black-robed Fathers,
who bore crosses of mahogany wood, and chanted with
loud voices.

Then our chief and all the young chiefs made haste,
and went out to welcome the Palefaces.   They gave them
water to drink in gourds, and ripe pears of the cactus,
blood-hearted, and very cool to the traveler.   They also
brought them to sit under shady arbors, and gave them
whatever things else, either pleasant to eat or to drink,
were in their village; for our fathers rejoiced greatly at
their coming.   And the Palefaces ate, and drank, and
talked with them.   Last of all our chief talked with one
of the black-robed Fathers, but his words were interpreted
by another.   Yet they spake not well together, but were
of different minds.   And it came about that the black-
robed Father said to our chief:

"Dost thou believe on God?"

"Yea, my brother," said our chief; "we believe in
God, even the Great Spirit, from whom we have our
spirits, and our sacred country, Aztlan."

"But thy god is a heathen god, and we account him less than nothing, and as a delusion and a snare."

"We know not, brother, if he be a heathen god, nor yet what heathen may be. We only know he is very kind unto us, and gave us our Great Mother, Aztlan, to nourish us, and all these shady trees, and the sacred Gila for water."

"But thy god cannot save thy soul from hell when thou diest."

"Tell me, what is hell, brother? Our prophets and medicine-men have spoken nothing of it at any time. Hell may have terrors for the Paleface, if his God made it; but, for the Pimo, none. If thy God be not able to save all from hell, but only a portion, as thou sayest, then Aztitli pities the Paleface.

"We believe that every Pimo, when he dies, is carried to the banks of the great and rapid Colorado; and that the spirit of every brave then takes up its habitation in some green and mighty tree which waves upon his banks, or stands upon the lofty mountains which he washes. The spirit of every squaw is carried into one of the clouds, those silvery, golden, and rosy clouds thou seest yonder. He who was bravest in this life, and slew fierce and many enemies, shall dwell in the loftiest tree, which waves in the sweet air the Great Spirit hath made, and lifts up its head proudly toward the Sun, and holds converse with the spirits of the clouds that settle round his head. But he whose soul was base, and whose life was a shame, shall inhabit the lowest tree, which dwells down in perpetual darkness and dampness, never beholding the Sun, or the golden clouds, or the sweet light of heaven. The clouds shall never settle fondly round his head."

"Ah, vain and babbling Pagan! What can all these thy wicked and idle imaginings avail thee against an offended and consuming God? Fall down humbly upon thy knees, and beseech the Holy Virgin, Mother of God, to intercede with her Son for thee, that the abounding efficacy of his death upon the cross may be applied to save thee from the wrath to come."

"Nay, my brother, hear me yet. Is not the Great Spirit very good toward the Pimos? Thou hast not shown me that thy God is any better. When our squaws cast seed into the ground, behold, does it not sprout? Does the sacred Gila ever forget his appointed floods? Does not our maize blossom in our fields, and bring milk in the husk, and after that the yellow ear? When have our squaws been stricken down in time of harvest, or given up their lives to black death upon their childbeds? Does not the Sun shine gloriously here, as in the country whence thou comest? And, indeed, I know not whether the same Sun shines upon thy fields, or whether thou hast any Sun; else wouldst thou be of a stronger color. Thou seemest to me altogether bloodless, and as a plant growing beneath a tree."

When he did not, therefore, bow himself before the cross, but rather stood up the more stiffly, and did not humble his neck, the black-robed Father drew near, and smote him with his hand full upon the forehead.

"Thou infidel dog!" cried he, "thy god has not even a name, nor yet any habitation; and thou darest set him above the Holy Virgin and the Almighty Maker of heaven and earth!"

Then there arose a great uproar in the village, and the young braves of the Pimos would have slain the braves of the Palefaces, and not left one of them remaining upon the earth. But the thing which the black-robed Father had done was displeasing to the chief of the Palefaces, and he rebuked him, and appeased the Pimos, and there was peace again in the village.

After that the band of the Palefaces visited all the lands of sacred Aztlan, and were well pleased with them, and remained many days. Many feasts did they eat, feasts of cakes of maize, with calabashes of yellow whey, and fat beans of *mesquite*, and rich, roasted bulbs of *mescal*, with curds, and gourds of *pinole*, sweet and good with sugar of maguey, and gourds of *pulque*, and blood-hearted pears of the cactus.   And the dark-eyed daughters of the Pimos ministered unto them, and brought them clay to anoint their heads, and mats, and they 'danced before them.

Now, it came about that a maiden of the Pimos loved a young brave of the Palefaces, and was loved by him again.   But the laws of the Pimos, in those days, guarded their women straitly, that they should not be given in marriage to strangers; and the maiden sighed within her for the love she had to the Paleface, but she dared not make it known to her tribe.   But when she could no longer conceal how it was with her, the Palefaces had already gone three days' march from sacred Aztlan. Then they used upon her all the awful tortures wherewith the Pimos of old were wont to punish a woman guilty of adultery, and commanded her to give the name of her betrayer; but when she continually refused, the tortures were made double, and again double, until the breath went out from her body; but she uttered never a word nor cried aloud.   But when the babe was ripped from the womb, the doer of this horrible deceit was discovered.

Then straightway a band of young braves, led by the maiden's brother, went forth with all haste, and, at the end of the second day, they came to the camp of the Palefaces. When they demanded the man, at first the chief of the band refused to send him forth; but when he saw that the Pimos were more numerous than they, and were greatly more fierce in their countenances than was their wont, he consented, and yielded up the seducer.

Then it came about, when they were even commencing their tortures upon him, that there came a strong and swift rushing, like that of a mighty wind from the desert; and there appeared unto the Pimos a glorious and fearful figure, shining as an angel from heaven, that stopped and stood still above the sacred Gila. Yet was he not young, like an angel, but ancient, and his hair was long upon his shoulders, and sad was his visage. Upon his head there was a *panache* of green plumes, and his robe glittered with emeralds and *chalchivitl*, and was bound with a golden girdle, and the soles of his sandals were as of burnished gold. Then this figure stood, and lifted his hand slowly toward the setting Sun, and began to speak unto the Pimos; and at the sound of his words, the souls of the Pimos became as water for terror, and they fell upon their faces to the ground:

"O Pimos! O my children! I am your Great Father, Montezuma. Lift not up your hands to slay the Paleface.

"Even now I ascend up from the city of my people, the great city Tenochtitlan, unto the bosom of the Sun.* Into this, the city of my people, are the Palefaces come, and rule in it supreme; and the ancient monarchy of the Nahuatlecas, the kingdom of the Seven Peoples, is forever overthrown. At the first, I prayed with strong crying and agony unto our great god, Mexitli, the God of

---

* The reader of Aztec history will detect the anachronisms of the legend.

Battles, for mine armies, that he would send them victory; but he gave them defeat. Nevertheless, my hope was not cast down, even as the mystic cactus, when it is cut down to the ground, dieth not, nor withereth.

"Then, on a time, there came upon me a troubled and fitful sleep, and I dreamed. There stood before me seven men of noble mien and stature,—the first an Azteca,—one for each of the Seven Peoples, the Nahuatlecas, who ruled in the land to the borders of flowery Cholulu. But, while I was looking, there came a Paleface, and touched the Seven, and they vanished utterly, insomuch that half their names were forgotten on earth. Then I cried aloud, in my grief for my beloved Aztecas, and for all the Seven Peoples, and awoke. But, when I slept again, behold, the Paleface was no longer the same, but his face was changed, like unto my people. And, when I looked yet another time, the Seven were there whom I beheld at the first, and the Paleface was one of them, and half of them bore his names.

"When I awoke, and mine eyes were opened, and I saw clearly the meaning of the vision, I commanded mine armies, and said unto them, 'Make no longer war against the Paleface, for ye shall not prosper, for ye are of one blood with him.' But they would not hearken. They stopped their ears; they ran upon me; they stoned me with stones, for their hatred to the Paleface. I was a friend to him, and for that I died at the hands of mine own people; and even now I ascend up into the bosom of the sacred Sun.

"Ye and the Paleface have one God, the God by whom we live, omnipresent, who knoweth all thoughts, and giveth all gifts, without whom man is as nothing. Ye have one God; yet your lives are given to contention.

"O Pimos! O my unhappy children! Mine eyes

are filled with tears for you, when they see the things which ye shall suffer before ye shall come to me at the last. The Paleface is great, he is proud, he is strong. Ye are weak, ye see not far, ye are vindictive. He cannot stoop to you. He does you wrong; and ye, in your littleness, avenge yourselves twofold; and then he makes no ending but with your death.

"O Pimos! O my unhappy children! My heart is filled with bitter grief for you, when it remembers the things which ye shall yet suffer. Each circling year, when I look down upon you from the bosom of the gorgeous Sun, I shall see your little tribe grow less. Ye are dearer to me even than they of the city of my people, the great city Tenochtitlan, because ye left not sacred Aztlan. But make no longer war against the Paleface. Remember what our holy men have said: 'Keep peace with all; bear injuries with humility; God, who sees, will avenge you.' So long as the sacred Gila rolls down his waters toward the All-mother of Oceans, so long shall God watch over you in heaven, and so long shall ye have, in your Great Father, an advocate to plead for your weakness and your littleness. Be ye steadfast. The trees which ye see on yonder desert take no root, and are beaten and broken in every wind; but behold the lordly *pitahaya*, which sends down his roots deep, and makes the desert glorious with his sap and his greenness.

"And when, at the last, your sufferings are too great for you, I will come to you in the chariot of the rising Sun, and ye shall be delivered from your sorrows. In the bosom of the gorgeous Sun there are many abodes, and thither shall ye come to me at the last. There shall your souls enter into the shining clouds, which float alway before God in Paradise, and into the singing-birds which dwell there. There shall ye see also the Paleface,

23*

"O Pimos! O my children! hearken well unto the words which I speak. When the evil days come upon you, ye shall certainly look for my coming in the chariot of the rising Sun, and set a watchman to watch for every village. Let the doors of your wigwams look toward the morning, and let them never be closed, for sad will it be with that one who shall not be ready at my coming."

When he finished speaking, the Sun was setting, as you see yonder now; and the Pimos heard a strong rushing, as at the first, and when they looked up, they beheld a swift and shadowy figure, which winged its way toward the setting Sun.*

*   *   *   *   *   *   *

As old Miliano concluded, in his broken Spanish, the story, of which the above is a somewhat embellished translation, the sun was setting. While we sat beneath the *mesquite* bush, the sky had clouded over, and just then there fell a little shower between us and the sun. The falling luminary looked through a chink in the clouds, and, shining through the wonderful tropic atmosphere of Arizona, turned all that rain into dropping blood. Then the river Gila, with its long and winding thread of green, and those immeasurable, deadened plains, so strangely dotted with the gorgeous emerald shafts of the *pitahaya*, and all the encompassing mountains, were, for the space of two or three minutes, red-lighted with an imposing and

---

* I care not to argue whether the Pimos are, or are not, of Aztec descent. It is sufficient for my purposes that they believe they are, and are looking for the second coming of Montezuma, and invariably make their doors open to the east, as I have abundantly seen for myself. Torquemada asserted they were Aztec; Coronado believed it; Pedro Font believed it; but Mr. Bartlett rejects the theory on linguistic grounds. I do not know how thorough was his examination; but he does not appear to have learned that they look for the second coming of Montezuma, nor to have noticed the singular fact respecting their doors.

lurid grandeur, as if an angel, great and glorious with the radiance of Paradise, swung already in the heavens the flaming firebrand of doom.

For several minutes we sat beneath the *mesquite*, contemplating in silence a scene which seemed to me like a prelude to the ushering in of eternity. I looked at old Miliano. Could it be, perhaps, that the soul of the old man, weary and sick with watching for the coming of Montezuma, was exulting in the belief that to-morrow's sun would bring him sweet release? Alas, I trow not; for presently he wreathed his skinny face into a most exquisitely hideous smile, held out his hand, and asked for a piece of tobacco. For once in my life, I sincerely regretted that I did not use the insane weed, for I should have given him all I possessed.

Then I arose, musing, and walked on alone down my long way westward. O too credulous and superstitious Pimo! by your constancy you rebuke the Paleface. But sad would be the face of Montezuma, if he came. You once were happy. Who brought you this your ceaseless dull pain, and your unrest and vague groping, and your despair? In the very presence of the Paleface, though you welcome him, you can see nothing but a monitor of swift-hastening annihilation.

As I passed through the last village, the inhabitants were sitting beneath their rude bush-arbors to take the breeze of the evening. Many of them had painted streaks of red ochre beneath their eyes, so that they seemed to weep incessantly tears of blood. Never can I forget the dull and stolid sorrow with which those big black faces—descended from a once mighty race, ancient, perhaps, already when the Old World was young, but touched now by the thickening miseries and the melancholy of their impending and relentless doom with yet sadder and darker lineaments—looked out upon a restless wanderer, sprung from a race which the wind blew yesterday over the sea; straying from the far-off East to molest with questions their ancient solitary customs and their immutability.

Not far distant, on the desert of Gila Bend, I passed within sight of Montezuma's Face. On the summit of a naked and wind-swept sierra, sculptured by Nature in the red granitic porphyry, that reclining face of the Great Father, unchangeable through wind, and tempest, and burning heat, and earthquake, sleeps on with the same sad, earnest, and tranquil mien, year after year, through these centuries of oppression and wrong, unmoved by the dying shriek of Pimo, or Apache, or Paleface, as they fall on the burning plain beneath him, because the fullness of time is not yet come when he shall awaken for the delivery of his waiting children.

TOM AND HIS WIFE.

> As through the land at eve we went,
> And plucked the ripened ears,
> We fell out, my wife and I,
> We fell out, I know not why,
> And kissed again with tears.
>
> TENNYSON.

TOM CULVER married simply because he was desperate. He had loved a fisherman's daughter in Maine, but his mother was one of those inscrutably absurd women who believe their children marry, not for themselves, but for them; and she decreed that Mary Milman was "beneath her son," and surreptitiously intercepted their letters until they became estranged, and one night the heart-broken girl threw herself from a cliff into the ocean. But at length Tom discovered the perfidy of his mother, and, with despair and bitterness rankling in his soul, he left her without a word of farewell, and sought that congenial refuge of broken hopes and embittered lives, the sunny, the wild, the all-forgetting California.

There, after long and aimless wanderings among the placers, he found, in Sacramento, Annie Donovan, a proud, willful, petted servant-girl. She was not beautiful, but she was vivacious in repartee, and to Tom Culver, in the blind and maddened bitterness of his despair, there was something unaccountably fascinating in the scorn which flashed in the black eyes and kindled the bloodless cheeks of this haughty little brunette, when she repelled his most careless advances.   What ! a little Irish servant-girl in California repulse him in that manner !   Tom had wellnigh lost faith in the virtue of womankind, and here was a phenomenon.   He set his heart recklessly on the conquest of that woman who dared repel him, especially as his rival was a State Senator, being determined, as he said, to "go him one better."

And he did.

Tom and Annie were married and took a little house, and the State Senator went home to his constituents.

But, now that Tom had triumphed through the mere recklessness of momentary devotion inspired, as it were, by his despair, the old bitterness of his early and only true love, forever blighted, gradually returned, supplanting this new and factitious sentiment.   With it also returned the old restlessness of a brooding and bitter-hearted melancholy.   His little wife was of that description of women with whom "love is love for evermore;" she loved her Tom with a passionateness he could not feel; and she was sorely puzzled at his moodiness and his incurable discontent.   She had married him without even knowing his occupation, much less his early history.   And, knowing it partially, the reader will, in the sad business through which we must conduct poor Tom, judge him more charitably than Annie could.

She could not discover that he had any occupation whatever.   He would peruse the morning newspaper until Annie announced breakfast, when he would carelessly sit by, absently conning a paragraph, then absently sipping his tea, and speaking only in monosyllables.   Then he would saunter forth into the city, with his hands pensively inserted into his pockets; return at dinner-time; then go silently and vacantly out again, and return late in the evening.

It was hardly a fortnight before the evening kiss, so eagerly exacted by Annie, and repaid at the highest rate of California interest, was omitted altogether. She felt greatly aggrieved, but was a thousand times too proud to ask him yet any reason wherefore.

Then again the inconsequent Tom would come home so early, whistling, and so blithe, so witty, so cheery in his manner, that she would forgive him everything, and the questions she had reserved for one of these happier moods were forgotten.

One morning, when Tom was unusually somber, they were sitting at breakfast in their little carpetless room, one of two in their little shell of a house. He tasted his tea, then shoved it quietly aside with an expression of listlessness.

"It's beastly cold, Annie."

"There, dear me, I forgot again," she said; and jumped up quickly, and set the teapot on the stove awhile.

He glanced with a troubled look into her face, then leaned over, thrust his hand into his pocket, and fetched out his purse.

"I'm going away to-day," he forced himself to say, in a faint, abrupt manner.

"Oh, dear, Tom, where?"

"Nevada."

She would have asked him why, but the extreme brevity of his reply nettled her a little, and she only looked piteously at him, and he looked at his newspaper. After he read a paragraph, he twisted the paper into a long stick, and, in an abstracted manner, pushed the purse across the table.

"That will keep you, I think, till I send you more from Nevada."

She brought the teapot, and poured out a cup, boiling hot, as he liked. There was something thick in her throat, and it took a whole cup of tea to wash it down.

"You'll come back—I mean you'll not—I hope your business won't keep you very long." So soon had her intense woman's curiosity begun to struggle with pride.

"That depends. If I make a big strike—it's uncertain."

He rose, to cut the parting short. He took Annie's hand, and, now that the struggle was over, he spoke more tenderly:

"Well, Annie, so long—so long!"

Then he walked away, with his hands deep in his pockets, but nothing else—"dead broke."

Day after day passed away, and no letter came from the wanderer. Morning, noon, and night, day after day, she set their little pine table in the little unplastered room, with Tom's plate in its place; and sometimes she dropped a tear when she looked at it; and sometimes she stormed to and fro in the lonesome room.

Ah! this living death, this utter silence and absence of those who are loved! It is unspeakably worse than the grave, for the grave has a voice, and when that speaks, we are silent and question no further. This relentless, unbroken silence! To live this day through in hope of to-morrow; to dream the weary night away; to awaken to nothing, ever and again nothing; and then to dream over and over again, and wander ten thousand times through the same maze of doubts, and hopes, and fears, and deaths, and still nothing but silence, unbroken and impenetrable silence. Ah, God! if she might know only one word! Dead or alive?

One morning there came a long and a strong rapping at the door. When she opened it, there stood a man in a double-crowned, white pith hat, with a vulturine nose, and immense black whiskers. He jerked his right hand half way up to his head, and nodded with his chin.

"Morning, m'm. Husband at home?"

"He is not. What did you wish?"

"No? Sorry, m'm," said he, leaning with one hand on the doorpost; "have to take the furniture away."

"What do you mean, sir?" said Tom Culver's brave wife, pulling down her black eyebrows in a very portentous manner.

"Sorry, m'm; but it's not paid for. Sheriff's attachment. Sorry; but can't be helped."

Now, the little woman had the murkiest possible notion what an attachment was, for she had not then lived long enough in California, where, as has been botanically ascertained, attachments used to grow on a species of shrub. But those other words, "not paid for," were dreadfully intelligible. So, without more remonstrance, she dismissed the fellow with the assurance that everything should be ready at eleven o'clock. Next, she hurried down to the furniture-rooms, and found the story was true; then to the landlord of her house, whom she notified and paid; then to a vacant room on N Street, which she rented; then back to her house again. She stacked the furniture neatly together in the middle of the room, gathered all her little possessions of trinkets, swept down and tidied up, took her broom in her hand, shot the bolt into its place, left the key in the lock, and reached her room before ten o'clock, with only a dollar in her possession.

Hitherto her deeply wounded pride had buoyed her up; but now that she was secure for a month once more, she wept bitter, passionate tears. A bride of only four months, and her husband ignominiously absconded, and the very chairs dragged from her house on an attachment ! That hateful, mean, ugly, disgraceful thing !

But she was not a woman to be dismayed, and she set herself resolutely to earn a livelihood by sewing. And now, at last, there came a letter from Nevada. Tom wrote cheerily :

" VIRGINIA CITY, NEVADA.

" MY OWN ANNIE,—Here is a lifter that will fetch you to me—$500. Ere ever the gourd blossoms again on my shanty, or the tree-toad singeth thrice in the sage, let me see you in Virginia. I've struck color, and have a pocketful of dust; but there's a hole in my pocket, and it's all running out. I think you can mend that pocket, my daisy, without taking a stitch. I'm afraid they took the furniture away from you. I forgot it teetotally. Pay whatever is due."

When Annie read this letter, she forgave her truant lord in a moment, and had absolutely no other wish but that she possessed a pair of wings, that she might fly to Virginia. But she was obliged to content herself with the lumbering stage-coach.

Tom received her at the stage-office, in holiday attire, purchased at a fabulous expense, and conducted her proudly, among the wondering and admiring bachelor miners, to his lowly shanty. The interior of it was wonderfully prinked up for this special occasion ; the earth floor had been scrupulously swept, and on a scantling behind the blackened and shining stove, each on his several nail, in perpendicular array, were a holder, a lifter, a sage-hen's wing, an iron stewpan, and a polished tin dipper.

The satisfaction which Tom took in introducing his little black-eyed wife to his brother miners, the expensive dinners he gave, the marvelous silks and satins he bought for her, were wonderful, and to her positively alarming, for she could not wholly forget the attachment. I think anybody would have laughed for very joy to see how proudly Tom strutted among the swarming bachelors with his Annie on his arm; how he tried to be exceedingly polite, but would be a blunt and hearty miner in spite of himself; and how he would pluck one by the sleeve in the street with: "I say, Jim ——, Mrs. Culver;" or how, when another was about to pass him with only a side glance, doubting whether he would wish to be recognized in company with so much silk, he would say: "No corner-lots to-day, Sammy. A front view. Mrs. Culver— my friend, Sam."

He always emphasized "Mrs. Culver," and if anybody had omitted to call her by that title, Tom would have knocked him down before he could say "Jack Robinson." To be able to say "Mrs. Culver," in those regions, was worth a quartz-mill.

But, after a few weeks, Tom began to grow restless and moody again. Was it because the presence of his wife reminded him of her who had perished broken-hearted in the ocean? Annie was gradually learning the melancholy secret of his life. By one of those inscrutable intellectual processes which women use, she hated Tom's mother, virtuously, for Tom's sake, but she hated the betrayed and perished woman, viciously, for her own sake. Instead of seeking to smother the early flame in his heart, she seemed rather to kindle it afresh, that it might consume itself.

But in process of time they accumulated large money, and then they cordially agreed upon one thing: that they would abandon the desolate region of the mines and go to San Francisco. That thing they did, and Tom secured a situation in the custom-house.

In the great city his generous soul quickly made him the center of a band of good fellows, whose society drew copiously upon his generous hand. This chapter is soon written. He loses his place, he is bailed out of the station-house one summer midnight by his weeping wife, and carried to his home on a dray. Very soon there comes another attachment, and Annie goes out to service in Sonoma, without a dollar, having expended her last to procure Tom a horse.

Upon this animal bestriding, he sets out for Idaho, a very sober and somber Tom, to "make his fortune" for the third time. Arrived in Boise City, he barters the animal for an axe, a plane, and a saw, and, what with his native ingenuity, in three weeks he is a successful carpenter, earning fabulous wages.

Months elapsed, and no letter came to Sonoma. After enduring untold anguish of suspense, of hope and doubt, of fear and jealousy, Annie went down to San Francisco, as a last resort, to inquire of persons arriving from Idaho if, perchance, somebody might have seen her erring and unhappy Tom. When nearly all her money was spent, "my uncle," with a round, white face and a blue eye-glass, arrived from those regions, and, upon being closely questioned, remembered a "French carpenter" who, he thought, nearly corresponded to Annie's description. She was puzzled and distressed beyond measure by this intelligence, and exclaimed, in feverish eagerness, "Part is Tom, and part isn't!" But, after a deal of cross-questioning, and the identification of a certain broken finger, this strange man was finally resolved into her American miner husband "that was." She was proud and delighted that he could learn carpentry so soon. But how had he learned French so quickly? That *was* a puzzle.

And then she was set in a delirium of distress and jealousy by the pawnbroker's exclamation of surprise:

"Is he your husband, madam? Well, he ought to be ashamed of himself! You must go to him right away."

She ran straightway out of the room, lest she should hear something worse. By using the utmost possible economy, she could make her thin purse carry her to Portland, and thence by stage to Boise City, and, without an hour's delay, she set forth.

In all the eleven miserable and weary days, amid the unutterable insults which came to a woman traveling to the mines in those times in the steerage, she scarcely slept. Scorned and despised by the few women who could take better passage, disdainfully refused even the poor loan of a pin, subjected to the brutal taunts of the sailors, she patiently and silently crouched in her wretched corner, bedraggled and bedabbled by the filthy decks, sleepless and haggard, and only creeping feebly at times to the guards, to solace her weary eyes with a sight of the rushing waters. Faster! faster! a hundred times faster! was her only thought.

Ah, Tom, Tom! if you had only understood the depth and the earnestness of that devotion, you could have forgiven many a little imperious jealousy and surveillance of its assertion. You married only in bravado, and so, in part, did she; but her love has increased with every year, while, I fear, yours has only grown feebler.

Boise City was reached at last, Tom was found, and they were speedily reconciled.

He was in possession of a mining claim, with several Chinamen employed; but Annie, determined that she would now get into her own hands the means for keeping a roof over their heads, against which all attachments would be powerless for evermore, set herself to washing. This was her personal and separate industry, and the rewards of it, which were enormous, were carefully hoarded. Tom was Tom—gay and melancholy by turns; and whether he was making any money from his claim, or not, she was profoundly unaware. Probably Tom did not know himself.

Eighteen months passed on thus,—happy months to Annie, because she was so rapidly getting the means to secure them a home which would endure,—and then it was agreed by them that she should return to San Francisco, and invest her personal savings in a house and lot, while Tom remained a few weeks longer, to close out the business to advantage.

She accomplished the journey with a little justifiable luxury, to recompense herself for the meanness and humiliation of the outward voyage. Before she had even become well rested from the journey, and shaken off the dust of travel, while she was looking over the "For Sale" columns in the newspapers, how great was her surprise to receive the following telegram:

> "PORTLAND, OREGON.
>
> "TO MRS. THOMAS CULVER, Russ House, San Francisco.
>
> "Send me up a hundred dollars, to pay my passage down to 'Frisco.
>
> "TOM."

On reading this message she laughed outright. She sent him the draft, however, by telegraph. It appears that the business had become perfectly hollow before she left Boise City. Her sudden departure aroused suspicion, unjust though it was toward her, an examination was made, and forthwith the water company gripped the unhappy Tom, attached his claim, and left him barely enough to pay his passage to Portland.

Arriving in the Golden City, he found his wife comfortably ensconced in a snug little house, and he registered a great oath to do better, and went to work, as never before, at carpentry. But Tom's chin was too short. He had no stick-to-it-iveness.

The story must now hasten on to its final stage. It is only necessary to say that they soon perceived another attachment looming up in the middle distance, and that Tom—willing to flee from temptation—went down to Los Angeles, bought a sheep-ranch in Annie's name, paid for it with Annie's money, and stocked it with sheep in his own name. With infinite ado he rived out enough "shakes" (long oak shingles) to construct a shanty, and in it, amid an indescribable clutter of tin cans, pet lambs, boxes, barrels, cats, dried apples, feather beds, etc., they lived the happiest winter they had ever spent together.

As soon as possible, Tom constructed a house, and then there was a house-warming which was characteristic of Southern California.

First, something as to the vicinity. The house stood at the foot of an easy terrace of foothills, thinly sprinkled over with oak-trees, just where they broke off, on the margin of an expanse of level open champaign. Tom whitewashed it and the two or three tiny structures about exceeding smirk and white, so that they looked very strange and toylike, standing on the edge of the naked waste. On all the dusty champaign, and under all the oaks, there was not one relieving thing, not a bush, in November, nothing but the burrows of ten thousand squirrels, which sat bolt upright on their little mounds, squeaking, and winking with their tails, in utter amazement at this invasion of their time-old dominions. The chickens wandered vacantly about over the nude expanse, and under the oaks, vainly cocking their eyes up and down, and all around, in search of a grasshopper, or any living bug; then they strolled disconsolately home, and seemed to lay eggs, because there was nothing else to occupy their minds.

Tom's dwelling was threefold. In the middle was a

house of one room; on one side, another house of one
room; and on the other side, the shanty of shakes. For
this occasion he made a chandelier of boards, with can-
dles in the ends. The estrade for the fiddlers was sufficiently elevated to allow the dancers room beneath.
There was a smooth floor beneath, a roof overhead, and
a shell of redwood boards—nothing else.

As fast as the people arrived, their horses were taken
into the *corral*, which was made like a stockade, of mighty
logs planted in the ground. Some clean barley hay was
deposited under their noses on the ground, while the gentlemen made their toilets in one end of the shanty, and
the ladies in the "parlor," the dance-room being between
them.

Tom was in an ecstasy of happiness, introducing people
to one another—for some had come thirty miles—now
running out to the hen's-nest in the forked oak beside the
parlor door, and now mixing a glass of eggnog for some
new arrival. He and Annie were arrayed in all the correct elegance of San Francisco. There were a number
of local wool-kings, rather uneasy in their unaccustomed
immaculate broadcloth, leaning most of the time against
the scantling posts of the veranda and smoking, but going
into the dance occasionally with an extreme vivacity;
five or six creamy-complexioned, dark-eyed *señoritas*, the
perfection of natural grace, with pale beauties from Texas,
and a superfluity of shaggy-whiskered shepherds, jiggling
and shaking themselves about over the floor in a comical
manner.

It was very pleasant to see these happy, awkward
couples, whirling in the lively dance, under the fiddlers,
under the board-chandelier, getting drops of tallow on
their heads, then away up, and back, and down the middle, straining their heads away from each other, as if in .

a frantic effort to separate. Annie was everywhere among
the guests, saying a great many pleasant things ; and the
silks and calicoes rustled on the slivers of the wall ; and
Tom's terrier pup got into the dance, and jumped up and
down, and waggled his tail ; and the little Digger peeped
through the window, and grinned all night long till daylight ; and all enjoyed themselves very much indeed.

About midnight a long table of rough boards was
brought in, ranged under the chandelier, and Tom and
Annie, assisted by a jolly old millionaire, six feet high
and with a mighty Roman nose, the king of all wool-
kings, soon loaded it with substantial provisions. "Ladies
and gentlemen, fall to !" cried Tom.

The amount of broken pies and cakes, canned peaches,
oysters, and chickens which the little Digger privately
and publicly devoured in the shanty for the next two
weeks, was positively alarming.

But, now that the edge of novelty was dulled again,
Tom's life began to be clouded with the ancient and incurable melancholy. The life of a wool-king in Southern
California is nearly as dreary as can be imagined. Week
after week, month upon month, for nearly half the weary,
interminable year, the sun comes up in the tenuous air
of the mountains, as spotless as a new brass platter ; burns
all day in the bright heavens in uncurtained and undiminished whiteness ; then burrows into the dusty hill-
tops as unclouded, as pitiless, and as unwinking as he
arose. All through the summer he lives in a dun-colored
desert, with only scattered oaks visible on the distant
sierras. There are lovely sunsets and sunrises, but they
fall upon the weary eyes, being always the same, without
the variation of a cloud ; and the unequaled purity and
healthfulness of the air itself becomes a weariness to the
spirit of man, because it seems to correspond so well to

the utter nakedness of the earth in summer, and the absence of all sights and sounds, save the stupid bleating of the lazy, contented sheep. It is quite too healthy, too pure, too vacuous, too colorless, and one longs to have a little quinsy for variety, or at least the terrific crack and splitting of a thunder-storm once in awhile. It seems as if a man would live almost forever here, until he dried up to a mere stick, and shot off somewhere like a rocket.

Around his wretched tenement of boards, or of sun-dried brick, there is a pole-fence, standing out in such indescribably hideous contrast under these immaculately blue heavens—an insult to the very crows, which will not perch thereon. Or, perhaps, there are only vacuous spaces around, without even a pole to anchor the dust, which burdens the very air, that you sniff all day the sweltering smell of the ground. Close at hand, for safety against the wild beasts, are the noisome corrals, where the sunshine riots and dances in the vile exhalations.

As soon as his shepherds are gone to the mountains, where they drowse the livelong day, the wool-king saddles his horse, and hies away to the old Mission. In its cool, dark recesses, looking out upon the desert glare only through the doors of its ancient arcades,—long ago fallen away from spiritual to spirituous uses,—he meets his compotators for cards and drinking-bouts.

Tom is often here, fleeing from the domestic surveillance which is daily becoming more intolerable. He returns only to encounter Annie's ominous frown, and supper is eaten in silence. He goes out to see if the little Digger returns with the flock unharmed, bandies some tolerable California Spanish with some bad Digger Spanish, and learns that the coyotes have caught two lambs. He curses himself for his stupidity, goes in, sits down by his lonely stove, and slides down all in a heap in his chair. He knows what is coming.

Annie holds up a plate, wipes and wipes it, turns it over and over, stops, scratches it a little with her finger, then turns half way round toward him, and pulls down her black eyebrows sternly.

"I suppose, of course, Inez Dominguez is well to-day?" This in a cutting tone.

"And narrow is the way to destruction. I'm going to preach under the big live-oak to-morrow, Annie, and I want a handsome deaconess about like you, to take up a contribution."

"But you didn't answer my question. I am anxious to know how Miss Dominguez is to-day."

Tom commenced singing gayly:

> "When this cruel war is over,
> No Micky need apply,
> For everything is lovely,
> And the goose hangs high."

"Why do you always sing that to me? Because I am Irish? Do you sing that to Miss Dominguez?"

Tom reached and took a crumb of bread off the table, and gave it to the cat, to see him and the terrier pup squabble for it, at which he laughed heartily. "Nip him, Topsy! Nail him once or twice!" he cried.

Annie held the cup close to her face, and wiped very hard and fast, while her face began to ripple, and her mouth to tremble, for she was about to laugh, in spite of herself.

Tom clasped his hands over the top of his head, and slipped farther down in his chair.

"Annie, I saw to-day the strangest man I ever saw in my life. One side of his face was perfectly black."

Her intense feminine curiosity triumphed at once, and

she stopped, and looked straight at him, for the first time that evening.

"La me! and the other side was white!"

"'The other side was black, too."

It is an incredibly short time before Tom and his wife are chattering together as gayly as little children.

But the quarrel was ever renewed. We have seen how greatly superior Annie was in business; but Tom would come in at noon sometimes, hungry as a bear, after working hard over his smirk whitewashed toy-houses, and find the breakfast things still on the table, and one of Annie's innumerable pet chickens with the whole length of its neck down in the cream-pitcher, while its mistress sat by the stove, reading the *Ledger* or Dickens. He vexed his tidy soul from day to day with his slatternly shanty, and when chance made him master of it for a day or so, he would peel off his coat, as in the old mining-days, and sing and whistle the livelong day, jolly as a sand-boy, while he scoured up and hung up a thousand and one things. On the other hand, he was so offended at the rigorous precision with which she always seated herself at the end of the table opposite him, that she was obliged to sit at the side. And indeed it is a most dreary thing for a married couple to sit seven long years at opposite ends of a table, when no little high-chair comes meantime to be drawn up to the side. So Tom thought, at least, and he often sighed and said to himself, "Ah! if I only had a child to love, my life might be mended yet."

To Annie's great distress, Tom *would* sit in his shirt-sleeves, even when Judge Haskell was there to dinner. And he could not endure to see her so fussy as to hand him bread on the plate, but she must pass him a slice "in her fist," and that not delicately, but as fearlessly as he would seize a crowbar.

The married life of Tom and Annie had been hitherto sadly at sixes and sevens, though it had partaken largely of the character of a farce; but now it darkened down, apparently, toward a swift and awful tragedy. Naturally of a jealous nature, and wedded to a man too proud to protest his innocence every day of his life,—for Tom *was* innocent now,—she found herself in a loneliness where she was left to be preyed upon by her own morbid im-aginings. The only woman she saw for months together was a little, withered, green-eyed hag, who had conceived a spite against Tom, for some reason, and supplied his wife to surfeit with infamous daily slander and lies.

Tom's most harmless business letters were by her in-vested with mystery and wickedness. She fancied im-pending over her all that was terrible on earth—some dark and secret plot of divorce, abandonment, infamy, beggary, imprisonment, friendless and hideous death. Sometimes she shuddered as she allowed herself to pro-nounce even the dreadful word "murder."

All the stern and grim suffering which is depicted in that weird, awful, and lurid story of "The Scarlet Letter" became her portion. Sitting in her lonely house at even-ing, far from human habitation, when Tom was absent hunting his horses, at the dismal yelling of the coyotes, or the boding screech of the owl, she would shriek in terror, run, and fall lifeless upon the Indian-boy, only less frightened than his mistress. A band of thieves and mur-derers had their rendezvous near by in the mountains, and the faintest scream of the night-hawk or the ghostly moaning of the wind through the trees, her distempered imagination magnified into their approach.

Tom was distracted almost to madness. He hardly dared leave her sight. He dreaded only less than death the quarterly journey to Los Angeles for supplies, which occupied nearly three days, lest he should return only to find Annie a raving maniac. With all his earnestness he warned her against the mousing visits of the evil-minded hag who was destroying her life, and he even threatened to expel her by violence; but he perceived that it would only add fuel to the flame of jealousy, and intensify Annie's suspicions. He abandoned his visits to the Mission, except on the most urgent necessity.

The time arrived again for another of his regular journeys to Los Angeles, and, parting from Annie with unwonted tenderness, he set out with a promise to return speedily. During his absence the lying hag spent day and night with Annie, and poured into her ears, itching with that strange and infatuated eagerness of jealousy, all her envenomed hate against the absent husband.

Tom kept his promise, and returned promptly in two days, bringing his wife an elegant gold watch and a rocking-chair. But no Annie came forth to greet him. Seeking her in her room, with a smile and a hearty, "Well, my dear, how has the time gone?" he found her silent and delirious with jealousy. She turned her face away to the wall, and refused to speak.

Not only was Annie indeed sick, but she feigned to be dying. For days together she persistently refused all nourishment at his hands, but kept some concealed, of which she secretly partook in his absence.

Does the reader, upon this announcement, cry out against the woman, and feel disposed to reproach me for having even described such a character? It is hard to look with allowance upon such a wickedness as this, and perhaps few of us would have done it, but we must be lenient in our judgment. We must pardon many an offense, heinous and despicable though it may seem, to the weakness and the madness of a jealous woman. She stooped to this base act of wickedness to try if her cup of married love was wholly drained; and in that awful night when Tom sat beside her whom he thought dying, far from any habitation of man, with no one near but the mute and stricken savage, crouching in the corner and rigid with terror, with no sound borne on the midnight air but the dismal yelling of the *coyotes*, as they dashed themselves against the wattled corral, and were hurled back upon the ground, he spoke to her with such true and piteous tenderness of love, that her sick heart returned from its wanderings, and she told him all, with tears, and begged forgiveness.

After seven years of married life, Tom was still so little learned in the devious ways of woman's jealousy, that he could not look upon this misdeed with any allowance. He forgot the large and generous pity of that saying of Seneca, "*Quem pœnitet peccasse pene est innocens.*" Forgive her! the act seemed to him so inexpressibly despicable that he turned away in silence and in loathing.

He took his rifle, and walked forth in the clear, crisp moonlight. After the first burst of passion had passed away, his soul was filled with that saddening and ineffable bitterness which longs for death, and the sweet and quiet rest of the grave, and he murmured: "Ah, Mary! my lost, lost Mary!"

Hardly knowing whither he went in his blinded and bitter despair, he approached his corral, and saw the coyotes dimly fleeing away across the champaign. Mechanically, he cocked the rifle, and put it to his shoulder. Then he brought it down, and placed the muzzle against his cheek. He touched the trigger, and in the very last moment he dashed it away, and, with a keen and hellish shriek, the bullet cut the still moonlight.

Next day he saddled his favorite horse, and, after a cold and careless farewell, he rode away. Week after week passed away, and there came no tidings of his rovings; month passed into month, and brought no report from the wanderer. What his wife endured from suspense can only be imagined,—

> "The hope, and the fear, and the sorrow,
> All the aching of heart, the restless, unsatisfied longing,
> All the dull, deep pain, and constant anguish of patience."

What was he doing? He penetrated the savage wilds of Arizona. He made long journeys across its trackless deserts, without any aim, and returned on his trail, without any purpose. Now he mined a little, and now he joined himself to a squadron in pursuit of Apaches, and, leaping in his stirrups with the old ringing yell of his youth, he sought death at the hand of the tawny savage. An arrow-wound, which brought him to the very mouth of the grave, brought him also to remorse, and to a yearning for his home. While he was yet convalescent, he set his face steadfastly homeward—an old man at thirty-two, with his cheeks seamed and bronzed, and his fine, black, curly poll half turned to gray. But he was still Tom, and his better nature had only slumbered.

The story ends well. Alas, alas! for both of them, it had not ended so years before. At last he is approaching his house. It is evening. He sees the familiar light of his " parlor" window shining under the old forked white-oak. He spurs his jaded horse into an amble. Hark! There is borne to his ears, on the still evening air, a feeble and uncertain squeal. What! Is it possible? Is it a——

He spurs his horse again, and the old fellow almost

jams his nose against the parlor door.   Tom alights, and flings the rein over the horseshoe nailed to the oak.   He knocks, and they open.   He enters.   Exclamations all around.   He looks about him.   They go to the bed, and gently turn down the counterpane.   Upon my word, it is a——

Tom settles back on one foot, plants the other ahead, folds his arms across his breast, and, with a perfectly unmoved countenance, but with a light of infinite gladness in his eye, and of a reconciliation never again to be broken, he salutes:

" Ah, he's a buster!"

25*

HISTORICAL.

A ROYAL ROAD TO HISTORY.

> Well—were it not a pleasant thing
>   To fall asleep with all one's friends;
> To pass with all our social ties
>   To silence from the paths of men;
> And every hundred years to rise
>   And learn the world and sleep again;
> To sleep through terms of mighty wars,
>   And wake on science grown to more,
> On secrets of the brain, the stars,
>   As wild as aught of fairy lore;
> And all that else the years will show,
>   The Poet-forms of stronger hours,
> The vast Republics that may grow.
>
> TENNYSON.

TO the youthful student who aspires to "climb the steep where Fame's proud temple shines afar," no part of that steep looks more formidable than the mountains of History. It is not their ruggedness, but their sheer height. Let us be thankful that the clean beasts and the unclean and the fowls of the air were so numerous in Noah's Ark as to leave no room for whatever parchment records that wise patriarch may have preserved. When the conquering Caliph applied the torch to the vast magazine of papyrus scrolls in Alexandria, he said, "If there be anything good in them it is contained in the Koran, and whatever is bad in them ought to be destroyed." When any other than one of those inscrutable persons, of whom the Chinese say, "If there is anything he does not know, he is ashamed," or one who, unlike the Admirable Crichton, is not prepared to dispute *de omni re scibili*, contemplates the above decision, he is disposed to cry out from the depths of his gratitude, "Thank Heaven for the Caliph!"

And yet, as time rolls on, and the busy hand of History is piling up Pelion on Ossa of the world's chronicles, the poor span of human life is yearly growing shorter. I have often cherished a secret rebellion against the historians themselves, as being largely responsible for this deplorable result; and if matters go on this way much longer, the mighty back of the world will be broken under its own accumulated history, and we shall all go down together in one desperate last floundering under our books.

It is a source of positive mental dissipation to be confronted with so many histories, for one feels all the while the spurrings of conscience that one ought to read them; and so, not doing it, one becomes intellectually debauched and reckless, like him who harbors in his bosom a secret deed of murder. O Methuselah and Mehujael, and all ye long-lived brotherhood of antediluvians, happy were ye that no Grotes, or Gibbons, or Bancrofts existed in your days, to pester your patriarchal tranquillity, and eat away your lives with a consciousness of duty unfulfilled!

Not many weeks after the great battle of Sadowa the school-children of Moscow wrote a letter to Bismarck, in which, with childish frankness and enthusiasm, they thanked him for ironing out some of the wrinkles of that part of European geography which had always given them so much trouble. When will some Bismarck arise to hew off a few of the branches from the "historical trees" which are a terror and a nightmare to our childhood?

There is rich and large material for a skeleton history in the political catch-words found in the literature of every nation, especially in our own. Every great crisis in human affairs produces one or more men, its "noblest offspring," who stamp their ineffaceable impress upon it, among other ways, by moulding certain apt phrases for affairs; for those epochs most prolific in noble deeds, "God's sons," also nourish the fairest generations of "men's daughters,"—words. It is these terse, clear-cut utterances of such periods that become the heirs and transmitters of their best or worst endeavors, as it were the high- and low-water marks of history. This article is simply an experiment in the construction of such an outline history, an attempt to indicate some of the possibilities of the topic.

Passing over all the Colonial and chaotic period, when we were no nation, let us begin with the Revolution, when we became such in substance, as a little later in name.

As in all history the grandest results have often grown from the most trivial causes, so here the spark that ignited the great magazine of war was only a little bit of "stamped paper" dropped into a few caddies of "gunpowder tea." That bowl of cold tea made in Boston harbor was as eventful as the one flagon too much of wine drunk by Alexander in the alabaster cup. But behind these mere trifles lay the great principle, "No taxation without representation." As a matter of fact, that was the whole head and front of the rebellion for a year, at least with the great majority. Franklin philosophically said, "Where Liberty is, there is my country;" but Paine, speaking to the fact, added a word: "Where Liberty is *not*, there is my country." Yet the real "Liberty Party" in the early days of the Revolution was small in numbers, even under the clarion eloquence of Henry, "Give me Liberty, or give me death!"

Thus the battle was joined. Having solemnly and dispassionately pledged to each other "their lives, their fortunes, and their sacred honor" for their common defense, and for the achievement of independence, they were not dismayed or faint-hearted in the day of sore calamity. "Independence forever!" cried Adams. Paine wrote, "These are the times that try men's souls;" but, fortunately for us, the pillars of the Revolution were made of sterner stuff than the ratiocinative souls of Paine and Franklin. We know what a disastrous shipwreck Bacon made of statesmanship.

Not only in the beginning of the war, but throughout, the authority of Congress was very weak; there was no President with even advisory powers. "There was a state without King or nobles; there was a church without a Bishop." Some good souls interpreted so ill the great movement they were engaged in, that they believed themselves still fighting under the banner of George III.,—for him, and against his usurping ministers,—just as, later in our history, some held to the impossible power of "constitutional resistance" and of "peaceable secession." Accordingly, when bold Ethan Allen laid siege to Ticonderoga, although the substance of royalty was gone out of him, the phantom of "divine right" still hovered over the vacuum, notwithstanding he was an infidel, and he issued his summons "in the name of the great Jehovah and of the Continental Congress."

That notion of "divine right" was driven out of the Fathers' minds far more by the whips and scorpions of war than by the philosophy of Jefferson, leading him to that great word, "Governments derive their just powers from the consent of the governed," and that the source

of all authority in government is, "We, the People."
Jefferson might write (poaching on the North Carolina
doctrines) "All men are created equal;" but the somewhat humiliating quarrels of the Fathers about grades of
authority did more to put that equality into effect than
did the Declaration of Independence.

Having no President, and only a very shadowy Congress, they were often in dire chaos. Washington was
elected to the chief command to restore order. Repair-
ing to New England to organize his little army, and finding matters in sad confusion, he said, playfully, referring
to the Governor of Connecticut, "We must consult
Brother Jonathan on the subject." Brother Jonathan
helped them.

The "Cowboys" on the Tory side, and the "Skinners"
on the Patriot flanks, were probably about like the modern
guerrillas and bushwhackers on the Rebel side, and the
"bummers" on the Unionist. There were some as
anxious to "take protection" from the British com-
manders as Southern families were to secure "protection-
papers" from soft-hearted Union generals.

The war was ended at last, independence was established, and the nation staggered along as best it might
without a head. The Tory McFingal scornfully but
truthfully said:

> "For what's your Congress, or its end?
> A power t' advise and recommend;
> To call forth troops, adjust your quotas—
> And yet no soul is bound to notice;
> To pawn your faith to th' utmost limit,
> But cannot bind you to redeem it."

The Articles of Confederation were found to be a
"rope of sand," and men began to say of them as poor
humpbacked Pope said of himself, "God mend me!"

But the wiser ones answered as the link-boy replied to his master, "God mend you? It would be far easier to make a new one." And they made a new one. They also gave the nation its present name. To our ancestors, just emancipated from dependence, and occupying only the edge of the continent, which the rising sun of empire had barely fringed with civilization, as the morning sun gilds the overhanging cloud, the name "America" might have seemed too pretentious; but it would not have been more assuming than "Continental Congress." It would have been more convenient than "United States."

To form a national banner to supplant the multitude of snakes, pine-trees, bears, and other grotesque devices carried through the Revolution, they

> " Tore the azure robe of night,
> And set the stars of glory there."

Trumbull puts into the mouth of his hero the contemptible objection which was urged against the flag at that time, that it was

> ' Inscribed with inconsistent types
> Of Liberty and thirteen stripes."

As though, forsooth, the Fathers designed to symbolize the lashes of slavery in its sacred folds! Yet we know very well, from the cooler erasures and interlineations which Jefferson drew through the white-hot first draft of the Declaration, and the still further omissions made by the Committee, that they did not by any means regard slavery with the abhorrence that young Jefferson did.

The national motto was probably taken from a modest metrical composition by John Carey, of Philadelphia, entitled "The Pyramid of Fifteen States," in which occur the following verses:

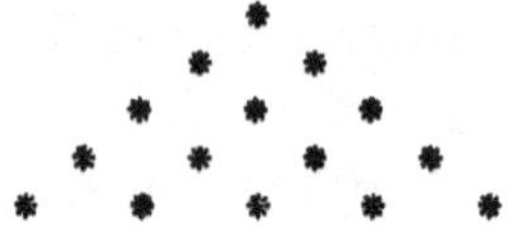

> "Audax inde cohors stellis *e pluribus unum*
> Ardua pyramidos tollit ad astra caput."

These three words occur as a motto on the title-page of the *Gentleman's Magazine*, published in London in 1731; but whether Carey or the Fathers ever saw them there I am not informed.

In 1796, C. C. Pinckney, having received a mercenary proposition of alliance from the French Directory, wrote home his great word, "Millions for defense, but not one cent for tribute!"

Two years later, in the midst of the partisan clamor and dissensions that distracted the country, in sympathy with the frenzied madness of the French Revolution, the voice of Hopkinson was heard above the din, summoning his countrymen to concord and fraternal love:

> " Firm, united let us be,
> Rallying round our Liberty—
> As a band of brothers joined,
> Peace and safety we shall find."

But suddenly every note of passion and of discord was hushed. There went a voice of mourning through the Republic, at the sound of which the stoutest hearts were awed, and the eyes of grim veterans were suffused with tears. He of whom it was said that "he had no children that a nation might call him father," went to his long home. Before the assembled Congress, Henry Lee pronounced his noble and memorable eulogy, "To the memory of the Man, first in war, first in peace, and first in the hearts of his countrymen."

Already, before the close of the century,—such was the strong recuperative power of the young country,—the Republic had so far recovered from the shocks of the Revolution, that the eaglet was hatched that was destined to develop into the "Birdofredum Sawin ;" and Timothy Dwight was moved to unpack his swelling patriotism in voluminous poetical compositions. He gave the nation its right name in the following couplet :

> " Columbia, Columbia, to glory arise—
> The queen of the world, and the child of the skies."

The national money, after the conclusion of the war, became so worthless as to furnish us a proverb to this day : "Not worth a Continental." But as early as 1811 the national finances appear to have become greatly improved, for in that year honest, indignant Josiah Quincy said in a speech, "Why, sir, we hear the clamor of the craving animals at the treasury-trough here in this Capitol." In this year, too, the Massachusetts politicians taught the country how to "gerrymander ;" so it was evident that "Young America" was making quite as rapid progress, both politically and financially, as was healthy. He was already looking well after the "Almighty Dollar" and the office.

The Federalist party took the lead during the Revolution and for some years after it, because, like their modern successors, the Republicans, in the war of the Rebellion, they were the party of strength and centralization. But the Democratic reaction came and swept them from power, bringing in Jefferson.

During the stately administration of Washington there was in the Capital a "Republican Court," and especially a brilliant galaxy of female beauties clustering about Mrs. Washington. When Jefferson rode down to the Capitol on horseback, and entered it in his dirty boots, all this was changed into "Democratic simplicity." The sturdy old Ironsides of the Federalist party became unpopular; being in the minority, they were necessarily "treasonable." The suite of rooms in Washington occupied by Pickering and Hillhouse were the Federalist headquarters, and were known as "Treason-Hall." The party name was becoming so unpopular that, a few years later, it had to be abandoned.

Jefferson originated the cry of "British influence," if not that of "British gold," which has hounded many a man to political death. He earnestly sympathized with France, and in 1809 he sought to cripple English commerce by the "Embargo;" but this harmed New England's commerce even more. Upon its enactment, therefore, her orators dramatically cried out, "Liberty is dead!" and the Boston newspapers appeared in mourning. Yankees disposed to jest—though not much humor had yet appeared in New England—anagrammatically called it the "O grab me."

The Republic went to war against England to resist the pretended "right of search." But "Brother Jonathan" grumbled loudly, because this war would ruin his commerce and his codfishing business; so he had to be degraded from the chief command, and replaced by the less provincial and more catholic, if coarser, "Uncle Sam," who was born in 1812, and had for his birth-record the head of a commissary barrel of beans.

Under this greater leadership the nation made gallant head in the war on the ocean, where it never "gave up the ship;" but on shore there seemed to prevail a "masterly inactivity," as John Randolph said. So sturdy was the opposition of New England to the war that certain persons along the shore of Connecticut (it was asserted) hoisted "blue lights" at night, to show British smugglers where to land; and thus added another phrase to the vocabulary of treason. The commerce of New England was literally going to grass, and the virulence of her opposition developed an intense party spirit. In 1814 met the famous Hartford Convention. It is wonderful how this assembly of twenty-six eminently respectable gentlemen scared Madison and his Cabinet; and yet not wonderful, when we consider the anger of New England, and the fact that these gentlemen dared even whisper the fatal word "Disunion."

Advancing upon New Orleans with the (alleged) rallying-cry of "Booty and Beauty," the English received their final and crushing defeat at the hands of "Old Hickory." The war of 1812 was ended.

The great "Northwest Territory" had been sacredly consecrated to liberty, but the ever-aggressive slave-power, stimulated by the new and great value given to cotton by the invention of Eli Whitney, cast greedy eyes upon this fair region. In the memorable struggle of 1820, terminating in the "Missouri Compromise," a noble State was lost to slavery, although, for the rest, the line between freedom and slavery, the old "Mason and Dixon's Line" (latitude 39°), was replaced by one further south, that of 36° 30'. But it was a gain to slavery on the whole. John Randolph denounced this compromise as a "dirty bargain," and the eighteen Northern Congressmen who helped strike it, as "dough-faces."

The advocacy of "Disunion" had already migrated from Hartford to Charleston. But it had not, in either case, reached the masses; and when Webster (1823) lifted up his voice in behalf of "Our country, our whole country, and nothing but our country," his words awakened, North and South, an approving response.

About this time the nation was gratified by Monroe's declaration of the principle, really originated by J. Q. Adams, that "the United States would view any attempt of the Allied Powers to extend their system to any portion of this hemisphere as dangerous to our peace and safety."

Reassured by the valorous assertion of this principle, dear to every American heart, and released by compromises from the baleful struggle with slavery, the Republic now entered upon the "Era of good feeling," which characterized Monroe's administration.

About the year 1828 a new fountain of bitter waters was opened up in the discussion of the tariff. Some stoutly defended the "American System," as alone patriotic; others insisted that the "Foreign System," or English free trade, could alone protect the finances of the country. Jackson advocated the rather indeterminate measure of a "judicious tariff." The manufactures of New England and the Middle States vigorously demanded "Protection to domestic industry;" but John Randolph, speaking for the cotton-growing, free-trade South, replied, "I would go half a mile out of my way to kick a sheep."

With the accession of Jackson came a new rule in politics. In 1832 Marcy gave it felicitous utterance in the Senate: "They see nothing wrong in the rule that to the victors belong the spoils of the enemy." Blair and Kendall, composing Jackson's famous "Kitchen Cabinet," on this new principle decapitated many a Whig, and roasted him on the Democratic spit.

The Federalists had long since transmuted themselves into "National Republicans," which name still indicated their centralizing theories. But about 1829 that was in turn abandoned for "Whig," although, after both these new births, the party still appeared wrapped in the swaddling-bands of the slave-power. The fierce attacks of the tariff party upon the Democrats forced them also, for a time, to seem to abandon their ancient name; at least they tacked on it as a shield the word "Republican," becoming "Democratic Republicans."

The Southern opposition to the tariff, under the leadership of Polk, began as early as 1828, and the war of words speedily waxed to threatening proportions. Hayne fired a great gun never heard before, "A State can commit no treason;" and from Garrison came back the answering defiance, "No union with slaveholders." Calhoun took up the word: "Each State has an equal right to judge for itself, as well of the infraction [of the Constitution] as of the mode and manner of redress;" and the Massachusetts "Come-outers" again retorted, "The Constitution is a covenant with death, and an agreement with hell." The South cried out, "Let us alone!" to which Garrison a third time made reply: "Our country is the world; our countrymen are all mankind."

Amid all these low, sullen mutterings of the approaching tempest, while the red glare of the lightnings was already playing along the horizon, and the heavens were darkened by black and gusty clouds, and the hearts of the mariners quailed with fear, there was heard the steady voice of the master, the "Expounder of the Constitution," warning his fellows to stand by the old ship, and giving them for a watchword to the end of time, "Liberty and Union, now and forever, one and inseparable!"

Holding the Constitution to be only a "compact," South Carolina invented a word of new and baneful import, "Nullification." But Jackson declared that the Union "must and shall be preserved," and his vigorous proceedings cleared the political atmosphere of South Carolina wonderfully.

Jackson fully restored the prestige of the ancient party name, and they now dropped their shield, and became once more (1834) simple "Democrats." The Whigs being now fully organized as such, received from Choate a popular rallying-cry, when he wrote to their convention, "We join ourselves to no party that does not carry the flag and keep step to the music of the Union."

The trifling incident of the so-called "Locofoco cigars" in Tammany Hall gave the Democrats a new nickname, which became popular.

In the famous "Hard-cider campaign" of 1840, for and against "Tippecanoe and Tyler too," the country first began to hear of, and to assemble in, "mass-meetings." Before this, too, not much had been heard of "available candidates." The West being now fully opened up, the business of "stump-speaking" and "log-rolling" began to flourish, though both were quite honorable and above-ground compared with the New York operations of "pipe-laying" and "repeating." When Vice-President Tyler became President, and turned away from the party which elected him, men revived the old Virginia doctrine (known also to the Magyars centuries ago) of the "right of instruction."

The great slave-power was now waxing so bold and so powerful in the land, that it was hard for both the two great parties to remain any longer neutral. The Whigs, under the lead of Webster and Clay, claimed to be the least subservient to it, but they began now to be sore pushed in their neutrality. As early as 1841 the seeds of their final ruin were planted; they became divided into "Conscience Whigs" and "Cotton Whigs,"—names which graphically explain themselves. Of the former division, Charles Francis Adams and Wilson were prominent leaders.

The slave-power had long had a wistful eye on the great and rich region of Texas, and in 1844 Polk was elected on the distinct platform of "Annexation," or "Reannexation" as some preferred to call it, which the Democratic party pronounced to be a "political necessity." Despite the imposing petition sent to Congress by the Conscience Whigs, the new "Liberty party," and the "Abolitionists," Texas was annexed by joint resolution. There was war with Mexico, and five Whigs in Congress made themselves immortal by "firing in the rear." Corwin virtually hoped the Mexicans would "welcome with bloody hands to a hospitable grave" every invader of their country. The animosity between the Conscience Whigs and the Cotton Whigs became intense; party spirit ran as high as in 1812.

At the same time with the Mexican war the country escaped with the skin of its teeth from another with England about the Oregon boundary. "Fifty-four forty, or fight!" was the popular cry, both North and South; but our government was obliged to yield its claims, although it compensated itself by seizing upon the peerless domain of California, at Monterey, scarce twenty-four hours in advance of the English admiral.

Jefferson's foreign policy, which consisted simply in avoiding "entangling alliances," expanded, under Polk's Administration, to this formula: "Ask nothing that is not right, and submit to nothing that is wrong." Both were rather vague.

Notwithstanding the great immigration all the while, our people still regarded foreigners with a certain amount of distrust, and used toward them a rather illiberal policy. Accordingly, when Bishop Hughes sought to organize an Irish party, his attempt not only failed, but produced a violent reaction (1844) which filled the land with the cry,

"Native Americans," "America for Americans," and subsequently gave birth to "Sam" and the "Know-Nothings." Our countrymen seemed to forget that it was foreign men coming to America, and not, as in the case of Poland and Ireland, foreign governments.

In 1850 the country was again alarmingly convulsed over the proposition to admit California as a free State. Webster virtually joined himself to the Cotton Whigs by advocating the infamous Fugitive Slave Bill. He asserted that "there are times when we must learn to conquer our prejudices," and that it was useless to attempt to "re-enact the will of God" concerning the destination of New Mexico. But a rupture was again staved off for awhile by Clay's "Omnibus Bill," which brought in California free, New Mexico and Utah as Territories, without mention of slavery, the abolition of slavery in the District of Columbia, and the Fugitive Slave Bill. This news was received in far-off California with wild delight, making "Admission Day" a joyful anniversary forever, to be celebrated with bonfires, cannon, and bell-ringing. But this bargaining with the slave-power shattered the Whig party, and it went down soon after in hopeless and irremediable disaster.

The arrogant attitude and demands of the slave oligarchy were now driving men from both the great parties toward a separate organization. Some came from the Democracy, but most of them were earnest men fleeing from the fast-sinking and dishonored ship of Whiggery, who, together with their few Democratic allies, launched a new vessel on the political seas, and named it "Free Soil." In 1848 it was fully rigged, and ready to sail. The two "healthy organizations" chose their captains for the coming contest,—Taylor and Cass respectively,—and now was opened an opportunity for the new party to win a splendid triumph. But, unfortunately, acting too closely upon their motto, "Success is a duty," they selected a feeble leader, Van Buren, and in the ensuing election they came out disastrously in the vocative. Their failure barely escaped contempt.

But now came up a new apparition, one of the most wonderful in all the erratic career of American politics,— the Know-Nothing party (1853). Like an uncalculated comet, it blazed through the heavens on its brief but astonishing career, smashing Whig and Free-Soil utterly, and shaking Democracy to its center. It seems almost like a providential intervention in history, in that it ground so thoroughly to powder the feeble parties which had hitherto made sham battles against the slave-power, reducing all to a common level, and thus clearing the ground of old and false traditions, preparatory to the rise of a new organization squarely confronting the oligarchy.

This new party called itself "Republican," thereby shaking off old and painful memories of disaster, and unhappy traditions connected with dishonored names. In 1856 it went forth to battle with the rallying-cry, "Frémont and freedom!" and, though beaten, was beaten without disgrace to itself.

In response to the demand for "free soil" in the Territories, the South replied, "We have a right to take our slaves wherever you take your horses." This was the first exchange of shots at long range between the outposts. In 1850 Seward said in the Senate that there was a "higher law .   .   .   which regulates our authority over the domain;" but there came back from Hammond the proud response, "Cotton is king."

In 1854 Burns was carried back to Virginia and slavery in a government cutter, and the New York *Tribune* passionately declared the flag that fluttered above him was a "flaunting lie." But Chief Justice Taney calmly replied that the negro "had no rights which the white man was bound to respect." Douglas protested against the quarrel over the negro, declaring that this is a "white man's government."

Through the action of Douglas the Missouri Compromise was repealed, thus throwing Kansas open to slavery; and Chief Justice Taney ruled that the Constitution "made no distinction between the right of property in a slave and any other property held by a citizen," which opened even the Free States to slavery. But the North was busy in hurrying emigrants into Kansas, and the "underground railroad" in carrying slaves out of it. Douglas offered his mediative principle of "Squatter Sovereignty" in the Territories, but it availed little for Kansas. There followed in that unfortunate State a long, miserable, and desolating struggle between the inhabitants and the Border Ruffians of Missouri; but the former triumphed over all at last, rejected the last plan of humiliation concocted by Congress, called the "English Compromise," and entered the Union free. The day of compromises was fast passing away.

Clear-sighted men saw the great battle was at hand. In June, 1858, Lincoln declared, "The Union cannot exist half slave, half free;" and four months later Seward announced to a startled and incredulous nation the "Irrepressible Conflict."

Parties were swiftly rushing to desperate measures. In May, 1859, the Southern Commercial Convention boldly affirmed the unconstitutionality of the laws forbidding the foreign slave-trade. Five months later old John Brown made the South tremble by his mad sally at Harper's Ferry.

The near approach of war oppressed thoughtful men with dread and melancholy, and the timorous separated themselves from the strong. Political parties multiplied on every hand, as the physicians assemble thick about the bedside of a dying man. In one great camp was seen the banner inscribed, " Congressional interference in the Territories *against* slavery;" in another the device, " Congressional interference in the Territories *for* slavery." Between these two remotest camps was another on whose ensign was written, " The great principle: Congressional non-interference;" and another with this motto, " The Union, the Constitution, and the enforcement of the laws." There was a multitude of separate brigades and regiments, as "Abolitionists," " Fire-eaters," "Silver Grays," " Old Hunkers," " Barn-Burners," " Co-operationists," etc.

The election of 1860 let slip the dogs of war. As one after another of the " erring sisters" took her departure from the ancestral hearth-stone, there were some who cried out, " Let the Union slide !" but the " old public functionary" shed tears. Some called earnestly after them, that they meant to leave their " peculiar institution" unharmed, but these protests of the weak-kneed were no longer of any avail. So great was the distress and alarm of the majority of the people, both North and South, that one good old man was encouraged to attempt once more the work of compromise. But the " Peace Congress" was laughed to scorn.

All patchwork of diplomacy was rudely swept aside by the attack on Fort Sumter, which commenced a war on " the best government the world ever saw." But in thus " firing the Southern heart" the Rebels fired also the Northern, and then came a wild cry for " blood-letting." The great word was spoken: "If any man attempts to haul down the American flag, shoot him on the spot !"

Maryland "had no quarrel with the Union," and then there came from the North a fierce cry, "Through Baltimore, or over it !" This was followed by "On to Richmond !" The raw and untutored army made a blundering pass at Manassas, had victory just in its gripe, then ran away in a bloody and disastrous panic, and a well-known voice cried, "Peace on the best attainable terms !" Then for weary months all remained "quiet on the Potomac," and the heart of the people grew sick and sad with hope deferred. But they were listening meantime to the marvelous narratives of the "reliable gentleman" and the "intelligent contraband," who related to their gaping auditors such accounts of the doings of the dreadful and mysterious "masked batteries" of the Rebels as made each separate and particular hair on our heads stand on end.

They had not yet learned in Washington to let headquarters be in the field, whence McClellan, after a series of dreadful battles, had to "change his base" before Richmond. This emboldened Lee to change his base into "Maryland, my Maryland," from which Antietam caused him to change it back again. Instructed by these bitter experiences, the government had allowed Pope, as Lee jestingly said, "to have his headquarters where his hindquarters ought to be ;" in consequence of which proceeding the "Mackerel Brigade" performed some most wonderful and astounding evolutions, in a race with the Rebels for Washington.

But in the mean time, happily, Grant was learning out West how to "move on your works ;" Sherman, how to "make a flank movement ;" and Sheridan, how to "do things."

There was a deal of bad management everywhere; a good deal of "shoddy" was distributed to the brave boys in blue; and the bacon was often rancid, or lacking altogether. Many a poor fellow who enlisted to do hard fighting, but was allowed to rot in ignominious inaction along the banks of the James, the Rappahannock, the Tennessee, and the Mississippi, lost the number of his mess, and was carried out feet foremost from his little "chebang" to his long home. Billy Jones "jumped the boun-ti-ee;" there were "Copperheads" in the grass, ready to strike the boys in the rear; there were infamous contractors getting rich on their sufferings. The "K. G. C." abounded; the "Butternuts" obstructed. The deserted and lonely maidens began to sing "When this cruel war is over." Many declared the "war was a failure," and all were at least ready to admit, with the President, that it was a "big job,"—bigger even than "Crazy Sherman" had predicted, and not to be ended in "ninety days" by any means. Those were dark, dark, sad days for all who loved the Republic.

But the people never desponded, whatever weak-kneed officers might do; and to the call for more troops they gloriously responded, "We are coming, Father Abraham, with three hundred thousand more;" and the tramp of armed myriads was heard from the piney forests of Maine to the broad prairies of Kansas. The "War Democrats" did nobly. Hooker fought his "battle above the clouds;" Rosecrans "went down to take Chattanooga,—and there he was."

Hitherto many good men had not been able to decide within themselves whether "the war was prosecuted to put down slavery, or slavery was to be put down to prosecute the war," or neither; but all the while "John Brown's soul was marching on" to its inevitable goal. At last the

President grew to the stature of the times, and felt himself strong enough to proclaim emancipation. This was a grievous stumbling-block and rock of offense to many good friends of the Republic; and they were hardly persuaded by the argument of "military necessity." The people drifted as slowly to emancipation as they did, in the Revolution, toward independence.

Better days were coming now. Grant sat doggedly down and pounded at Vicksburg for months. At last he and Pemberton met under a tree, and in the course of two or three hours broke a celebrated "backbone."

The navy was "stopping up the rat-holes" faithfully. Grant was assisted in the capture of Vicksburg by "an iron fleet with a wooden commander;" New Orleans was taken by "a wooden fleet with an iron commander."

As for the Rebels, so thoroughly had they believed in "peaceable secession," thinking the North too mercenary to fight, that many a vainglorious orator offered to "drink all the blood that would be spilled." Even should there be fighting (as Northern men also asserted), "one man would whip ten." At first there was division in their councils, some wishing all the Southern States to "co-operate;" but the capture of Sumter so turned the Southern head that opinion was reduced to an almost absolute dead level of unanimity, and "secession," pure and simple, every State going out for itself, was the order.

At first the leaders inflated the popular hopes with "foreign recognition;" then later, when the battle was beginning to go sore against them, with a "revulsion of popular feeling in the North."

The Rebels too often had to defend their cities, as Bragg said to Davis, "with five proclamations and one brigade." "Political Brigadiers" were the curse of their armies. Deserters abounded at the front, and "bombproofs" at home. The secret "Red and White League" —not daring to add the "blue," but repudiating the "red"—sapped their Georgia regiments. Discipline was nugatory; the order to charge or to fall back sometimes proceeded from some Stentor of a private. "Lee's miserables" were so ragged that he "was always ashamed of them except when fighting." Memminger's "graybacks" would not feed them, and Nature's "graybacks" devoured them.

Stonewall Jackson performed prodigies of daring and valor, and made Frémont his "Quartermaster." Johnston made a masterly retreat in Georgia; and then Hood "fout and fout" in Atlanta, and afterward was driven away from Nashville with ignominy.

But it was all of no avail. Their great "interior circle," on which Albert Sydney Johnston counted so much, became daily narrower and more hollow. "Cousin Sal" was impetuous and brave, but no match for her persistent and hard-headed old Uncle. To replenish their wasted regiments, they were driven to "rob the cradle and the grave." The fatal end drew near. "Submissionists" began to rear their heads. Men began to talk of "dying in the last ditch."

Meantime, Grant was pounding at Richmond with his accustomed doggedness, determined to "fight it out on that line, if it took all summer." It took all summer, and all winter. Sherman conceived his daring project, asked and received permission, and then went "marching through Georgia." Sheridan took a memorable "ride" up the Shenandoah Valley, then hastened down, and fell upon Petersburg.

One Sunday morning, after reading a mysterious telegram in church, Davis made ready in all haste, and fled

with his Cabinet from Richmond. On his way through
North Carolina he made a speech, in which he affirmed
that the "war had entered upon a new phase." That
new phase meant for him a "Yankee Bastile."

It was a "lost cause." The Rebels were "overpowered,
but not whipped." They were "outnumbered by the
Northern scum."

The government did not hang Davis on a "sour apple-
tree," or any other, but proceeded quietly to the great
work of "Reconstruction." "My policy" did not prevail, but Congress deemed it necessary to "reconstruct
reconstruction." "Universal amnesty and universal suf-
frage" was refused, though the Northern people were disposed to treat the fallen Rebels with great generosity.
There followed a long and disgraceful wrangle between
Congress and the President, continuing until the incoming
of a new administration, with a motto which the people
took up with that great joy that comes of weariness: "Let
us have peace." But, alas! the South had been "reconstructed" so much, and yet so ill, that there was no peace
there; but the unhealed and rankling malady of disfran-
chisement within burst forth in the violent eruptions of
the "Ku-Klux."

The North had said, "The negro troops fought nobly,"
and therefore demanded for them the ballot. But the
negro himself responded:

> "Shoo, fly! don't bodder me,
> For I belong to Company B."

This history may properly end with the latest sectional
mottoes. New England says, "Boston State-House is the
hub of the Solar System." The West, speaking through
General Logan, replies with arguments about the "geo-

graphical center." The South says, "In Dixie land I'll take my stand." On the Pacific slope the word is:

> " That for ways that are dark,
> And for tricks that are vain,
> The heathen Chinee is peculiar."

GERMAN STUDENT FRATERNITIES.

PERHAPS it would be impossible to give a clearer and yet more comprehensive epitome of German political history for the last three centuries than is found in the student fraternities. Of course, they do not present an actual epitome of that history, but only an imitation performed by boys; but the doings of boys are so much simpler and withal so much more attractive than their fathers' actions, and, in Germany, have been such an exact imitation of the same, that their history is altogether the most interesting. Görres says, "If a boy does not at ten run around with all the *gamins* he can find, and at twenty become a red-hot republican, he will come to nothing." But the university boys of Germany are not all red-hot republicans at twenty, and we shall therefore find in their doings all forms of government typified.

The fraternities correspond exactly neither to the secret societies of our American colleges nor to the literary societies; for, unlike the first, their constitutions and proceedings are open, and, unlike the second, they pay small attention to that kind of peculiarly American oratory which frequently smacks, as the French say, *de la blague,* and more to the cultivation of a slightly maudlin patriotism which is known in Germany as *Deutschthaumelei.* As in America, there are two classes of organizations, quite as distinct as ours, and a third party of neutrals, though these latter are far less numerous proportionately than in American colleges. The most numerous and powerful class of fraternities, especially in North German universities, is the corps; and the others we may call, for lack of a more accurate word, literary clubs, though this is by no means a translation of their title (*Burschenschaften*), but only an approximate indication of their character. Besides these, there are a few theological fraternities, found principally in Catholic universities and in Switzerland; and fewer still of what may be called classic fraternities, as, for instance, that of Berlin devoted to the study of Thucydides. Both the corps and the literary clubs have, as in America, a common organization in many universities, though this community is less perfect than ours, extending usually only to the most general regulations as to duels, beer-courts, etc., and the correspondence between them is irregular. Each university has its own special beer-code and duel-code, established by its General Convention, by which all beer and sword-duels must be regulated; but the different lodges of the same organization have an arrangement of cartel between them which entitles students moving from one university to another, or students fighting a duel in another university than their own, to certain rights and privileges. Some of them may have secret grips or pass-words, but, if so, it is in violation of agreements made with the faculties, and I have never discovered any evidence of them. The principal mode of salutation consists in an embrace and a good, broad, " clamorous smack." As to badges, colors, uniforms, and present general character, it will be more appropriate to speak after some consideration has been devoted to their origin and history.

The existence of these fraternities reaches far back into the seventeenth century, and the earliest form which they assumed was that of national clubs (*Landsmannschaften*) founded solely on the principle of a common nationality.

When the student came to the university he was a stranger, far from home and in need of friends; he found there many different dialects of German, less intelligible to each other than now, and many varieties of national costume and customs. Nothing was more natural, therefore, than that he should seek out men from his own province, speaking his own dialect. They would console each other in their loneliness, and "drink brotherhood" together, that is, holding the beer-mugs in locked arms.

Of course, the constitutions and laws of these clubs were at first very ill defined, and their amusements were of the rudest and often the most scandalous description. Many students wore swords, and their favorite pastime was to slap the street-boys (*Gnoten*) with the flat of the sword, or to terrify children and nurses at night with hideous ghostly apparitions. The "captain joke" was to annoy the "rattlers," as they called the policemen, by thumping on their doors and crying "Murder!" to see them gather up their loins and run through the streets.

"Pennalism," or the system of fagging, existed then in its worst shape; and in many universities the student did not become a "moss-skin," that is, entirely free from servitude, until the seventh semester, or beginning of the fourth year. German historians assert that this custom, or one very like to it, existed in the schools of Athens. The Senior Convention was absolute. It was its influence principally which gave the clubs so great a supremacy in the universities as to force nearly all the students to join them, will they, nill they. As the university was imported into Germany from France, so the cumbrous title, national club, presently yielded to the French designation *corps*, though the fraternity was sometimes called a circle (*Kränzchen*). The constitution of the Senior

Convention, as it existed before the nineteenth century, was substantially as follows :

1. All students who wish to have a voice in the regulation of public affairs in the university must belong to some corps.   In most universities the names of all corps that may exist there have been already permanently established, so that any new organization springing up must take a name now vacant, by which it becomes entitled to a vote in the Senior Convention ; or, if not satisfied with an old name, must approve itself in the duello with all the existing corps.   The new name will then be recognized by the Senior Convention.

2. Each corps has one vote in the Senior Convention. This body exercises all legislative and administrative functions in public affairs, and wields executive power through a committee of three (*Chargirte*).

3. No honorable student can permit himself to be slandered or insulted.   He must, within the lawful time (generally three days), either exact an explanation or challenge the offender to a duel.

4. When the student's personal honor is wounded by insult or slander, it can be restored by the duello (with the sword) alone.

5. Regulations as to methods of challenge, weapons, seconds, distance, etc. are different in different universities.

6. Regulations as to the degree or amount of disgrace attaching to every dishonorable action, such as a breach of the word of honor, certain verbal and personal injuries specified in the code of honor, but, above all, refusal to fight when challenged, are generally prescribed by the Senior Convention.

7. Another matter over which the Senior Convention exercises control, is the rights of the students among

themselves.   During the existence of the system of fagging, the regulation of the relations of fags to the other students occupied most of the legislative activity of this body.   (The precise definition of the nature and position of a fag appears to have given students much trouble a century ago.   An old Heidelberg code defines a fag as "A piece of flesh without mind, wit, or sense, but who always carries a great quantity of cigars and tobacco about him."   Another at Halle summed them up thus, "Pennals are sly, but they do not think.")

The corps, as inspired and guided by the Senior Convention, exercised a relentless tyranny, and their influence was in many respects then, as it is to-day, deplorable.   All who would not join them, preferring to avoid the duel and to give their evenings to study, were branded as "finches," "camels," "savages," and were treated with unmeasured contempt.   Kobbe, writing of the period which followed the Thirty Years' War, says: "In that dark epoch it was, when the national heart was crushed and broken, that the germ of our liberties, or, if the name is preferred, the spirit of youthful chivalry, took refuge in the universities; and that of which people had no enjoyment elsewhere they consoled themselves with to the fill during their three years' residence at the university.   In this way, then, the old university freedom soon degenerated.   The staid old men gave the institution their sanction only because the youth could therein find vent for their buoyancy, and run out their horns. The wilder the better, said they, and so that which was originally designed to make the soul really free, and to elevate the intellect above the conventional, and give it strength for coming life, became a sort of opium-eating, which wasted the intellectual powers, perverted the ambition, and left behind a corresponding insipidity and hollowness, and that which the state, as it was left by that unhappy war, could best employ—machine-laborers.''

About the middle of the eighteenth century there spread out from Scotland, all over Europe and into the German universities, a sort of Freemasonry, which threatened, for a time, to extinguish the earlier national clubs or corps altogether. They disregarded nationality, and selected members solely on the principle of congeniality. The students went mad over these follies, and for a quarter of a century, corresponding with the Storm-and-Stress Period in literature, Germany was filled with signs and wonders, stories of pale riders on horseback, terrific caged goats, heated gridirons, etc. Fearful rites of initiation were employed, which made '' each particular hair to stand on end.'' The national clubs almost entirely disappeared from some universities, being supplanted by these new orders, of which the most widely ramified and popular was the *Amicisten Orden.* Their device consisted of a kind of cross, with the letters V. V. A. (*vivat vera amicitia*) above it, and V. A. F. H. (*vivat amicitia fructus honoris*) below it.

Toward the end of the century these fooleries fell away, and the year 1798 tumbled them into their grave. The old national clubs everywhere experienced a resurrection, with their ancient names, Saxonia, Westphalia, Bavaria, Rhenania, etc.; but the *furore* of Scotch-German Free-masonry had had this effect, that it destroyed the principle of association by nationalities, and henceforth these national clubs were called corps, as now, and selected their members entirely on the basis of congeniality. Thus this half-mad folly from Scotland had done something to break down provincialism in the universities, and so far forth was useful.

A writer describing the costumes of the corps in Erlangen, about 1800, says they generally wore leather breeches, like the Bavarian peasants of to-day, usually black or brown and ornamented with looped braid ; cannon-boots, very high, with the trousers worn inside ; tall, pointed, black felt hats, ornamented with long white cock's-feathers ; spurs, gauntlets, and a light straight sword (*Stossdegen*). This last article they carried a great portion of the time. Their long swan-neck pipes were ornamented with the corps colors, and sometimes they wore a leather helm, like that of the Bavarian army. In other universities the modern jaunty little cloth cap was already introduced.

Such were the fraternities at the outbreak of the French Revolution. The great Napoleonic wars decimated the universities only less disastrously than the Thirty Years' War ; nearly half a score of them totally disappeared, professors and students going into the ranks. The tyranny of the French rallied all to the front, and in the momentous years 1814–1815, when old Germany boiled like a pot, the enthusiasm which ran through that phlegmatic people, as the mighty game which had been played by giants for a quarter of a century was drawing to its grand close, was only equaled by our vast uprising of 1861. Jena sent half a regiment. The student Stapps shot at Bonaparte in the garden of Schönbrunn, and five hours afterward he was fusiladed. His death wrought miracles, —for every drop of his blood so dastardly spilled there sprang up a thousand of his comrades to avenge his death.

Bonaparte was crushed. Many of the students returned to the lecture-room to complete their studies, boys no longer, but broad-shouldered and bearded men, the veterans of many a hard campaign, leather-hided and brawny, decorated with crosses and epaulettes and honorable scars, their white, thin skins tough as shagreen. Should they now go back to the petty squabbles of their vealy days? Should men who had fought for all Germany, bared their breasts to its foes on many a gallant field, and drained the bowl around many a bivouac-fire beside the Rhine to the united Fatherland, now draw their toy-swords for Saxonia, or Lusatia, or Rhenania? Absurd! They must have a fraternity founded on a broader basis.

Scarcely, therefore, had the peace of Vienna been concluded, when one Jahn, a Jena man, sent out a circular to all the students of Germany, glowing with patriotic fervor, and containing the kernel of a constitution for such a new and broader sodality. In it he named the magic word *Bursch*, for which the English has no full equivalent. Eleven men of Jena, from the four corps there existing, met and organized the first literary club, but did not awaken the enthusiasm they expected, and presently the project fell through. Another small club, calling itself the Sulphurea, having no constitution but the motto, "Death to the duello!" died even more quickly.

But one Kaffenberger, also a man of Jena, saw that the corps, backed by the great and ancient prestige of the duel, must be attacked more craftily. He took Jahn's constitution, but popularized it by adding many of the least objectionable laws of the corps, and founded thereon, June 12th, 1815, the *Christlich-deutsche-Burschenschaft*, with the motto, "Honor, Freedom, Fatherland." This is an important date in the student life of Germany, as marking the first great step of revolt against the duello. Kaffenberger took away the despotic power given by the corps to the oligarchic Senior Convention, for which body he substituted the General Convention, wherein every student, except Freshmen of the first semester, had a voice.

This latter body was a return to the old Athenian *ecclesia*, and was the ultimate authority; but his President and council, with their combined executive and legislative powers, mutually supplementary, curiously resembled our President and Senate. They made small war on the duello as yet, even fighting themselves when unavoidable, and their principal object was to cultivate patriotism. The greatness, the unity, the invulnerability, the incomprehensibility of Germany, etc.,—this was their weakness, or rather their strength, for the new doctrine now began to multiply on the face of the earth. About the only good thing these enthusiasts accomplished was to give to Germany some of its most beautiful songs, for which the appreciative American student will ever be grateful to them. The glorious drinking-songs of Arndt, Rückert, Körner, and others, such as the "Gaudeamus," "Landesvater," and

"Wir hatten erbaut ein stattliches Haus,"

were first heard then in many a roistering beer-cellar, and, to the great advantage of morality, soon supplanted the smutty or maudlin effusions which had descended from the age of Louis XIV.

In less than a year after their foundation the literary clubs had rooted out all the corps in Jena except one dwindling lodge, and the faculties negotiated with them as constituting the entire body of students. On the first anniversary of the Vienna peace they marched in gorgeous procession through Jena, and received from the young ladies a silk banner bearing their colors (black, red, and gold), which afterward had a history more mysterious and celebrated than any other ever known in Germany. A year later they carried it in gala procession again, and immediately afterward it was stolen and no trace of it could be found,—a circumstance which created an excitement as profound as the abduction of Morgan. Thirty years afterward a man who had belonged to the only corps that was left, confessed on his dying bed that he had hidden it in spite; but to this day there are hundreds of thousands of superstitious Germans who still believe that old flag is hidden somewhere about the Wartburg, sacredly guarded by the patron saint of Germany, who will bring it forth in triumph on the day of Germany's final union.   Its appearance is now due.

In 1818 these literary clubs held their first great reunion, and at that time they were firmly established in eleven universities.   Haughty and aristocratic Göttingen and Breslau were the only strongholds that had not been wholly or partly carried by this half-mad *Deutschthaumelei.* America is called the peculiar dwelling-place of humbug and "sensations;" but does the marvelous history of Know-Nothingism or of the *morus multicaulis* furnish anything surpassing this?

Jena was the only university where the corps had entirely succumbed, but in a few cities they still held out in undiminished strength, and in others shared the dominion pretty equally with their young rivals.   On the whole, Germany was more equally parceled out between them than at the present day, the literary clubs being weaker now, which fact is significant, since they represent socialistic democracy, while the corps stand for the old feudal aristocracy.   Since they now (about 1818) stand over against each other most equally matched and in full battle-array, let us take a survey of their respective uniforms.

The literary clubs called themselves Old Germans, and affected something of the simplicity and more of the extravagances of their mediæval ancestors.   Their gala uniform was generally a close, short, black tabard, with a stiff narrow collar, and, turned over it, a wide shirt-collar, ornamented with embroidery, spangles, etc.; bare neck; long hair; a black bonnet on the head, garnished with feathers and a gold acorn.   On particular days they wore a red scarf bordered with gold fringe; a long, straight, slender sword (not the pointed rapier, for the stab-duel, but a sword with a knob on the point, for the stroke-duel); gold spurs of great size; and had their coats bordered with velvet scollops and gold fringe.   Sometimes they trained in the linen uniforms of the Turners, as we see them to-day.

The corps, inconsistent with their real principles, called themselves Young Germans, and chose the then most modern costumes.   They wore cavalry collars; cannon-boots, the same as now; immense spurs; sometimes military helmets, but oftener the modern caps; uhlan casques; hussar cassocks; Polish coats with an abundance of loops and braid on the breasts; and on their trousers galloons as wide as one's hand.   They generally carried yet the pointed rapier suited for the stab-duel.   Mayer's article on the universities, from which I derive many facts, and the Breslau pamphlet entitled "*Der Unsinn des Duells*," differ somewhat as to the date when the corps abandoned the stab-duel for the less ferocious stroke-duel, but it was somewhat later than the time under discussion.

The literary clubs, as we have seen, came in on the mighty flood-tide of enthusiasm following the expulsion of Bonaparte, but that flood-tide was already ebbing. The Germans having healed their wounds were beginning to dream again, and to burrow in their book-dens like troglodytes.   Arndt says, "People have sometimes done us Germans the honor to call us the Greeks of the modern world, and the thoughtful people who have been designated by God to think and invent for the peoples of

Europe. . . . But we are for all other Europeans and above all others the dreamers, and have thereby suffered to fall into the hands of subtle and crafty strangers a great part of that which we had earned with our sweat and blood." For this reason the literary clubs were already showing the yellow leaf, when there fell a stroke which cut them up by the roots. The Confederate Parliament, in Frankfort, passed a series of resolutions which set forth that "the so-called literary clubs, now existing in certain universities, and carrying on a secret correspondence that extends all over Germany,—an institution that is dangerous to the liberties of the people, as well as corrupting to public morals, and cannot therefore be tolerated,—be, and the same are, hereby forbidden." They further enacted that any person convicted of belonging to one of these pestilent clubs after the enactment should be declared forever incompetent to hold a public office! So another reunion took place in Jena in 1819, and with solemn and imposing ceremonies the literary clubs were dissolved *as public organizations.* Whereupon there was great rejoicing among the corps, and much accession of beer and new members. The literary clubs deserved their fate, not for their sins, but for their follies. Patriotism with them became a disease. With all their scandalous sins of sottishness, outrageous quarrelsomeness, and vainglory, the corps were the more respectable, even if their souls were so dead that none ever to himself hath said, "This is my own, my native land." They were too proud to make themselves fools.

Of course, as the reader has foreseen, these literary clubs, being publicly suppressed, gradually sprang up again as secret societies. In Jena alone did they maintain an open existence, but did it at the expense of all their old principles and their patriotism, fought duels, and despised the non-fraternity men, the "camels," as heartily as did the corps.   In the universities, too, where they lived only in profound secrecy, they abandoned the notion of saving the Fatherland, and gave their attention pretty exclusively to the question of the relative disadvantages of the fore-stroke and the back-stroke.   Within three years after their formal dissolution they had secret lodges in most of the universities where they existed before ; but the university police hunted them so keenly that many of them dared have no written constitution, and were liable at any moment to be seized and ignominiously cast into the pit, whence they might dolorously cry out of the deeps, *O quid agis ?*

But as time rolled on, and the statute began to acquire a covering of dust, this severity relaxed.   In 1824 the remnants of the old literary clubs in Erlangen ventured to reorganize themselves into a body to which they gave the cautious name of the Generality (*Allgemeinheit*), and by conducting themselves with great discretion, in a year they transgressed with impunity the Bavarian law which forbade any but the corps from wearing colors.   They assumed uniform caps.   But from the day of their foundation there had been growing up among them a division of sentiment, one section acquiring the title of the Pathos party, while the others became known as Bummers.   The first hankered after the flesh-pots of the old Jena literary clubs, were the dreamers, the maudlin patriots, the troglodytes of the university ; but the second had caught a partial inspiration of real human life, and were less anxious to save the Fatherland than to find out the best quality of beer and swig the same.   Having before them a goodly keg (*Fass*) of mellow old hock, they would cry out in the words of the moral Seneca, "*Hoc* absit ne-*fas !*" The Pathos worshiped the Muses and the Graces, and wept over the downfall of the Fatherland; the Bummers worshiped the graces who lived in Erlangen, could quaff beer, and trip it "on the light fantastic toe," and as for the Fatherland, their creed was—to commit a slight violence on a venerable text—*ubi puella, ibi patria.* In the picnics in the vicinity of Erlangen, the Pathos would wander off alone, and frequently improve the opportunity in the silent forests to debate and reason together upon the affairs of the nation, or—

> " Retreated in a silent valley, sing
> With notes angelical to many a harp;"

while the Bummers danced, and rollicked, and occasionally fleshed upon each other the latest fashion of saber from Suhl. They were captured by the police so often when they were enjoying their Attic nights, and incarcerated in the dungeon, that they made a song about it, of which a couplet may be thus rendered:

> "Think you this joke annoys me, chum?
> No; prison-life is frolicsome."

German students are generally good draughtsmen, and they had such frequent and admirable opportunities for developing their gifts in this direction, that the walls of the old university dungeons look like a geometrical palimpsest.

In a year after its establishment the Generality split, the Bummers becoming the Germania, and the Pathos the Arminia. The former adopted the colors of the old literary clubs and white regulation-caps. This date is important, because the Germania eventually became the widely-ramified literary clubs of to-day, a fine body of men, who have been an honor and a benefit to the universities; and we must overlook their origin when we remember the human material out of which Rome was builded. Freshmen were now for the first time in history admitted to a perfect equality with the older classes in all elections and other privileges, their sole lingering badge of inferiority being the tricolored guards which they wore instead of the white ones of the older classes. This year, therefore (1825), marks the final abolition, at least by this new order of fraternities, of the odious and barbarous system of fagging; and it is greatly to the credit of Catholic Erlangen that it was in advance of the Protestant North German universities in adopting this reform. But the duello was still retained in a milder form, for no fraternity could hope to live in open revolt against it, and it was by this alone that the Germania fought its way to a vote in the Erlangen Senior Convention. On the other hand, the Arminia with their foolish *Deutschthaumelei* allied themselves with the Philistines (citizens), thus covering themselves with fresh contempt, and speedily went into nothingness.

Jena also had a revival of the old literary club, and it likewise split into Pathos and Bummers. The Pathos occupied themselves with such questions as these, Ought the Almighty or Mephistopheles to have won his wager on Faust? and, Ought grace to be said at table aloud or in a whisper? They adopted the Erlangen names, Germania and Arminia, but both retained the duello, and one day they assembled in battle-array, thirty on a side, in a pinery near Jena, fell to at a given signal, and made no end until they had fought three-quarters of an hour. One student was killed on the field, two others had to have arms amputated, and none of them escaped without serious stabs or slashes. The Arminia was beaten, and consequently was expelled from the Senior Convention with ignominy.

In 1832 came the bastard Frankfort revolution, an affair

as contemptible in every way as our John Brown raid, but it scared the German governments greatly. The Germania now had numerous chapters, and some of their men were foolish enough to join in the Frankfort fiasco, or to cause suspicions that they did, and forthwith the storm burst over their heads again. All the governments in Germany, with the single exception of Würtemberg (now, perhaps, the most stupidly illiberal in the empire), issued rigid decrees against the Germania men, and swept them all away smack-smooth. In Tübingen alone did one chapter remain in open existence. All other universities compelled the student to promise on matriculation that he would join himself to no secret fraternity, and some, as that of Vienna, included secret and open, though they left a loop-hole where-through a man might creep, by adding, "or that you will abide all the penalties thereto attached."

Of course, the Germania men had to burrow in secret again and live the lives of ground-moles. After a few years they began to come up again ; they picked up the best men from the scattered remnants of the poor Arminia ; purged their ranks of the help-drinks (*Mitbummler*) and the bottle-tails (*Kneipschwänze*) whom they had taken in the day of prosperity merely to equalize their numbers with their enemies the corps ; and so began slowly to come to the surface once more. In some universities the storm had wrecked everything, clubs and corps alike. This was the case in Jena, and for several years there ensued a dreary interregnum, an arid waste in college life for lack of the social vivacity of the fraternities, until in 1837 there came up the Unsinnia, a club of wits and scholars, like the Owls of London and our own Phi Beta Kappa. These men gradually drifted into the again rising tide of the literary clubs or Germania men, and by their eminent respectability gave them impetus and *éclat.* In 1848 the Germania may be considered to have regained all the ground lost by the blunder of 1832, and they were now pretty much everywhere either tacitly or directly recognized by the faculties. That year, therefore, may stand as the date when the corps and the literary clubs were fully organized and developed as they stand to-day.

Among the elegant and haughty swashbucklers of Göttingen the literary clubs never got any considerable foothold in all their vicissitudes. The great storm of 1832 swept away even the corps in Göttingen, but after their revival they began to find rivals in fraternities founded much on the same principle as obtained in the ancient national clubs. These men called themselves Lüneburgers, Bremeners, etc.; but the haughty young gentlemen and sprigs of Hanoverian nobility in the corps dubbed them "guzzlers," implying that they assembled for no purpose but to swig beer. They also accused them of *Deutsch-thaumelei* or Jena Red Republicanism,·and this brought a great explosion in 1840, which I find reported in an old number of the *Rheinische Zeitung;* but the examination instituted by the faculty cleared them of the charge. The corps also tried to root them out by throwing themselves on them and contracting innumerable *pro-patria* duels with them; but the nationals got themselves privately coached in the use of the sword, and the only result was that they became as good strokes as the corps men, and gave them as good as they sent. The prime cause of the hostility of the corps was that the guzzlers were too democratic to submit to the oligarchic tyranny of the Senior Convention, and also wished to substitute a court of honor for the duel. The quarrel waxed so fierce at last that the faculty intervened, punished the corps men severely, distributing among them fifteen hundred days of imprisonment, and gave some of them the *consilium abeundi*. They obliged them to enter into cartel with the nationals; recognize the court of honor, if the nationals preferred it to the duel; and also abide by the decisions of the General Convention in all matters affecting equally corps men and nationals, although the former still retained the Senior Convention as the highest authority in matters between the corps alone. Preposterous as it may seem, the mystic letters G. C. and S. C. were never spoken but in a whisper (so says this *Rheinische Zeitung*) as being the awful depositories of power, though every bootblack in the town knew on what evenings they met. About the only difference between the corps and these nationals in Göttingen was, that the former fought more duels, and developed more vociferous ability in "throating." A duel with them generally created a great clamor as to whether a stroke had "set," whether or not it was "on," or was a "back-stroke" or a "fore-stroke," so that one duel usually begot another among the seconds or witnesses.

Thus we have briefly traced out the corps, beginning before the Thirty Years' War, and the literary clubs which arose in 1815. The first represent the old feudal aristocracy; the latter, democracy. The subject cannot be dismissed without a word or two of comment.

One of the greatest benefits which the club men have helped to confer on student life is the mitigation of the duel. Coming originally from Italy, the dark and treacherous, the duello prevailed for centuries in Germany in the frightful form of the thrust-duel. The first step of reform was to cause a large hilt, as broad as a dinner-plate, to be made on the rapier, to catch the point of the adversary's weapon. Then a knob was put on the point, and the thrust-duel was abandoned for the stroke-duel, which is far more honest, manly, and consonant with that Teutonic genius which invented the war-club swung so lustily in the time of Tacitus. That hideous weapon the three-edged rapier, bearded like a sickle, so that when it was thrust into the body it could not be drawn out, was forbidden by the university statutes. Jean Paul cynically said of that barbarous form of duel that it was well enough, for it was killing off the fools; but, unfortunately, so great was the strength of a false public opinion, a good man, unskilled with the sword, could be forced to fight and be killed by a brainless coxcomb who would escape unhurt. Next the whole breast, throat, and right arm were muffled in stout leather, and the eyes protected with wire goggles, so that a man could get no slashes except on his cheeks and on the top of his pate. The present mode of duel is very seldom fatal, almost never unless the rapier breaks, as happened a few years ago, when the point broken off pierced a student's heart. Club men are inclined to avoid the duel, and appeal to a court of honor; but the corps push dueling to a ridiculous and outrageous excess. Rival corps often egg on their best strokes to settle a long-standing feud between them, like the Horatii and the Curiatii. In Heidelberg, for instance, when a student wishes to fight another, he has only to look hard at him in a peculiar manner, when the other asks, "What do you want?" and the first one replies by asking him to name his seconds. In one respect the corps are superior, for they never descend to the base American fisticuff, or the "hustle" in the university halls, or the caning (*Holzerei*), while the club men sometimes so forget their dignity as to engage at least in the "wooden." It is the one solitary palliation of German dueling that it prevents men from fighting on the spot, brutally, and in the red heat of passion, and adjourns the matter to a cooler moment. The corps never fight a Philistine, unless he be a military officer; but the club men will not refuse a "towny" satisfaction, but prefer to carry the dispute before the university senate.

On the other hand, the beer-duels are, if possible, more ridiculous and puerile than the contest with the rapier. The club men are even freer than the corps to swig off fifteen or twenty glasses in a "salamander," or drain their glass after each stanza of the long song:

> "In Leipzig angekommen,
>   Als Fuchs bin aufgenommen,"

or to resent the insult of being called "Pope," or "doctor," or "sage," or "beer-baby," by challenging the adversary to an expiation of this mortal offense by a duel of two, three, or four glasses, the first one through being winner.

> "Und de more you trinks, pe cerdain,
>   More Deutsch you'll surely pe."

And is it not the darling purpose of the club men to be as German as possible, and to save the Fatherland?

Göttingen, Heidelberg, and Würzburg are the strongholds of the corps, while the literary clubs are potent in Jena, Erlangen, and Munich. Thanks to the young scions of nobility who keep up the corps in Göttingen, that institution has been a bane to Hanover and to all North Germany. Go almost any evening to the "Kaiser" or other favorite student resort in that city, and about the only topics you shall hear broached will be duels, love-intrigues, or the qualities of the dogs kept there by the young noblemen. If sometimes they so forget their frigid dignity as to join in a song, they do not, like the "sholly

poy" of the literary club, choose the beautiful songs of
Fred. Rückert, Arndt, or Schenkendorf, but rather the
scandalous effusions of the French Rococo age. It is the
acme of wit to narrate some belittling and vulgar anec-
dote of a professor, as it is the acme of stupidity to mention any topic of his lecture, and who does it is soon
enough silenced with "sage." Göttingen is praised for
its outward decorum, the students daintily prink and
polish their apparel, and you shall not hear a tenth part
of the vulgar but honest noise resounding in that cellar
where Goethe once helped to make night hideous; but
nowhere in Germany is there another body of students so
hollow-hearted and so eaten up with conceit. The German language has no equivalent for the word *gentleman*,
and it is said to have been introduced and naturalized by
the young Hanoverian snobs of Göttingen in the time
of George IV., a prince whom they had given to England. As for their studies, they consist simply in parrot-
ing certain necessary facts, which they arrange as on a
string and mechanically cram for examination-day. They
are too proud to endure the disgrace of being plucked,
but as for any enduring and assimilated knowledge, it is
not in them. Göttingen is a memorizing machine.

It is not to be denied that the corps are schools of a
certain independence, a certain formation of gentlemanly
character in the external sense; but the independence
nurtured by them is founded on an immeasurable conceit,
and the character is one of unmitigated selfishness and
arrogance. The whole body of corps laws and their
esprit de corps are filled with a contempt for everything
not reducible to certain formulas of honor, falsely so
called, and especially for the Philistine, the plain citizen.
One of the most hateful characteristics of the upper
classes of Germany is their despotism over the humble

and their cringing servility before the great, and it is in no small degree traceable to the teachings of these university corps. An Italian nobleman may be of the most exalted rank and yet be a liberal; but no sooner does a German get a title and a kingly cross on his bosom than he hastens to *kow-tow* before the throne.

If the club men sometimes, nay, often, bubble quite over with a certain namby-pamby patriotism, they are at least greatly and honestly in earnest. Give me a man, says Emerson, who has a bias in his convictions. The literary clubs are less devoted to dreamy and worse-than-useless Platonic-Republic-building than they were twenty-five years ago. The one great excellence in them is that they are schools of practical oratory. Jean Paul says, "The man can dispense with the savant, but not the savant with the man." What the German universities need above all things else is schools of practical men of affairs, of statesmen who can make kings tremble instead of laughing, as now, over their lamentable and egregious follies. The literary clubs teach men how to stand up and reason on their legs, how to hit straight out from the shoulder of their argument. Anything and everything is good for a German that will rouse him out of his bed, out of his easy-chair, out of his book-den, or any other place, attitude, or atmosphere whatsoever which is conducive to his fatal habit of searching for the unseen, and inject into his veins some of the fresh blood of solid facts, and rack his brain with some of the hard knocks of everyday political and social human nature. If the literary clubs will make debates on fresh practical topics a specialty, they will be worth more as educators of public men than all the universities together.

CALIFORNIA saved the Republic once, and was saved by it in return. How did California save the Republic?

The discovery of gold in the placers at Coloma turned us away from Mexico, which is political death. Before that discovery, and especially after the conquering heroes of Buena Vista and Chapultepec had marched through and spied out the land, there was a current of adventure and speculation steadily setting toward her fabulous riches of silver; but the fame of California turned it aside, let us hope, forever. American men and American money would have grouped themselves gradually about the richest mines, and, becoming compactly knit together in strong towns, would have revolted, as the Lone Star Republic did, and brought province after province knocking at our doors.

The Roman Empire girdled nearly all the known world with victories, but when its armies went down to Egypt, there was opened a fountain of corruption and contention which overthrew the empire. In the day when we add Mexico, it becomes our Egypt.

To many this may seem a shadowy and altogether insubstantial peril which was thus averted. But there was a very positive and tangible element of salvation which California digged, and washed, and pounded out, in the shape of $191,300,000 in gold, produced during the years of the war, to say nothing of the million or more which the people contributed, out of their prodigal generosity, to the Sanitary Fund. There never was any adequate official acknowledgment of this mighty succor given by California to the struggling nation. But Congress understood it well, when, in the midst of an unparalleled civil war, there came a sudden dread and a peril, lest some losel rebel should fall foul of the monthly argosy, heavy with *oro Americano,* off the coast of Mazatlan, and when in all haste it voted millions, though in the darkest days of a frightfully expensive war, to set the overland railroad a-digging. General Grant understood it well, when he congratulated the people in his message that they were gotten now in a position to reach across quickly, and finger their "strong-box" in the day when they needed money.

But our principal concern is with the second question: How did the Republic save California? And, first, it is necessary to state at considerable length the condition of affairs present and impending, from which the coast was thus rescued.

Not many months after the completion of the overland railroad everybody was asking his neighbor, "What ails California?" In many of the mountain mining towns, which once resounded with the blast of the powder, the clank of the quartz-mill, and the merry click of the pistol, the doors were shut in the streets, and the sound of the grinding was low. The silver mills were dry, the gold ran thin in the sluices, in many places the harvests were shortened, and the "blanket men" were abroad in the land in ominous numbers. Real estate fell from the very top-round of the ladder of an unprecedented inflation down to the fourth or fifth step. Mortgages on real estate in San Francisco mounted up to the alarming figure of $30,000,000, a sum nearly equal to all the deposits then in the savings-banks of California. The enormous cash rent which small farmers were paying for wheat-fields, with money borrowed at an exorbitant interest,—thereby often spending in one year's rent nearly the whole actual value of the farm,—was sinking them deeper than luckless Digger ever floundered in the wintry *adobe* of Salsapeutos.

Sü, the venerable and godlike, says: "Every good and bad deed will in the end receive its merited recompense; fly high or run far, still will it be difficult to escape." Wherein had California sinned, that its sin had found it out so swiftly and so surely? We must, to use a mining phrase, go down to the bed-rock, and patiently scrape together all the elements of the false position.

The vast mineral wealth of California had a deplorable effect on great masses of the early population, in a two-fold manner. First, it infected men with that restless fever which clung to them through life, even until they made their last little entry of real estate, and "took up a claim," seven feet by three. Second, many miners were attracted by the admirable adaptation to viniculture of the soil in the Sierra Nevada foothills, and gradually beat their picks into pruning-hooks, and their long-handled shovels into plows. This was fortunate, so far, and illustrates the remark of Humboldt, that the influence of mines on the progressive cultivation of the soil is more durable than the mines themselves. The placer gold was soon exhausted, and then the land became more valuable for agricultural purposes; but, unfortunately, the government refused to sell it or give any title for it, still holding it for "mineral land."

Fifteen or twenty years thus spent by the farmer, in the hope of some time getting a title to his little homestead, had a most disastrous effect, both on himself and his children. His family grew up unstable and uncertain. His manly arm was unnerved by insecurity. For the sake of a few paltry and delusive particles of glittering dust which yet lingered in the creek-bed or in the boulders among his clambering vines, any lawless rover might tear up all his terraces, uproot all his carefully-cultured vines and trees, for whose fruit he had toiled and waited, and leave him utterly without redress. Thousands of families grew up in this manner, making only a miserable shift until they might be certain of their possessions, and then abandoned them in despair at last,—all the best years of their lives wasted, their energies gone, and idleness and shiftlessness woven into the very life-web of their characters.

At last the government was induced to set about the survey and sale of these equivocal and fatal lands, but not until irreparable mischief had been done. The amount of "poor white trash" (I beg pardon of the reader for using this mean phrase, for no other is so expressive) which this state of things, together with other causes, produced, and turned loose upon California, especially the southern portion, it is deplorable to contemplate.

Such a course wrought such an effect in the fruit-growing foothills, and a different cause produced a like effect in the great valleys. To liken great things to small, the condition of California resembled that iniquitous old monopoly, the Roman Empire, as it was in the third and fourth centuries, when the homeless and landless hordes of savages began to surge against its borders, and strain their bloodshot eyes across its walls toward the riotous opulence within.

A man in the Tulare valley owns $1,000,000 worth of land for his herds to roam upon, yet he comes up to Sacramento, stands up in his place in the Legislature, and fights like a brigand against a projected railroad, be-

cause, forsooth, it would pierce his principality, and induce settlement; while the farmers, for lack of that railroad, pay half the value of their wheat for transportation.
Another in Kern valley owns 230,000 acres, yet sixty
families go home to Texas, because they can find no useful land.   Another near Santa Barbara claims 247,000
acres, and the citizens of that town hold an indignation
meeting, because this one man is throttling their life like
an anaconda, and no farmers can settle near them.   And
even mutton is not cheap.

"Coyotes" is getting to be the cant name for the poor
in Southern California.   There is no place for them on
top of the land, and they must dig underneath.

Travel anywhere in that section, and you shall find
them.   Between the great hills, all softened with a lilac,
chiaroscuro film of haze, brightly evergreen on the north
side with *chamizal*, but on the south side nibbled bare and
dusty by the swarming sheep, you shall anywhere find one
of these families, in an abandoned shepherd's-hut or a
wretched cabin of logs.   A spring of water is hard by;
under the vast overshadowing live-oak hangs a half-eaten
carcass of venison (fortunately, the atmosphere is very
pure); and in the cabin there is a can of wild honey.
They are a lank and sallow couple, with the Piké-county
twang, and seven white-haired daughters.

Come farther north, and journey over the great plains
of the Sacramento and San Joaquin valleys.   In the midst
of an almost boundless expanse of wheat, there stands a
mean, unpainted, unfenced shanty.   For days and days
the whistle of the steam-thresher can be heard, here to-
day, there to-morrow, but all the while on the ranch of
him who lives in that shanty.   The grimy gang of laborers
follow it through the season, for it is their principal "job"
of the year.   When the summer is over, and the harvest

is ended, they betake themselves to the towns; and then, as soon as they and their money part company, which is quickly enough, they sally forth again, sweating under their rolls of blankets,—aimless and incurable vagabonds.

California had no more grievous a system of land-monopoly than Michigan and Illinois formerly groaned under. Why, then, was it not broken up small, like those States?

The answer to that question is, that the Chinese scared away the immigrants whose crowding and attrition could break it up small. Why do Germans avoid the South? Many of them do, because they learn in infancy to run and hide their heads when the *bonne* cries *Schwarzer Mohr!* Mongolophobia did for California, to no little extent, what negrophobia did for the South.

The influence of the Chinese race in bolstering up these evil and ominous monopolies was twofold :—they scared away Caucasian immigrants, who would have forced a division of them; and they enabled them the better to be kept together, inasmuch as they prefer to labor in gangs, for the sake of companionship and protection, and do not care to hire themselves to small farmers, or buy farms of their own. In a word, the curse of California always was, that it had an excess of mere hirelings, and a lack of families; and, as the Chinese seldom bring their wives, they tend to keep up this worst of all social conditions.

The peculiar circumstances attending the genesis of California created a state of affairs not a little resembling the English system of primogeniture, with its train of evils. Men who were here before the discovery of gold "had greatness thrust upon them" by that event, while those who "came in '49 or the spring of '50," with reasonable prudence and energy, could hardly choose but achieve greatness. The immense grabs which were made in that famous year into this unmeasured and unhandled wild became the foundations of monopolies such as no other country ever beheld. The "Pioneers" became demigods. There was scarcely a member of Stevenson's Regiment who did not become rich and famous. For twenty years the State had only two governors, and San Francisco only two mayors, who did not "come here in '49 or the spring of '50." "Opposition" in California meant "the second son;" it meant a losing game. Monopoly was the very breath of the life of business.

On the one hand, there were the many, the unfortunate, and the wicked (regarded in Chinese philosophy as identical), the wrecks of the mines.

On the other hand, there were these fortunate or energetic few, under whose magic touch everything had turned to gold. They were strong, and great, and happy. They held California in their gripe. They had banks, and ranches, and steam-lines, and stage-lines. They were anxious to see California grow, partly because of a commendable public pride, partly because its growth was their wealth. It irked them to see "enterprises of great pith and moment" languish for want of laborers. Many of them were parvenus, and hardly brooked the lordly uses and the arrogance of the sometime miners and speculators, who had drifted down from loss to loss, and lodged at last, as common laborers, with soured tempers and broken bodies, in this soft and sunny clime.

Here stepped in the Chinese. We cannot refuse to believe the employers of California when they affirm, as most of them do, that they prefer white laborers to Chinese; and this makes it the more certain that it was the former who, by their absurd arrogance, wrought their own harm, and fastened the Chinese upon the country. It seems as if, almost in proportion as white laborers in California were worthless, in that proportion were they stubborn and dictatorial. The Chinese are even tamer in soul than the negroes, they are exceedingly imitative, and, in certain small and nimble labors not much exposed to the sun, they are notably industrious. Hence they were even better material than the negroes for an aristocracy to build upon.

California always will have an excess of "those unfortunates, the Helots of mankind," who come out ruined from the mines, and whom it will always tax the rural population to absorb and neutralize. More than that, the vast plains and valleys of the interior, being adapted to wheat culture, naturally gravitate into large ownings, on account of the facility and profit of machine-work; and this circumstance tends to make the body of laborers bachelor hirelings. In short, the main great agricultural system of California, instead of serving as a reclaimer of vagabond miners, has a tendency to keep them vagabonds.

If the Chinese brought their wives and stayed, their imitativeness would soon make them good citizens, and their willingness to work up the little odds and ends of farms would render them admirable chinking and filling between these great wheat-ranches. But, as it is, they not only do not become citizens, but they scare away people who would. Hon. F. M. Pixley, in a public lecture in San Francisco, affirmed that they have frightened away thirty thousand men. They make California empty of citizenship. They rot out the heart of the people, as the slaves of Italy, in the later days of the Roman Empire, rotted out the independent peasantry, and drove them into the cities.

Of all things, California most needs a stable, hard-fisted class of small farmers, to redeem her from the infamy of money-jugglers on one hand, and of vagabonds on the other. As the heart needs its good red blood, so does California need, on the great plains of the interior (for there is no danger of this great ranch system in the mountains), to make every man who labors there an owner and a voter. There is already a pernicious tendency to absenteeism in California; that is, men owning great ranches leave them to lieutenants, and spend their lives in hotels in the cities.

A few figures here set down will show that California was at one time rapidly approaching a point where the Chinese immigration would have exceeded the Caucasian. In the decade ending with 1850 only 35 Chinese arrived in the country; in that ending with 1860, 41,396; 1870, 68,475. In 1865 the Chinese immigration formed thirteen per cent. of the whole; over eighteen per cent. in 1868; nearly forty per cent. in 1869; and over twenty-one per cent. in 1870. The crisis was passed in 1869. But, while many Caucasians came only to go away, the Chinese permanent gain was larger. Thus, the Caucasian gain of arrivals over departures during the last three years of the decade was only a little over one hundred per cent.; while the Chinese gain was over one hundred and seventy-five per cent.

These figures are anything but pleasant to contemplate, or were at that time. The point was, not that California had not room for millions, but that, almost inversely as the Chinese immigration increased, the Caucasian diminished.

And what was, if possible, still more deplorable, was that the greatest organs of public opinion were almost as effectually estopped from even pointing out the evils of

Chinese immigration, as ever the press of the South was gagged against attacks on slavery. The wild and brutal atrocities of the mob, and the *ad captandum* diatribes of the demagogues, created a fierce party sentiment, and men brought over Chinamen from spite. The innocent Chinamen served, as the negroes did in the South, and do still when liberated, to separate the rich man more hopelessly from the poor. With the Chinamen present, the rich and great would infallibly put their hands on their shoulders, and lift themselves head and neck above the multitude. No Chinaman helped a laboring man to get on, but he made the poor poorer, and the rich richer. The Chinaman served as a wedge, to cleave the extremes of society further and further apart.

Under the influence of this sad and miserable political antagonism, the sentiment of the ruling classes was becoming oligarchic, plutocratic. Their talk had in it the old arrogant fallacies of the Southern planter. A quotation from one of their most authoritative utterances will illustrate:

"If society must have 'mudsills,' it is certainly better to take them from a race which would be benefited by even that position in a civilized community, than subject a portion of our own race to a position which they have outgrown."

How much that sounds like the old *ante-bellum* reasoning of Governor Hammond and *De Bow's Review*, by which it was conclusively demonstrated that the presence of the negro was the elevation of the white man! And the "poor white trash" to-day show what the results were. "The Chinese are just so many human machines," was the utterance of another high authority; and this was the burden of the general argument. Ignorant and fanatic workingmen have often, in modern history, made bloody

riots because of labor-saving machinery; but none ever
made war upon machinery persistently for twenty years.
And no mere machinery ever degraded any part of the
laboring masses to the condition of "coyotes."

There was a little golden-walled empire here, isolated
from the great world almost as effectually as China itself,
and full of notions of its own greatness as an egg is full
of meat.   It was prosperous beyond all that men read of
in history.   California was sailing down a glittering track
of prosperity toward industrial and social ruin.   The
minds of business men were provincial and supercrafty,
but narrow as their own range of physical vision.   Much
money had made them mad.   One of the most amusing
instances of this perverted judgment, as it were turning a
summersault in an oyster-shell, is found in the same
authoritative utterance above quoted :

"The clear-headed capitalist rejects the present one
per cent. per month for the future five per cent. per
month on his capital, and adds thereto the gratification
of having done his part in forwarding the interests of all
mankind."

Thus far the article has been devoted to a consideration of the condition of California from which it was
rescued by the Republic.   It turns now to narrate briefly
the circumstances of that change which linked the Pacific
coast to the great world.

On the 10th day of May, 1869, the golden spike was
driven on Promontory Mountain which united the East
to the West.   That was the signal for the dismissal, by
the Central Pacific alone, of an army of 16,000 laborers,
who surged back upon California.   One-half of them were
Chinese.   This great multitude swamped the labor market
in a twinkling.   The hundreds and thousands of butchers,
bakers, grocers, etc. who had supplied them, were sud-

denly without customers. The golden stream of a million dollars per month, which had poured out of the coffers of the Central Pacific, ceased to flow. The fifty ships per month which had sailed up the Sacramento, laden with materials for the mighty work, bumped their barnacled hulks idly against the wharves of San Francisco.

Real estate suffered an extraordinary collapse. The drummers and the runners of Chicago swarmed in the land like the locusts of Egypt, while the merchants of San Francisco sat in their office chairs, cocked up their heels on "the great resources," serenely smoked the cigar of "the laws of trade," and saw the Territorial merchants go off arm-in-arm with Chicago. Hundreds of wagon-makers, grocers, and merchants barely escaped bankruptcy with the skin of their teeth, by dismissing hands and cutting down expenses; while scores sold out everything at a ruinous sacrifice, and with the little remnants bought a piece of a ranch. The rush of Eastern competition and Eastern goods was too great for the market, and, for the time, the whole bottom dropped out. An extraordinary and ominous number of "blanket men" were abroad, and that winter the streets of San Francisco rumbled to the tread of three thousand hungry men, clamoring for work or bread.

Never since the day when Babel heaved its high walls in the face of heaven have men more thoroughly accomplished the opposite of what they sought. It was thought the railroad would straightway bring the starving East and Europe to California, in search of land; but the first task the railroad had to perform was, to carry homesick California to the East on a visit. It was confidently believed by many that it would restore the ever-lamented "flush times" of 1850; but, so far from that, it sunk

California, temporarily, to the profoundest depths of de-
pression.

It was amusing to see the commercial wincing and wry
faces with which it was reluctantly acknowledged at last
that "the railroad was not an unmixed good," and to
see even a great newspaper array itself lustily against it
and take up the championship of the stage-coach! In
fact, California had fallen into a deep and gentle slumber,
lulled by the pæans of her own greatness. The first
through train, coming laden with the belated thunders
of Gettysburg, and with the big hoarse music of the noisy
and justling East, was as if a six-cylinder press had suddenly been heard clanking in the Happy Valley of Ras-
selas and Imlac.

And now for the first time it went hard, in good sooth,
with poor John Chinaman. Who killed Cock Robin?
The Central Pacific, his best friend. It was a new thing
under the sun to hear a Chinaman complain of "hard
times," and to see him going about soliciting little jobs
of washing or dish-washing. Eastern competition was
ruining him also. It began to be the common remark
among them that California was little better now than
China. Thousands of them, who had prodigally gambled
away their seven fat kine in the years when the Central
Pacific was building, and were penniless, now circumscribed
all their ambition to the single purpose of saving enough
from their seven lean kine to carry them home to China.

And then came, in the summer of 1870, the famous
manifesto of the Six Companies, which was posted on all
the dead walls of the Celestial Empire, warning their
countrymen to remain at home. Then, in process of
time, the splendid steamers of the Pacific Mail no longer
staggered wearily into the Golden Gate, after their long,
long flight across the waters, with nine, ten, eleven hun-

dred yellow faces staring curiously out from their decks upon the shores of the Kingdom of the Flowery Flag. They came now with a hundred, seventy-five, fifty; and went away reeling under hundreds. The Chinese percentage of the whole immigration fell off in one year from forty to twenty-one.

Those two car-loads of Chinese bones, digged up in the Nevada deserts along the line of the Central Pacific, and carried home for burial in the Celestial Empire, were the vanguard of the final exodus.

"And Moses took the bones of Joseph with him: for he had straitly sworn the children of Israel, saying, God will surely visit you; and ye shall carry up my bones away hence with you."

And, after their hard labor and bondage in the desert, let them depart in peace. They have done their great work. They have made their bricks without straw, a railroad where there was no wood. Let them spoil us, the Egyptian taskmasters, if they will, and carry home their poor little remnants of gold and their silver. They have earned it well.

With the departure of the Chinese will come the long-awaited immigrants. With them will come the just partition of the soil. With that will come white competition in labor, to which the workmen need no longer be ashamed to yield. With that will come cheap capital, busy to seek out the development of the land, instead of burying itself in dead bank-vaults, or wasting itself in wild and frantic speculations.

Thus it was that, at the last ringing stroke of the sledge upon the golden spike, all this colonial narrowness and colonial inflation, all these false ideas and false systems of labor, vanished like gibbering ghosts at cockcrow, and a new and true foundation was laid, although at great present loss, whereon to build the future of this peerless California.   Not less auspicious for America was the hour when those two locomotives rubbed their pilots together, in friendly greeting, on Promontory Mountain,

> " Facing on the single track,
>   Half a world behind each back,"

than was for Europe that day when Charles Martel smote hip and thigh the Saracenic hordes before the walls of Tours.   Alexander Dumas says Africa begins at the Pyrenees.   We did not want Asia to begin at the Sierra Nevada.   Thanks to the overland railroad, it shall not.

FREEDMEN'S BUREAU.

ALL that is necessary to be said of the Freedmen's Bureau may be grouped under four heads.

I. In the organization of it a mistake was made in not committing the whole matter to the control of the army. Obloquy necessarily attached to the functions of the Bureau among the Southern whites; and as it was the army, in very many cases, which was the *ultima ratio* and only final enforcer of the Bureau's decrees, the Regulars, both officers and soldiers, conceived a rooted hatred both for the Bureau and the freedmen, because they were through them brought into odium with the citizens. Hence they often obstructed the one and shamefully abused the other, which they would not have done if acting on their own orders.

In the appointment of the head of the Bureau, a gentleman was chosen who, as a soldier, was brave as a lion, as a Christian, was thoroughly earnest, but as a man, was narrow, jealous, and easily deceived. Consequently, he appointed many subagents who, like himself, were, as Talleyrand says, "too full of zeal," and whose total ignorance of human nature made them disqualified above all men for an office wielding such great discretionary power. On the other hand, the most worthless of the volunteer officers were precisely those who were most reluctant to be mustered out, because they were conscious they could make an easier living in the army than under their own vine and fig-tree. By writing patriotic letters, full of sympathy for the freedmen, these fellows often induced the over-zealous head of the Bureau to appoint them agents.

'Thus, what with the foolish zealots and the worthless volunteer officers, more than half the agents were totally unfit for the office.

From the above facts resulted, (1) that, for a short time after the establishment of the Bureau, the planters were excessively fined and humiliated, which created in them an exasperation that wreaked itself directly upon the freedmen ; (2) that, as the agents gradually settled down among the people, and found it necessary to cultivate friendly relations with them, since they were to live there several years, they yielded to cajolery, and fraternized with whites against blacks. By the end of 1866 there were as many agents who sold the freedmen justice, or did them absolute injustice, as there were in 1865 who did the same by the planters. In the first months of 1868, when I walked a thousand miles through the South, I found, by innumerable inquiries of the negroes themselves, the following state of affairs : *There were thirteen agents of whom most negroes spoke with more or less bitterness, and only six whom they generally agreed in praising.*

II. The first work of the Bureau was, necessarily, one of demolition. The surrender destroyed the form of slavery, but not its traditions and its airy and impalpable fetters. The freedmen had a universal and instinctive desire to wander (which they seldom could explain), founded on a vague notion that they were not free at all if they remained on the old plantation. They must demonstrate their freedom with their legs, just as an infant wanders into every corner of its room. The old masters, of course, dreaded this disruption, and tried to prevent it. Governor Marvin, of Florida, a wise and noble man, was great enough to feel and appreciate this longing of the freedmen, and he advised them to wander to their hearts' content, till they fully felt and knew they were free, knowing as he did full well that most of them would ultimately return. But most planters were too narrow and short-sighted to foresee this, and, by tacit (sometimes by expressed) neighborhood agreement, it was made a mean-spirited and unhandsome thing for one planter to employ another's late slaves. Some neighborhoods organized, and expressly agreed among themselves that no one should employ another's freedmen unless they could produce a written recommendation, which, of course, was not given.

In thwarting these tendencies, the Bureau was infinitely useful. Whenever the freedman wanted to rove until he could feel the uttermost length and breadth of his freedom, the Bureau insisted on his right. This wandering was absolutely necessary, in order that the idea might fully dawn upon their poor darkened souls that they were not bound to call any man master. We who have always had our liberty can hardly understand how necessary it was for the freedmen to swing like a pendulum, to tramp day after day for weeks, and never find the end of the rope and be obliged to give an account of themselves. They were the merest children, and this was healthy for them. They got their lungs full of good wide breath. They got hungry. They knocked about the world, and found the need of a home. Then they were ready to go back to the old plantation, and live content, knowing they were absolutely free.

This work of the Bureau was like that of the farmer who tears down his old fence and builds a new one. If he is a good farmer, he pitches all the rails about and handles them roughly, so that all may be broken which are not fit to enter into the new fence. Of course, the Bureau broke

many a negro rail in thus pitching them about, sent many
a one to the penitentiary or under the sod sooner than he
would have gone; but this was inseparable from the general benefit.   Many an idle and worthless negro, whom
force had hitherto kept in some decency, under this new
relaxation speedily went to the bad; but this new and
broad notion of liberty gotten by the others was worth
unspeakably more than the lives of these few vagabonds.

III. The second great work of the Bureau was to re-
build.   After the freedmen had wandered to their hearts'
content, more than three-fifths of them (I speak from wide
observation) returned to the old plantations.   The Bureau
did great service in leading them back to steady habits,
by solemnizing contracts for labor with formalities which
impressed their imaginations.   This helped to build up
that in which life-long slaves were almost utterly lacking,
that is, a sense of legal responsibility.   Without the intervention of the Bureau, the old courts of planters would
have flogged the negro on the spot, as a legal nonentity.
It was an herculean task to make the negro understand that
he had a right to go to the penitentiary, or to be hanged
by process of law.   It was an infinite labor to lift the
freedman up high enough to understand that he was not
to be whipped as a child, but was to be tried like a citizen.   This the Bureau did.

The Bureau made it, for the time, fashionable among
the freedmen to go to school (for there is no other race
in the world so absolutely governed by the fashion of the
hour).   Its agents established an immense number of
schools.   Yet I consider the benefit thus conferred on
the freedman almost incomparably less than the practical
sense of equality, the knack of affairs, the *savoir-faire*,
knowledge of the great world, and ability to knock about
and make a living, which the Bureau greatly helped to

build. There is not another race in the world in whose heads book-learning is so little turned to bread-and-butter uses as in the negroes.

As to the evils of the Bureau, a word. It has often been charged with having encouraged the freedmen to expect confiscation and distribution of lands, and thus kept many in absolute idleness, and many more working for wages, as a mere temporary expedient until they should get land thus, instead of contracting for a share of the crops. There is no doubt that this expectation of confiscation wrought untold evil on the freedmen; but the Southerners themselves are responsible for it, not the Bureau. They talked confiscation all through the war, in hearing of their slaves, as a *bête noir* to frighten each other to do desperate battle for their homes. But many of the agents sinned in this, that they did not take enough pains, or took none at all, to assure the negroes beyond all doubt that no confiscation would take place. I doubt if any agent ever actually encouraged the negroes to expect land.

In needlessly prolonging the dole of rations, the Bureau encouraged beggary. With all its hideous wickedness, slavery never encouraged the negro to beg, tobacco alone excepted.

IV. To recapitulate: Slavery practically taught all negroes to steal; the Bureau taught many to beg. Slavery made the race very fruitful, for its own profit; the Bureau removed its restraints, without being able to cure their inherent licentiousness. Slavery drugged the slave with a few moral maxims, which were, for the most part, of no effect whatever; the Bureau awakened an unprecedented desire for learning, as a fashion. Slavery treated the negro as an animal, and, as an animal merely, he was happier then than after he was liberated; the Bureau lifted him to the level of a man, and gave him the keen pangs and the keen transports which attend all higher life. Slavery developed the negro downward, and attached him to the soil; the Bureau opened his eyes to a self-understanding, to freedom, to restlessness, to ambitions which can never be fulfilled so long as he remains among the whites, and thus planted the greatest amount of seed for Liberian colonization which has ever been scattered in the South.

THE END.